BLOOD GUILT

Ben Cheetham's short stories have been widely published in the UK, US and Australia. He lives in Sheffield.

BEN CHEETHAM

BLOOD GUILT

HEAD
of
ZEUS

First published as eBook in the UK in 2011.
This paperback edition first published in the UK
in 2013 by Head of Zeus Ltd.

9 7 5 3 1 2 4 6 8

A CIP catalogue record for this book is available
from the British Library.

Paperback ISBN 9781781852484
Ebook ISBN 9781781852491

Printed and bound by CPI Group (UK) Ltd,
Croydon, CR0 4YY.

Head of Zeus Ltd
Clerkenwell House
45–47 Clerkenwell Green
London EC1R 0HT

www.headofzeus.com

For Clare

Prologue

With cold, sweaty hands, Harlan Miller unconsciously reached into his pocket and pulled out his Marlboros. Shooting nervous glances all around the room, he withdrew one and moved it towards his mouth. It was a sterile-smelling room, furnished with a desk, a phone, three chairs, and a doctor's examining couch. On the walls hung some framed medical certificates, and a picture of a sperm wriggling its way into an egg with the words *It takes more than this to be a parent* underneath. It wasn't until Eve gave him a frowning look and hissed his name that Harlan noticed the cigarette. 'Sorry,' he said, returning it to the packet. Managing a strained little smile, Eve reached to give his hand a squeeze.

Harlan jerked around at the sound of someone entering the room. As soon as he saw the doctor's face, he knew it was bad news. He'd always had a talent for reading people. It was part of what made him so good at his job. He had a sudden urge to jump up and run from the room. As if sensing this, Eve tightened her grip.

The doctor sat down, looking first at Eve. 'I'm afraid it's good news, bad news time. The good news is, you have no fertility problems.' His gaze shifted to Harlan. 'The bad news is, you have a very low sperm count and a high percentage of your viable sperm are abnormal.'

A tightness rose in Harlan's throat, giving his voice a husky edge. 'What do you mean, abnormal?'

'They have misshapen heads or tails, which severely reduces their chances of reaching the egg.'

'So basically what you're saying is I'm infertile.'

'You're not completely infertile, but as things stand you're going to find it very difficult to conceive.'

Harlan shook his head in stunned bewilderment. 'But I never had a problem before.'

'You're thirty-five now. Fertility goes into decline after thirty.'

'Is there anything he can do to improve it?' asked Eve.

The doctor started talking about diet, vitamins and exercise but Harlan wasn't listening. He was thinking about Thomas, about the way he'd looked the last time he saw him. He'd looked perfect, except his cheeks were very pale and the edge of a bruise was visible on his forehead by his hairline. It was a freak accident, a doctor had explained. Kids fall like that all the time. They usually walk away unharmed, or at least they walk away. Not Tom, though. Eve had told Harlan that Tom never even cried out when his head hit the ground. He'd just lain with closed eyes, motionless as a doll.

The urge to leave came over Harlan again, stronger than before, irresistible. It pulled him to his feet, wrenching his hand out of Eve's. 'Harlan,' she called after him as he hurried from the room. He didn't stop, didn't look back, didn't reply. Eve caught up with him on the steps of the clinic. 'Wait. For Christ's sake, wait! Where are you going?'

Harlan avoided Eve's eyes as if he had something to be ashamed of. 'I don't know. I just couldn't stay in there any longer.' He took a shuddering breath. 'Jesus, I can't have children any more.'

'That's not what the doctor said,' Eve gently pointed out. 'He said it'd be difficult, not impossible. There's still a chance.'

'What chance? My sperm are crippled. How are you going to get pregnant if the little fuckers can't even swim to the egg?'

Eve tried to put her arms around Harlan. 'Come back inside and talk to the doctor.'

He shook his head, pulling away. 'I just need some time alone.'

For hours Harlan wandered the city's streets. He bought a litre of Scotch and drank it like water. Somehow or other, he found his way to the playground where the accident had happened. He sat on a bench, zombie-eyed, just staring. He watched parents watching their children. *That will never be me*, he thought, and a sense of crushing loss almost as painful as when Thomas died hit him, wrenching a sob from his throat. Noticing that he was drawing glances from the people around him, he stood to leave. His mobile phone rang, Jim Monahan's name flashing up on its screen. Harlan stared at it, trying to decide if he was up to taking the call. Probably not, he decided. But the pain was so unbearable he knew he'd better do something to distract himself before he completely lost the plot.

Taking a steadying breath, he put the phone to his ear. 'What's up, Jim?'

A voice roughened by years of smoking replied, 'We've got a body. Man about thirty or thirty-five years old.'

'Homicide?'

'Uh-huh.'

'Where?'

Jim told Harlan the address, and Harlan told him he'd be there as soon as possible. He left the park and hailed a taxi. It was a bright, cold afternoon, but during the drive dirty white clouds moved in, obscuring the sun. When the taxi arrived at the address, a uniform waved it to a stop. Harlan flashed his ID and the uniform stepped aside. The street was clogged with police vehicles. Another uniform stood at the end of a large detached house's driveway. Forensic bods in white suits were visible through the house's windows. Jim was waiting at the front door, wearing his usual alert but world-weary veteran's expression. On seeing Harlan, he said matter-of-factly, 'You look like shit.'

'I'm fine. So, what's the story?'

'Married couple. Name Lee and Susan Burke. Mrs Burke says they were in bed having sex when—'

'A married couple shagging on a weekday afternoon,' Harlan broke in doubtfully, following Jim into the house. Somewhere overhead a woman was sobbing hysterically.

A crooked smile tugged at the corners of Jim's mouth. 'Yeah, I know. That's what I thought too. Anyway, she says they were doing the business when they were disturbed by the sound of breaking glass downstairs. Mr Burke went to investigate while Mrs Burke phoned us.'

Mr Burke was lying naked, face down in the kitchen, limbs splayed like a dried starfish, his back a bloody latticework of cuts and stab wounds. Glass from a broken window was scattered over the lino and the corpse. The half-brick that'd been used to smash it lay against the foot of the opposite wall. 'Twenty-eight, twenty-nine, thirty...' a forensics guy was saying, as he counted the stab wounds. A raw breath of air that smelled of snow blew into the room and everybody shivered, except the dead man and Harlan. The whisky sloshing around inside his otherwise empty stomach insulated him from its touch.

'She's lying,' said Harlan, blearily studying the corpse.

'What makes you think that?'

With his foot, Harlan rolled the body onto its side. 'Hey!'

said the forensics guy. 'What do you think you're doing?'

Harlan ignored him. 'There's glass on and around the body, but not under it. Which means the window was smashed after he died. And which also means Mrs Burke is a lying, murdering bitch.'

Harlan spoke loudly – loud enough for anyone within fifty feet to hear – with a harsh slur in his voice. When he finished, the house was silent. Everyone in the room – uniforms, forensic bods, photographer – stared at him. He lifted his eyes and called at the ceiling, 'That's right, lady, don't waste your time blubbering. Call a lawyer because you'll need one.'

'Detective, can I speak to you outside?' said Jim.

'Sure.'

Somewhat unsteadily Harlan stepped over the body, leaving a partial footprint in the blood pooled on the lino as he headed for the back door. Frowning, Jim followed him. 'What the hell were you trying to do in there?' he demanded.

'My job.'

'Yeah, well you won't have a job much longer if you keep this up. When word of this gets back to the DCI, you'll be lucky if he doesn't bring you up on disciplinary charges.'

Harlan's lips curled into a sneer. 'Aw, fuck Garrett.'

A few flakes of snow hung in the air. Several of them turned to droplets of water on Harlan's bottle as he took a hit from it. 'Jesus, Harlan,' said Jim, 'put that away before someone sees it.'

Harlan returned the bottle to his pocket, then started back towards the house.

Jim placed his hand on his partner's chest. 'I can't let you go back in there.'

'Are you saying I'm not fit for duty?'

'I don't want to get into an argument. We'll talk about this later.'

'The fuck we will. We're gonna talk about this right now.'

'Look,' sighed Jim, 'I don't know what's going on with you today, but this isn't the time or place to get into this. So here's what's going to happen. You're going to go home and sleep this off and when you wake up you're going to phone this number.' He scribbled down a number on a notepad, tore out the sheet and handed it to Harlan.

'What's this?'

'The number of a therapist.'

'A *therapist.*' Harlan said the word as if he had a nasty taste in his mouth. 'What do I need a therapist for?'

'Because Garrett might go easy on you if he knows you're trying to get your head straightened out. Her name's Linda Harris. She's helping me through my divorce.'

Harlan stared at the number, forehead rutted into furrows as deep as the sadness in his eyes. 'There's no getting through this.' Crumpling the sheet of paper into a ball and tossing it aside, he stepped around Jim.

'Where are you going?' Jim asked, as Harlan headed down the side of the house.

'Where do you think? Home.'

'One of the uniforms will give you a lift.'

'I'd rather walk.'

Shoulders hunched, breath steaming the air, Harlan made his way along the street. Tears misted his eyes. He swiped them away savagely before they could fall. He finished his whisky in one long swallow, and the pain retreated to lurk like a stalker in the shadows at the back of his mind. He thought about the dead man. What was his name? Lee Burke. Yes, that was it. He'd got it in the back. No defensive wounds. Probably died instantly without pain. 'You're one of the lucky ones,' he murmured, as the snow came down in larger powdery flakes.

By the time he got home, the pavement was white.

Harlan stared at the house – a semi, nothing spectacular, a family home. He used to love its solid, suburban comfort, its large child-friendly gardens. Now he hated it for the same reasons.

Heaving a breath, he entered the house. He made his way upstairs, pulled down the loft ladder and climbed. The box was in a far recess of the attic. His thoughts flashed back to the day he'd put it there. That day, like so many other days during the first year after Tom's death, he'd spent hours in his son's shrine of a bedroom, crying. Eventually, Eve had come into the room and said, 'Enough is enough, Harlan. Tom's gone and it was no one's fault and there's nothing we can do about it except get on with our lives.'

Her words had felt like a betrayal. Harlan remembered how he'd bitten his lip to keep from speaking, afraid that if he opened his mouth all the things he'd wanted to say so many times before might come spilling out. Things that he knew were unfair, yet which he couldn't help but think. Things like: you were his mother, you were supposed to be watching him, making sure he came to no harm. Things that, if voiced, would destroy what little was left of their relationship.

'I love you but you're killing me,' Eve had continued. 'If you carry on like this, it'll be the end of us.'

Harlan had known she meant it, and suddenly his anger had disappeared and panic had risen in him at the thought of losing the only thing left for him to love. 'You're right,' he'd said. 'I've got to stop doing this.'

That same day Harlan had cleared out Tom's bedroom and taken down every photo of him in the house. 'You don't need to go that far,' Eve had said, shocked.

'Yes I do,' he'd replied. 'If I'm going to put this behind me,

7

I can't be surrounded by things that remind me of him.'

So Harlan had pushed the memories down. Down and deep. He'd locked them away and swallowed the key, and for a while it'd worked. They'd got on with their lives, even trying for a baby. Trying and trying but not succeeding. After a year, Harlan had started to get scared. 'Maybe we should see a doctor,' he'd suggested to Eve. She'd agreed.

Harlan didn't want to look inside the box but somehow he couldn't stop himself. With hands that would've trembled but for the alcohol flooding his veins, he pulled away the masking tape and opened it. Thomas's rosy-cheeked face beamed up at him from a photo frame. He had Harlan's intense dark eyes and thick brown hair, and Eve's full lips and cute snub nose.

Harlan's breath came out in a sudden gasp, as if he'd been punched in the stomach. The tears welled again. This time he couldn't stop them. They fell onto the photo, onto Thomas's favourite teddy bear, onto his lucky pyjamas. He slumped forward, pressing his face into the box's contents, inhaling deeply, smelling the remnants of his son. He was still in the same position an hour later when Eve poked her head into the attic. 'Harlan?' she said.

His mouth twitching with resentment, Harlan raised his tear-stained face to glare at Eve. His anger was almost tangible, filling the space between them like invisible tentacles ready to strike. 'Go on, say it,' said Eve, her voice flat, emotionally drained. 'Say what you're thinking. It was my fault, right? I should've been watching him more closely.'

'Yes!' The word came out in a loud hiss, like a release of pent-up steam.

They stared at each other. Harlan was struck suddenly by how much Eve's face had changed since Tom's death. Everything about it – skin, smile, eyes – had once been soft. There was no softness now. Her face was thinner, worn into hollows beneath the cheekbones, her eyes were sharp, and lately her mouth had assumed what seemed to be an almost permanently downturned position. She looked older – not old, but not young any more either – and very tired. Like that day in Tom's bedroom, the tentacles of Harlan's anger suddenly withered and sucked back in on themselves. He made to speak, to apologise, but before he could do so Eve ducked out of sight. He hurried after her into their bedroom.

'I'm sor—' Harlan started to say, but he broke off as Eve pulled a suitcase down from the top of the wardrobe. 'What are you doing?'

Eve didn't reply. She started flinging clothes into the suitcase. When Harlan caught hold of her arm, she jerked around to glare at him with such implacable fury that he released her and took a step back. She stormed past him into the bathroom, returning with an armful of cosmetics. As she hauled the suit-case downstairs, Harlan said, 'Please, Eve, don't do this. I'm sorry. I should never have said what I did.'

Eve paused at the front door, turning to Harlan. 'Why not? It's what you think, isn't it?'

He dropped his gaze from hers, his broad shoulders slumping like a defeated boxer's. Sighing, Eve continued a shade more softly, 'I should've done this months ago but I stupidly kept telling myself there was still a chance we could make it in time. Now I know what you really think. And no amount of time will be enough to change that. It's over, Harlan.'

As she turned to head for her car, Harlan's mind reeled with conflicting desires. Part of him desperately wanted to try and stop her. Another part told him to let her go. After all, whether or not she was right, what future did she have to look forward to with him? Maybe in time he could come to terms with Tom's death. But he'd always be sterile. And as far as he was concerned, a childless future was no future at all. No, better to let her go while she was still young enough to start a family with someone else.

He watched Eve get into her car, watched her pull away. Then he too left the house. He didn't close the front door behind him. He didn't care if the place got ransacked and trashed. All he cared about was getting so drunk he'd forget everything, even his own name. The snow came down in swirling flurries, settling in a rapidly thickening layer on the ground. He almost slipped over several times on his way to the pub.

It was a Friday, and despite the weather the pub was busy. A large group of men and women occupied several tables in the centre of the bar. From their flushed faces and loud, laughing voices, it was clear they'd already knocked a good few back. As Harlan made his way past them, he tripped over an outstretched foot and staggered against a table, knocking over a glass of wine.

'Fuckin' watch it!' yelled a shaven-headed man about Harlan's age, wearing a T-shirt that showed off bulging tattooed biceps. The kind of tough guy type Harlan used to deal with every day of the week when he was walking the beat.

'Shit, I'm soaked through!' said a woman at the man's side, springing up. She was a little younger, thirty or so, bottle-blonde, a pretty face hidden behind too much make-up. White wine streamed down her figure-hugging dress. 'Look at my dress, it's ruined.'

'Sorry,' said Harlan, taking out a handkerchief and proffering it.

Standing, the man slapped his hand away. 'You trying to touch her up or something?'

The man fixed Harlan with a practised hard stare; he was a couple of inches taller and more heavily built. But his muscles were running to fat, whereas Harlan's were whipcord tight beneath his clothes – the result of a youth spent in sweaty boxing gyms. Harlan held his gaze, not aggressive, but letting him know he wasn't about to be intimidated. The man blinked, obviously not used to someone standing up to him.

'Look, let me buy you both a drink to apologise,' offered Harlan.

'Fuck drinks. That dress cost a hundred quid. What you gonna do about that?'

'Well I'm not going to give you a hundred quid.'

The two men faced each other silently. Some part of Harlan wanted the man to go for him, wanted to feel the good, clean pain of punching and being punched. That kind of pain he could handle. 'Leave it, Rob,' said the woman. 'It'll come out in the wash.'

'You sure?'

'Yeah.'

Rob's face relaxed into a mean little smile. 'I'll have a lager, she'll have a large white wine,' he told Harlan.

Faintly disappointed, Harlan approached the bar and ordered the drinks, plus a double Scotch for himself. He took the couple their drinks, not bothering even to look at their thankless faces. Then he returned to the bar and went to work on the whisky. At first he was half aware of Rob shooting an occasional dark glance his way but after a while he noticed nothing, except whether his glass was full or empty. At closing time, he reluctantly made his way outside, taking small, jerky steps like a toddler learning to walk.

It'd stopped snowing, and the pale luminescence of a full moon made the streets seem paved with shattered glass. A group of people were throwing snowballs at each other in the road. Harlan barely gave them a glance. He was thinking about the house. A shudder passed through him at the thought of spending the night there with only the ghosts of unwanted memories for company. He took out his mobile phone and speed-dialled Jim. After four or five rings, his partner picked up. 'What is it, Harlan?'

'Eve's left me.'

'Shit, I'm sorry to hear that.'

'Can I come over?'

Jim sighed. 'Sure.'

'Thanks, Jim.'

As Harlan hung up, a voice rang out behind him. 'Hey, fuckhead!' He glanced over his shoulder, and a snowball hit him hard in the face. He wiped it away and through a blur of tears saw Rob approaching him with that same smile on his face. The woman was dragging at Rob's arm, slowing his progress. He jerked free of her and pointed at Harlan. 'You owe me a hundred quid.'

The woman grabbed his arm again. 'Please, Rob,' she said, her eyes pleading with Harlan to walk away. But Harlan wasn't about to walk away, not until he was sure Rob wouldn't rabbit-punch him. Rob stopped about fifteen feet away from him, and Harlan thought, *This guy's all bark and no bite*. He turned and started walking to jeers of, 'Wanker!' from Rob's mates. Another snowball hit the back of his head. *Just keep walking*, he told himself, gritting his teeth. A third snowball burst on his back. He stopped and turned to face Rob. Even as he did so, his mind said, *What are you doing? Don't be stupid*. But his heart was almost grateful to Rob. Here was a chance to take out his anger and frustration on someone who needed teaching a lesson.

As Harlan advanced towards him, Rob spread his arms and shouted, 'Come on then!'

Harlan swung wildly, something between a straight punch and a wide-sweeping haymaker. Somehow, by some quirk of luck, his fist connected flush on Rob's chin. Both feet shot out from under the bigger man and he catapulted backward. As his head hit the pavement, there was a sound like breaking eggs. A sickening, stomach-churning sound. He didn't cry out, his arms twitched a little spasmodically, then he lay still, eyes closed.

'Rob!' cried the woman, dropping to her knees, putting her ear close to his mouth, frantically checking for a pulse. 'Oh God, he's not breathing. I can't feel his pulse. Shit, shit—' Her shrill voice choked off into gasping panic breaths.

'Call an ambulance!' yelled someone.

Harlan just stood in mute, uncomprehending stupefaction, watching blood spread like a halo through the snow under the prostrate man's head. The blood looked oily black in the moonlight.

'Help him! Help him!' shrieked the woman.

Harlan flinched like someone jerked out of a trance. He stooped towards Rob. The woman screamed, her eyes swollen with fear, anger and hatred. 'Get away! Get away from him, you murdering bastard!'

No, not murder, said the policeman in Harlan. *Manslaughter*. 'I know CPR.' His voice sounded eerily distorted in his own ears, like an echo. A strange feeling of disconnection came over him, reinforced by the dreamlike hush of the snow-muffled city. The feeling was dispelled by the sting of the woman's nails raking at his face. Two of her friends grabbed her.

'No!' she wailed, as they dragged her away. 'Rob! Rob!'

Harlan felt for a pulse. Nothing. He listened for breath. There was none. He gently tilted Rob's head back, opened his mouth and checked nothing was obstructing his windpipe. He pinched Rob's nose shut and breathed twice into his mouth.

13

Then placing his hands, one on top of the other, on Rob's breastbone, he compressed his chest. He checked for breathing and a pulse again. Still nothing. He thumped Rob's chest.

'Stop him!' The woman's shrill, sobbing voice cut through the air. 'Call the police!'

I am the police, thought Harlan. His next thought was, *No you're not. You're not a policeman, you're not a husband, and you're not a father. The man you were is as dead as this poor bastard. Everything he was is gone. It's over. Finished. Nothing can bring him back.*

He stopped the CPR. Slowly, as if he was being dragged down by some irresistible weight, he bowed his head until it rested in the snow.

Chapter One

With a smooth, effortless motion, Harlan did push-ups on his cell floor. On reaching the required number, he picked a diary off his narrow bunk and totted up the final tally. Four hundred and ninety-two thousand mind-numbing push-ups in four years. Making a mental note that he was never going to do another one, he glanced at his watch. Nine a.m. Not long now.

His gaze travelled blankly around the cramped segregation cell where he'd been kept for his own protection since word somehow got out that he used to be a copper. Four, three, even two years ago, his sharply chiselled features would've assumed an expression of disgust verging on hatred, as he took in the drearily oppressive walls, the barred window with its plastic curtains, the stark fluorescent light, the small television, and the stainless steel integrated toilet and sink unit. But at some point – he couldn't remember exactly when – a kind of resigned acceptance had kicked in. *Just do the time and let everything else go*, he'd told himself. Only he hadn't been able to let everything else go. Each night at lights out, he'd focused on the continuous din of his fellow inmates calling to one another, vainly trying to stay in the here and now. But his mind was stuck in a loop, constantly being drawn back to the moment of drunken rage when he'd deprived a wife of her husband, and two young boys of their father – he'd found out at the trial that the man he killed had two sons, aged four and eight. At the time, he'd become so filled with self-hatred that he contemplated suicide. Even now, thinking about it made him unconsciously clench his hand and pummel it into his thigh.

A guard opened the windowless steel door and wordlessly motioned for Harlan to follow him. They made their way along a corridor lined with cells to a heavily barred door. Several more corridors and barred doors brought them to the reception area, where after having his ID verified and signing a bundle of forms, he was handed his street clothes, his personal belongings, an envelope from the housing advisor, forty quid and a travel voucher. After getting changed, he was escorted to the outer door. And then, suddenly, he was outside in the car park. He stood there a moment with the cod-medieval battlements of HMP Leeds looming behind him, just breathing in the morning air and feeling the sun on his face.

'Harlan!'

Harlan blinked in surprise at the sound of his name being shouted. He wasn't expecting anybody to be waiting to meet him. Recognising the deep, smoke-roughened voice, he looked in the direction it'd come from and saw Jim Monahan approaching. Jim hadn't changed much, except his hair was thinner and his belly rounder. 'Jim, what are you doing here?'

'What do you think? I wasn't about to let you walk out of here alone.'

'But how did you know I was getting out today?'

'Eve told me. She was going to come herself but she didn't think you'd want to see her.'

'She was right. Me and Eve, we're the past, and wallowing in the past wouldn't do either of us any good.' Harlan's voice was full of conviction but a vague flicker of disappointment showed in his eyes. From inside the prison came the muffled clang of a door closing. A shudder passed through him. 'Where are you parked?' Jim pointed and Harlan started towards the car.

After they'd driven a couple of streets and the prison had been blocked from view, Harlan asked, 'So how is she?'

'She sounds good.' Jim gave him a hesitating glance. 'You know she's living with someone?'

A sudden deep ache filled Harlan's chest. 'I do now. That's good. I'm glad. Glad she's happy and getting on with her life.' Even in his own ears his voice sounded too controlled to pass as natural. The policeman in him would've characterised it as revealingly unrevealing. For the first time in years, he found himself wanting a smoke. 'You got a cigarette?'

Jim handed him a pack of cigarettes and a lighter. He sparked up and leaned his head against the headrest, gazing out the window. The streets looked grubby and unwelcoming; the buildings drab and depressing. People were rushing around, each caught up in their own little world, their faces as cheerless as their surroundings. He sighed. 'Some shit never changes.'

'So where do you want to go?'

'The housing advisor sorted me out a flat.' Harlan took a sheet of paper out of the envelope and showed Jim the address.

Jim frowned. 'Bankwood House, Callow Mount. That's a shithole of a tower block in a shithole neighbourhood.'

'Yeah, well, you should've seen my last place.'

'Tell you what, why don't you doss down at mine? Just until you've had a chance to find your feet.'

'What about Garrett? He's not gonna be impressed if he finds out you're associating with an ex-con.'

Jim grinned. 'Aw, fuck him.'

'Thanks for the offer but it wouldn't be fair on you. Besides, and don't take this the wrong way, but I can't be around that right now.'

'Around what?'

'Y'know, police talk.'

'Oh right, so I'm the past too, am I?'

Harlan made no reply. They headed out of Leeds, following the signposts for Sheffield. Jim made a couple of attempts at small talk, but when Harlan's responses were brief or non-existent, he gave up and they rode in silence. An hour or so later, they pulled into the car park of a tower block, one of a cluster of six clad in various shades of green and brown, like colossal trees of concrete and steel. A gang of sullen youths, all bling, white trainers, tracksuits and baseball caps, loitered against a graffiti-tagged wall. In the centre of the car park a stripped car squatted on its wheel-less axles.

'Well, here we are,' said Jim. 'Home sweet home.'

Harlan collected his few belongings from the back seat. 'Thanks for the ride.'

'No problem. You want me to come up with you?'

'I think I'd rather be alone right now.' Harlan managed a smile. 'Besides, from the look of those kids, leave your car here and you'll be lucky if it's still got wheels when you get back.'

'Listen, Harlan, I know you feel you need to make a clean break, but if you change your mind about my offer, or if you just want go out for a drink, or whatever, give me a call.'

'I will. See you, Jim.'

As Harlan headed into the stairwell, the youths cast knowing glances at his sallow, sun-starved face and the prison-issue plastic bag that contained everything he owned. He caught the lift to the twelfth floor. The first thing that struck him on entering his flat was the acrid stink of cleaning chemicals, behind which lurked a faint tang of something else, something coppery sweet. He knew what the smell meant. Someone had recently died in the flat, and their body had lain undiscovered

18

long enough to begin decomposing. He made a quick tour of his new home: whitewashed walls; cheap, thin carpets; a bedroom with a bed and bare mattress; a tiny kitchen; an equally tiny, windowless bathroom; a living room with a hard-looking sofa, a fold-up table and two chairs. He opened a grimy, weather-stained window as wide as it would go, then pulled a chair over to sit in the current of air. He thought of Eve living with someone else. Loving someone else. And again an ache filled his chest. 'Let it go,' he murmured, closing his eyes. 'Let it go, let it go...'

Chapter Two

Harlan quickly settled into a routine that left little time for reflection. Seven nights a week, at eight o'clock, he started work at the warehouse where his parole officer had found him a job loading and unloading delivery vehicles. It was long hours of arduous, mind-deadening work, but that was fine with him. He slept – more often than not with the help of a Valium – from seven in the morning till two in the afternoon. That left six hours until his next shift. Those empty hours were the most difficult. Sitting in his flat with only the sound of the wind shrieking against the windows for company, time seemed to stretch out like an elastic band before him. So he took to walking the streets, but that didn't stop him from thinking, didn't stop his mind from endlessly looping back. A feeling was growing in him. He tried to ignore it but as the weeks drifted by it strengthened almost to a compulsion. He had to find the woman. He had to see her. Not speak to her, just see her, see how she was doing.

It wasn't hard for Harlan to find her. He looked up her name – he'd learned that at the trial too – in the phonebook. Susan Reed. A common name. There was almost a page of them. Now he had something to fill the empty hours. A purpose. Every afternoon, he headed out with a list of names and addresses in his pocket. He worked methodically down the list, staking out the addresses until he was sure the Susan Reed he was looking for didn't live there. Of course, he realised, there was always a chance she'd moved away from the area. But he didn't think it was much of a chance. She was a local girl, uneducated, a mother. Not the type to uproot and start again somewhere else.

After a fortnight he found her. He was nursing a coffee in a scruffy café opposite a row of two-up, two-down terraced houses when he saw her. He almost didn't recognise her. Her once bleached-blonde hair had grown out to its natural mousy-brown colour. It hung in greasy strands around her unmade-up, puffy-eyed face, as styleless as the clothes that hung around her body. She'd lost weight, but not in a good way. There was a brittleness about her movements, a jerkiness that spoke of nerves stretched close to breaking. Two boys trailed behind her, dressed in school uniforms. Ethan and Kane. Her sons. Her fatherless sons. They'd be about eight and twelve years old now. Ethan, the younger brother, bore little resemblance to his father. He was small for his age and had pale, delicate features and dreamy, introspective blue eyes. Kane, on the other hand, was the spit of his dad. He was as tall and well built as a boy of fifteen or sixteen, with short-cropped hair and a flushed frowning face. They were kicking a football along the pavement. Suddenly, for no reason Harlan could see, Kane hoofed the ball at Ethan's head. The smaller boy staggered and almost fell, clutching his face with both hands. Susan turned and snapped something at Kane. She clipped him across the ear, before stooping to examine Ethan's smarting cheek. Kane made to retrieve the ball but Susan snatched it off him and stalked away with it under one of her arms and Ethan under the other. Kane dragged his feet after them, the sullen resentment of an older sibling towards a younger one glimmering in his eyes.

Harlan watched them enter one of the houses. Through the downstairs window he saw them take off their coats and dump their bags. A television flickered into life. Ethan sat on a sofa in front of it, his face palely illuminated, while his brother followed their mother into the back of the house. Maybe Harlan was just seeing what he expected to see, but the boy's expression seemed to speak of someone who'd known more sorrow than happiness, more anxiety than contentment. A kind of sick, guilty agony burned through him. He hurried from the café, hurried all the way to the bank. There was just over ten thousand pounds in his account – his share of the equity from the house. He hadn't wanted it but Eve had insisted. He emptied his account, put the cash in an envelope and wrote *Susan Reed* on it. Then he returned to the house and posted the envelope through the front door. Ten thousand pounds. Not much in return for the loss of a husband and father, but something. Before he could turn away, the door opened. It was Ethan. He looked curiously up at Harlan, his mouth a flat line.

Harlan couldn't help but blink. Not wanting to scare the boy, he smiled, but the smile felt unnatural, more like some strange kind of grimace. He pointed at the envelope. 'That's for your mum. Tell her I'll send more as soon—' He broke off as, to his horror, tears spilled from his eyes.

'Are you OK?' asked Ethan.

Harlan nodded, quickly wiping his tears away. 'I... I'm...' he stammered, his voice catching.

'Ethan!' The shout came from the rear of the house.

'That's my mum. I have to go see what she wants.' Ethan bent to pick up the envelope. 'Bye.' He shut the door.

'I'm sorry,' murmured Harlan, before turning and moving slowly away.

He headed to work, even though there were a couple of hours till his shift started. The foreman was happy to let him start early, just so long as he didn't expect to be paid extra.

He threw himself into the work with even more than his usual fervour, blotting out Susan Reed and her sons' faces through a blank repetition of monotonous movement. But after work, lying in bed, he saw them again, and it burned him worse than battery acid.

Harlan was floating on the edge of a Valium-induced haze when a hammering at the front door jerked him upright. Groggily, he pulled on his jeans and made his way to the door. The instant he opened it, a wad of banknotes hit him in the chest. 'I don't want your fucking blood money!' hissed Susan Reed, her face contorted into sharp lines of rage. Harlan made no attempt to dodge out of the way as she drew her arm back to fling another fistful of fifty-pound notes at him. 'You think you can buy away your guilt? Well you fucking can't. It's yours for the rest of your pathetic little life, and I hope it eats at you every second of every day.' She stabbed a trembling finger at Harlan. 'Come near me or my boys again and I'll fucking kill you. You hear me, you bastard?'

Without waiting for a response, she turned and stalked away. Leaving the money scattered over the carpet, Harlan made his way to the sofa and dropped onto it as if his body was impossibly heavy. So that was that. There could be no redemption. She would give him no chance.

His mobile phone rang. It was Jim. 'I've been trying to get hold of you since last night,' he said. 'Has she been to see you yet?'

'If by "she" you mean Susan Reed, then yes.'

'Shit. She phoned me demanding to know where you live. Sorry, Harlan, but I had to tell her, otherwise she was threatening to tell your parole officer what you did. Just what the hell were you thinking? If she reports you, you could get sent back to prison.'

I already am in prison, thought Harlan. *A prison that holds me captive more securely than any man-made structure could.* He said with a fatalistic calmness, 'Maybe that'd be for the best.'

'What are you talking about? Are you OK? Do you want me to come over?'

'No, I don't want you to come over. And don't ring me again either.'

Harlan hung up. He returned to bed and lay awake, embracing the guilt, letting it consume him. The phone rang several times. He ignored it. When the sun softened to twilight he got up, haggard and sunken-eyed. Mechanically, he dressed and ate. Mechanically, he made his way to work.

Chapter Three

After work, on his way back to the flat, Harlan bought a bottle of whisky. He poured a shot and swallowed it – the first drop of alcohol he'd put to his lips since that tragic, fatal day. Jesus Christ, it tasted good. Then he popped all the Valium he could find out of their blister strips and lined them up on the table. Finally, he propped a photo in the centre of the table of himself, Eve and Thomas. They were on a seaside pier, Eve hugging Tom, Harlan hugging both of them. Behind them the sea sparkled in the sunlight. All three of them were smiling. Harlan stared at the photo, a sheen of tears over his dark eyes. He was still staring at it an hour or so later when someone knocked at his door. He ignored the knocking. It came again, louder and accompanied by a terse, insistent voice. 'Mr Miller, if you're in there, open up. This is the police. We need to talk to you.'

Harlan's first thought was, *So she's reported me*, but then a wrinkle of doubt formed on his forehead. Even if he was right, his parole officer would've surely been in touch to get his side of the story before sending some uniforms around to pick him up. 'Who's we?'

'DI Scott Greenwood and DI Amy Sheridan.'

Harlan knew then that this was about much more than him. No way would they send detectives to deal with a parole violation. Something big-time serious had happened, was happening, and he was under some kind of suspicion. He swept the sleeping pills off the table into the tumbler and put it out of sight. Then, trampling banknotes underfoot, he opened the door just wide enough so that he could peer out. 'What's this about?'

'Can we come in and ask you some questions?' said DI Greenwood, a stocky man with steely, watchful eyes.

It was phrased as a request but it wasn't one. If Harlan said no, he knew he'd be in cuffs before he could blink. 'Sure.'

He opened the door fully. DI Sheridan, a poker-faced blonde of about thirty, pointed at the banknotes. 'Can you explain what that's about?'

'Susan Reed threw them there.' Harlan saw no point in dancing around their questions. Susan, or something connected to her, was the only reason he could think of for the detectives to be here, which meant they almost certainly knew about his visit to her house. His mind raced over the possibilities of what might've happened, and quickly came to the conclusion that the most obvious likelihood was that Susan or one of her sons, or maybe the entire family, had been hurt or killed in suspicious circumstances.

'Why?'

'I tried to give them to her. She didn't want them.'

'Do you mind if we take a look around?' said DI Greenwood.

Another question that wasn't a question. Harlan shook his head. The detectives worked their way methodically through the flat, checking under the bed and in the wardrobe and cupboards, testing to see if the side of the bath could be removed, even lifting the sofa. Harlan knew what that meant. It meant someone was missing, which was a small relief because it also meant there was a chance no one was dead.

'Do you have a garage?' asked DI Greenwood.

'No.'

'What about a car?'

Harlan shook his head.

'Where were you last night between the hours of twelve and four o'clock?'

'I was working. But you already know that, don't you? Otherwise I'm guessing I'd be down the station helping with enquiries, or maybe even being read my rights by now.'

'Tell us exactly what happened with Susan Reed,' said DI Sheridan, pen and notepad at the ready.

Harlan gave them the full story. 'I know it was a foolish thing to do but I had to do something to try and help her.'

'And since then you've not attempted to make further contact with her?'

'No.'

'When you were staking out Susan Reed's house, did you see anybody else visiting or hanging around?'

'No.'

'One final question, Mr Miller. When you were in prison, did you speak with any of your fellow inmates about Susan Reed or her children?'

A cold fist seemed to close around Harlan's heart. So this did concern the children. Otherwise, why mention them? 'Never. Look, why don't you tell me what's going on. Then maybe I can help.'

'We can't discuss the details of an ongoing investigation, Mr Miller. You should know that,' said DI Greenwood. 'Thanks for your cooperation. We may need to talk to you again later.'

The detectives headed for the door. Harlan stood at the living-room window. After maybe a minute, the detectives emerged from the stairwell and got into an unmarked car. As they drove away, another car pulled into the car park. *So I'm being watched*, he thought. The realisation didn't bother him. He'd had four long years to get used to the view from the other side of the fence. What tormented him was not knowing why. His gut instinct, which he'd learned over the years to trust, told him it had something to do with the children, and that that something involved the disappearance of one, or both, of them. Working on that assumption, it followed that the police hadn't ruled out the possibility of abduction. It also followed that it could be a simple runaway case. A sick feeling settled in his stomach as it occurred to him that maybe it was no coincidence that this was happening so soon after his visit to Susan Reed's house. Maybe his actions had somehow sparked off a course of events that led to one of the boys running away. Unconsciously, he put a clenched fist to his mouth and bit his knuckle hard. If that was the case, if he was the source of yet more pain and loss in that poor woman's life then… well, then there would be no more hesitation. He would swallow the whisky and pills, and do the world a big favour.

Harlan reached for his phone and called Jim. The instant he picked up, Harlan said, 'What the hell's going on, Jim?'

'A whole lot of crazy shit. That's what's going on. Christ, you're lucky you've got a cast-iron alibi, otherwise Garrett would've had you strung up by your balls. Hang on.' Harlan heard the faraway sound of Jim talking to someone else, then his voice came down the line again. 'I've got to go. I'll call you back as soon as I get a chance.'

'Wait. Just tell me one thing, tell me this isn't my fault.'

'Believe me, Harlan, this isn't your fault.'

The sudden release of Harlan's suppressed breath filled the line. 'Thanks.'

'Watch your back. Garrett's gunning for you.'

Harlan gave a mental shrug. He wasn't concerned about his own back. He would've gladly returned to prison to serve out the remainder of his sentence if it meant Susan Reed and her boys would be OK. He hurried from the flat, pausing only to snatch up a fistful of banknotes. He headed to a nearby row of shops, half an eye on the plain-clothes who got out of the unmarked car and followed him at a discreet distance. He bought a television from a pawn shop and hauled it back to his flat. In missing-person cases the most important time was the first four days – especially when that person was a child. Most missing children were found or returned home of their own free will within that time-frame. Those that weren't tended to be dead. So it was crucial to get the news out there as quickly as possible. He tuned into the twenty-four-hours news channel and settled down to wait for the news to break.

Shortly after midday it broke like a bomb, knocking the breath from Harlan's lungs. 'Police are investigating the abduction of an eight-year-old boy from his bedroom in the middle of the night by a masked armed intruder,' a newsreader gravely announced.

Harlan gaped at the television. He'd been prepared for something sinister but this – this was insane. A child being abducted from the streets was rare enough, but this kind of thing was almost unheard of.

The news cut from the studio to a live shot of a reporter on the pavement across from Susan Reed's house. The street behind was lined with police vehicles. Several uniforms and detectives were gathered outside Susan's front door. Figures in white plastic suits were visible through the windows. 'Here's what we know so far,' said the reporter. 'Sometime last night, eight-year-old Ethan Reed was abducted at gunpoint from the bedroom he shares with his twelve-year-old brother, Kane.'

'Gunpoint,' murmured Harlan, thinking, *This just gets crazier and crazier.*

'Neither Kane nor his mother, Susan, were hurt during

the incident,' went on the reporter. 'At this time that's all I can tell you. The police are going to be making a statement shortly...' A sudden buzz of activity at the front door of Susan's house attracted the reporter's attention. 'In fact, I think... yes, here's Detective Chief Inspector John Garrett to give us that statement.'

The camera homed in on a late-middle-aged man, with a smooth, polished public-school face, and close-set eyes that seemed to be doing their best to appear full of gravity and fortitude. Harlan couldn't help but curl his lip at the sight. He'd never much liked Garrett as a man or a cop. He found him arrogant and condescending, a persuasive talker and shrewd political negotiator, but lacking a cop's compass, that intuition or gut instinct or whatever you wanted to call it that you only got through years of 'dancing with the street', as Jim used to call pounding the beat.

As a half-moon of reporters thrust microphones at him, Garrett began, 'As you know, at some point between the hours of midnight and four a.m. last night, an intruder forced entry to the house behind me and abducted Ethan Reed. We're circulating this recent photo of Ethan.' He held up a photo of Ethan's fragile, androgynous face, and Harlan felt a sharp little sting in his chest.

'In terms of physical description,' continued Garrett, 'Ethan is around four feet five inches tall and slimly built. At the time of his abduction, he was wearing red and blue Spiderman pyjamas. We believe this abduction wasn't an act of impulse. The intruder appears to have known which room Ethan slept in. This leads us to conclude that the intruder may have watched the house prior to taking Ethan. With this in mind, we're urging members of the public to get in touch if you saw anybody in the area over the past few days or weeks who may have looked out of place or who you haven't seen previously. Similarly, did you see any vehicles in the area that you haven't seen previously? However irrelevant you think what you saw might be, please contact us. A coordinated search of the local area is being carried out, involving more than two hundred officers and thirty detectives. We're searching houses, open land, outbuildings and sheds, as well as stopping and questioning motorists. But we're also asking the public to keep their eyes open. Ethan may be with a dark-haired white man of medium height and build.'

Jesus, no wonder they're watching me, thought Harlan. The description fitted him perfectly. It also fitted thousands of other men in the city.

'Susan Reed has asked me to read a brief statement on her behalf,' said Garrett, transferring his gaze from the camera to a sheet of paper. 'To whoever's got my beautiful son, Ethan, please don't hurt him. Please let him go. If you or anyone else knows where Ethan is please bring him home safe. Ethan is my life and my love. Knowing he's out there somewhere and not here where he belongs is devastating beyond anybody's ability to describe. Please do the right thing and give me back my little boy.'

Garrett thanked the reporters, and as they fired a barrage of questions at him, turned to re-enter the house. The camera cut back to the studio. The newsreader said something, but Harlan wasn't listening any more. He was desperately trying to process everything he'd just heard. What the hell was this all about? Ethan obviously hadn't been snatched in the hope of extracting a ransom from his family. And there was no domestic angle. Which suggested the motive was sexual. He winced like someone in pain. If that was the case, experience told him Ethan was almost as good as dead. The only slight positive he could see to hold onto was the fact that Susan and

Kane were still alive, even though, presumably, at least one of them had seen Ethan's kidnapper. Which meant that whatever else the kidnapper might be, they weren't an out-and-out killer.

The television was now showing an aerial shot of Susan's house and the surrounding area. A forensic tent had been erected in the tiny yard at the back of the house, covering the door and downstairs window – one of which, no doubt, was the point of entry. Uniforms were combing an alley beyond the yard, some leading hounds attempting to pick up Ethan's scent, others leading German shepherds specially trained to sniff out human remains. Further afield, more uniforms were talking to local residents. It was off camera, though, that the work which Harlan knew was the real key to finding Ethan was taking place. Detectives would be building up a picture around the boy – scrutinising his family, extended family and school friends; trawling through phone records and computer files; calling on local sex offenders; looking for that vital scrap of evidence, that tiny piece of the jigsaw that would crack the case.

His phone rang. He snatched it up. 'Are you watching it on the telly?' asked Jim.

'Yes.'

'Insane, isn't it? I mean, what kind of fucker snatches a kid from his bed like that?'

'So how did it go down?'

'Like Garrett said, sometime between twelve and four someone forced the kitchen window and took the boy.'

'Come on, Jim, you've got a lot more than that.'

Jim was silent a moment, then he said, 'First you've got to promise me you'll stay away from this case.'

'How am I supposed to do that when I'm a goddamn suspect?'

'Don't be coy with me, Harlan. You know what I mean. I can hear that cop's brain of yours cranking into motion. You want to play armchair detective, fine. Just make sure it goes no further. Besides, no one here seriously considers you a suspect, not even Garrett.'

'Then why am I being watched?'

'Procedure. We can't take any chances in a case like this. You know that.'

'Look, I'm not about to start tearing this city apart searching for Ethan Reed. All I want is to hear the details of the case, see if anything jogs in my memory. After all, I was sat outside the vic's house for several hours two days before all this happened. I might've seen something without realising it.'

'OK, but I'm trusting you as a friend not to get any more involved than you already are.' Jim took a breath, and as if reading from a sheet of paper, continued in an atonal voice, 'Ethan shares a bunk bed with his brother, Kane. Both were in bed asleep by ten. Susan went to bed at midnight. Sometime after that, Kane woke when he heard his brother say, "Who are you?" He saw Ethan stood in his pyjamas facing a figure dressed in a black sweatshirt, camouflage trousers, gloves and a balaclava. The figure whispered to Ethan, "Be quiet or I'll kill you and your brother." Kane pretended to be asleep, but kept his eyes open just enough to see that the figure's wrists were white with dark hairs on them. He also saw that the figure was holding a handgun. The figure led Ethan from the room. Kane remained in bed, terrified that if he moved or made a sound the figure would return and carry out his threat. At approximately four o'clock he went to his mother's bedroom. It took him a while to wake her up because, like most nights since her husband's death, she was out of it on sleeping pills and alcohol.'

Guilt loomed like a tainted shadow at Harlan's back again. He shook it aside. This was no time to give in to emotion. If he was going to be of any help he had to keep his head clear. 'Maybe the kidnapper knew Susan was on sleeping tablets.'

'Maybe. Maybe our guy knows her. Or maybe the brothers confided in their friends and teachers about her problems. Or maybe one of Susan's friends or someone in her family or extended family talked with their spouses or friends about her. Or maybe our guy doesn't know Susan and was crazy or stupid or desperate enough to do what he did anyway. Or maybe—'

'All right, I get the point. What about leads? Any concrete leads?'

'Just one. At approximately three a.m. a milkman saw a silver VW Golf with tinted windows cruising up and down the street. He thought the driver might be aiming to rob him, so he took down the number plate.'

'What's the reg?'

'I don't think you need to know that.'

'You're right, it probably won't make any difference. But why take the chance?'

'No, I think I've told you all I want to for now. I've got to get back to it. Remember what I said, Harlan. Keep your head down.'

'Just tell me one more thing. What does your gut say? Dead or alive?'

Jim considered this a brief moment. Then he said, 'Dead,' and hung up.

Chapter Four

Dead. The word kept ringing in Harlan's mind. Dead, or soon to be dead. That's what his gut told him too. Everything he'd heard pointed to a sexual motive. And no sexual predator willing to go to such extremes to get their hands on Ethan was going to leave him alive to tell the tale. Harlan figured the police had a window of maybe two days to find Ethan. After that, forget it.

The television was showing Ethan's photo again, alongside a grainy photo of his mother's grief-stricken face. With a jolt, Harlan realised he recognised the photo – it'd been used in a newspaper article about Susan's husband's death. If the media hadn't done so already, Harlan knew it was only a matter of time before they made a connection between his release and Ethan's abduction. Then his face would be splashed all over the news too. He'd be named as a person of interest, held up for public scrutiny. Regardless of his innocence, the stigma of association would make his life a hell on earth. He wouldn't be able to leave the flat without attracting hostile looks and verbal abuse. He frowned in distress. Not that he was bothered what the general public thought of him – fuck them. What bothered him was the thought of the pain that the media picking at the scars of past wounds would cause Eve – especially as it occurred to him that they might well try to draw some kind of spurious link between Thomas's death and Ethan's disappearance.

Once again, Harlan thrust his emotions aside and focused on what needed to be done. Nothing mattered now, except finding Ethan. He hurried into the hallway, grabbing his jacket and scooping up most of the remaining banknotes on his way out of the flat.

In the lift, Harlan phoned the warehouse foreman and told him he wouldn't be able to make it in to work. 'Good,' said the foreman. 'And don't bother coming in tomorrow either. You're fired.'

The foreman hung up. Harlan sighed, thinking, *So it's already started*.

He made his way to a nearby public library, logged onto a computer and searched the local business directory for milkmen. Darren Arnold & Sons served Susan Reed's neighbourhood. He phoned them, and when a man picked up, he said, 'This is DI Greenwood, Mr Arnold. I'm just going over your statement and I need you to confirm the registration number of the VW Golf you saw.'

'KY09 SGE.'

'Thank you.'

Harlan hung up, navigated to a car registration checker website, and typed in the reg. *Renault Clio 1.2 16V* came up on the monitor, which meant the milkman had either got at least part of the reg wrong or the plates were stolen. He phoned the local DVLA and asked for Pete Devlin – a guy he used to know back when he regularly needed to trace vehicles.

'Harlan, how the Christ are you?' said Pete. 'When did you get out?'

'A few weeks ago. Listen, Pete, I need a favour. I'm trying to trace a car that pranged me and didn't stop.'

'What's the reg?'

Harlan gave Pete the number.

'Renault Clio,' said Pete.

'That's the one.'

'I shouldn't be doing this, but seeing as you're an old friend. It's registered to a James Barnshaw. Thirty-four Chatfield Crescent.'

'What about the car's history?'

'It's clean.'

'Cheers, Pete. I owe you.'

Harlan Googled James Barnshaw and the address. Nothing came up. He navigated to the phonebook website, found Barnshaw's number and called it. A woman answered. She sounded middle-aged and middle-class. 'Can I speak to James Barnshaw, please?' said Harlan. 'My name's Detective Inspector Greenwood.'

'Is this about James's number plates being stolen?'

'Yes, I just need to confirm exactly what happened?'

The woman sighed as if she was tired of repeating the story. 'When James left the house last Wednesday morning, his number plates were missing. We didn't hear or see anything.'

'What about your neighbours? Did any of them see anything?'

'No.'

Harlan thanked the woman and hung up. The fact that the plates were stolen gave credence to the idea that the Golf had been cruising Susan Reed's street on some criminal expedition. But it also meant the lead was a dead end, unless the car had been caught on camera speeding, or driving away from a petrol station without paying, or some such thing – and even if it had, he didn't have the means of finding out. The best use of his time at present, as far as he could see, was simply to get out there and search the streets for the Golf. He glanced out the window at the plain-clothes sheltering from a sudden downpour in a shop porch. He deleted his browsing history, left the library and made his way hurriedly to the nearest second-hand car dealership. There was a souped-up black VW Golf on the forecourt that was about as fast as any car in its class. He went into the dealer's office and slapped down the cash to buy it.

Harlan cruised the streets, searching for silver VW Golfs, scanning licence-plate numbers. There was little hope in it but – for the moment, at least – he could see no other course open to him. He switched the radio on and tuned into the news, which was playing an edited version of Garrett's statement. There was no mention of the Golf. It was always a tricky question – whether and when to make such information public. On the one hand, someone who'd seen the car or knew its owner or the owner themselves might well contact the police. On the other, if the car's owner and Ethan's kidnapper were one and the same, they might try to hide or destroy the car, or even worse, they might be panicked into killing the boy. Harlan guessed that if the information was released at all, it wouldn't be until the four-day mark passed. After that, in their minds Ethan was dead, so they'd have a shit lot less to lose by going public.

All day long Harlan vainly searched for the Golf, circling outwards from the city centre, paying special attention to the uninhabited houses, cadaverous factories and pockets of woodland and wasteland in the lonelier parts of the urban sprawl. He wasn't the only one searching. Almost everywhere he went there were uniforms doing their thing. Police helicopters hovered and circled over the city. He didn't stop to eat, he only stopped to fill up on petrol. As the hours flashed past like lightning, a sense of frustration swelled in his gut. Outside the official information loop, he felt blind and helpless. He tried several times to ring Jim but got no reply. He supposed his ex-partner was either too busy or pissed off at him to answer – Jim would certainly have heard by now what he was up to.

Harlan's stomach gave a lurch when he heard his name on the radio. 'Detectives are speaking to persons of interest in the case,' said the newsreader, 'including ex-police officer, Harlan Miller, who was recently released from prison after serving a four-year sentence for the—'

Harlan reflexively snapped the radio off. After the space of a breath, he turned it back on, wondering who the other persons of interest were. But no more names were mentioned.

Before the news report was even finished, Harlan's phone rang. A number he didn't recognise flashed up on its screen. He answered the phone and waited for whoever it was to speak. His stomach gave another lurch when Eve's voice came over the line. 'Harlan?'

Harlan hadn't spoken to Eve since starting his prison sentence. She'd written to him, asking if she could visit. He'd written back, saying it would be for the best if she stayed away. He'd also told her he was sorry. It'd been wrong of him to blame her for Tom's death – in some perverse way, killing Robert Reed had made him see that. Finally, he'd told her that the one thing she could do to help him through his sentence was to get on with her life. It'd hurt him deep and long to write that, but it was necessary.

Eve's voice sounded different – no, not different, just changed. There was a softness to it that reminded him why he'd first fallen in love with her. A thickness rose in his throat. He swallowed it in a lump and shoved it far down. 'I assume Jim gave you my number.'

'He's worried about you.' There was a slight hesitation, then she added, 'We both are.'

'Well don't be. I'm not worth your worry.'

'That's not true. You're a good man.'

'Good men don't kill.'

'You lashed out in a moment of madness and despair at a man who severely provoked you. Yes, that man died, but you've paid for—'

'You're wasting your time,' broke in Harlan. 'This is something I've got to do.'

'They'll send you back to prison.'

'If they do, they do. Susan Reed's already lost her husband. I can't let her lose her son as well. You of all people should understand that.'

Eve was silent a moment. When she next spoke, Harlan could tell she was struggling to keep her voice from shaking, and it hurt him to hear. 'But what can you do on your own?'

'I don't know. Probably nothing. But I've got to try.'

Eve sighed. 'OK, if I can't change your mind then all I can say is good luck. Find that boy. Find him and return him where he belongs.'

Another silence passed between them. Harlan waited for Eve to say goodbye – he'd never been any good at goodbyes – but instead she said hesitatingly, 'Maybe we could meet up sometime.'

Christ yes, his heart said. How he would love to meet up with her, listen to her soft voice, smell her, touch her. He suddenly found himself remembering how it felt to kiss her, the way she used to murmur his name as he nuzzled her neck, her ear. And the memory of it made his blood quicken. But he knew he couldn't allow himself to follow his heart. After all, what did he have to offer? Nothing but memories and misery. 'I don't think that'd be good idea.'

'Yeah, I guess you're right. I don't know why I even suggested it. Take care, Harlan.'

'You too.'

Harlan hung up, releasing a heavy breath. 'Focus,' he said

sharply. He returned his attention to the street shining wetly beneath the orange glow of the lamp-posts, telling himself, *That life is gone. This right here, this is all the life you've got left, so make it count.*

All night he searched in vain. When darkness began to give way to the blue of dawn, he grabbed a bite to eat at a café. The breakfast news blared out of a television on the wall. The waitress served him in silence then quickly retreated behind the counter where she fell into a whispered conversation with another woman. Both women shot him uneasy, frowning glances. He ignored them, concentrating on eating and the news. The police were having no more luck than him, it seemed. There had been no reported sightings of Ethan, and the police had expanded the focus of their search beyond Sheffield into the surrounding regions, particularly the north-west where there'd recently been a suspected child abduction – Jamie Sutton, an eleven-year-old boy, had disappeared while out riding his bike in Prestwich, a northern suburb of Manchester, nearly two months ago. A massive search had been conducted, thousands of missing-person posters had been distributed, private donors had put together a reward of two hundred thousand pounds for anyone who came forward with solid information that led to the boy's rescue. All to no avail. Jamie Sutton, it seemed, had literally vanished into thin air.

Harlan considered expanding the focus of his search too, but quickly decided against it. The connection between the cases was too tenuous. For starters, it was impossible to say with certainty that Jamie Sutton had been abducted. He might've been the victim of a hit-and-run, met with some kind of accident, or maybe even be a runaway. Secondly, if Jamie had been abducted, then the kidnapper's MO was significantly different, more suggestive of an opportunistic mindset. Thirdly, Jamie was a very different boy from Ethan – Jamie had a broad face and bold, self-confident eyes, whereas Ethan looked shy and timid. Finally, and most importantly as far as Harlan was concerned, he saw little hope in himself succeeding where the best efforts of the police had failed. Better to continue the search here, where the trail was still fresh.

It was midday when the posters started appearing on lamp-posts and in shop windows. They featured close-ups of Ethan taken from different angles and with different expressions. Above his face in big letters was the word *KIDNAPPED*. Below were the numbers of a couple of freephone tip-hotlines. There were also groups of people on the streets – not police, but volunteers – handing out leaflets to passers-by and motorists. Harlan rolled his window down to take one from a woman. 'There's going to be a march through the streets around Ethan's home tonight,' she said. 'Everybody's welcome.'

'Everybody doesn't include me,' said Harlan, and he drove on, working his way methodically through the city.

New information trickled through the radio. Police dogs had picked up Ethan's scent but the trail they'd found ended several feet from the backyard gate. Detectives were holding a local man for questioning. William Jones, a fifty-two-year-old, unmarried, unemployed steel worker with convictions for child sex offences, had apparently been seen on several occasions recently hanging around outside Ethan's school and at a nearby play-park that the boy frequented. Jones was well known in the community as a sex offender, and his home and car had been vandalised many times in the past. In a brief statement to the press, Detective Chief Inspector Garrett said that Jones was on the Sex Offenders' Register and was considered a medium risk.

Harlan pulled over at a café with internet access, navigated to the website of a local newspaper, typed *William Jones* into the search-term box, and scanned down the list of related articles until he came to the headline: *Man Jailed For Child Sex Offences*. He clicked the link and skim-read the article it led to. Jones had been sentenced to a year's imprisonment in 2005 for ten counts of making indecent images of a girl under fourteen years old, and one count of indecent assault. There was a photo of him – overweight, vein-streaked alcoholic's cheeks, receding grey-brown hair. Although, at a stretch, Jones might fit the kidnapper's description, Harlan dismissed him as a suspect. The guy was a relatively low-grade offender with a taste for young girls. A nasty piece of work but not the type to snatch eight-year-old boys from their bedrooms. That didn't mean it wasn't worth bringing him in and grilling him for a while. After all, birds of a feather flocked together – especially when no one else wanted anything to do with them – which meant that characters like Jones were often the best source of information about offenders operating under the police radar in an area.

Harlan returned to his car and the search. Afternoon wore away like a corpse in a hot climate. Five o'clock, six, seven... Every time he glanced at the clock, another hour seemed to have passed. He swallowed ProPlus tablets with black coffee, but even so his vision began to grow blurry as if he was looking through a haze of tears. It'd been nearly forty-eight hours since he last slept. Reluctantly accepting that if he continued searching he'd be likely to miss more than he saw, he headed back to his flat.

Remembering about the march, Harlan flicked the television on and found himself confronted by Susan Reed's haggard, almost cadaverous face. She looked like she'd aged two years for every day that'd passed since he last saw her. Her eyes, which peered out from under tear-swollen lids, had a glazed look about them. More than likely she'd been given a mild sedative. A man had one arm cupped around her narrow shoulders as if to hold her up. He was maybe five or ten years younger than her, tall and skinny, with a pale, lumpy face, and a fine fuzz of blond hair on his skull and above his upper lip. Watery blue eyes – it was difficult to tell if they were watery with tears or just watery – peered at the cameras through cheap-looking spectacles. Harlan wondered who the man was. A friend? A relative? No, his body language spoke of a different kind of intimacy. A boyfriend, maybe. A person of interest, definitely.

A gang of reporters pushed microphones closer to Susan's trembling lips as she opened her mouth to speak. 'Ethan...' Her voice cracked and she seemed to lose her breath. She was silent a moment, wrestling with her emotions, on the edge of being overcome with grief. 'Ethan, if you're out there and you can hear me, we're doing everything we possibly can to find you.' She looked away from the cameras, steadying herself, then she addressed the kidnapper. 'Please let my beautiful little boy go. Please! Please!' She couldn't hold it together any longer. Tears spilled down her cheeks. She dropped her head, shoulders quaking, and the man at her side gently guided her away from the microphones.

The camera panned around to focus on a crowd about four- or five-hundred strong, many of them carrying flowers and lighted candles. At the front of the crowd a line of children held a large banner with two pictures of Ethan flanking the words *HELP FIND ETHAN* and a telephone number. The crowd applauded as Susan and the man joined them. They set off along the streets, chanting Ethan's name. Their voices were full of a kind of sad enthusiasm, but suddenly a discordant, angry note came to the fore. The crowd bunched into tight knot outside a dilapidated two-up, two-down terraced house. The house's downstairs window was boarded with warped, rain-stained chipboard on which was graffitied in red paint *Pedo Scum*. As the camera homed in on the graffiti, a voice-over explained that the house belonged to William Jones.

Jones was lucky the police were holding him, Harlan reflected. He knew from experience how quickly a peaceful gathering could transform into a lynch mob. He'd once been part of a task force set up to investigate the death of a convicted paedophile whose house was ransacked by an angry mob, some of whom were only a couple of years older than Ethan.

He phoned Jim. This time his ex-partner answered. 'Who's the guy with Susan Reed?' asked Harlan.

'Forget it, Harlan. You're not getting anything else out of me, not after the way you've behaved. I thought we had a deal that you were going to keep away from this thing.'

'You thought wrong. Look, Jim, all I'm doing is searching the streets. I owe Susan Reed that much at least. Besides, the guy went on the national news with her. His name's going to come out soon enough anyway.'

'I'll tell you this much. He's clean, no warrants, no record, and he's got an airtight alibi.'

'He could have an accomplice.'

Jim sighed and tried to change the subject. 'Have you spoken to Eve?'

'Yes. She asked if I wanted to meet up.'

'And what did you say?'

'I said no.'

'You want a piece of advice from someone who's let pride get in the way of happiness. Call her back, tell her you've changed your mind.'

'I can't do that.'

'Why? She still loves you.'

'I know. That's why I can't see her.'

Jim huffed his breath into the receiver. 'Christ, I've never heard such a load of bollocks. If you think you're doing Eve a favour by staying away from her, you're wrong. All you're doing is making both of you miserable. But then again, maybe that's what you want. Maybe prison's turned you into the kind of guy who enjoys misery, wallows in it like a pig in muck.'

'Maybe so.' Harlan's eyes were drawn to the television by the sound of smashing glass. Someone had hurled a bottle at Jones's house. The police quickly moved in to usher the crowd onwards. The camera homed in on Susan Reed, milking every ounce of agony and despair. Her boyfriend, or whatever he was, looked pale and uncomfortable, like he wanted to be somewhere else. 'So what's the guy's alibi?'

'Jesus, Harlan,' snapped Jim, and he hung up.

Harlan switched off the television and headed for bed. He set the alarm clock for two hours hence and shut his eyes. As he drifted off to sleep, he thought about what Jim had said. Jim was wrong, prison hadn't changed him – at least, not in the way he meant. He'd always needed a bit of misery in his life. As a detective, he'd needed it the way an oyster needs sand to form pearls. It'd provided him with the edge and insight required to do the job. The difference was that back then he'd used his misery, controlled it. Now it was the other way around.

Chapter Five

All that night and the following day and night, Harlan relentlessly scoured the streets. He saw dozens of silver VW Golfs but none of their number plates came close to being a match. If the car belonged to the kidnapper, chances were the plates had been switched anyway. He simply had to hope the kidnapper was too incompetent to have done so. It wasn't much of a hope, but it was a possibility. Experience told him that the average criminal was just as likely to be brought down by their own stupidity or simple oversight as detective work.

As the hands of time ticked mercilessly towards the four-day mark, his searching became ever more frantic. One time, after glimpsing a silver car in his rear-view mirror, he did a high-speed U-turn and gave chase. A mile or so later, leaving a trail of blaring horns in his wake, he caught up with the car only to find it wasn't even a VW.

There was little new to be heard on the news. For some undisclosed reason, a pond was dragged but turned up nothing. William Jones was released without charge. The police issued warnings that vigilantism wouldn't be tolerated. They also put up a ten-thousand-pound reward for information that would lead them to Ethan. Their search was building to fever pitch too – over a third of the regional force's manpower was now involved. An army of volunteers wallpapered the city with

Ethan's picture and handed out reams of leaflets. Susan Reed spoke to dozens of journalists, making a series of increasingly desperate appeals. But answers seemed non-existent and fear swelled like waves of fire, ready to consume the city. Parents kept their children indoors. Home security companies couldn't keep up with demand. Police were inundated with reports of suspected prowlers.

On the evening of the third day, Garrett gave another press conference at which he admitted that the police had few clues to go on and called on people not to lose hope. Don't lose hope! In the past, Harlan had spoken those same words to the families of missing and kidnapped persons, and they'd rung as hollow on his lips as they did on Garrett's. He glanced at the clock. Half past seven. There were approximately eight or nine hours of hope left. After that, anyone who knew anything about child abductions knew that Ethan would almost certainly be dead.

Time wore on. Ten p.m., eleven... one a.m., two... Harlan didn't stop for food, didn't stop for red lights, barely stopped to breathe, until the clock hit four a.m. Then he pulled over and sat for a long moment with his head pressed against the steering wheel, eyes closed. 'It's over,' he murmured to himself, and he turned the car to head back to his flat.

He dropped like a stone onto his bed but despite his exhaustion it took him hours to get to sleep. And when he did eventually manage to drop off, his sleep was one long, sweaty nightmare in which he was chasing a silver Golf through the city. A child's terrified face was pressed against the car's rear windscreen, but that child wasn't Ethan it was Thomas. On and on the chase went but Harlan never got any closer to the car. He awoke choking on tears of frustration and rage. 'It's not fucking over!' he gasped, shaking his head. With or without hope, he had to continue searching.

He yanked on his clothes and checked the news to see if there'd been any developments – there was one: the identity of Susan Reed's companion had finally come out. His name was Neil Price. He was thirty-one years old and worked as a night porter at the Northern General Hospital – which explained his airtight alibi. He was referred to as 'Mrs Reed's media-shy boyfriend'. The way the newsreader said it, as if there was something intrinsically dubious in being media shy, made Harlan's toast stick in his craw. There was no suggestion that Price was under any kind of official suspicion but a criminologist in the studio insidiously invited viewers to regard him with narrowed eyes by describing the classic profile of a potential abductor – white male, early thirties, unskilled worker. Harlan found himself wanting to speak up in Price's defence – not because he thought there was no possibility the guy was involved but because he despised the media's tactics. He'd seen too many lives indelibly marked by shit-flinging journalists.

Over the next few days, Harlan spent every waking moment searching for Ethan. He trawled the suburbs, peering over fences and into garages. He drove around supermarket car parks, and multi-storey car parks, and industrial estate car parks, constantly moving, constantly looking.

Nothing. It was as though the VW didn't exist. Harlan began to wonder whether the milkman had got the car's make wrong. If so, he might as well be out hunting for a ghost. Whenever he returned to the flat, bone-weary though he was, he lay awake with doubts swirling inside him.

Days stretched into weeks. Harlan hardly slept, ate or washed. Telephone calls from his parole officer – he'd failed to report for a meeting – went unanswered. Mail piled up unopened. He was searching further and further afield. Villages and towns he'd never been to before. Sometimes he didn't return home for days. He stayed in cheap hotels and B&Bs, and when nowhere else was available, he slept in his car.

With every passing day, the media and the public's interest in the case waned. News reports got shorter and less frequent. Newspaper articles were relegated from the front pages. Volunteers pasting up posters and handing out leaflets disappeared from the streets. Ethan's sun-and-rain-faded face was gradually blotted out by fly-posters, defaced by graffiti, even torn down – some people, it seemed, objected to being constantly reminded that something so terrible had happened in the place they lived.

There was no longer a plain-clothes on Harlan's tail wherever he went. The police's search – at least on a street level – was winding down. In the north-west, whatever leads they'd been following had apparently led to nothing. Locally, they'd searched hundreds of addresses, spoken to thousands of people, pried into every corner of Ethan and his family's life, but all their efforts had failed. The jigsaw remained incomplete.

Exactly a month after Ethan's abduction a local Baptist preacher named Lewis Gunn whipped up interest in the case by appearing on the news to urge church members nationwide to continue the search. He announced that an all-night prayer vigil was to be held at tabernacles across the city at which he would be collecting donations for a reward to be offered on top of the police reward. Harlan had previously stayed away from all such gatherings, partly out of fear of being recognised, but mainly because he knew Garrett would use his presence as an excuse to haul him in for further questioning, maybe even try to get his parole revoked. But now that he was no longer being followed he saw no reason not to go along. And there was little chance of him being recognised – he barely recognised himself with several weeks' growth of beard on his sleep- and food-deprived face.

He went first to Lewis Gunn's tabernacle – an ugly brick building with a huge concrete crucifix over its entrance. Its car park was crammed with cars. People, many of whom held lighted candles, were filing inside it. There was a solemn hush over the gathering and, indeed, over the surrounding streets, as if the whole city held its breath in silent prayer.

Harlan was about to get out of the car when he saw Susan flanked by Neil and the preacher – a vigorous-looking middle-aged man with a bushy head of grey–black hair. It hurt Harlan like a knife to see Susan, her face devoid of colour, her eyes devoid of expression, like something dead but alive. Walking slowly, like an old woman crippled with arthritis, she headed into the church. Harlan left the car and made his way around the car park, checking number plates. His heart gave a double thump when he saw the silver VW Golf with tinted windows. His eyes darted down to the number plate. KY09 SGE. An exact match! But why the hell, he wondered, would the kidnapper – if that was who the car belonged to – risk coming here? Several possibilities occurred to him. Maybe the kidnapper was somehow connected to the church, and it would look odd for him not to be here. Or maybe he was someone from the local community who was trying to distance himself from the crime by staying close to it – there were plenty of cases where murderers had got involved in the search for their victims. Or maybe he was simply the kind of guy who got a kick out of seeing first-hand the pain he'd inflicted.

Harlan snatched out his phone to call Jim but it just rang and rang. Staying on the line, he pressed his forehead to the car's rear window, cupping his hand against the glass to cut out the reflection of the street lamps. He could vaguely make out some kind of shape on the back seat, a rucksack perhaps, or possibly a bin liner stuffed with something. It crossed his mind that maybe this sick fuck was crazy or arrogant enough to bring Ethan – or rather, Ethan's body – here. Maybe it gave him some kind of twisted thrill. Whatever it was in there, Harlan felt compelled to get a proper look. He ran to fetch the wheel-nut wrench from his car. As he returned to the Golf, Jim finally answered. 'Jesus, Harlan, what do you want?'

'I found the silver Volkswagen.'

'Holy Christ! Where?'

'The Baptist tabernacle on the Attercliffe Road.'

'Stay where you are. Someone will be there as soon as possible. And for God's sake, don't do anything. Do you hear?'

'Uh-huh.'

Harlan hung up and raised the wrench overhead to smash the passenger window. Before he could do so an angry shout rang out, 'Hey you! What the fuck you doing?'

A heavily built man dressed in jeans and a leather jacket was approaching fast. He was about Harlan's height and age but his close-cropped hair was ginger, not dark.

His hands were up in a fighting position, and Harlan noticed that the backs of them and his wrists were greenish-black with spidery jailhouse tattoos – tattoos which in a semi-dark room to a terrified twelve-year-old's eyes might conceivably be mistaken for hair. One look at the man's expression told him there was going to be serious trouble if he didn't act fast. He shoved the wrench in his jacket pocket. 'Police. Is this your car?'

The man stopped a few feet away from Harlan, uncertainty puckering his forehead. He took in Harlan's unkempt hair and creased clothes. 'You're police? Let's see your ID.'

'Is this your car?' Harlan repeated more forcefully. The key to these situations, he knew from experience, was to take control, and to do so quickly with a calm aggressiveness.

'You're not police. You look like a fuckin' scag-head to me.'

'Sir, this vehicle is suspected to have been used in a crime. I need you to accompany me to the station for questioning.'

The lines of doubt on the man's face deepened at Harlan's official-sounding language. For an instant, he looked as if he was going to accept Harlan's claim to be a police officer but then the pinpricks of his pupils flared. 'Either you show me some fuckin' ID, pal, or I'm gonna fuck you up so bad you'll wish you were dead. You get me?'

The two men stared silently at each other. Adrenalin poured into Harlan's bloodstream. He knew what he had to do – he had to put this fucker on the ground and kneel on his back until the uniforms showed up – but he couldn't do it. His body was rooted, paralysed, while his mind looped back to the image of Robert Reed going over like a skittle. Yet again he heard the sickening crunch, yet again he saw the blood diffusing like wine through the snow.

The man swung at Harlan. Automatically, he jerked his arms up to block the punch. The man swung again. Harlan swayed out of his reach. 'Motherfucker!' roared the man, throwing a flurry of punches, all of which either deflected off Harlan's arms or missed their target. The man backed away, breathing heavily, a new wariness in his eyes.

Again, they faced each other silently for a moment. Then the man pulled out a key and unlocked the car. 'Stop. I can't let you leave,' said Harlan, but he made no attempt to prevent the man from ducking into the car. It wasn't until the engine revved into life that he darted forward and tried to yank open the driver's door. He was dragged along, stumbled to his knees, and as the car turned sharply, narrowly avoided getting pulled under its wheels.

As the car accelerated onto the road, Harlan sprinted to his own car. He slammed it into gear and pushed his foot down hard. He'd been trained in pursuit driving, and he knew the area well, so he was confident the Golf wouldn't get away from him. Accelerating smoothly through the gears, he quickly caught up with it. Its driver put on a sudden burst of speed at a junction, narrowly avoiding clipping another car. Harlan was forced to briefly mount the pavement in order to swerve around the same car. Zigzagging through traffic, careening wildly around bends, they roared through the streets at blurring speeds. Horns blared, tyres squealed and brakes screeched as the Golf's driver attempted to shake off his pursuer by going the wrong way around a busy roundabout. There was the sound of grinding metal as Harlan's car scraped along the side of an oncoming bus. For an instant, he thought he was boxed in, then the traffic parted like the Red Sea, and he was charging after the Golf again. Its driver was going like a mad thing, overtaking blindly, cutting across streams of traffic, forcing Harlan to take crazy risks just to keep him in view. *This is going to end badly*, thought Harlan, and a second later it did. The silver Golf took a corner too fast, skidded out of control, hit a kerb and flipped. Once, twice, three times it rolled across a grass verge, tearing up huge chunks of turf, before coming to rest on its roof against a wall.

Harlan sprang out of his car and ran to the Golf. He tried to open the driver's door but it was wedged shut by the car's buckled roof. He kicked in the window, already shattered by the impact. Ducking down, he saw the man lying in an unconscious heap, his face crushed and bloody. Scattered all around him were clothes, which appeared to have come from a holdall that'd burst open during the crash. Harlan felt for a pulse and, to his relief, found one, although it was weak and thready. The man groaned as Harlan hooked his hands under his armpits and gently as possible pulled him from the wreckage. His breath gurgled and grated as if something was broken inside his chest. Blood welled from a deep gash on the palm of one of his hands. Harlan took off his jacket and covered him with it, before ducking back into the overturned car to grab an item of clothing to staunch the bleeding. It was then that he saw the gun. It was an Olympic .380 BBM revolver – a starter pistol favoured by criminals because it could easily be purchased and just as easily be converted to fire live ammo. Careful not to touch the gun with his hands, he wrapped it in a T-shirt and pocketed it. Then he tore another T-shirt in two and bandaged the man's hand as best he could with the strips. The man's eyes flickered open, showing white for a second before the pupils rolled down. He tried to sit up.

'Lie still,' said Harlan, holding him down.

'I can't breathe.' The man's voice came in a strangled gasp. 'Where is he?'

'I need an ambulance.'

'I'll call one as soon as you tell me where Ethan Reed is.'

'How would I know that?' the man groaned. Spittle muddied with blood dribbled from the edges of his mouth.

'Listen to me, you've probably got serious internal injuries. You might not have long left to live. This could be your last chance to make amends, to save your soul. So why don't you tell me where Ethan Reed is?'

'Oh God,' whimpered the man. 'Oh God. I didn't want to hurt anybody... I didn't... I...' His voice faded out and his eyes rolled again.

'Stay with me,' urged Harlan but he couldn't keep the man from slipping back into unconsciousness. He checked through his pockets and found a wallet. Inside it there was some loose change, a baggie containing a small amount of white powder and six credit cards, each with a different name. In the distance, he heard the wail of approaching sirens.

Chapter Six

Harlan examined his arms. Bruises were already beginning to flower where the punches had landed. He folded his hands – which were trembling from the fading rush of adrenalin – together on the table in front of him. He looked at the uniform standing by the door of the interview room. 'Don't suppose you could get me a coffee and some painkillers?'

The uniform nodded and turned to leave. A short while later, Jim entered the room and put a polystyrene cup and a couple of tablets on the table. 'How you doing?' he asked.

In answer, Harlan held up his shaky hands. 'What about our man?'

'Still unconscious.'

'Will he live?'

'The doctors aren't saying.'

'Who is he?'

'We don't know. We're running his prints.'

Harlan took out the gun. 'I found this in his car.'

Jim looked at it with distaste. 'Seems like every scumbag out there is carrying one of those pieces of crap these days. You're lucky you didn't get a bullet through your damn fool—'

Before Jim could finish Garrett stormed into the room, and planting his hands on the table, said to Harlan, 'Just what the fuck did you think you were doing? You put innocent people's lives at risk out there tonight. Detective Monahan told you to stay put and do nothing.'

'I'm not a cop any more, and I don't take orders from anybody.'

'That's right, Miller, you're not a cop.' There was a tone of stung pride in Garrett's voice. It was deeply embarrassing to him that one man, regardless of who that man might be, had succeeded where several hundred officers and detectives under his command had failed. Moreover, it was a blow to his career – it was no secret that he was an ambitious man with an eye on the chief superintendent's office. 'You're an ex-con who's failed to show for a meeting with his case officer. That's a serious parole violation. I could have you put back inside.'

'So do it.'

The two men stared at each other, neither flinching. Garrett shook his head. 'No. As much as it pains me to admit it, our main suspect would still be on the streets but for you. That's why I've spoken to your case officer, explained that there were extenuating circumstances for your failure to show.'

'Do you expect me to say thanks?'

'No. I expect you to go home and get on with your life. I don't want to hear your name in connection with this case again. If I do, I won't hesitate to have you thrown back in prison. Do I make myself clear?'

What fucking life? Harlan felt like saying, but he said, 'Perfectly.'

'Good.' Garrett straightened, casting Jim a stern glance as he turned to leave the room. 'As soon as you're finished here, DI Monahan, I want to speak to you in my office.'

'Yes, sir.'

Garret paused by the door and looked at Harlan. 'To think that you were once one of our most promising young DIs. Looking

57

at you now it, well, it just makes me very sad.'

Despite himself, Harlan blinked from Garrett's gaze. A familiar surge of self-loathing burned through him as he caught sight of his ragged reflection in the room's one-way observation window. There was nothing left of that young DI to see. There was only a pitiable, broken creature, with the desperate, bloodshot eyes of an animal in pain rather than a human being. He fought a sudden wild urge to snatch up the pistol and put a bullet in his reflection.

'Patronising bastard,' muttered Jim, once they were alone. 'You deserve gratitude, not pity.'

'Forget it.' Harlan forced a smile. 'Sounds like I've got you in trouble.'

Jim smiled crookedly in return. 'So what else is new?' he sighed. 'Sometimes I think I'm getting too old for this job.'

'Bullshit. You're the best copper this force has ever had.'

Jim gave Harlan a meaningful look. 'No I'm not. Come on, I'll walk you out.'

As they made their way past the booking area to reception, Jim said, 'Garrett's got his head so far up his arse he can't see for the shit in his eyes, but he said one thing that makes sense – get on with your life.' He stopped at the front entrance and looked Harlan in the eyes. 'Eve called me again. She's broken up with her boyfriend.'

An involuntary rush of something close to elation swept through Harlan. 'Why?' he asked, keeping his voice carefully level, not daring to acknowledge, even to himself, the strength of his feelings.

'Call her and find out.'

They shook hands. 'Call her,' Jim shouted, as Harlan made his way to his car.

Harlan took out his phone and found Eve's number. His

finger hovered over the dial button, his face screwed up with indecision. One minute passed. Two minutes. Suddenly, as if it'd burned his hand, he threw the phone onto the passenger seat. Fatigue heavy in his bones, he drove back to the flat and fell into a dreamless dead sleep.

When Harlan awoke it was afternoon of the next day, and hunger gnawed at the pit of his stomach. He went to the kitchen and opened a cupboard, at the front of which was the tumbler of sleeping pills. He stared at it a moment, then reached past it for a box of cereal. He switched on the television and sat eating at the table. Eve smiled at him from the photo next to him. Catching himself drifting into a fantasy about her in which they were talking and embracing, he reached to flip the photo face down. The sound of Garrett's voice drew his eyes to the television. He was standing outside the police station, saying, 'All I can tell you at this time is that there have been significant new developments in the case.'

'Can you confirm the rumours that these developments are related to an incident which took place at St Mary's Baptist church last night?' asked one of the gathered journalists.

'No I can't. No more questions right now. There'll be a full press briefing later today. Thank you.'

Garrett turned and headed into the station. The cameras cut back to the studio where, after speculating about what the developments might be, the newsreader announced that nearly twenty thousand quid had been raised by the all-night vigil to add to the ten thousand already on offer. Harlan's thoughts began to slide away from the TV back to Eve. He closed his eyes, feeling her fingers crawl up his back, her mouth nuzzle his neck. As if she was right there in the room with him, he heard her murmur, 'I love you.'

I love you too, Harlan thought. But before the words could form on his lips, he shook himself free of the fantasy. He jerked to his feet, grabbed his jacket and left the flat. He needed to walk, to clear his head. As he pounded the streets, though, scenes of Eve tumbled through his mind in rapid succession, threatening to overwhelm his consciousness. He was holding her, kissing her, tasting her, smelling her. They were in bed, making love. Then he was watching her sleep, stroking her hair. Memories mixed intoxicatingly with imagination, like colours on a palette, until one became indistinguishable from the other. In a kind of daze, he took out his phone and called her.

'Harlan?'

The sound of Eve's hesitant, hopeful voice jolted Harlan back into the moment. He gripped the phone to his ear, heart thumping.

'Harlan?' she repeated. 'Are you there? Are you OK?'

This is crazy, Harlan thought. *It can only lead to more pain and suffering. Just hang up, hang up...* But he didn't hang up. Instead, he said, 'I'm sorry, I shouldn't have called.'

'No, I'm glad you did.'

Harlan was aware that his breathing had quickened. There was a slight quiver in his voice as he spoke. 'Jim told me you broke up with your boyfriend. But he didn't tell me why.'

'I realised I didn't love him.'

Eve's answer led Harlan to another question, one he didn't dare ask – what made you realise you didn't love him? A moment of silence passed. 'I'm sorry,' he said again, for want of something to say.

'Don't be. It's not your—' Eve broke off.

It wasn't hard for Harlan to figure out what she'd been about to say. *It's not your fault.* The implication behind her silence – that it *was* his fault – sent a rush of blood through him. Suddenly, he knew that he had to see her. He just had to, no matter how his guilt burned at his heart. 'Where are you?'

'At work.'

'Can you get away?'

'Why?'

'I want—' No, *want* wasn't the right word. 'I need to see you.'

'OK. We can meet at my flat, if you like.'

'Where is it?'

Eve gave Harlan the address, and he told her he'd be there as soon as he could. He ran back to his car, not wanting to give his guilt a chance to steal his need, his desire. When he got to her place – a one-bedroomed, modern apartment close to the city centre, about as different from their suburban semi as you could get – she was waiting for him. She not only sounded different, she looked different too. Her hair was shorter, more styled. Her make-up was more carefully applied, more sensual. She'd put on a little weight, but in a good way. She looked more like the girl he'd fallen for than the wife he'd divorced. He stared at her awkwardly, suddenly conscious of his unkempt hair and the scruffy growth of stubble on his pinched cheeks.

'Hello, Harlan.' Eve smiled but Harlan could tell she was as shocked by his appearance as he was surprised by hers.

'Hello, Eve.'

She motioned for him to come in, and he followed her into an open-plan living area furnished with a cream three-piece suite that wouldn't have lasted ten seconds with Tom's muddy feet jumping all over it. There were pictures on the walls – including several photos of Tom at different ages, from baby to shortly before he died – and books and ornaments on a set of shelves, as well as other knick-knacks that marked the flat out as a home rather than merely a place to sleep. Sliding glass doors led to a balcony that overlooked what seemed a different city from the one visible from Harlan's flat. He was glad to see that she was doing so well, but it also made him think, *This isn't right, you shouldn't be here.* 'You look great,' he said.

'Thanks. You look...' Eve hesitated.

Harlan could see she was reluctant to say anything that might upset him, so he spoke for her. 'I look like shit.'

'I was going to say you look like you're ready for a good meal and a good night's sleep.'

'And a bath and a shave.' Harlan heaved a sigh. 'It's been a long few weeks, and the last twenty-four hours have just about finished me.'

Eve looked at Harlan searchingly. 'Did you have anything to do with this incident they mentioned on the news?'

Harlan nodded, reflecting that even after four years apart Eve could still read him better than anybody else he'd ever known. Her eyes widened as he told her what'd happened. 'So you caught the kidnapper.'

'Maybe. I guess we'll have to wait and see.'

'You could be in line for the reward then.'

Harlan frowned. 'I honestly hadn't thought about that. I didn't do it for the money.'

'Of course you didn't. I know that. Just like I know you're already thinking about refusing the reward. Well you shouldn't. That money could give you a fresh start. You owe it to yourself to accept it.'

I owe myself nothing, thought Harlan, his desire evaporating like dry ice. *The only debt I have is to Susan Reed and her children.* The idea that he might profit from their loss was almost enough to nauseate him. He looked away from Eve, turning as if to leave. 'Do you want something to eat?' she said quickly. 'I can make you a sandwich or whatever.'

'I don't know. Perhaps I should go.'

'Stay a while longer. If you're not comfortable talking about Susan Reed, I won't mention her name again.' Eve reached out to touch Harlan's hand. It was only the lightest of touches but it reignited his desire like a fire in a haystack. 'Please, Harlan.'

'OK. I tell you what I'd really like. I'd like some spaghetti, if that's not too much trouble.' Harlan had always loved her pasta. He hadn't eaten a meal that was worth tasting in years, and just the thought of it made him salivate.

Eve smiled again. 'Of course it's not.' She headed into the kitchen. 'Look, why don't you get a bath while I'm cooking?' She pointed to a door. 'The bathroom's in there.'

Harlan hesitated but she wafted him towards the door. Like the rest of the flat, the bathroom was clean and comfortable and smelled of Eve's perfume. He set the water running and poured bubble bath into it. As he undressed, he noticed a razor and shaving foam on the side of the bath. He lathered his cheeks and shaved at the sink, before getting into the bath. He stretched out, releasing a long breath, and for the first time in as long as he could remember, he felt the knot of tension in his belly start to uncoil.

After luxuriating for a time, Harlan towelled himself down, dressed and returned to the living room. He inhaled the scent of cooking and his stomach growled. Like a moth to a flame, his gaze was drawn to the photos of Tom. He was amazed to realise he was smiling. 'Beautiful, isn't he?' said Eve. Harlan turned and saw that she was watching him intently from the kitchen doorway, as if trying to gauge his reaction to the photos.

'He's the most beautiful thing I ever saw.' There was still sadness in his voice but no trace of the old bitterness.

Eve's features relaxed. She approached Harlan and stood close enough that he could smell her wine-sweet breath, studying his face as if she'd never seen it before. 'I used your razor,' he said, dry-mouthed, restraining an urge to grab her and crush her to him. 'I hope you don't mind.'

She shook her head. Hesitantly, she reached to stroke his cheek. 'The food won't be ready for a little while,' she said, as he shuddered at her touch.

He opened his mouth to reply, but before he could do so she kissed him. He kissed her back, hard. The sensation was familiar, yet new at the same time. Blood pounding in his head and groin, he ran his hands up and down her back. Urgently fumbling at buttons and buckles, they undressed each other. Then they were on the floor, limbs entwined, hips grinding, rushing towards orgasm. Afterwards, they held each other close for a long while. When they finally drew apart, Harlan saw that there were tears in Eve's eyes.

'What's the matter?' he asked softly.

'Nothing,' she said, turning her head away as if embarrassed.

'Tell me.'

'It's just I haven't felt anything like that since, well, since we were first together.' She stood up and pulled on her underwear. 'I'd better check on the spaghetti.'

Harlan stretched out naked on the rug, his body suffused with an almost floating sense of relaxation. It was as though, for a brief time at least, Eve had drawn all the guilt out of him and absorbed it somewhere deep inside her. She returned with a tray loaded with two bowls of pasta and crusty bread. They ate on the rug, Harlan shovelling his food down as if there was no tomorrow. Eve laughed when he asked if there was any more, and fetched him a second helping. When he was finished, he rested back against the sofa and sighed contentedly. He would've liked nothing better at that moment than to curl up in bed with Eve and drift off to sleep. 'God, I've missed this,' he said. 'I've missed you.'

'I've missed you too, Harlan. More than I ever thought I could.' The tears were back in her eyes. She swiped them away and cast him a glance, half hopeful, half fearful. 'So what happens now?'

What happens now? It was a question that tore away Harlan's thin layer of contentment, gripped him by either hand and pulled in opposite directions. On the one hand, he desperately wanted to be with Eve. On the other, he didn't know whether he could allow himself to be with her. It wasn't simply that he was an infertile ex-con with zero career prospects – although that was a big part of it. It was the guilt. Already he could feel it creeping back over him like a vine. Soon the weight of it would be enough to drag him, and maybe Eve too if she was with him, back down into a pit of self-loathing and despair. He would've rather swallowed the tumbler of sleeping pills than do that to her again. He had to climb out from under the guilt. But he couldn't do it by himself. He needed help. And the only person who could help him was the person who hated him most in the world – Susan Reed. He didn't expect forgiveness, but he hoped that if he helped get her son back, she would ease his burden enough to let him have a life.

Harlan was reluctant to explain the way he felt to Eve, knowing his words would cut deep. Bitter experience had taught him that concealing his feelings wasn't an option either, though. He sat trying to work up the nerve to put his thoughts into words, but when he eventually opened his mouth all that came out was a lame, 'I don't know.' He dropped his gaze. Suddenly conscious of his nakedness, he started pulling on his clothes.

'Why don't we go to bed?'

Harlan looked at Eve uncertainly. A few minutes earlier he wouldn't have hesitated to go along with her suggestion but with so many conflicting thoughts and feelings battling for space inside him he knew he wouldn't be able to sleep. 'We don't have to talk,' she continued. 'We can just hold each other and forget the world for a while.'

'Forget.' Harlan said the word with a sigh of longing. 'OK.'

Eve took his hand and led him to bed. He nestled into the soft, clean-smelling sheets with her head on his shoulder and her leg crooked over his, feeling the heat of her breath against his skin. At first, her breathing was a little shallow and her body occasionally spasmed – she'd always suffered from hypnic jerks when tense. After a while, though, he felt the heaviness of sleep overtake her. He watched her and tried to exist only in that moment, but it wasn't possible. In the end, he gently disentangled himself from her, gathered up his clothes, went into the living room and switched on the television to check for any breaking news. There was none. The promised press conference hadn't yet occurred.

His phone rang. It was Jim. Heart thumping, wondering if this was going to be the call that changed everything, he answered. 'What's happened?' he asked, his voice eager but apprehensive.

'Our man came out of his coma last night,' Jim said. 'His name's Carl Gallagher. He's thirty-two years old and a real piece of work. He's got a record for breaking and entering, GBH and, get this, the statutory rape of a fifteen-year-old girl. He also has warrants out on him for a string of armed robberies in the city.'

'So it was him. He took Ethan.'

'He's denying any involvement.'

'Of course he is. They always do. But he did it, right? I mean, what other reason could a scumbag like him have for cruising Ethan's street in the middle of the night?'

'He says he was visiting a girlfriend, a married woman. He cruised the street several times to make sure her husband wasn't home.'

'Does his story check out?'

'Yes.'

'What about forensics?'

'We've searched his car, and we're still searching his last known address, but so far we haven't turned up one scrap of physical evidence to connect him to Ethan.'

Harlan rested his head against his clenched fist, disappointment coursing through him. 'Where's Gallagher been hiding out these past few weeks?'

'He's been sleeping rough in some woods near Wharncliffe.'

'What was he doing at the church?'

'He was going to rob the donation box.'

It was the answer Harlan had expected. As far as he could see, there were no holes in Gallagher's story, no unanswered questions. The lead was a dead end, which meant his life remained a dead end. He ground his knuckles into his forehead in frustration. 'Thanks for letting me know, Jim.'

'No problem. I don't give a toss what Garrett says, you deserve it after what you did.'

'Have you got any other leads?'

'You know I can't tell you that.'

There was a weariness in Jim's voice that answered Harlan's question well enough. 'You haven't, have you?'

Jim was silent a moment, then he admitted, 'We've got shit all. Unless we get a lucky break, I can see this one going on and on.'

On and on. Harlan grimaced as the words echoed like a bell inside his head. *On and on*, like being trapped in a waking nightmare. Without knowing what happened to Ethan, there could be no funeral for him, no closure for his family, no time to grieve or heal. All there could be was uncertainty and pain. The thought of it was almost too much to bear.

Harlan tried to say goodbye to Jim but his throat was closed up so tight the words wouldn't come. He hung up and lay back on the sofa, eyes closed. He wasn't floating any more, he was falling, plunging helplessly into darkness. He jerked upright at the sound of Eve calling to him from the bedroom. He couldn't let her see him in this state. He had to get out of there. Pulling his clothes on as he went, he rushed out the front door.

Chapter Seven

For days Harlan hermited himself away in his flat, ignoring phone calls and knocks at his door, venturing outside only when he ran out of food and to report to his case officer. He didn't watch the news any more – hearing about the police's continued lack of progress only made him feel his helplessness with an even more oppressive weight. He spent most of his time in bed seeking the blankness of sleep, or sitting staring out the living-room window at a world he was in, but wasn't part of. He could see no way forward, no way back. He was at a dead end, stuck in a morass of confused thoughts and emotions. What to do? What to do? Sometimes he'd jerk awake clutching his head as if to keep it from exploding.

After maybe a week – he'd started to lose track of time – Eve came knocking. It wasn't the first time she'd tried to contact him. His phone was full of messages from her, asking and then pleading with him to ring her back. 'Harlan, are you in there?' she called.

Harlan approached the door but made no reply.

'Please speak to me, Harlan. You don't have to open the door. Just let me know you're OK.'

Harlan's face creased in distress. It hurt him to hear Eve sounding so worried. But still he said nothing.

'I'm not angry with you,' she continued. 'I understand why

you left like that the other day. I've spoken to Jim. I know how much it must've hurt you to find out the man you caught wasn't the kidnapper.'

'Please go away,' Harlan murmured, barely audible.

'I'm not leaving until you speak to me.' Eve's voice was as resolute as it was concerned. 'Do you hear me, Harlan? I don't care if I have to stand here all night.'

He knew she meant it. She could be as stubborn as him when she wanted to be. That was one of the reasons they'd worked so well together. 'Please go away,' he repeated louder, his tone apologetic.

He heard her draw a breath of relief. 'If that's what you really want, I will. But not until you tell me why.'

'You don't need me in your life, Eve.'

'Why don't you let me be the judge of what I need.'

'I'll just end up hurting you again.'

'Better that than going through life feeling nothing, which is what I've felt these last four years.'

'You wouldn't say that if you could feel what I feel.' Harlan's words came in a pained, weary breath. 'I'd give anything to feel nothing.'

'But then you wouldn't be you, and I wouldn't love you like I do.'

Harlan closed his eyes, pressing his forehead against the door. It made him want to weep with joy to hear Eve say she loved him, but it also made the guilt flare like a furnace in his heart. How could he let himself love and be loved when Susan Reed and her family were enduring such torment? Bile rose up his throat at the thought of him enjoying himself while Ethan, if he was still alive, was subjected to God knows what kind of horrors.

As if reading his thoughts, Eve said, 'It seems to me that you want to punish yourself because you think you're somehow to blame for what's happened to Ethan. But you're not to blame.'

'How do you know? If I hadn't killed his father, he might not have been taken.'

'Maybe that's true, maybe not. But either way, it doesn't change the fact that you've paid for what you did.'

'I've paid my debt to society, but not to them, not to Susan Reed and her kids.'

'You've done everything you could possibly do to try and get that boy back.'

'Have I? I don't know. Maybe there's something else I can do.'

Eve released an exasperated sigh. 'If there was, you'd be out there doing it.'

She was right, Harlan knew. He'd racked his brain for some other line of inquiry to follow but there wasn't one. He ground his forehead against the door in frustration.

'You have to forgive yourself for what happened,' continued Eve, 'because there's no way of going back and changing it.'

He shook his head, muttering with savage self-recrimination, 'I can't forgive myself.'

'If you don't, you'll throw away any chance of happiness we've got.'

'You don't need me to be happy.'

'There you go again. Telling me what I need. Believe me, Harlan, I've tried to move on from you. I thought I had done, until I heard your voice. Christ knows why after everything you've put me through, but the fact is I need you. I need to be with you.'

Again, Harlan's chest ached with a contradictory mingling of joy and guilt. 'You don't seem to understand. I can't wipe this blood off my hands. It'll be there for ever, tainting everything I touch.'

'No, you don't understand. I'm not scared by that. I'm scared of being alone.'

'I don't want to be alone either.' Harlan's voice grew low with longing. He'd learned all about loneliness in jail – the kind of loneliness that was so severe you felt it like a physical pain. 'I want to fall asleep with you in my arms every night and wake up with you beside—' He broke off. He could feel his resolve weakening with every word. He pushed himself away from the door. 'I'm sorry, Eve, I can't talk any more.'

'So that's it.' A firm, almost forceful note came into Eve's voice. It took hold of Harlan and stopped him from retreating any further. 'You're just going to hide in there and drive yourself crazy agonising over something you can't do anything about.'

'Please go. Please!'

'OK, but first I want you to promise me that you won't do anything stupid like kill yourself.'

'You don't need to worry about that.' The thought of suicide hadn't crossed his mind since Ethan went missing.

'Promise me.'

'I promise.'

'I'll be back tomorrow to make sure you've kept your promise. I'm not going to give up on us so easily.'

As Harlan listened to Eve's footsteps echo away, an urge came over him to tear the door open, run after her and fling his arms around her. Resisting it with a wrench of will-power, he fell back against the wall, hugging himself, sliding to the floor. 'She's coming back,' he murmured, lips twitching as if they didn't know whether to smile or grimace.

He held onto that thought, using it to get him through the long night when he was being tortured by images of what he'd done to Robert Reed and what others might be doing to Ethan. The next morning he woke up telling himself he wasn't going to be in when Eve came knocking. But all day he sat in the living room, listening out for her. To kill time, he turned on the television. Susan Reed appeared on the lunchtime news wearing a T-shirt with Ethan's face on it and the words *Have you seen ETHAN REED?* She spoke to the newsreader from her tiny kitchen, which was crammed with people sorting through boxes of posters and leaflets. Her expression was no longer dazed. Her frowning, bloodshot eyes somehow managed to simultaneously convey a sense of fatalistic weariness and steely determination. The Baptist preacher, Lewis Gunn, stood grave-faced at her side, resting a supportive hand on her shoulder.

'The search for my son will continue as long as it takes,' Susan told the news reporter. 'We'll never give up hope of finding him.'

When Susan finished speaking, the preacher, in his usual vigorous manner, informed the viewers that he was organising several events to raise money for the reward fund. He appealed to people to give generously and read out a telephone number for donations. Harlan greeted the announcement with mixed feelings. The offer of a large reward often led to an influx of new information, most of which, although of little or no use, was given in good faith. But it also brought out the chancers and scammers, passing the police weak or even knowingly false information in the hope of getting their hands on the money.

The knock eventually came late in the afternoon. Harlan sprang up and hurried to the door. 'Eve?'

'Hello. I told you I'd be back. I've brought you some pasta.' Eve waited a moment to see if Harlan would open the door, before adding, 'I'll leave it out here for you.'

Saliva filled Harlan's mouth – he hadn't eaten a decent meal since visiting her flat. He looked at the door handle, swallowing. Hating himself for it, he slowly reached for the Yale lock and opened the door. His gaze flicked from Eve to the plastic carton of pasta she held, as if he couldn't decide which he wanted more. In return, her eyes moved over him anxiously as if searching for signs of illness or self-abuse.

Wordlessly, he motioned for her to come in. She moved past him, glancing from side to side, her gaze lingering on the sheets scrunched at the bottom of his otherwise bare mattress, the bathroom with its mound of dirty clothes and towels, and the kitchen work surfaces cluttered with unwashed pots, half-eaten cans of baked beans and spaghetti, and mould-flecked bread. 'Cosy, isn't it?' Harlan said, with a crooked smile.

In the living room, Eve handed him the pasta and sat on the sofa watching while he voraciously consumed it at the table. 'Why are you doing this to yourself?' she asked when he'd finished.

'You know why.'

'Jim says the boy's dead.'

Eve's words laced Harlan's forehead with lines like cracked clay. 'He can't know that for sure.'

'No, but that's what he and all the other detectives on the case think. That's what you think too, isn't it? I can see it in your eyes.'

Harlan broke his gaze from Eve's, looking at the sheer cliffs of concrete, glass and steel outside his window. 'We could be wrong.'

'Even if you are, there's still nothing you personally can do about it.'

'There might be. I might think of something.'

'Like what?' Eve's voice was gentle but her question contained a note of challenge.

'I... I don't know. I just know that I owe them this.'

'No you don't!' Eve was on her feet suddenly, moving towards Harlan. He flinched at her touch and held her at arm's length,

74

as if afraid she'd catch something nasty off him. 'You owe yourself. You owe us.'

Harlan shook his head fiercely, still not looking at her. 'There can't be any us.'

'This is crazy.' Her voice was hard, but the hands that clasped Harlan's arms were tender. 'I love you. Fuck knows why. Maybe it's because only you really understand what I've been through. And you still love me. You don't need to say it. I know you do.' She tried to pull him to her. His arms trembled, but didn't bend. 'How can that be wrong? How can love be wrong? If you can tell me, I'll leave right now and never bother you again.'

Harlan couldn't tell her. Suddenly his arms gave way and he collapsed into Eve's embrace. Uncontrollable tremors ran through him. This was what he wanted more than anything, yet part of his mind, his soul, railed against it. He tried to draw away from her but she held him tight, as though trying to squeeze every last drop of resistance out of him. 'Don't,' she said.

'Look at me.' Harlan made a sweeping gesture at the room. 'Look at this place. I'm no good for you.'

'You are good for me,' Eve soothed. 'I love you. I want to be with you no matter what. And as for this place, well, you don't have to stay here. You can move in with me.'

Harlan shook his head. 'I need to be here.'

'Why?'

'In case.'

'In case of what?'

'She... Susan Reed, she knows I live here. So she knows where to find me if she needs me.'

Eve looked at him with a baffled frown. 'Why would she come to you for help? She hates you.'

Harlan's mouth screwed into a grimace. 'I know it's absurd, I know, but I've got to be here for her. I've got to.'

Eve stroked his face, the angular jut of his cheekbone, the roughness of his stubble-flecked jaw. 'OK, stay here, and I'll stay here with you.'

'But this place is a dump.'

'It's not so bad.' Eve smiled. 'Nothing a woman's touch can't fix.'

Harlan smiled faintly too, remembering how she had transformed the first place they'd lived in together – a dingy one-bedroomed flat above an off-licence – into a comfortable love nest.

'So it's settled,' continued Eve.

'I... I'm not...' Harlan mumbled uncertainly.

She tilted up his chin and looked him in the eyes. 'It's settled. I'm going to fetch some clothes from my flat. I won't be long.' She leaned in and kissed him. At the touch of her lips, the last of his resistance seeped away.

'OK.'

As Harlan saw Eve to the door, guilt gnawed at him with sharp teeth. He returned to the living room and stared out the window, half watching for her, half studying his own reflection, wondering how it was possible to feel so good and so bad at the same time. Perhaps there was no way to reconcile his longing for her with his sense of obligation to Susan Reed. Perhaps he was just going to have to accept it, let it wash over him, see where it took him. He knew one thing – if his future with Eve was uncertain, without her it was non-existent.

An hour or so later, Eve returned with a bag of clothes and a box of cleaning products. She set to work on the flat straight away, scrubbing the bathroom and kitchen till they gleamed, hoovering and dusting the living room and bedroom, bagging the dirty linen ready for the laundrette, changing the bedding. And when she was done with the flat, she set to work on Harlan, cutting his hair, running him a bath, climbing in it with him, soaping his back. Afterwards, they ordered takeout and ate it on the floor in front of the gas fire, talking and listening to the wind whip at the windows. They talked long into the night. Eve told Harlan about the new career she'd embarked on in the past year. She told him, at his insistence, about the relationship she'd had during his incarceration. He told her, equally reluctantly, what prison had been like. They talked with some sadness but no resentment about Tom – his seemingly boundless energy, his huge sense of fun, his cheeky laugh. When they were finally tired of talking, they undressed each other and made love and fell asleep in each other's arms.

Chapter Eight

Over the next few days Harlan and Eve hardly spent a moment apart, except when she was at work. They bathed together, ate together, slept together. She dragged him out to restaurants, to the cinema, even to an art gallery. It felt both unnerving and exhilarating to him, doing normal things as if he was a normal person. Sometimes, in the middle of a meal or whatever, he'd find himself staring off into the distance with eyes that were adrift in a sea of guilt. At other times, he'd wake in the middle of the night, lathered in sweat, chest heaving, grinding his teeth, trying to push Eve away. But she wouldn't let him. She'd hold him to her, stroking his hair, shushing him as if he was a child that needed calming, until his body relaxed back into the bed. Occasionally, when the guilt burned and bit so deep he felt like bashing his head against the wall, he'd shout, 'This is wrong!'

To which Eve's reply was always the same. 'Love's not wrong.'

Gradually, as days turned into weeks, normality started to feel less unnatural to Harlan. The attacks of guilt became more and more infrequent. He went a minute without thinking about what he'd done to Robert Reed and what was happening to the family that'd survived him, then five minutes, then fifteen, then half an hour. One day, as he and Eve sipped coffee in the café of a department store where they'd been shopping for cushions and curtains and other items to make the flat more homely, it suddenly struck him that he hadn't felt even a twinge of guilt all day. He lowered his cup, his throat so tight he couldn't swallow. 'You've got that look on your face again,' said Eve, reaching for his hand.

Harlan flinched from her touch, jerking to his feet so hard he nearly knocked the table over. 'I've got to get out of here.' His voice trembled with urgency. 'I've got to get back to the flat right now.'

'Calm down, Harlan. Sit back down and let's talk about this.'

He shook his head, turning to leave. Gathering up the bags of shopping, Eve hurried after him, pausing to pay the bill, not waiting for her change. She caught up with him at the store's entrance and gasped, 'Wait! Slow down.'

He ignored her. As if he was being pulled along by an invisible chain, he ran through the streets to his car. One image kept wrenching at him – Susan Reed hammering at the door of his flat, calling his name. Calling to him for help. When he got to the car, Eve was no longer behind him. He didn't wait for her. He jumped into the car and accelerated, tyres squealing out of the car park. He drove back to his block of flats like a man possessed, and sprinted up all twelve flights of stairs. Breathing raggedly, he arrived at his floor fully expecting to see Susan stood at his door. She wasn't there, of course.

Harlan's shoulders sagged as though from unbearable weariness. Feet dragging, he entered the flat and crumpled onto the sofa. He sat with head hanging and eyes closed. Half an hour later, when Eve came into the flat, he looked at her and said, 'I'm sorry.'

A faint, tender smile passed across her features. 'There's no need.' She sat down next to him and gently took hold of his wrist. 'We'll get through this. I promise you. We can get through anything as long as we're together. Say it to me.'

Reluctantly, without much conviction, Harlan repeated Eve's words. 'Say it again and really mean it,' she said, placing her hands on either side of his face and holding his gaze with her own. He took a breath and said it, and this time he felt the words in his heart and head, reassuring him, calming him.

They held each other for a while, then they set about preparing a meal. 'You know what we should do,' said Eve. 'We should get out of the city for a few days. Go to the east coast. You remember that little B&B we used to stay at?'

Harlan remembered, but he made no reply. The mere thought of leaving the city was almost enough to tip him back over into the seething storm of guilt.

'I know you're not comfortable with the idea,' continued Eve, 'but I really think it would do you the world of—' She broke off at a knock on the front door.

Harlan stiffened as though the sound frightened him. He looked towards the door, eyes popping out of their sockets.

'You want me to see who it is?' Eve tried to sound casual but a note of unease crept into her voice, as though, despite her best efforts, she was starting to be infected by Harlan's mood.

He shook his head. He knew who it was. He knew it in his bones. His movements tense, he approached the door and opened it. And there she was, Susan Reed. She looked even thinner than she had done on the television, almost anorexically so. Her hair was greasy and uncombed. There were bluish smudges like bruises under her eyes. Her arms were hugged across her stomach as though she was in pain. For what seemed a long moment, she stared silently at Harlan, then she said, almost murmuring, 'Can I come in?'

Catching a faint tang of alcohol on her breath, Harlan stepped aside. Warily, as if entering enemy territory, she moved past him. He bit back an urge to apologise as she paused at the kitchen door, looking at Eve, who'd turned noticeably paler under her make-up. Their faces set into hard masks, the two women stared at each other for a few seconds. A bitter little smile of understanding tugging at the corners of her mouth, Susan continued into the living room. 'Nice place you've got here,' she said without a hint of sarcasm.

This time Harlan couldn't hold his apology in. 'Sorry.' The word came out in a tortured whisper.

Susan made a contemptuous hissing noise, as if to say, *Yeah, sure you are.*

'What do you want?' Eve asked, her voice polite but cold.

Susan shot her a savage glance, as if she considered her presence to be some kind of betrayal. 'I want to speak to your boyfriend or husband or whatever he is alone.'

Eve folded her arms. 'Well you're going to have to say what you've got to say in front of me, because I'm not going anywhere.' She turned to Harlan. 'Am I?'

Harlan struggled to return Eve's gaze. 'I'm sorry, Eve, but I think you should leave. I'll call you later.'

Eve stared at Harlan a moment, the hurt plain on her face. She leaned in close to him and her voice came in an aggrieved but concerned murmur. 'Just remember what I said. You owe yourself. You owe us.' Then she snatched up her coat and handbag and left.

An uneasy silence descended between Harlan and Susan. He motioned for her to sit on the sofa, but she shook her head. 'Do you want a cup of tea or something?' he asked. Again, she shook her head. She fidgeted with her hands, her eyes darting around the room as if searching for something.

At last, she began. 'I need—' But she broke off, struggling

to bring herself to say what was on her mind. Swallowing a breath, she forced herself to look Harlan in the eyes. 'I need your help.'

'I'm willing to do anything I can to help you.'

'Do you mean that? You'll really do *anything*?'

Susan's voice carried an edge that made Harlan hesitate a second before nodding. 'I just don't see what I can do that the police aren't already doing.'

'You can talk to William Jones.'

'What would be the point of that? The police obviously don't think he's involved.'

'Yeah, well they're wrong,' Susan returned with a sneering scowl that mingled contempt with barely suppressed rage. 'That fucker's hiding something.'

'What makes you think that?'

'Cos I saw him. I saw that sick pervert watching my Ethan and the other kids come out of school. And I saw him in the park with his paints and things, painting pictures of the kids in the playground.'

'That's certainly incriminating but as I understand it Jones goes for girls, not boys.'

'He goes for little kids. Girls and boys. Ask anyone around where I live and they'll tell you what that filth, that fuckin' vermin goes for.'

As Susan spoke, her voice grew loud and splotches of angry red stood out on her pale cheeks. Harlan held up his hands in a calming gesture. 'OK, let's assume you're right. If the police can't get him to talk, what makes you think I can?'

'Because you can do things the police can't.' Susan's eyes glittered with the same brutal intent that suffused her voice. 'You can make Jones talk.'

The deep creases that marked Harlan's face grew deeper.

The idea of trying to beat a confession out of a suspect went against both his natural instincts and everything he'd been taught. As far as he was concerned, police who used violent tactics were little, if any better, than criminals themselves. But even if he'd been willing to do as Susan asked, he wasn't sure that he could. Merely thinking about it brought on a twinge of the same paralysis that'd gripped his limbs like a vice when Carl Gallagher attacked him. He dragged his feet across the room to the window and stared at the leaden grey sky.

'You said you'd do anything,' Susan reminded Harlan, her voice insistent and pleading at the same time.

'I know, but...'

'But what?'

Harlan turned to Susan. 'I can follow Jones night and day. He won't be able to make a move without me knowing it. I can even break into his house and search it while he's out.'

She shook her head. 'The police have already done all that and it got them nowhere. Why do you think I'm here?' For a second, tears trembled on her eyelashes. She swiped them away as if she hated them, and when she next spoke her voice was edged with steel. 'You want a chance, don't you? A chance to wipe your conscience clean. Well this is it, and you better fucking believe me, it's the only one I'm ever gonna give you. You do this one thing and then you can forget about me and my kids for ever.'

Not forget about you, thought Harlan. *Never that. Never completely. But maybe, just maybe, move on from the memory enough to start rebuilding my life properly.* He heaved a sigh. 'OK, I'll do it.'

Susan matched his sigh with a sharp breath of relief. 'What will you do to him?' There was something almost ghoulish in the trembling eagerness of her question.

'I don't know,' admitted Harlan, his voice tight with strain. 'Before I do anything, I need to ask you a couple of questions.'

'Go ahead.'

'Does anyone else know you're here?'

'No.'

'Good. Let's keep it that way. Have you made any public threats against Jones?'

'I've only said the same as everyone else in my area's been saying for years, that he needs his balls cut off and put in his mouth.'

Harlan frowned thoughtfully. 'With Jones being so widely hated, there won't be any shortage of suspects for an attack on him.'

'Yeah and you don't have to worry about anyone saying anything to the coppers. They'd all be too busy celebrating if the bastard got killed.'

Harlan looked hard at Susan. 'No one's going to get killed.'

Her bitter blue eyes returned his gaze with a sudden flash of hatred so intense he involuntarily winced. 'Not deliberately, but as we both know sometimes things happen that we don't intend to happen.'

A sense of immobility spread through his body like an injection of cement. Lumps stood out at the corners of his jaw where his teeth locked together. When he spoke his voice had a hoarse, hollow sound. 'After I do this, the police are going to come straight to your door. So you've got to make sure you and your boyfriend have got solid alibis.'

'Neil works at the hospital from six until six every night except Sunday.'

'That's good. Have you got a mobile phone?'

'Yes.'

'Give me your number.' As Susan told Harlan her number, he punched it into his phone. 'I'll call you and let you know when I'm gonna do it. Whatever you do, don't come here again.'

'I won't.'

A moment of silence passed between them. She continued to look at him, her expression bouncing back and forth between anger, hate, fear and desperate hope so rapidly it made his head reel. Blinking from her gaze, he motioned towards the door. With a strange, hesitating reluctance, she headed into the hallway. She turned suddenly and gripped Harlan's wrist with her cold, damp hand. All that was left in her eyes was the agony of a mother fearing for her child. 'I'm not stupid. I know that the chances are Ethan's dead. But I've got to believe he's still alive. And even if...' Her voice caught in her throat. Swallowing her pain, she continued, 'Even if he's not, I still want him back.'

'You realise it could take years to find him.'

'I don't care how long it takes. The moment Ethan went missing my life stopped. Since then time has had no meaning.' Susan's nails dug into Harlan like thorns. 'Just get my little boy back for me.'

'I'll try.'

Susan shook her head frantically. 'Don't try. Do it. Do whatever it takes.'

'I...' Harlan's tongue could barely force the words out through his teeth. 'I will.'

'Promise me.'

'I promise. Whatever it takes, however long it takes, I'll find Ethan.' As Harlan spoke, a sick feeling settled in his stomach. It was madness to make such a promise. A life of fruitless searching or a long jail sentence; as far as he could see those were the most likely outcomes of his words, but even so his conscience compelled him to say them.

A little of the tension left Susan's face. She released Harlan's arm, and with a seemingly unconscious movement, wiped her palm on her coat as if she'd touched something dirty.

Harlan opened the front door and poked his head out, glancing in both directions. When he was certain there was no one lurking about, he said, 'Put your hood up and keep it up until you're off the estate.'

Susan pulled up her hood. 'When will you call?'

'Soon.'

Harlan watched her get into the lift, before shutting the door. He moved to gaze out the window again. She emerged from the tower block and hurried, head down, across the car park. Harlan scanned the streets for anyone who appeared to be watching her. There was no one. When Susan disappeared from sight, he lifted his gaze to the heavy-bellied clouds. He had his chance but it was as thin as a razor blade. An all-or-nothing chance that would either allow him to retrieve his life completely or completely consume whatever was left of it.

He took out his phone. A long moment passed before he worked up the nerve to call Eve. She was on the other end of the line in a couple of rings. 'I can't see you for a while,' he told her.

'Oh really? Why's that?' Eve didn't sound surprised. There was a fatalistic quality to her voice, as if she'd prepared herself to hear what Harlan was saying.

'I can't tell you why. And if anyone asks, you never saw Susan Reed at my flat. OK?'

'Well if I'm going to lie about that, I might as well go the whole hog and provide you with an alibi as well.'

'Why would I need an alibi?'

Eve huffed her breath. 'Don't bullshit me, Harlan. I can deal with all the other crap. Just don't bullshit me. OK?'

'OK.'

'I don't suppose there's any point trying to talk you out of whatever it is you're going to do.'

'No.'

'You're going to end up back in prison. You know that, don't you?'

'It doesn't matter what happens to me.'

'Of course it bloody matters.' Eve's voice was sharp with irritation. But it softened as she added, 'It matters because I love you and I want to be with you.'

I feel the same way, thought Harlan. He didn't say the words, though. It wouldn't have been fair.

'So when can I see you?' asked Eve.

'I don't know.'

'What do you mean, you don't know? How long are we talking about here? Days? Weeks? Months? Years?'

'However long it takes.'

'However long it takes.' Eve repeated the words as though struggling to understand them. 'So I'm supposed to spend my life in limbo, waiting for you.'

'I'm not asking you to wait for me. I'm just trying to be as straight as I can with you.'

'Oh, thanks.' Eve's voice was loaded with sarcasm and hurt.

'I'm sorry, Eve.'

She sighed, not angry any more, just sad and full of yearning 'Don't be sorry, Harlan, just promise me one thing. Promise me that after all this is over you'll come back to me.'

'I promise.' Harlan's voice was thick with suppressed emotion. He knew he couldn't allow himself to feel too much, not while faced with the task before him. He had to be hard in thought and feeling, or else the paralysis would seize him and he'd be powerless even to leave his flat. 'I've got to go now, Eve. Take care.'

Before she could reply, he hung up. As he turned away from the window, the clouds burst and dirty black rain pelted the glass, ushering in an even dirtier, blacker night.

Chapter Nine

On his way to Jones's house, Harlan bought a hooded sweatshirt, a rucksack, a torch, a screwdriver, a crowbar, leather gloves, a balaclava and a roll of duct tape. He spread his purchases around several stores, paying with cash. He parked in an unlit side street half a mile or so from his destination, pulled on the sweatshirt and, head bowed against the rain, continued on foot.

By the time he reached Jones's street, the lamp-posts were blinking into life. Jones's house was in the middle of the terrace, its front door soot-blackened from what appeared to be a recent arson attack, its boarded-up windows daubed with fresh graffiti. *DEAD MAN WALKING* proclaimed blood-red letters a foot high. No light seeped out from around the edges of the rainbowed chipboard. The house wore an air of desertion.

Harlan slowed his pace, scanning the vehicles parked along the kerb. None of them were occupied. His gaze lingered on a black van across the street. Yanking his hood as far down over his face as it would go, he walked past Jones's house. Near the far end of the street, he darted into a ginnel between two unlit houses. His eyes flicked back and forth from the van to Jones's house. Neither showed any sign of being inhabited. Considering the amount of time that'd elapsed since Ethan's abduction, he doubted Garrett would be keeping Jones under surveillance – unless it was for his own protection. Looking at the dilapidated, battered house, he also doubted whether Jones continued to live there. More likely, he reflected, he'd been put up in an ex-offender's hostel until the anger against him died down. Guilt-tinged relief seeped through him at the thought.

When a car pulled over outside the ginnel, Harlan moved off. Behind the row of terraces there ran a cobbled alley flanked by high brick walls and sturdy wooden gates with their house numbers painted on them. As he neared Jones's gate, Harlan saw that he'd been wrong – a faint glimmer of light was visible through an intact upstairs window. His heart began to palpitate. A glance at the wall told him there was no way he was going over it – at least, not without tearing his hands to shreds. It was topped with a layer of cement in which was embedded nails and shards of glass. He turned his attention to the gate, which had a heavy-duty lock. He headed back to his car, stopping at a phone box to call Susan Reed. The instant she picked up, he said, 'You should stay in tonight.' Before she could make a reply, he hung up.

Harlan sat hunched down in his car, watching the rain, trying to focus only on what he needed to do. But his mind kept turning to Eve – her face, her voice, the way her body felt when he held her in his arms. He turned on the radio to drown out his thoughts. There was no mention of Ethan's abduction on the news. The media were losing interest. They'd wrung every last drop of drama out of the story as it stood. Now they were eagerly awaiting new developments.

The hours crawled by as if they were as weighed down with anxiety as Harlan. At one a.m. he packed the gear into the rucksack, shouldered it and left the car again. Keeping to the shadows, he made his way back along the alley to Jones's house. There was no light in the upstairs window now. He took out the crowbar and, after a quick glance to check no one was around, set to work. He jammed the crowbar between the gate and its frame and threw his weight against it, heaving it back and forth until the muscles of his arms burned. The wood cracked and splintered and finally, with a groan, the lock gave way. He found himself in small concrete yard strewn with the debris of material Jones had used to repair and reinforce his house – rotten wooden boards, bags of mouldy cement, rusty screws and nails. He crouched in the darkness, barely breathing, listening. There were no sounds of movement from inside the house.

He pulled on the balaclava, then picked his way across the yard to the back door. He briefly aimed the torch beam at it. The door was reinforced with steel panels and deadbolts. It would take a battering ram to break it down. He turned his attention to the downstairs window, which was protected by wire mesh screwed into the brickwork. The window had no visible lock. He took out his screwdriver and set to work removing the screws, many of which were almost ready to drop out of the crumbling mortar. He piled up some bags of cement and stood on them to reach the uppermost screws. When they were all out, he peeled away the mesh, jimmied the blade of the screwdriver under the rattling, rotten window frame and dislodged the latch. Seconds later he was wriggling in through the open window, pulling aside the curtains and lowering himself to the floor. There was a hollow clink of glass bottles as his feet came into contact with a plastic bag. He froze, ears straining. Again, there was no sound of movement.

Nose wrinkling at a pungent smell that was part fried food and alcohol, part stale cigarette smoke and even staler sweat, part mildew and something else he couldn't quite place, Harlan reached for his torch. Its pale yellow beam revealed what the something else was – an easel was set up in the centre of the room, holding a canvas thickly encrusted with gaudy, glistening acrylic paint. The painting depicted a group of children at a playground, kicking their legs high on some swings, their heads thrown back, their mouths wide with laughter. It would've been a perfectly innocent scene in any other context, but seeing it here gave Harlan a cold feeling in his stomach. The feeling intensified as he shone the torch around the walls, which were covered with dozens of paintings and drawings. Some hung in cheap frames, others were simply tacked to the yellowed woodchip wallpaper. Some portrayed scenes similar to the canvas on the easel, others showed children at play in schoolyards, children riding bicycles, children eating, children reading, children sleeping. All the paintings' subjects were rendered in too-bright colours, so that they seemed to possess a heightened reality. There was nothing overtly sinister about any of the individual artworks, yet collectively it was one of the most sinister things he'd ever seen. He realised now why Jones stubbornly refused to leave his house. This collection was clearly his pride and joy – his life's work.

The cold feeling came stronger and stronger. Harlan let it rise into his gullet, hard and big as a fist, knowing he'd need it when he came face to face with Jones. A cursory examination of the remainder of the room revealed a threadbare sofa and two armchairs piled with boxes of paint, brushes and blank canvases; no carpet, only bare, paint-spattered floorboards; bin liners bulging with empty cans of super-strength cider and bottles of cheap sherry; the greasy remnants of a meal; the ashes of a long dead fire. There were three doors. One stood open, leading to a small, pot-cluttered kitchen. Very quietly, very slowly, he opened one of the other doors. It led to a hallway that terminated at the front door. The third door opened onto a flight of stairs. Wincing at every creak, he padded up them. Like the living room, the stairwell was papered with artworks. Halfway up, Harlan paused as one in particular caught his eye. It depicted two figures drawn in silhouette – an adult and a child holding hands at the entrance to a yawning black tunnel. Harlan wondered whether the drawing represented reality, or whether it was some kind of symbolic representation of Jones's relationship with children. Whatever the case, the grim little drawing was somehow truer and less distorted than its more garish neighbours.

He stiffened at a sound from upstairs – a sort of asthmatic snuffle followed by a phlegmy cough. He waited until silence resumed, before climbing to the landing. To his right a short hallway led to a bathroom, from which emanated a tang of stale urine. To his left was a closed door. Pressing his ear to its chipped paintwork, he heard a low snore. He switched off his torch and waited a moment for his eyes to adjust to the darkness before easing the door open. In the faint ambient glow of the city that filtered through the bedroom curtains, his eyes traced the outline of Jones's sleeping figure on a single bed. He was on his back beneath a tangle of blankets, his round bowl of a belly gently rising with each snore. His right hand gripped what looked like an old-fashioned police truncheon. Harlan couldn't clearly make out Jones's face, but he knew from the newspapers that he was a late middle-aged man with the vein-streaked skin and puffy eyes of a heavy drinker. The vinegary smell of cider hung in the air like an invisible smog.

Keeping his breathing low and shallow, Harlan approached Jones. He paused at the bedside, staring down at the sleeping man. A tremor ran through him as the image of Robert Reed wormed its way into his mind. With a shake of his head, he shoved it back down through the layers of his consciousness.

In its place he pictured Ethan – Ethan stood hand-in-hand with Jones at the entrance to a tunnel. The image seared through him like cold flames. It took hold of him and made him reach to snatch away the truncheon.

Jones's eyelids flickered. 'Wha...?' he slurred.

With a fluid, practised movement, Harlan flipped Jones onto his belly and twisted his arm up behind him. Jones struggled furiously to break free, bucking like a maddened bull as Harlan straddled his squat, powerfully built body. Harlan twisted harder. Something popped. Jones gave out a muffled scream and his struggles subsided. For a moment both men were still and silent, except for the sound of their accelerated breathing. Then, his voice ragged with pain and fear, Jones said, 'What do you want?'

Harlan pressed the point of his screwdriver against Jones's neck. 'Move and you're dead,' he hissed, trying to disguise his voice by talking through his teeth.

'Please, you don't need to hurt me any more, I'll—'

'Shut the fuck up. Don't speak unless I ask you a direct question.'

Harlan took out the duct tape. Jones whimpered as Harlan wrapped it tightly around his wrists and ankles. When he was done, he rolled Jones onto his back again. The beam of his torch explored the bedroom – more paintings; some cheap-looking furniture; a bedside table cluttered with brown plastic pill bottles; a stack of newspapers, the uppermost carrying a photo of Ethan. The light lingered on some pale rectangles on the tobacco-stained walls where pictures used to hang, before landing on Jones's face. Jones's bloodshot eyes blinked in their folds of bruised-looking flesh. Quivers ran through his sallow, stubbly cheeks. His chest rattled as he sucked in deep, panicky breaths. Harlan picked up the truncheon and balanced its skull-cracking weight on his palm. 'I'm going to ask you some questions and you're going to tell me what I want to know,' he began in a quiet, tightly controlled voice. 'What do you know about Ethan Reed's abduction?'

'Only what I've read in the papers.'

Harlan hefted the truncheon menacingly. 'You know a lot more than that.'

Jones flinched, pressing back against the pillows and speaking in a trembling whimper. 'I don't. Honestly. Why do you think the police let me go?'

'You know where Ethan goes to school and which park he plays in, don't you?'

'I've seen him around,' admitted Jones.

'Have you painted him?'

'I dunno.'

Harlan aimed the torch at the pale rectangles. 'Where are the pictures that hung there?'

From the flash of anger that passed over Jones's face it was clear the question touched a sore spot. 'The police took them.'

'Why?'

'They thought one of the children in them looked like Ethan.'

'And was it him?'

'I told you, I dunno. Maybe. I paint so many that I forget.'

'You like painting kids.'

It was an observation, not a question, but Jones spoke anyway, a fiercely protective note vying with the fear in his voice. 'Yeah. So? It's not illegal, is it?'

'No, but abducting and molesting them is.'

'I've never abducted a kid in my life.'

'You've molested them, though.'

Red splotches rose up Jones's throat, mottling his skin. 'I

took some photos of a girl once, for artistic purposes. But I never laid a hand on her.'

'That's not what she said.'

Jones jutted his chin up at Harlan. 'Yeah, well she was a lying little slut.'

'Forensics don't lie,' Harlan pointed out, his voice growing cooler as Jones's grew more heated. The old feeling of controlled calmness he used to get from fazing suspects and pushing their buttons was seeping back in. 'I've read the newspaper reports. Traces of your semen were found on her clothes.'

Jones's eyes narrowed a fraction, as if something had just occurred to him. He heaved an asthmatic sigh, the defiance draining from his features. 'OK, so I did some... some bad things once. But I haven't done anything like that in years. Not since I started painting. You see, painting, well, it's an outlet for my emotions. It's what keeps me straight. As long as I can paint, I'm all right.'

'And do you only paint what you see?'

'Yeah. I'm a realist. I can't allow myself to fantasise.'

'So where did you do that drawing of the man and the boy holding hands outside a tunnel?'

Jones was silent a moment, brows drawn together, as if unsure which picture Harlan was referring to. Then he said, 'Oh that little thing. I did that years ago, while I was doing my time. It's... it's nowhere. It's what's inside me. The darkness that calls to me. Y'know?'

Harlan knew. He'd spent years trying to see through other people's darkness. He also knew deceit when he heard its hesitating voice. He brought the truncheon down with concussive force inches from Jones's head. The bound man flinched and quivered and gave a choking little sob as his captor snarled, 'Either you stop bullshitting me, or I'm gonna start breaking bones.'

'Don't hurt me, please! It's the truth. So help me Christ, it's the truth.'

'Christ can't help you now. Only you can help yourself.' Harlan leaned in close, applying pressure to Jones's injured arm. 'Where did you do that drawing? This is the last time I'm gonna ask nicely.' His voice was full of quiet menace but inside his heart was thumping wildly.

Jones grimaced, tears spilling over the piggish folds of skin beneath his eyes. His mouth opened. It closed. It opened again, but still no words came. Finally, his breath coming in rancid gasps, he screwed his eyes closed and shook his head. Seeing that he wasn't going to get another word out of his captive unless he followed through on his threat, Harlan raised the truncheon high. His own breathing grew more rapid despite his best efforts to keep it regular, as the truncheon hung in the air for one second, ten seconds, thirty seconds, a minute. Tremors passed up his body into his arms. He seemed to be struggling against some invisible force that prevented him from striking Jones. It was hot under the balaclava, and worms of sweat slithered into his eyes, blurring his vision. He swiped a hand across his eyes, trying to wipe the stinging sweat away, but also vainly trying to rid himself of the image of Robert Reed that loomed before him, blood fanning from his shattered skull. He made as if to look away. But there was no looking away. Suddenly, as if he'd been punched in the solar plexus, his body sagged and his arms dropped limply onto his lap. He sat for long seconds, staring at the threadbare carpet, though seeming to stare at nothing. Letting the truncheon fall to the floor, he staggered from the room.

Harlan's legs almost gave way as he squirmed through the window and dropped to the ground. He squatted on his haunches for a few seconds, yanking off the balaclava and sucking in lungfuls of the cold, cleansing night air. Then he approached the gate and, after a glance to make sure the alley was clear, set off walking fast – but not too fast – in the direction of his car.

He detoured down some steps at the side of a bridge to toss his gloves, balaclava, sweatshirt and the contents of his rucksack into the River Don's murmuring waters. Looking at the deeper darkness under the bridge, he thought about the drawing. He felt in his bones that Jones knew something about something. It was another question, however, whether that something had anything to do with Ethan's abduction. Jones was obviously a dangerous man – a predatory pervert with a few brushstrokes of fragile paint on canvas between himself and his next victim. But was he the type to go breaking into someone's house and snatching a kid? Harlan doubted it. He was more the type to patiently groom his victims, ply them with gifts and favours, gain their trust. He was also a bit long in the tooth and heavy in the gut to be climbing through windows and creeping about houses. What really made Harlan doubt Jones's involvement, though, were the paintings. There'd been no trace of hesitation in Jones's voice as he spoke about what they meant to him. As repulsive as they were, they were clearly a sincere attempt to channel his thoughts, his emotions, his desires into something that, as he'd said, kept his darkness at bay. Of course, the attempt might've been unsuccessful. But even if that was the case, it seemed highly unlikely that Jones would look so close to home for his victims. That would've been a suicidal move for someone so locally notorious. And Jones wasn't suicidal. He was a realist. A survivor.

As Harlan drove to his flat, he wondered what he was going to tell Susan. Whatever he told her, he knew she was going to be as angry and dissatisfied with him as he was with himself.

Why hadn't he been able to do what needed to be done? What was he afraid of? Not prison. Prison held no fear for him. It wasn't simply that he was afraid of hurting others, either. It went deeper than that, right down to the roots of his psyche. He'd seen the darkness that existed there. He knew what it was capable of. And that was what scared him more than anything else.

At the flat, physically and emotionally spent, Harlan crashed into bed fully dressed. Within seconds he was dreaming. Tom was standing at the entrance to a dark tunnel. Jones was next to him. They were holding hands. Tom was looking at Harlan. He didn't seem scared. There was a strange, sorrowful blankness in his eyes. Jones bent and whispered something to Tom. To Harlan's horror, the two of them turned and headed into the tunnel. 'Tom, stop!' cried Harlan. 'Don't go in there.'

Tom didn't seem to hear.

'Let my son go,' yelled Harlan. 'Let him go or I'll kill you.' He tried to give chase but his feet felt glued to the ground.

The darkness closed like a fist around the two figures. 'Tom!' screamed Harlan. 'Tom!' There was no reply, except the echo of his own voice. He collapsed to his knees, weeping with impotent despair and rage.

Chapter Ten

Harlan was woken by an insistent and ominously regular knocking at his door. It was a knock he recognised, a knock he'd fully expected. It sent a thrill down his back. Not rushing, he rose and went through to the toilet. By the time he was done in there, he'd composed his thoughts and appearance. 'Mr Miller,' shouted a male voice, impatient but professional.

'Coming,' called Harlan, flushing the loo. He opened the door and found himself confronted by the steely-eyed DI Scott Greenwood and his po-faced partner DI Amy Sheridan. 'Sorry about that. How can I help you?'

'We'd like you to accompany us down to the station,' said DI Greenwood.

'Why? What's going on?'

'We're just here to fetch you. The DCI wants a chat.'

'A chat?' Harlan frowned. 'About what?'

DI Greenwood's purse-lipped expression made it clear that whether or not he knew the answer, he wasn't about to tell Harlan.

'Am I under arrest?' asked Harlan.

'No.'

'And what if I don't feel like going down the station?'

'We can do this the easy way or the hard way,' put in DI Sheridan. 'The choice is yours.'

'It doesn't sound like I've got a choice.' Harlan pulled on his shoes and coat and followed the detectives to their car. They rode to the station in silence, punctuated by brief spurts of gabble on the two-way radio.

DI Greenwood led Harlan to an interview room while DI Sheridan went to inform Garrett of their arrival. When the DCI entered the room, Harlan asked with feigned puzzlement, 'What's this about?'

A scowl creased Garrett's pink, well-scrubbed face. 'Don't play games with me, Miller. You bloody well know what this is about.'

'Sorry, but I—'

Before Harlan could finish, Garrett brought his hand down on the table with a bang that reverberated around the room. 'Where were you last night?'

'At my flat.'

'All night?'

'Uh-huh.'

'Alone?'

Harlan nodded. He expelled an impatient breath through his nostrils. 'Look, either you tell me what I'm doing here or I'm leaving.'

Garrett regarded him with narrowed, probing eyes. 'William Jones. Recognise the name?'

'Of course. It was all over the newspapers.'

Garrett gave a small wince, as if the fact pained him. 'Have you ever met him?'

'No.'

'You sure about that?'

'Well, not a hundred per cent. I've met a lot of scumbags in my time. You know how it is. After you've been on the job for a few years, the faces and names all start to blend together.'

'I'm not—' began Garrett, his voice rising. He stopped himself, took a breath and continued in a controlled voice. 'I'm not talking about when you were on the job. I'm talking about since Ethan Reed's abduction.'

Harlan gave a wry inward smile. Garrett was usually a calm, competent interviewer, but something about Harlan got under his skin. It wasn't hard to guess what that something was – Harlan had been one of Garrett's protégés, fast-tracked through the ranks. He was supposed to be part of a new breed of detectives, someone who was as likely to solve a crime using a computer as they were chasing down suspects on the streets. Garrett had once regarded him as one of his greatest successes. Now the exact opposite was true. 'In that case, the answer's a definite no. So what's happened to Jones?'

'What makes you think something's happened to him?'

'Well it's obvious something's happened, otherwise I wouldn't be here.'

Garrett glanced at DI Greenwood. 'Tell him.'

Flipping open his statement pad, the detective recited, 'Sometime between one and two a.m. last night a masked intruder broke into William Jones's house. The intruder bound Mr Jones's hands and feet before questioning him about Ethan Reed's abduction. When Mr Jones said he knew nothing about it, the intruder threatened to torture him. Mr Jones said again that he knew nothing, at which point the intruder left. At approximately five a.m., Mr Jones managed to free himself from his bonds and phone the police.'

'And you think I was the intruder.'

'I don't think, I know,' stated Garrett.

'Really? How do you know? Where's your evidence?'

Garrett shot Greenwood another look, and the DI said, 'Certain phrases the intruder used, in particular the way he referred to forensic evidence relating to Mr Jones's conviction made him suspect that the intruder was, or had once been, a policeman.'

With a look of incredulous surprise, Harlan's gaze flicked between his interviewers. 'Is that it? Is that your evidence?'

'That's all we have right now,' said Garrett, bending in close to Harlan. 'But soon we'll have more evidence. Hard evidence.'

Harlan didn't flinch from Garrett's gaze. 'I can see how embarrassing this must be for you. But what did you think would happen once the media got hold of Jones's arrest? You might as well have painted a target on the guy's back. Half this city's out for his blood because of you. And now you want to make an example of someone, so that no one else dares touch him. I understand that. I'd do the same in your position. But I'm not the guy you're after. Since we last talked, I've steered clear of everything to do with Ethan Reed's abduction. I haven't even followed the case on the TV.'

As Harlan spoke, Garrett's pink complexion deepened into an angry flush. 'You're right. That's what I'm going to do. I'm going to nail you up for everyone in this city to see. Then I'm going to bury you so deep you won't see the light of day for years. You've made a fool of me for the last time, Miller.'

'Is that it? Are we done? Or are you going to arrest me?'

'We're done. For now. I could have your property searched but I don't suppose you'd be stupid enough to have left anything for us to find.'

'I don't suppose I would, if I had anything to do with this.'

As Harlan stood to leave, Garrett added with a note of genuine sadness in his voice, 'Do you know what the real shame of all this is? You were the brightest and best DI I ever had. I had such high hopes for you, Miller. Such high expectations. I gave you the opportunity to go as far as your ability could take you, but you threw it away.' He shook his head. 'Such a waste.'

A ripple disturbed the calm surface of Harlan's expression. 'That's what life is – a waste, a fucked-up joke.'

'If that's really what you think, why bother going on?'

'Sometimes I don't know. I really don't.'

The two men stared at each other a few seconds more, then Harlan turned away. DI Greenwood escorted him from the station. 'Do you want a lift home?'

Harlan shook his head. He needed to walk and think about what he was going to say to Susan Reed. Besides which, he'd suddenly noticed how hungry he was. He set off in the direction of a nearby café he knew from his police days. As he rounded a corner, a hand touched his shoulder. He turned and saw that it belonged to Jim Monahan. 'Christ, Harlan, tell me you didn't do it,' he said.

Harlan answered with silence.

Jim's face ruckled in dismay. 'For fuck's sake, have you lost your mind? Just what the hell were you trying to achieve? We questioned that nonce, Jones, for two days and got zip from him. What made you think you'd do any better?'

Because I can do things the police can't, thought Harlan, but he remained silent.

'Jones is in hospital, you know.'

Harlan's heart gave a quick thump. It flashed through his mind that Jones might've suffered a heart attack or something but he dismissed the thought – if that'd been the case, Garrett would've used it to try and get him to come clean. 'Nothing serious, I hope.'

Jim shook his head. 'A dislocated elbow.' He looked at Harlan as if trying to recollect a face he hadn't seen for a long time. 'What's going on with you? Intimidation was never your bag.'

'Who says it is now? Who says I had anything to do with what happened to Jones? Maybe I was at the flat all night, like I told Garrett.'

'And maybe I was having dinner on the moon.' Jim sighed. 'How did this happen? I mean, what made you do this? Just the other day Eve phoned to tell me how well you were doing. She sounded happier than she had in a very long time. She said the two of you were really making a go of things.'

A familiar bite of guilt gnawed at Harlan. 'Yeah, well, she was wrong. I was wrong too. I allowed myself to think I could be with her. But I can't be. Not now. Maybe not ever.'

'That's just crazy talk, Harlan,' snapped Jim, a sudden anger flaring in his eyes. 'Do you want to know something? That woman's worth ten of you. And you're gonna let the chance to be with her go by, for what? So you can go on some insane hunt for a boy who's already dead.'

'You don't know that. You don't know for sure that he's dead.'

'Yes I do. And you do too, only you won't admit it to yourself.'

'Maybe, but it doesn't really matter if he's alive or dead – at least, not in the way you mean. This isn't just about Ethan. It's about the people who love him. One way or another, they need closure.'

'And what makes you think you can give it to them? Come on, Harlan, you know how it is with cases like this. We might get a lucky break and catch the fucker who took Ethan or—'

'Or you might never catch him,' interrupted Harlan. 'Yeah, Jim, I know how it is.'

'But that doesn't make any difference to you, does it? You're gonna keep at this until you're in jail or dead, aren't you?'

Again, Harlan said nothing, but the fixed set of his jaw and the way he stared unflinchingly at Jim told his ex-partner all he needed to know. Jim heaved another sigh. 'OK, you win. Look, I'll tell you what, if you keep me in your loop, I'll do the same.'

'Why would you do that?'

'Because if I can't talk you out of this, I might as well use you. Besides, I'd rather you come to me than pull another stunt like last night.'

'What about Garrett?'

Jim smiled. 'You know what Garrett can go and do.'

A thin smile played on Harlan's lips too. 'OK. Maybe between us we can solve this thing.'

'Maybe.' Jim sounded unconvinced. He glanced over his shoulder in the direction of the police station. 'Listen, we'll be seen if we talk here much longer. Let's go somewhere where we can pick each other's brains.'

Harlan was about to say OK, but his thoughts returned with a falling sensation to Susan Reed. 'Some other time. There's something I need to do.'

'Just do me a favour and try to keep a low profile for a few days. Garrett's spitting blood about what happened to Jones. He knows he fucked up releasing Jones's name to the press, and he's desperate to make an example of someone.'

'I'll try.' Harlan held his hand out and when Jim took it, he said, 'Thanks.'

'No problem,' Jim paused a breath, before adding meaningfully, 'partner.'

Harlan smiled again at the word. 'I'll see you.' His hunger forgotten for now, he made his way along the street until he saw a phone box. He called Susan Reed. She picked up instantly, as if she'd been waiting.

'I heard what happened. Mr Garrett sent a couple of his detectives to see me. Don't worry, I stayed right here all night with Kane, just like you told me to.' Susan's tone was breathless with eager inquiry. 'What did you find out?'

There wasn't much to tell, but what there was Harlan was unwilling to say over the phone. 'Let's meet and I'll tell you.'

'OK. Where?'

'Tom's Café.' It was a grotty little backstreet greasy spoon where Harlan used to meet his informants. He'd used the place because of its privacy and because its name was a reminder of something that was innocent and worth preserving, worth fighting for. He hadn't been there since Tom's death. 'Do you know it?'

'No.'

Harlan described where the café was. 'Do you think you can find it?'

'Don't worry, I'll find it.'

'I'll see you there in half an hour or so.'

Harlan headed to the café. He watched carefully for any sign that he was being followed but there was none. Just in case, he went into a busy indoor market, weaved his way quickly between the stalls and dodged out of a side entrance. When he got to the café, he ordered a fried breakfast and wolfed it down while he waited for Susan. As usual, the place was empty except for a few shady-looking characters and a craggy-faced old guy behind the counter who'd been a permanent fixture as long as Harlan had been going there.

Harlan had just finished eating when Susan turned up. To his dismay, she wasn't alone. Her boyfriend, Neil Price, was with her. Harlan took in Price's cheap, baggy clothing and even cheaper haircut as, holding hands like teenage lovers, the two of them sat down opposite him. Up close, Price looked both younger and older than he had done on the television. The watery blue of his eyes, which blinked nervously at Harlan from behind thick lenses, was lined with red. And the surrounding flesh was tired, grey and marked with crow's feet – no doubt the result of years spent working nights. But the awkward way he held himself and the ratty fuzz of hair on his chin and upper lip gave Harlan the impression of an adolescent desperately trying to be an adult.

Frowning hard, Harlan shifted his attention to Susan. 'I told you to come alone.'

'You can trust Neil,' she assured him.

'I don't give a toss if I can trust him. He shouldn't be here. I thought you understood, this was supposed to be between just you and me.' Harlan released an angry hiss of breath. 'Give me one reason why I shouldn't get up and walk out of here right now.'

Susan's eyes swelled with alarm. 'Please don't.'

'I'm here because Susan needs support,' said Neil, his voice reedy and tremulous. He tried to hold Harlan's gaze but his eyes dropped to the table after a few seconds.

Harlan scrutinised Neil, wondering what Susan saw in him. He didn't seem her type at all – his nervy demeanour and thin, gangly frame were about as dissimilar from her husband as could be. Maybe that was it, he reflected. Maybe, consciously or unconsciously, she'd gone for someone who wouldn't stir up bad memories every time she looked at him. Harlan sighed, his anger fading a little in the face of Neil's timidity. 'Wait outside.'

'There's no point.' Neil worked up enough courage to look briefly at him. 'We don't keep any secrets from each other.'

Harlan shifted his gaze to Susan. 'Either he leaves or I do.'

'Do as he says, Neil,' she said.

A look of hurt flashed over Neil's face but he removed his hand from hers and obediently headed for the door. Harlan's eyes followed him, then returned to Susan. 'I hope you're right about him.'

'I am.' Susan bent forward, her voice dropping. 'So what happened with Jones?' Her mouth twisted as if the name had a taste that made her want to spit.

'We'll get to that in a moment. First I want to ask you a couple of questions about Neil.'

Susan made an impatient gesture. 'The coppers have already asked me a thousand questions about him, and I'll tell you what I told them – Neil hasn't got anything to do with any of this.'

'You realise he fits the classic profile of a potential abductor – white male, early thirties, unskilled—'

'Yeah, I know,' cut in Susan. 'But I also know that he's the kindest, sweetest man I've ever met. He couldn't hurt a fly.' Susan glanced at Neil, who was leaning with his back to the window, hands thrust in his pockets, staring at the pavement. 'I mean, for Christ's sake, look at him. He jumps at his own shadow. Do you really think he could've taken my Ethan?'

Harlan had to admit that Price looked about as harmless as they come, but he also knew that appearances could deceive, that the sheep could turn out to be a wolf. 'Where did you meet him?'

Susan heaved a sigh. 'At the hospital a couple of years ago. Ethan got ill – some kind of blood infection. He was in hospital for a week. Neil was a porter on his ward. He looked out for Ethan. He looked out for all the kids. Brought them comics from his collection. Anyway, one day we got talking and, well, things just kind of happened.' A note of some old guilt entered Susan's voice. 'Not that I was looking for a relationship, or anything. Neil's the first man I've been with since... since...' She trailed off.

'Where does he live?' Harlan asked quickly, as reluctant to hear the name on Susan's tongue as she was to say it.

'With his parents over on Manor Lane.'

'What number?'

Susan told him, adding, 'He's saving to buy a place of his own.'

Harlan wasn't in the least surprised to learn that Price still lived with his parents. It was written all over his thirty-year-old teenager's face. 'So he's got money of his own.'

'Well, he's not with me for my money, is he?' There was a sharp, ironic edge to Susan's voice.

'What I mean is, does he live off his parents?'

'More like the other way around. His dad's an unemployed brickie and his mum's a dinner lady at Ethan's school.'

Harlan's eyebrows lifted at this. It was a seemingly small thing, but as the cliché went, the devil was often in the detail. 'What are his parents' names?'

'George and Sandra.'

'Did Sandra know Ethan before you and Neil got together?'

'She knew him to look at, if not to talk to.' Susan blew out her breath in frustration. 'Look, Neil's got an alibi, right. He was working the night Ethan was taken. On top of which, the sicko that took my baby boy is dark haired and about your height and build. If you hadn't noticed, Neil's over six foot, blond and weighs about nine stone soaking wet.'

'Maybe he's got an accomplice.'

'An accomplice? And just who the hell might that be?' Susan's raised voice barely drew a glance from the other customers – Tom's Café was a place where people knew to mind their own business.

'Does he have any friends?'

'Yeah. Brian and Dave who he plays darts with down the Three Tuns.'

Harlan recognised the pub's name vaguely from his days on the beat. 'Anyone else?'

'Some old schoolmates he sees occasionally. No one important.'

'Everyone's important in a case like this. Everyone and every detail. That's how to crack a case, by finding that one tiny little piece of the puzzle.'

'I know, but I've been through all this dozens of times before with Mr Garrett's lot. And they've spoken to Neil and everyone he knows, and found nothing to make them think he's got anything to do with this.'

'I understand, and I know how hard this is for you. But if I'm going to have any chance of finding Ethan, I need to build up a complete picture of your life. And the only way I can do that is by asking the same questions the police asked.'

'I didn't come to you so you could ask those questions. I came—' Susan broke off, her eyes flitting around the café. She continued more quietly, but no less vehemently, 'I came to you because you can do things the coppers can't. So come on, out with it. What happened? What did you find out?'

'A couple more questions. Then we'll get to Jones. How is Neil with Ethan and Kane?'

'He's great. And before you ask, no he's never done or said anything inappropriate. He's a good, decent man. Do you hear? I know he comes over as kind of immature, but let me tell you this, there's a shit lot of so-called real men out there who'd run a mile from a woman like me.'

'And there are also men out there who specifically go for women with young children.'

'Enough!' Susan brought her hands down on the table hard enough to make the crockery jump. 'I won't hear another word against Neil. If it wasn't for him, I don't think I'd have made it through these past few weeks. And I won't answer another of your questions until you tell me what fuckin' well happened last night.'

Harlan guessed she wouldn't be in any kind of mood to answer his questions even once he'd told her what she was so desperate to know. But he saw that he'd pushed her as far as he could. She sat glaring at him, little tremors of pent-up, barely contained pressure running through her body. He took a breath and came out with it. 'I don't think Jones is involved in Ethan's abduction.'

'Not involved,' Susan said slowly, as if she wasn't sure whether to be relieved or disappointed. 'How do you know he's not involved?'

'Well for one thing, he doesn't fit the profile. He's too old, too cautious. For another, he doesn't fit the physical description.'

'Yeah, but like you said, there might be an accomplice.' As Harlan shook his head, Susan continued insistently, 'It's possible though, isn't it?'

'It's possible, but I don't think it's the case.'

'Why? If you're willing to suspect someone like Neil, then why not a pervert like Jones?'

Harlan sighed. 'I'm sorry, but I... well, I just don't believe Jones is our man.'

Susan frowned, picking up on Harlan's hesitation. 'You still haven't told me what happened last night. Not really.'

'You know what happened. I went to Jones's house and questioned him.'

'Yeah, but did you do it like I asked you to? Did you *make* him tell you the truth?' When Harlan gave no reply, the lines on Susan's forehead intensified. 'You didn't, did you?'

'I questioned him thoroughly.'

Susan dismissed Harlan's words with a contemptuous hiss. 'The coppers questioned him thoroughly. They questioned the shit out of him for two days and got nothing. I wanted you to do more than just ask questions. That was the whole reason I came to you for help.'

'I know.'

'So why didn't you do it?'

Harlan blinked as the image of Robert Reed lying on the snowy, blood-stained ground flashed through his mind. 'I did what was necessary.'

'No you fucking didn't. Not unless you beat that bastard until he was nearly dead.'

'I... I...' Harlan stumbled over his words, as if he were struggling to make a shameful admission. At last he spoke in a sudden rush. 'I couldn't do it.'

Susan rose from her seat, white with rage. 'Oh, so you could kill my Robby, but you can't hurt that filthy paedo!'

This time Susan's savage words were enough to draw glances, even in that place. Harlan raised his hands as if to say, *Calm down*, but his gesture only angered her more. 'You know what you are?' she hissed. 'You're a coward. A sick, twisted coward!'

'Sit back down.'

'Fuck you.'

'Please, let's talk some more.'

'I've got nothing left to say to you.' Susan's voice dropped a tone but remained taut with emotion. 'Not unless you'll go back there, back to that fucker's house and do what I asked.'

The suggestion was enough to make Harlan's pulse beat in his throat. 'Even if I agreed to do that, I wouldn't be able to get near him. The police will be watching his house. Garrett can't afford for anything else to happen to him. His reputation's on the line.'

'So don't go to his house. Get him when he goes shopping or whatever. I don't give a toss how you do it, just do it.'

'This isn't the way to go. There are other avenues, other lines of investigation I—'

'No. This is the way, and this is the only way for you. Do you fucking—' Susan's voice caught in her throat. Tears swelled into her eyes. Her lower lip trembled briefly. Then she got hold of herself and continued, 'Do you understand?'

Harlan stared at Susan with a kind of pleading in his eyes but her resolve didn't waver. His body leaden with anxiety, he nodded. She frowned at him a few seconds, as if trying to work out whether or not she believed him. Then she turned and hurried from the café into Neil's arms. Her self-control crumbling like a sandcastle in front of a wave, she pressed her face against his shoulder and sobbed. Neil shot Harlan a glance that almost dared to be angry. This time it was Harlan who dropped his gaze to the table top. When he looked up a minute or so later, Susan and Neil were gone.

Noticing how dry his mouth was, Harlan swilled back the dregs of his coffee. He approached the counter and held up fifty quid. 'If anyone asks...' He trailed off meaningfully.

'I never heard nothin',' grunted the man behind the counter.

Harlan handed him the money and left. Head lowered in thought, he made his way slowly along the quiet street. He imagined himself beating Jones with the truncheon until his flesh was a pulpy mass and blood oozed from his face. He began to feel light-headed, dizzy. Susan's bitter words echoed in his ears. *You're a coward. A sick, twisted coward.*

Maybe she's right, he thought. *Maybe that's what I am. A sick, twisted coward without the courage to do what needs to be done, without the courage to live, without the courage even to end my own misery.*

He didn't hear the fast-approaching footsteps until they were right behind him. Before he could turn to see who they belonged to, something hit the back of his head hard enough to stagger him. White sparks exploding silently in front of his eyes, he flung up his arms to shield his head. A second blow deflected off his forearm, sending an electric current of pain up to his shoulder. A third found its way through to his skull, connecting with an ugly, hollow sound, buckling his knees. As he went down, he managed to drop his shoulder and roll away from his attacker. Through a haze of tears, he saw a baseball-bat-wielding figure looming over him. Even dazed as he was, he made a mental note of his attacker's physical characteristics – five foot five or six, medium build, wearing baggy blue jeans and a black hooded sweatshirt with the hood up. A scarf was wrapped around the lower half of the figure's face, so that all Harlan could see was a pair of eyes – young-looking, hazel–brown eyes so swollen with hate they seemed ready to pop out.

As the figure raised the bat for another strike, Harlan kicked upwards. His foot slammed home. With a loud 'Oof', the figure doubled over. For a second or two, Harlan and his attacker writhed separately, each lost in their own pain. Then Harlan grabbed his attacker's arm. Jerking free, the figure straightened and began to stagger away. Harlan attempted to follow, but as he pushed himself up onto his knees his vision blurred in and out. He reached up and felt a wetness on his scalp. He looked at his hand. Blood. He could feel it now, trickling warmly down the back of his neck. Groaning with the effort, he clutched a lamp-post and dragged himself upright. The figure was almost out of sight at the far end of the street. As he stepped away from the lamp-post, the pavement seemed to dip, then drop away vertiginously from beneath his feet. He felt himself tumbling through the air, then he slammed into the ground with enough force to wind him. He lay face down, his eyeballs rolling, struggling vainly to rise onto his elbows. Then he was falling again, going down, down into impenetrable blackness like a well.

Chapter Eleven

After what might've been minutes or hours, a voice called Harlan back to the conscious world. 'Mister,' it said, urgent and concerned. 'I saw what happened.' His eyes flickered open. He was on his back now. Whether he'd rolled over by himself or someone had turned him over, he didn't know. A young woman gazed down at him, her face blurry in patches. 'Just lie still,' she continued, as he tried to sit up. 'I've phoned for an ambulance.'

Her words lent Harlan the strength to clamber to his feet. The police wouldn't be far behind the ambulance, and that would mean serious trouble. 'I'm fine,' he said groggily, brushing away the woman's helping hands. Using the buildings for support, he slowly worked his way along the street. Dimly aware of sirens away in the distance, he went into a public toilet, washed the blood from his hands and applied a wad of tissue to the back of his head. Then he staggered to a nearby taxi rank and ducked into a black cab.

'You OK, mate?' asked the cabbie.

Harlan nodded and wished he hadn't when a blinding pain pulsed from his skull. He gave the cabbie an address not far from the Northern General Hospital. As the cab negotiated the congested roads, he closed his eyes and summoned up an image of his hooded assailant. Who could it be? Not Ethan's abductor

– when Harlan had grabbed his attacker's hand he'd noticed it was as hairless as a child's. The attack hadn't been random, though. That much was obvious from the hate in those hazel–brown eyes. It was equally obvious that the attacker must've followed Susan and Neil to the café, since he was certain no one had followed him. Which meant either that one of them had told someone else about the meeting, or the attacker had overheard them discussing it. If what Susan had said about Neil was true – which he had no reason to suspect it wasn't – the second possibility was the most probable. And there was only one person he could think of who could easily get into close enough proximity to overhear them – Kane. What's more, the boy was the same height and build as his attacker, and he certainly had more than enough motive to want to hurt him.

Harlan paid the driver and, swaying like a drunk, made his way to A&E. He gave the receptionist a false name and address and told her he'd tripped and hit his head. Under local anaesthetic, a doctor stitched and bandaged the lesions on his scalp. Then he was given a head X-ray. 'There are no fractures and no signs of serious brain injury,' said the doctor, examining his X-rays. 'Luckily for you, you've got a remarkably thick skull. I've seen people end up in a coma from less severe injuries.'

I've seen them die, thought Harlan. 'So I'm OK to go?'

'You have a concussion. As a precautionary measure, we'd like to admit you overnight for observation.'

'I'd rather go home.' By the morning, Harlan knew, there was every chance the police called to the scene of the attack would trace him to the hospital.

'Well that's your choice, although I'd strongly advise against it. Where do you live?'

Harlan's head throbbed with the effort of remembering the false address he'd given the receptionist.

'You mustn't drive for forty-eight hours. Is there someone you can call to pick you up?'

'Yes,' lied Harlan.

'Good. Also, you need to rest, but you should try to stay awake for the next twelve hours. If you do fall asleep, you need to be woken every two hours at the most to make sure you don't fall into a coma. And don't rely on an alarm clock to wake you.'

Harlan thanked the doctor, and trying to appear less groggy than he felt, made his way out of A&E. He caught a taxi to his flat. After swallowing some painkillers, he got into bed. He lay glaring at the ceiling, his fingers convulsively clenching and unclenching as he thought about those hazel–brown eyes. His anger wasn't directed at Kane – he felt nothing towards him except guilt, sadness and sympathy – but at himself. It made him want to tear his own guts out to think that he was the cause of such fury, such hate.

After a while, without even realising it, he began to drift into a dream. He was at the entrance to the tunnel again. Only this time he was standing in Jones's place, holding Kane and Ethan's hands. He looked down at each boy and saw that their faces were masked with blood. And the boys looked up at him and spoke. 'Dad,' they said in unison.

With a gasp, Harlan dragged himself back to wakefulness. Fighting an urge to vomit, he rose and tottered through to the kitchen to make a strong black coffee. He lay cradling it on the sofa, watching the television. There was nothing on the news about what'd happened to Jones – no doubt, Garrett was doing everything in his power to hush it up. As he listened to the droning voice of the newsreader, an immense weariness came over him, as if lead weights were attached to his eyelids. This time the sound of his mug clattering to the floor jerked him back from the edge of sleep.

He fetched a tea towel to mop up the coffee. The effort of doing so was enough to make his skull feel as if it was splitting apart. Not knowing what else to do with himself, he sat at the table, head on his hands. Alternating waves of nausea and drowsiness broke over him. Realising he'd be swept away by them unless he did something, he took out his mobile phone. He thumbed through the contacts list to Eve's name. He stared at it for a long moment. Heaving a sigh, he pressed the dial button.

'What is it? What's happened?' Eve asked on picking up the phone, her voice swaying between hope and anxiety.

'Can you come over?'

'Have you found Ethan?'

'No.'

'Oh.' The word came out in a breath of disappointment. 'Then what's changed?'

'I'm too tired to speak over the phone, Eve.' Harlan spoke slowly, but even so his words blurred into each other.

'Are you OK, Harlan? You sound strange.'

'I'm fine. I just need to see you.'

The line was silent for the space of a few breaths. Then, with a sharp little sigh in her voice, as if she was irritated with Harlan or herself, or both, Eve said, 'OK, I'll be there as soon as I can.'

Harlan moved his chair to the window and sat in the gathering dusk, watching for Eve. His forehead was nodding against the glass when her car pulled into view. He dragged his feet to the front door, reaching it as she knocked. The look that came over her face when she saw him added one more thin layer to his guilt. She put her hand to her mouth, shaking her head. 'I'm sorry,' Harlan said. 'I wouldn't have called you, only I need someone to help me stay awake. I've got a concussion. It'll be

OK, but the doctor says I shouldn't sleep for longer than two hours at—' He broke off, swaying on his feet.

Eve darted forward to support him. She helped him into bed and sat on the edge of the mattress, gazing at his pale, drawn face. 'Aren't you going to ask me what happened?' he said.

'I'd say it's fairly obvious what happened. Susan Reed thinks that man they released, William Jones, may know something. And she asked you to question him. And when you did, he attacked you.'

Harlan smiled faintly through the pain in his head and heart. 'Not bad. That's almost exactly right. Have you ever considered a change of career? You'd make a pretty good copper.'

'No I wouldn't. I don't enjoy sticking my nose into other people's business. And I don't like the police much, anyway.'

'I don't blame you.'

'Besides, you said almost right. What did I get wrong?'

'Jones didn't do this to me.'

'So who did?'

Harlan took a long breath and told her everything. She deserved that much at least. Besides, it felt good to get it all out. When he came to the part about how he hadn't been able to bring himself to hurt Jones, his eyes dropped away from hers. 'Susan Reed thinks I'm a coward.'

'A coward is the last thing you are, Harlan. You've just seen too much hurt.'

'Maybe not a physical coward, but a moral coward. I mean, for Christ's sake, I killed an innocent man but I couldn't hurt a child abuser who might hold the key to finding Ethan.'

Eve shook her head. 'You've got it the wrong way around. You'd be a moral coward if you hurt Jones.'

Harlan made no reply but his expression was unconvinced.

'Do you really think Jones knows where Ethan is?' asked Eve.

Harlan was momentarily silent in thought, then he said, 'No. But he knows something about something.'

'What makes you think that?'

'Just a hunch. I've questioned enough people to know when someone's hiding something.'

A ripple of unease passed over Eve's features. 'You don't think Jones is...' she paused and gave a little shudder, before continuing, 'doing something to some other child, do you?'

Harlan thought about the paintings. 'I don't know. I think he's fighting what he is, but maybe it's a battle he's losing.'

Eve's frown deepened. 'It horrifies me to think that there are people like that out there.'

'Then don't think about it. You've no need to.' The instant Harlan said the words he wished he hadn't.

'Why haven't I?' Eve demanded to know, the hurt plain in her eyes. 'You don't need to be a mother to feel that way. You just need to be alive and human.'

Alive and human. The words seemed to throb in Harlan's mind. It'd been a long time since he'd truly felt either of those things. 'I'm sorry.'

Eve's features softened. 'Forget it,' she sighed. 'So what happened after you left Jones?'

Harlan told the rest of the story. When he finished, Eve asked, 'Do you have any idea who attacked you?'

'Kane.'

Eve's eyebrows lifted. 'Ethan's brother? How can you be sure it was him? You said your attacker wore a scarf over their face.'

'Yes, but not his eyes. You should've seen his eyes, Eve. The hate in them...' Harlan's voice trailed off with a tremor, as a pain that was nothing to do with the lesions on his scalp poured out from his brain.

A moment of silence passed between him and Eve. He could

see she wanted to say something to comfort him. But he knew as well as she did that there was nothing she could say. He cleared the knot from his throat. 'Susan wants me to question Jones again, properly this time.'

'And are you going to?'

'I don't think I can.'

'So what are you going to do now?'

'I'm not sure. All I know is I've got to do something. If nothing else, I must make Kane see how sorry I am.'

'How? By spending your life searching in the shadows for a boy you'll probably never find?'

Harlan looked at Eve with a desperation close to tears. 'What else can I do to make him stop hating me?'

'Oh, Harlan,' murmured Eve, compassion shining in her eyes as she reached to touch his face.

'Don't.' Harlan moved his cheek away from her. 'I don't want sympathy. I just want to stay alive until this thing's done.' He stared out the window. All he could see was blackness and stars. A strange sensation came over him, as if he was falling into the night sky. His eyelids drooped. 'Wake me in two hours,' he managed to mumble before sleep overpowered him.

Seemingly only seconds later, Harlan felt himself being shaken awake. 'It's been two hours,' said Eve.

As he rolled over to look at her, pain crackled through his skull. 'Painkillers, please,' he groaned.

Eve fetched him a couple of tablets and a glass of water. 'Are you hungry?'

'No.'

Eve watched with an air of resigned sadness as Harlan shakily swilled back the painkillers. She said nothing. There was nothing left for her to say. After a while, he closed his eyes and fell back asleep.

Eve woke Harlan three more times during the night. The final time, it was getting light and she held a tray with toast and tea on it. After a silent breakfast, Harlan went through to the bathroom. He still felt headachy and dizzy, but when he looked in the mirror he saw that his pupils were no longer dilated with concussion. When he left the bathroom, Eve was waiting for him in the hallway. She had her coat on.

Harlan managed a thin smile, although a heavy, hollow ache wrung his chest at the thought of her leaving. 'Thanks.'

Eve nodded, turned and left.

From the living-room window, Harlan watched her get into her car and drive away. Swallowing a sigh, he dropped onto the sofa and watched the morning news. Still no mention of Jones. Garrett was doing a good job of keeping a lid on the whole affair. It was only a matter of time, though. Not that there was much chance of Jones going to the media – characters like him thrived in the shadows. But every police department had its leaks.

What are you going to do now? Eve's question came back to Harlan. The answer was simple. He was at a dead end, and there was only one thing he could do – turn around and go back over old ground, see if he'd missed anything. He retrieved his phone from the table and called Jim. 'Tell me about Neil Price.'

'I've already told you everything you need to know. He's clean as a baby. Never even had a speeding ticket.'

'Everybody's got some dirt somewhere.'

'The guy doesn't do drugs, he doesn't gamble, his computer's clean. The only thing we dug up on him even vaguely interesting is that he got into some credit-card debt in his early twenties.'

'How much?'

'I can't remember exactly. Nine or ten thousand, I think. But he finished paying it off a couple of years ago.'

'No outstanding loans?'

'No. His credit record's clean now.'

'What about to loan sharks?'

'Not that we know of.'

'Yeah, but we know he has the potential to get himself into debt.'

'Don't we all? I'll bet if I added up how much I owe on credit cards, car loans and all the other crap, it'd be a good few thousand quid.' Jim let out a sigh. 'Look, I'm telling you, Harlan, he's just some poor kid who got caught in this mess through no fault of his own. And besides, I don't think he's got it in him to pull something like this.'

'How do you mean?'

'If you'd met Price you'd know what I mean. He's the kind of guy who lets people walk all over him. He lives with his parents on the Manor. His mum's this little mouse of a woman. But his dad's a real tyrant. An unemployable drunk. The impression I get is that Neil and his mum spend most of their lives running around after him.'

'Maybe that's the angle, maybe Neil's sick of being a door-mat. We've come across dozens of people like that – people who live passively with anger and resentment for years until suddenly one day, pop!'

'He's not got the anger in him. I questioned him myself, pushed him real hard and he just took it. It was pathetic really. I almost felt sorry for him.'

A hint of a surprised smile tugged at Harlan's mouth. He'd never known Jim feel sorry for a suspect before. 'You must be getting soft, mate.'

'Maybe. Or maybe it's like I said the other day, I'm just getting too old for this kind of work. I tell you, Harlan, some days I'm so tired – tired of dealing with scum like William Jones and putting in fifty or sixty hours a week for sod all – that all I can think of is getting out of this job. But what else would I do, eh? This is all I know.'

'How is Jones?'

Jim gave a low whistle of contempt. 'Oh he's fine. Garrett wanted to put him up in a safe house, but he refused. So now a couple of uniforms are sat on him day and night. If you ask me, there's something warped about us babysitting that—' He broke off at a voice in the background. After a moment he came back on the line and said, 'I've got to go. Something's going on. I'll talk to you later. And Harlan, remember our deal, if you find anything out…'

'Yeah, yeah. I'll call you.'

Chapter Twelve

Careful not to wet his bandage, Harlan showered and shaved. Pausing occasionally to steady himself, he dressed and made his way down to his car. According to the doctor, he shouldn't drive for another twenty-four hours or so. But the thought of doing nothing was even more nauseating than his concussion. The effort of concentrating on driving made his head reel. Several times he was forced to pull over and wait for the world to stop spinning in front of his eyes.

Harlan didn't need an A–Z to find Manor Lane. He knew it all too well from his days on the force. It dissected the Manor – an estate with a bad rep as a playground for binge drinking, mugging, joyriding, happy-slapping hoodies. Neil Price's parents' house was at the lower end of Manor Lane, with a view overlooking the traffic-clogged Parkway and the industrial sprawl of Attercliffe and Tinsley. Harlan drove slowly past it and pulled over a few doors down on the opposite side of street. The house was a dirty red-brick semi with a small front lawn that managed to be both threadbare and overgrown. A beat-up Volvo was parked outside its front door. The neighbouring house, like numerous others dotted around the huge estate, was boarded up with metal sheets. Harlan reflected that there was certainly no shortage of places thereabouts to stash an abducted child. Both sets of upstairs curtains were drawn.

Harlan guessed that Neil and his dad were respectively sleeping off a night shift and a hangover. The downstairs curtains were open and the flicker of a television was visible. As he'd passed the house, he'd seen a late-middle-aged, mousy-faced little woman sitting in an armchair.

He tuned the radio to the news and settled back to watch the house. He wasn't worried about people wondering what he was doing there. Manor Lane was a busy road. Moreover, its residents were accustomed to turning a blind eye to what went on outside their front doors. Not that most of them weren't decent, honest people. Only they'd become hardened, worn down or simply desensitised by the relentlessness of their lives. And they were sick of being tarred with the same brush as the criminals. It all added up to a toxic cocktail of distrust, apathy and silence.

Harlan wondered how Neil Price had fared growing up on the estate. For someone as obviously sensitive as him, life must've been a bitter pill to swallow. Places like the Manor had a way of finding and homing in on weakness like a predator to prey. A gawky, skinny misfit like Neil would've been an easy target for the other kids to tease and bully. Surely somewhere beneath that timid exterior there was a store of pent-up anger and frustration simmering away. Or maybe Jim was right, maybe Neil really didn't have it in him. If the former was the case, Harlan was determined to find a line of attack to draw it out of him.

Harlan's attention was attracted to the radio by the sound of Garrett's voice. He realised why Jim had to get off the phone so suddenly as, after the usual preliminaries, Garrett said, 'The abduction of Ethan Reed clearly embodies people's deepest fears about the safety of their own children. I understand everyone's frustration and anger about the perceived lack of progress in this case, but vigilantism will not be tolerated in this city. Those engaged in such activities will be caught and prosecuted to the fullest extent of the law. We ask you to trust us to do our jobs. Over the past few weeks the incident room has been inundated with calls from members of the public who've provided us with information. This information is being scrutinised by teams of specially trained officers who are exhausting every avenue we're provided with. Our officers clearly won't be able to do that job as effectively if they also have to deal with citizens taking the law into their own hands.'

Harlan shifted his attention back to the house as Garrett continued to bang on about how his officers were resolutely following up every lead, while telling the media nothing about what those leads were. The obvious assumption was that the release of such information would compromise the investigation. In truth, Harlan suspected it was because the leads amounted to the same as they had on day one – zip, zilch, fuck all.

Shortly after midday, a set of upstairs curtains opened and Neil appeared at the window. He stood looking out at the street a moment, rubbing his eyes and yawning. Then he turned and moved from view. Half an hour or so later, he emerged from the house and got into the Volvo. Harlan slid down in his seat as the car reversed onto the road and drove past him. He waited until it was almost out of view before accelerating after it. He followed at an inconspicuous distance as Neil headed through Attercliffe towards Susan's house. Harlan pulled over at the end of her street, out of sight of her house. There was a chance that when Neil left he wouldn't come back this way. But it was a chance Harlan would have to take. Susan's house was almost certainly under surveillance.

At three o'clock the Volvo reappeared with Susan in the passenger seat. Harlan tailed it to a nearby comprehensive school. Children were streaming out the gates, some getting into cars and buses, others heading home on foot or bicycle. His stomach squeezed unexpectedly at the sight. Many were the age Tom would've been by now. Some even looked like he might have looked. Many times Harlan had tried to comfort himself with the thought that Tom's early death had saved him from the cruelty and pain of the world. That might've been true, but seeing the chatting, laughing, shouting throng drove home how hollow that comfort was.

As Harlan dragged in a shaky breath, he spotted Kane. The boy was slouched by the gates, hands thrust in pockets, eyes down. Susan got out of the Volvo and approached him. He followed her back to the car, dragging his feet, still staring sulkily at the pavement. Harlan could easily guess what the problem was – before Ethan's abduction Kane would, more often than not, have made his own way home, but now he was forced to endure the daily humiliation of being collected by his mum.

Neil returned to Susan's house. Again, Harlan waited outside her street. Thirty minutes passed. An hour. Neil reappeared on foot, carrying a bulging carrier bag. Harlan got out of his car. As he tailed Neil through the noisy, fumy rush-hour streets, the dull nagging ache in his head intensified to a severe throbbing. Neil handed out leaflets from the bag to everyone he passed. One man shoved the leaflet straight into a bin. Harlan retrieved it and saw a grainy black and white image of Ethan's smiling face. Occasionally, Neil went into a shop – no doubt, to ask if he could put a missing-person poster in the window. Slowly but surely, he worked his way to the Baptist tabernacle. The preacher, Lewis Gunn, met him at its entrance. They shook hands and went inside.

Glad for the chance to rest and let his headache subside, Harlan sat on a bench from where he could watch the church's door without being in its direct line of sight. His head felt heavy and sluggish, as if he'd just woken from a deep sleep. Time dragged by. His glazed eyes began to drift. His head lolled. An image of Tom came into his mind – not Tom as he'd been, but as he might be now if he'd lived. His hair cut into a trendy style. A few zits and a hint of bumfluff around his mouth. His cheeks starting to lose their puppy fat. But his smile the same. And his eyes... his eyes... Harlan felt his chin touch his chest. Jerking his head up with a sharp intake of breath, he saw that a double-decker bus had pulled over a hundred yards or so along from the church. People were boarding it, their features obscured by distance and the grime on the bus's windows. He caught a glimpse of a coat the same colour as Neil's. Was it him or was it just a coincidence? He jumped to his feet, squinting. But the coat had already disappeared into the stairwell. As the bus pulled away, Harlan made a mental note of its number – 77.

Muttering reproachfully to himself, he resumed watching the tabernacle. With every passing minute that Neil didn't emerge from it, he felt more certain it was him he'd seen. The daylight started to drop. Lamp-posts flickered into life. Number 77 buses chugged by at regular fifteen-minute intervals, heading to Grenoside – a solid working-class suburb on the north side of the city. By half past five, Harlan knew Neil was no longer inside the church, not if he started work at six. 'Shit,' he said, standing. As he headed off in the direction of his car, he reflected that he'd been an ex-cop so long he'd forgotten the number one rule: there's no such thing as coincidence.

Harlan drove back to the tabernacle and waited for a number 77 bus to pass. When one did, he followed it. Crawling through the traffic-clotted streets, the bus made its way to Grenoside, passing offices, shops, terraced houses, Hillsborough football ground, seventies high rises, modern apartment blocks, a suburban shopping centre, more terraces, semis, a new housing estate. Then, finally, the edge of the city – fields dotted with sheep; scattered farmhouses; purple-flowering moorland; and the vast blue–red expanse of the twilight sky. The bus pulled into a turning circle. It sat there for ten minutes before setting off back towards the city centre.

Harlan walked the circumference of the terminus, peering into the closely clustered ranks of pine trees that almost completely encircled it. Nothing to see but tree trunks and pine needles. He took a deep breath of the cool, head-clearing air, then returned to his car and the city.

He drove to the Northern General Hospital and cruised the car parks until he found Neil's Volvo. After parking in view of it, he bought coffee and doughnuts from a nearby shop. But even that wasn't enough to stop his eyelids from drooping. Realising sleep was going to win out anyway, he set the alarm on his phone for midnight, reclined his seat and closed his eyes. It seemed mere seconds later that the alarm woke him. The Volvo was still there. He reset the alarm for five thirty a.m. and fell back asleep. When he next awoke, he banished the fuzzy edges of sleep with the cold dregs of his coffee. Shortly after six, Neil appeared in his porter's uniform, his narrow shoulders scrunched against the chill morning air. He ducked into the Volvo and drove away. Harlan tailed him back to Manor Lane.

At seven o'clock the mousy-faced woman opened the downstairs curtains. She stood smoking a cigarette at the living-room window, the elbow of one arm cupped in the other hand. She turned suddenly and moved from view, as if someone had called for her. The morning dragged by. Some of the residents of Manor Lane headed out to work or school. Others came crawling home. As on the previous day, Neil surfaced at noon.

A few minutes later, the other set of upstairs curtains opened too, revealing a man who looked like Neil might look in twenty or so years if he spent the intervening time soaking himself in booze. The mousy-faced woman appeared and proffered a mug, which he pushed away. Moments later, Neil hurried from the house to his car. He drove to a nearby off-licence, bought some cans of lager and a couple of bottles of whisky, and returned home. He handed the booze to his mum at the front door, then got back into his car. Again, as on the previous day, Harlan tailed him to Susan's. Again, the two of them fetched Kane from school. But today, instead of going home, they went to the tabernacle. Lewis Gunn and a dozen or so other people were waiting for them in the church's car park, all of them wearing T-shirts printed with Ethan's face. The preacher shook Neil's hand and embraced Susan.

Harlan watched the group hand out missing-person posters in the city centre. Susan and Lewis Gunn also spoke to several journalists and the entire group posed for pictures, holding a banner that read *ETHAN STILL NEEDS YOUR HELP*. If nothing else, Harlan reflected caustically, his 'vigilantism' had fanned the media's interest back into flame.

At half-five Neil left the group and headed off to work. He parked in the same spot. So did Harlan. He bought more coffee and doughnuts, and a newspaper. The eye-catching front-page headline ran: *Police's Failure To Catch Kidnapper Prompts Vigilante Attack*. Beneath it there was a picture of Garrett at a press conference. It gave Harlan a small measure of satisfaction to note that there was a sheen of sweat on Garrett's forehead. He skimmed over the article. What little information the reporter had about the so-called 'attack' on Jones they'd got from a neighbour who'd heard him shouting for help. Jones himself had refused to speak to reporters, except to shout, 'Leave me alone!' through his letter box. The remainder of the article was made up by Garrett's platitudes, wild speculation about Jones, and the opinions of locals, which ranged from the relatively mild 'He had it coming' to 'I just wish that whoever it was had done the job properly and killed him'.

Frowning, Harlan tossed the newspaper aside. Part of him was irritated by the public's all too predictable indifference about what'd happened to Jones. But another part of him understood it completely. After all, people raising kids on Jones's street could hardly be blamed for wishing him dead.

The night passed the same as the last. With small variations in routine, so did the following day, and the day after that, and the day after that, and so on. Harlan didn't hear from Garrett. Not that he'd expected to after the precautions he'd taken to make sure he didn't leave any physical evidence behind. Of course, there was always the chance someone had seen him hanging around Jones's house, but if they had it was doubtful they'd be able to identify him. And even if they could, it was unlikely they would, not considering how hated Jones was. The general consensus on the street was that the vigilante was the hero, not the villain.

For a week, except for a brief visit to his parole officer, Harlan stuck to Neil like shit to a shoe. Neil spent his days doing things for other people – fetching booze for his dad, ferrying Susan and Kane around, handing out leaflets, meeting with Lewis Gunn. The only time he took for himself was a Sunday night visit to the Three Tuns – a little backstreet pub near the cathedral – where he played darts with two men, whom Harlan assumed to be Brian and Dave. Both men were a good few years older than Neil. Neither of them seemed to fit the kidnapper's description. One was blond. The other, although dark haired, was short and squat. They had beer guts and receding hairlines. They downed pints while Neil stuck to Cokes. They made a slightly odd trio – the beer-guzzling lads and the gawky oddball – but they seemed to get on well enough. No doubt, reflected Harlan, this had something to do with fact that Neil was the best player amongst them.

Susan, it seemed, had been right when she'd said Neil could be trusted. Harlan was beginning to wonder if he was wasting his time following him. More than that, he was starting to feel bad about it. Jim's words kept returning to him. *He's just some poor kid who got caught in this mess through no fault of his own.* Harlan was on the point of accepting that this was precisely what Neil was, and no more, when the number 77 bus chugged into view again. As previously, Harlan had tailed Neil to Susan's, then to the Baptist church. But unlike previously, this time Harlan saw him board the bus in his car's rear-view mirror. A little spurt of adrenalin racing through his bloodstream, he tailed the bus, pulling over at an inconspicuous distance every time it did.

Harlan kept thinking about the woods at the end of the line – how easy it would be to hide a freshly dug grave under the thick layer of pine needles beneath the trees. But after only a couple of miles Neil disembarked. Harlan parked up and followed him on foot along a busy road flanked by exhaust-stained terraced houses, pubs, small shops, restaurants and takeaways. Neil entered a rundown bookies. *ACE RACING* read the faded sign over its door. A heavily built, bulldog-faced skinhead stood behind a plexiglas screen at the rear of the bookies. Neil handed him some cash, which he counted out onto the counter, before pocketing it. Harlan estimated there to be one or two hundred quid. He dodged out of sight into a shop as Neil exited the bookies. What was the cash for? This question was uppermost in his mind as he watched Neil cross to a bus stop on the opposite side of the road. The most obvious answers were that Neil had either laid a bet or made a repayment on a line of gambling credit. But Harlan doubted for several reasons whether this was the case. For starters, the skinhead hadn't given Neil a betting slip or put the cash in the till, which meant the money wasn't going through any official books. More significantly, if Neil was a serious gambler, there was no way the police wouldn't have found traces of it on his financial history. There was another possibility, namely that Neil had paid off an instalment of a loan. Harlan knew from past experience that many bookies also ran a profitable sideline in illegal loan sharking.

As Neil waited for a number 77 to take him back into town, Harlan phoned Jim. 'I need some information,' he told his ex-partner. 'Ace Racing on the Penistone Road. Who owns it? What's their story?'

'Never heard of it. I'll make a few calls. Then I'll get back to you. I assume this has got something to do with Ethan Reed.'

'Uh-huh.' Harlan hung up. He wanted to get a clearer picture before saying anything more. He was in his car, tailing the 77, when his phone rang. He put it on loudspeaker.

'Ace Racing's owned by a guy called Gary Dawson,' said Jim. 'Nasty piece of work, by all accounts. Got his fingers in a lot of pies – dog fighting, fencing stolen goods, loan sharking.'

'Has he got a record?'

'GBH, demanding money with menaces, handling stolen property – all the typical crap you'd expect from a character like him. So are you going to tell me what this is about? Dawson's a scumbag but he's not exactly the type to be involved in something like this.'

Harlan hesitated. He wasn't sure he wanted to tell Jim. He was pretty certain that the first thing Garrett would do once the information filtered back to him would be to haul Neil in and sweat him for a day or two. Harlan suspected this wouldn't achieve anything besides putting Neil's guard up. Under immense scrutiny, Neil had managed to lie successfully to Susan and the police. Whether that lie concerned gambling or illegal loans or both was beside the point. The point was that beneath his timid exterior there lurked a steely resolve that few, if any, had detected. Harlan wondered what else was concealed in the shadows around and inside Neil. What hopes? What desires? What other secrets? And he figured that the best chance he had to find out was to keep tailing him.

'I tell you something, you tell me something. That was the deal,' said Jim.

'Trust me, Jim, I will tell you. I just need more time to work out what I'm on to here.'

Jim released a nasal sigh. 'You've got two days, then I want to hear everything you've got.'

Harlan knew there wasn't much chance of finding out the truth behind Neil's lie in two days. Not unless he got lucky. 'I need at least a week.'

'Four days. If I don't hear from you after that, I'm going to do some digging myself. See if I can't find out who owes Dawson what.'

Harlan smiled thinly. Jim might be getting a bit past it but he was still a shrewd operator. From his tone, it was obvious he suspected Harlan's interest in Dawson had something to do with Neil Price. And, adding two and two, it didn't require a huge intuitive leap to guess what that something entailed. 'OK. Four days.'

Chapter Thirteen

Time suddenly seemed to be on fast forward. With the speed of a thought that was gone before it was barely formed, one, two, then three days flashed by. Neil's routine, by now so familiar to Harlan, never once varied – work, sleep, off-licence, Susan's house, pick up Kane, hand out leaflets, work, sleep... The relentless tediousness of it numbed Harlan's brain, blotting away all thoughts except those that flowed from the question: why had Neil lied? The question whirled round and round in his head, even though he knew he wouldn't find the answer there.

On the fourth night, Harlan parked at the hospital, and as had become his habit, after watching Neil head into A&E, went for coffee and doughnuts. As he queued, he thought with mixed feelings about phoning Jim. On the one hand, he would've liked more time to follow Neil. But on the other, he was acutely aware that Susan deserved to know about Neil's lying, regardless of what lurked behind it – be it shame, fear or something more sinister. Harlan paid, turned to leave and found himself staring into Neil's eyes. Both men blinked in surprise. Neil's watery blue pupils darted around as if looking for a place to hide. 'What are you doing here?' he asked with a nervous little swallow.

Keeping his expression carefully deadpan, Harlan raised his box of doughnuts in answer. He stepped around Neil and headed for the exit. 'Fuck, shit,' he muttered under his breath, feeling Neil's eyes follow him until he was out of sight. The last thing he wanted was for Neil to realise he'd been tailing him. Not only because it would put him on his guard, but because if there was something sinister behind his lie it might panic him into doing something rash. He tried to phone Jim. No answer. 'I need to talk to you,' he told the answering service. 'Call me as soon as you can.' He waited five minutes, fretfully sipping coffee, then tried again. Still no answer. *For fuck's sake*, he thought. Jim was never without his mobile phone, so why the hell wasn't he answering? 'Price made me. We have to get him off the streets as quickly as possible,' he said, then hung up.

Ten more minutes passed. Harlan stared at his phone as if willing it to ring but it remained infuriatingly silent. Thrusting it into his pocket, he made his way back to his car. He approached it warily, scanning the car park for Neil. He was nowhere to be seen. He started up the car. As much as he was reluctant to leave Neil unwatched, he couldn't risk spending the night there. He pulled out of the parking space, jamming his foot on the brake as Neil appeared from behind a van. The watery eyes weren't dancing now. They were fixed on Harlan. Pushing his glasses up on his nose, he approached the driver's window. 'Are you following me?' He still sounded nervous but there was a kind of forced courage behind his voice.

Harlan motioned with his chin at the front passenger door. 'Get in.'

Hesitantly, Neil made his way to the door and ducked inside. Harlan accelerated towards the car park's exit. 'Hey, what you doing?' said Neil. 'I'm working. I only nipped out for a sandwich. I'll get in trouble if I'm not back on the ward soon.'

Harlan made no reply. As he pulled into the last remnants of the rush-hour traffic, he watched Neil out of the corner of his eye, studying every movement of his features.

'Where are we going?' persisted Neil. More stony silence. 'Hey, I asked you—' he started to say, but his nerves got the better of him and the words stuck in his throat. He sat stiffly with his thin hands clasped in his lap. His tongue flicked at his lips. His eyes flicked at Harlan. That dancing look came into them again as the car turned onto the Penistone Road. One of his hands moved towards his coat pocket.

'Don't,' said Harlan, his voice hard with warning.

'I just need to phone my manager, let him know I'm OK.'

Harlan shook his head, holding out his hand. 'Give me your phone.'

'What for?'

'Just fucking do it.'

Neil reluctantly handed over his phone. It started to ring. *Susan* flashed up on the screen. 'Who is it?' asked Neil. His eyes widened when Harlan told him. 'Let me talk to her. Please, it must be something important. She never usually rings me at work.'

Harlan put the phone in his pocket, watching closely for Neil's reaction. A slight flush rose into his cheeks. He opened his mouth to speak but closed it again without doing so.

'Go on, say what you were going to say,' said Harlan, wanting to see if he could draw some kind of angry response.

Blinking, Neil dropped his gaze to his lap. They drove on in silence, passing a number 77 bus. Neither of them exchanged a word until they pulled over outside Ace Racing. Then Harlan turned to Neil and gave him the hard stare he'd perfected as a cop, the one that said, *I know everything so you might as well spill it.* Neil's eyes flickered crazily all over the place but he held his silence. 'How much do you owe?' Harlan's voice was even and low but there was a weight behind it that was calculated to knock Neil off balance.

'I... I...' stammered Neil, then he sucked his lip into his mouth and pinched it between his teeth, staring at his clasped hands.

Like a father disappointed in a child, Harlan sighed and shook his head. 'Listen up, Neil, at the moment I'm the only one who knows about this. If you want to have any chance of keeping it that way, you'd better tell me what I want to know right now.' No matter what Neil told him, he had no intention of keeping it between them. Using a lie to uncover the truth always left a sour taste in his mouth but he'd long ago come to accept that the ability to do so was one of the most important tools in any detective's toolbox.

Neil released his lip suddenly and touched a finger to it. Blood. He stared at the crimson droplet as if trying to work out what it was. 'Nearly ten thousand.' His voice was tiny as the squeak of a mouse.

'Is it a gambling debt?'

'I've never gambled in my life. It was a loan.'

'What for?'

Neil gave a slight shrug. 'A car, clothes, furniture, rent for my flat.'

'But you live with your parents.'

'I do now, but a few years ago I moved out and lived in a flat in Ranmoor.'

Harlan's eyebrows lifted. Ranmoor was an upscale suburb on the south side. Neil obviously had ambitions to escape Manor Lane. 'That's a long way from the Manor.'

Neil's nose wrinkled as if the word 'Manor' smelled bad, but he said nothing.

'What's the flat's address?'

'Three hundred and forty Manchester Road. Flat one b.'

'Nice place was it?'

Again a shrug. 'It was just a one-bedroomed basement flat, but I liked it.'

'How long did you live there?'

'A couple of years.'

'So you lived above your means and ended up having to run home to Mum and Dad. That must've hurt.'

Neil remained silent but his expression said it all.

'Who put you in contact with Dawson?'

'A friend.'

'Name?'

'Dave Brierly. A guy I play darts with.' Neil's eyes blinked as though he had a pain behind them. 'He told me not to go to Dawson but I didn't listen. I must've been mad. I never seem to be able to pay off what I owe. The debt just keeps getting bigger.'

'That's how scumbags like Dawson operate.' Looking at Neil's tired boy–man face, Harlan felt a needle of sympathy. Alcoholic father, Manor Lane, no prospects – the kid hadn't exactly been dealt much of a hand. He pushed the emotion aside. He couldn't afford sympathy, not considering what was at stake. 'Why didn't you tell the police about your debt?'

'I've never told anyone about it. Not even my parents.'

'Why?'

Neil was silent a moment, then he said quietly, 'I was ashamed. When I had to give up my flat and return home, I felt such a… a…' He trailed off as if he couldn't bear to say the word.

Harlan said it for him. 'Failure.'

Neil nodded, his head hanging low as if a heavy weight was pressing on the back of it.

'And is that why you haven't told Susan either?'

'That and because, well, she's already got so much to deal with. I don't just mean with Ethan, I mean with her being a single mum and barely having enough money to get by. I was afraid that if she found out she'd leave me. You can understand that, can't you?'

'Sure I can, but I don't think that's all there is to it. Is it, Neil?'

Eyes wide and glistening, Neil jerked his head up. 'What do you mean?'

'A young boy's been abducted and you're hiding things from the police. You must see how that looks.'

'I know it looks bad but you've got to believe me it's got nothing to do with Ethan's abduction.' Neil pressed his hand over his heart in avowal. 'I love that boy. Since he was taken I've done everything I can to try and help get him back. I've handed out thousands of missing-person posters, I've helped organise fundraisers, I've—'

'Maybe you're just trying hard not to look suspicious,' cut in Harlan. 'I've been involved in plenty of murder investigations where someone's come forward to offer their help only to turn out to be the killer.'

'Why would I take Ethan?'

'Plenty of reasons. Maybe you sold him to a paedophile ring. Maybe you're a paedophile yourself. Or maybe you've cooked up some plan to get your hands on the reward money.'

Neil shook his head vehemently, eyes bulging at Harlan. 'You're crazy.' His voice rose as indignation overcame his sub-missiveness. 'I love Ethan.'

Ah, so you can get angry, thought Harlan, returning Neil's stare impassively. 'So you said.' He took out his phone and pushed its buttons as slowly and deliberately as he was pushing Neil's.

'Who are you phoning?'

'The police.'

A sick look came over Neil's face. 'But you said if I told you what you wanted to know you'd keep this between just you and me.'

'I said there was a chance of it. But you haven't told me anything that's convinced me not to phone them.'

'I... I—' Desperation made Neil's voice break. He cleared his throat, before blurting out, 'If you tell the police about me, I'll tell them about you and Jones.'

A hint of a crooked smile crept across Harlan's lips. The cracks in Neil's mask of timidity were rapidly growing. It wouldn't take much more pulling and prodding to reveal his true character. 'If you knew me, you'd know that wasn't a threat.'

Neil's eyes dropped apologetically from Harlan's. 'I shouldn't have said that. I didn't mean it.' He breathed a sigh of shame and despair. 'I know you're only doing what you have to do. But that's all I'm doing too. You see, the thing is, Susan's the first, the only woman who's ever looked twice at me. She means more to me than anything. If she leaves me I... I don't know what I might do. So I'm asking you, begging you, please don't tell the police.'

There was no lie Harlan could detect in Neil's voice. All he heard was a pleading, almost pathetic desire to love and be loved. Again, in spite of himself, he felt a stirring of sympathy. He knew what it was like to lose everything that meant anything. He knew what it was like to feel that life is too painful to live. The thought of inflicting that on someone, anyone, else was a torment to him. Again, he slammed a door in his mind, shutting the emotion out. As much as he wanted to believe Neil, he couldn't risk doing as he asked. 'I've got to.'

Neil's features crumpled like a cardboard box left out in the rain. 'OK, tell the police.' His voice was crushed by hopelessness to a whisper. 'But before you do, please will you let me tell Susan myself?'

Harlan considered this a moment, then nodded. He took out Neil's phone and scrolled through its contacts list for Susan's number. 'Tell her you want to meet at the hospital.'

'Can't I just go to her house?'

'No. I can't risk going to her house.'

'You mean you're going to be there when I tell her.' When Harlan nodded, Neil continued, 'I'm not sure I can do it with you there.'

'You've got no other choice.'

Harlan dialled Susan. When she picked up, he put the phone on loudspeaker. Her voice came down the line with urgency. She sounded different to how he'd ever heard before – unguarded, less angry, more fragile. 'I've been trying to ring you. Why haven't you been answering your phone?' Before Neil had a chance to reply, she continued, 'I rang Detective Greenwood and he said he didn't have time to talk. He wouldn't say why. I got the feeling something's going on.'

'You get that feeling every time you talk to the police,' said Neil.

'I know, but this time I'm certain of it. Something's not right. It's like I keep saying, the police know more than they're telling us. Oh Christ, Neil, what if... what if they've...' Susan's voice quivered breathlessly as she tried to bring herself to say what she barely dared think.

'Calm down, Susan.' Neil's voice was soft, reassuring. 'Remember what the doctor said to do when you feel like this, take a couple of deep breaths and count to five.' As Susan sucked in her breath, he counted slowly, 'One... two... three... four... five... That's it. Now exhale and say after me, if there were any important developments they'd have told me.'

'If there were any important developments they'd have told me.' Susan sounded calmer, but unconvinced. Harlan wasn't convinced either. Thinking about how Jim hadn't answered his phone, he suspected Susan's instincts were right. Something might well be going on. But what? Was it possible they'd found Ethan alive? No. If that were the case, they'd have told Susan. More likely they'd found a body and were waiting for positive identification. Or perhaps they had a new lead on Ethan's kidnapper. Whatever it was, it obviously didn't involve Neil, unless... It occurred to Harlan with a jolt that maybe *he* was the development. Maybe the police were surveilling them right now. His eyes scoured the street for potential unmarked police vehicles. There were none. He cut off his line of thinking, reminding himself that in all his days of tailing Neil he'd seen nothing to make him suspect the police were doing likewise. *Stop speculating on what you don't know*, he told himself sharply. *Focus on what you do know. The facts, only the facts.*

'There. Now don't you feel better?' said Neil.

'I suppose so. Thanks, babe. I don't know what I'd have done without you these past few weeks.'

'You'd have got through it. You're stronger than you think.'

'No I'm not.'

Neil looked meaningfully at Harlan, who was astonished to find himself questioning whether he was doing the right thing. Neil was Susan's main support. If he was pulled away from under her, there was no telling how far she might fall. *Do you really have to do that to her, after everything else you've done?* agonised Harlan. Almost the instant he asked the question, some other part of his brain shot back the answer: *yes*.

'Tell her you need to see her,' Harlan mouthed silently at Neil.

Neil's Adam's apple bobbed. His words came hesitatingly. 'Listen, Susan, I... we need to talk.'

'I thought that's what we were doing.'

'No, well, yes we are, but I need to see you.'

'What? Now?'

Wringing his hands, his voice nearly disappearing within the folds of its reluctance, Neil said, 'Yes. I've... er... got something to say to you.'

'So say it.'

'I can't. Not over the phone. It's too important.'

'What's so important you can't say it over the phone?' Harlan heard the frown in Susan's voice. He winced inwardly as, a note of panic creeping back in, she continued, 'Is it about Ethan?'

'No,' Neil said quickly. 'It's about me. Look, just meet me outside A&E as soon as you can, will you?'

'Can't you come here?'

'I can't be off the wards for that long.'

'What about Kane? I can't just leave him here on his own.'

'So drop him off at one of his friends' houses.'

'I don't know. It's getting a bit late for that and I... Look, can't you just tell me what you've got to tell me?'

Neil sighed. 'Will you come or not?'

Susan was silent a moment, then, sighing too, she said, 'OK, but you'd better have something big to tell me.'

Harlan hung up and returned Neil's phone to him. He turned the car and accelerated back the way they'd come. Neil sat slumped down in his seat, his expression swaying between misery and resignation. When the hospital came into view, he turned to Harlan suddenly. 'There must be something I can say to convince you this is unnecessary.'

'Maybe there is,' said Harlan, although there wasn't.

'I'm taking every extra shift I can to pay off Dawson. I've upped my repayments to two hundred a week. He says if I keep it up my debt will be cleared in a year and a half. Then I'll

be able to apply for a mortgage, and me, Susan, Kane and—'
Neil caught himself on the verge of saying 'Ethan'. 'We can
live together in our own place. And maybe me and Susan can
get married and have kids. We can have a real life together.
Don't take that away from us.'

A real life. At these words, an image came into Harlan's
mind of Tom playing with his toys on the hearthrug while he
and Eve chatted and read the Sunday newspapers. *A real life.*
A life that'd been taken from him through no fault or action
of his own. Anger suddenly surged up in him. 'I'm not taking
anything away from you,' he snapped. 'You've done that to
yourself.'

'I only did it to save Susan from—'

Harlan shot Neil a glance that silenced him. As they parked
outside A&E, Neil sagged back down into his seat, his eyes
glistening wet.

They sat in silence for twenty or so minutes, until a taxi
pulled up and Susan got out. 'Call her over,' said Harlan. When
Neil didn't make a move to do so, he added, 'Call her over,
or I will.'

Neil opened his window and shouted to Susan. When she
saw Harlan's car, the lines etched into her features by the weeks
of worry deepened. 'What's he doing here?' she demanded
to know, the openness that Harlan had heard on the phone
replaced by her familiar guardedness.

'Get in and I'll tell you.'

Susan hesitated to do so, suspicion rippling over her face,
her eyes flicking back and forth between Neil and Harlan, as
though she was trying to work out if they were in some way in
league together. With a slight shake of her head, she seemed to
dismiss whatever she was thinking. She ducked into the back
seat, but didn't shut the door. Arms crossed, she waited to hear

what Neil had to say. He stared at his lap, pale as a condemned man. His mouth opened and closed, but no words came out. 'Tell her or I—' Harlan started to say.

'OK, OK,' broke in Neil. With a tight breath, he lifted his gaze to meet Susan's. Her thin lips grew thinner still as he said, 'There's something about me I've been hiding from you. The thing is, Susan, I… erm… You know I said I was saving to buy a place of my own? Well I'm not. Not yet anyway. I am going to, but first I've got to pay off a debt. You see, I took out a loan from this guy, Gary Dawson.'

'How much?' Susan's voice was calm, but an undercurrent of growing anger was perceptible.

'Only four thousand, but now I owe him nearly ten.'

'And do the police know about this?'

'No.'

'So you've lied to me and the police.'

'Yes, but only because there's no need for them to know. This has got nothing to do with—'

Susan's hand lashed out and Neil felt the same sting of her nails that Harlan had on more than one occasion. 'Don't say it,' she hissed. 'Don't you fuckin' dare say my boy's name.'

Tears spilled over Neil's eyes. 'But it's the truth. Please, Susan, you've got to believe me.'

'How can I? If you'd told me about this right away after this all started, I might've been able to. But now…' Shaking her head, Susan repeated, 'How can I?'

'Because I love you and I love Ethan and Kane.'

'If you really loved us, you'd have told the truth.'

'I was trying to protect you.'

'No!' Susan stabbed an accusatory finger at Neil. 'You lied to protect your own pathetic hide. Remember what Detective Greenwood said – he said, "Somebody out there's holding that vital piece of information that's needed to solve the case, and they might not even realise it. So we need to know everything you know, no matter how insignificant you think it is." Do you remember that, Neil?'

Neil nodded desolately.

'How do you know it wasn't this guy, this Gary Dawson, who took Ethan?'

'He wouldn't do something like that.'

'Wouldn't he? Maybe he's using Ethan to force you to pay up.'

Neil shook his head. 'He's a loan shark, not a child abductor. And anyway, he doesn't need to force me to pay. I'm already handing over half my wage packet to him.'

'Neil's right,' put in Harlan. 'I don't know much about Dawson, but I do know it wouldn't make any sense for him to kidnap Ethan – at least, not on account of a ten-thousand-pound debt.'

'So you don't think this… this fucking nightmare has got anything to do with Neil's debt.' Susan looked at Harlan with a conflicted gleam in her eyes that suggested she was caught between the desperate desire to find out what'd happened to Ethan, and an almost equally desperate hope that it had nothing to do with Neil.

'I didn't say that.'

'It hasn't,' said Neil, shrill with the need to be believed. 'I swear on my life. I love you, Susan. I'd never do anything to hurt you. I know I've messed up big-time. I know I should've told the police, but I panicked at the thought that I might lose you.'

'You were right, you might have lost me,' said Susan. 'But now you definitely have.'

More tears bubbled up and ran down Neil's cheeks. He clutched at Susan's hand like a drowning man. 'Please don't do this. I'm so, so sorry. I'll make this up to you.'

Susan shoved his hand away. 'You can't. Not unless you can bring back my little boy.' She leaned forward suddenly, her eyes like needles. 'Can you do that?'

Neil's voice matched the intensity of Susan's gaze, as he said, 'No, but I can try. I'll do everything I can to prove how much I love you. Just give me a chance. I swear to God, I'll either make this right or die trying.'

Seemingly stunned by the force of Neil's words, her inner turmoil and uncertainty written in the shifting lines of her face, Susan hesitated to reply. She flinched at the shrill ring of Harlan's phone. He snatched it out, and seeing Jim's name on its screen, he said, 'I've got to take this.' Giving Neil a warning look, as if to say, *Don't even think about moving*, he got out of the car. 'I've been trying to call you,' he said. 'Why aren't you answering your phone?'

'I'll tell you in a moment,' said Jim, sounding utterly worn out. 'First you tell me why it's so important that we get Price off the streets.'

Harlan told his ex-partner about Neil's debt.

'Interesting.'

'I'd say it's more than interesting.'

'Where's Price now?'

'In my car.' When Harlan's reply elicited a hiss of displeasure, he added, 'And before you start getting shitty with me, I'm not forcing him to be there, he approached me to talk.'

'And what's he told you?'

'Nothing much I didn't already know. He claims he lied because he was afraid Susan would leave him.'

'That's most probably true.'

Harlan's eyebrows came together in a frown. 'What makes you say that? Come on, Jim, out with it. What the hell's going on?'

'First things first. Where are you?' When Harlan told him,

Jim said, 'Stay there. I'll send someone to pick Price up.'

'Why can't you come yourself?'

'Because I'm in Manchester.'

Harlan recalled that the police had been searching for connections between Ethan's abduction and a boy who'd gone missing in Prestwich. What was his name? Jamie Sutton. Yes, that was it. He'd gone out riding his bike and not come home. 'You've found the Sutton boy.'

'No. Another boy's been abducted just a few miles from where Jamie Sutton went missing. His name's Jack Holland, and he's seven years old.'

'Jesus. What happened?'

As though the words were heavy weights that had to be hauled out of him from a great depth, Jim said, 'Jack and his fourteen-year-old brother, Mark, were at some shops near their home. Mark went into one, leaving Jack playing on his scooter outside. When Mark left the shop approximately five minutes later, the scooter was still there but Jack wasn't. Mark saw a white transit van driving away fast from the shops.'

'Did he get the reg?'

'No.'

'Did anyone else see anything?'

'If they did, we haven't talked to them yet.'

'So you don't know for sure that the kid was abducted. He could've just wandered off.'

'He could have, but I don't think he did. I think he was abducted. I'll go even further than that and say that I think he was abducted by the same person who took Ethan Reed.'

Harlan puffed his cheeks. 'That's a pretty big assumption to make based on what you've told me.'

'If it was based on that alone, yes, it would be. But there's something I haven't told you yet. Something about Jack

Holland. Actually, maybe it'd be better if I just show you.'

'What do you mean, show me?'

'I'm sending you a picture of Jack Holland.'

Harlan's phone beeped as the picture came through. When he saw it, his mouth fell open. Jack Holland had the same pale, delicate features, the same faraway blue eyes, even the same wavy, straw-blond hair as Ethan Reed. There were differences between the boys – Jack had a dark mole on his left cheek, and his face was perhaps a shade chubbier. But at a glance they could've been mistaken for identical twins. 'Are they related? Jack and Ethan, I mean.'

'No.'

'So… so…' Harlan trailed off as his mind scrambled to make sense of all the possible implications of what he was seeing.

'So either this is just a monumental coincidence or someone out there has very specific tastes.'

'There's no such thing as coincidence.'

Jim grunted in agreement. 'Now you understand why I think Price is more than likely telling the truth. This isn't about money. This guy, whoever he is, is a predatory sexual deviant of the worst kind. And, as you know, scumbags like that usually operate alone.'

'Usually, but there's a chance this one doesn't, right? I mean, Jamie Sutton was a good few years older than Ethan and Jack. So either this perverted fuck goes for older boys as well, or he's got a partner with different tastes.'

'That's a possibility, assuming Ethan and Jack's cases are connected to Jamie's, which we're not convinced they are. But even if they are, it doesn't put Price in the frame. In fact, I'd say it does the opposite. Think about it. Assuming Price does have a taste for boys like Jamie Sutton, how come he's never tried anything on with Kane Reed?'

'Maybe he has.'

'If that were true, do you really think Kane wouldn't have spilled to us by now?'

No, Harlan didn't think so. He glanced into the car. Susan was staring at him as if trying to read his lips. Neil's head hung forward, eyes closed. He could've been mistaken for a corpse. Just one more casualty in the trail of desolation that lay in the wake of all such crimes. Harlan heaved a sigh. 'So who are you sending for Price?'

'Don't worry. It's someone you can trust not to tell Garrett about your involvement. Listen, Harlan, I can't talk any more now. Things are pretty hectic here. I'll call you if there are any new developments.'

'Good luck.'

Harlan hung up. He stared at the photo of Jack Holland a moment longer. Then, with a sick and weary look in his eyes, he got back into the car. 'Who was that?' Susan asked anxiously.

'A friend. A policeman. There's been a development.'

'I knew it! I knew something was going on.' Susan's voice grew hesitant, as if she wasn't sure she wanted to know the answer to her question. 'Have they found Ethan?'

'No. There's been another abduction.' Harlan showed Susan the photo. She sucked in her breath, putting a trembling hand to her mouth as he briefly filled her in on the details.

Neil craned his neck to see the phone's screen. His eyes widened, horrified, yet with a spark of wild hope mixed in. 'Don't you see? Don't you see, Susan? This proves none of this has got anything to do with me.' He turned to Harlan. 'Tell her. Tell her I'm right.'

'It's hard to say what this proves right now.'

'But if this sicko's snatching other kids, then—'

'Shut up, Neil,' broke in Susan, glaring at him as though

she might slap him again. Transferring her gaze to Harlan, she asked in a quiet, almost tender voice, 'Do you think your friend could get a message to Jack's parents? Just to let them know they're not alone. That I know what they're going through.'

'I'll ask him.'

Dropping her eyes back down to the photo, Susan reached to gently stroke her fingers over Jack's face. 'God, he's so beautiful.' She looked away suddenly, tears spilling down her cheeks, her expression contorting into a quivering scowl. Spittle flecked her lips as she said, 'It makes me want to kill, thinking about what might be happening to him.'

They sat unspeaking in the gathering gloom – Susan letting her tears fall silently; Neil pale, his lips drawn into a tight line; Harlan staring at the hospital, trying not to think or feel for a while, but knowing that was impossible. A car pulled up in front of A&E. DI Sheridan got out of it, glancing around. Harlan flashed his headlights and she headed in his direction. 'Get out,' he told Neil.

Neil shot Susan a final pleading glance. 'I meant what I said, Susan. I'm gonna make this right. You'll see.' When she refused to meet his eyes, heaving a breath, he got out of the car. DI Sheridan took hold of his arm, and with a brief nod at Harlan, guided him towards her car.

'Do you really think Neil's got anything to do with this?' asked Susan.

Harlan knew what she wanted. She wanted what so many others had sought from him in the past – hope. But as much as he hated to see her pained, imploring eyes he couldn't give it to her, not while there was even the slightest chance it might turn out to be false. 'I don't know.'

'Oh Christ, I hope he doesn't. I let him into the kids' lives. I'll never be able to forgive myself if he's part of this.'

Harlan started the engine. 'I'll give you a lift home.'

Susan looked at him uncertainly, as if she wasn't sure whether to accept or not. Then she let out a breath that seemed to come from her feet. 'I've got to pick up Kane from his friend's house.'

'What's the address?'

'Just drive. I'll tell you where to go on the way.'

Following Susan's directions, Harlan drove to a terraced house several streets away from her own. She got out and rang the doorbell. The door opened and Kane stepped out. Anger festered in his sullen, simmering hazel–brown eyes like an open wound. When he saw Harlan, his mouth twisted with bitterness. 'What's *he* doing here?'

'Giving us a lift home,' said Susan.

Kane glared at her incredulously. 'No way am I getting in that car!'

'Please, Kane.'

'No. No fuckin' way.'

Susan's voice rose. 'Don't you use that language with me.'

'You said you were going out to talk to Neil. You lied.'

'No I didn't. Look, Kane, something's happened. Something to do with—' Susan broke off, glancing around as if afraid of being overheard. 'This isn't the place to talk about this. Just get in the car, will you?'

Kane shook his head furiously. 'How can you have anything to do with him?'

'I don't want to, but I have to.'

'Why?'

'You know why. Now come on, get in.' Susan caught Kane by the arm, dragged him towards the car and opened the rear door. He kicked it shut, then kicked it again, denting it. 'Kane, stop that!'

Jerking away from Susan and darting Harlan a look of violent hostility, Kane ran across the street. 'Get back here,' shouted Susan. He ignored her. She ducked her head into the car. 'Sorry about your door.'

'No need,' said Harlan. He would've gladly let Kane work the car over with a baseball bat if it helped dissipate some of his rage.

'I'll have to go after him.' Susan started to turn away from Harlan, but hesitated. Not looking at him, her voice barely audible, she said, 'Thanks.'

Thanks. The word reverberated in Harlan's mind as he watched Susan chase after Kane. What did it mean? That she'd forgiven him? He dismissed the thought. She was grateful for what he'd done but that didn't mean she'd forgiven him. There was only one way she'd ever do that, and maybe not even then. Still, it briefly buoyed his spirits. But then his thoughts returned to Ethan and Jack, and everything inside him grew heavy again.

Chapter Fourteen

Harlan drove to his flat, stopping on the way to pick up some fast food – his fridge had stood empty for days. He ate mechanically, tasting nothing, lost in a fog of exhaustion. His meal half finished, he shuffled to bed. All he wanted to do was sleep, but the moment he shut his eyes he saw Jack Holland's face as if it'd been imprinted on the underside of his eyelids. Something else Susan had said came into his mind: *it makes me want to kill*. When Tom was alive, he'd said a similar thing to Eve once while investigating a particularly heinous crime. But when Tom died that part of him had been closed off. Now all he had the capacity to feel was a kind of soul-sick sadness. But it was enough to keep sleep away. After a couple of hours he got up and switched on the television. There was nothing on any of the news channels about Jack Holland's abduction. It wouldn't be long before there was, though. Then the media would go into a frenzy, pumping out fear like an overactive adrenal gland, making every man a suspect. And maybe they'd be justified in doing so, reflected Harlan. If, as seemed likely, Ethan and Jack's kidnapper was the same person, it was clear they wouldn't stop until they were caught.

He rubbed at his temples, trying to relieve the pressure lodged behind them, but it just built and built. He took out his phone and stared at Jack Holland's delicate, chubby face as if internally debating something. Suddenly, his expression tired but set, he grabbed his shoes and coat and hurried down to his car. Speeding along quiet night roads, he passed through the suburbs to the edge of the city and beyond. Following a sign marked *Manchester*, he turned down a slip road to the M1. He wasn't sure what he was going to do when he got there. All he knew was that he had to keep moving, keep searching.

Harlan was about twenty miles out from Sheffield when his phone rang. It was Jim. His weariness had been replaced with uncharacteristic excitement. 'You're not gonna believe this, Harlan. The kid, Jack Holland, he got away.'

Harlan's eyes popped wide. 'Fucking hell. How?'

'We're still getting the full story, but from what we know it went down something like this. Jack was grabbed from behind and thrown in the back of a white transit van. He was gagged and blindfolded and his hands and feet were tied. After what felt like hours to him, the van stopped and he was carried from it and put down on something soft. He heard his kidnapper moving away. He managed to work his hands free and remove his blindfold. He found that he was alone, lying on a mattress in a tunnel—'

'A tunnel,' broke in Harlan, frowning. 'What kind of tunnel?'

'I'll get to that in a minute. So anyway, the kid's in this tunnel and it's almost pitch black, but he can see daylight in the distance. He unties his legs and tries to make a run for it but he can't because his feet are numb from having the circulation cut off. So, get this, he crawls on his hands and knees until the feeling comes back. At the end of the tunnel there's an overgrown drainage ditch. As Jack's climbing out of it, he hears a man shouting something. He doesn't look to see who the voice belongs to. He runs into some nearby woods and hides. He hears somebody moving through the undergrowth, but he doesn't dare lift his head to look at them. When he can't hear anyone any more, he starts running again. Beyond the woods, there's a road. He flags down a passing car. The driver calls us. Turns out Jack was taken to a disused storm drain twenty or so miles to the east of where he was snatched.'

As Harlan listened to Jim, his frown deepened until a furrow like a knife wound was cut into his forehead. 'Are you at the storm drain now?'

'Yeah. It's a scary fucking place, right out in the middle of nowhere. You could scream your head off and nobody would ever hear.'

'Can you send me a photo of it?'

'Sure. But why? What are you thinking?'

'I'm not exactly sure. I just need to see it.'

'OK. Hold on a second. I'm sending it.'

Harlan's phone beeped. He opened the photo and stared at it in silence, his heart pounding in his throat. As Jim had described, the drainage ditch was choked with nettles and brambles. A path had been beaten through them to a circular brick drain protruding from the base of a steep, grassy bank. The drain's entrance was covered with a rusty metal grille that'd been bent outwards. Beyond the grille was a darkness so thick it seemed as solid as the brick encircling it. A shudder ran through him as his mind superimposed an image onto the photo of two figures drawn in silhouette – an adult and a child holding hands.

'So come on, Harlan, out with it,' said Jim. 'I can hear that brain of yours ticking over.'

Harlan opened his mouth to tell him about Jones's drawing but shut it again without saying anything. There was no way Jones was directly involved with Jack Holland's abduction, not with all the heat that was on him. And a drawing hardly proved that Jones knew anything about what went on at the storm drain. But Harlan felt certain down to the marrow of his bones that he did. He felt equally certain that the police wouldn't be able to get anything out of Jones, not unless they could find some physical evidence – DNA from a semen stain on the mattress, maybe – to link him to the drain. But even if they could, which seemed highly unlikely, that kind of forensic work took time – time Ethan, assuming beyond all optimistic hope that he was still alive, didn't have. If Ethan and Jack's kidnapper was one and the same, whoever it was would most likely be attempting to destroy any incriminating evidence, burning it, throwing it away, burying it. *You're the only chance Ethan's got*, thought Harlan with rising nausea, *you have to act, and act now.* Tyres screeching, he swerved sharply onto a slip road.

'Are you going to tell me what's on your mind or do I have to guess?' asked Jim.

'I can't talk any more right now.'

Jim's breath rasped down the line as if he'd expected that answer. 'One more thing before you hang up. We found some photos in the drain. Photos of boys, some of them little more than…' He trailed off, his voice suddenly clogged with rage and something else. Was he fighting tears? Surprise flickered in Harlan's eyes. He'd never heard such raw emotion in his ex-partner's voice before. The case had obviously got under even his thick skin. It was a few seconds before Jim could continue. 'Whatever you need to do to get this fucker, Harlan, you do it.'

'I will.'

Harlan hung up and concentrated on the road. He drove as if he saw Ethan in front of him, tied up, waiting to be slaughtered. He stopped to rush into an all-night supermarket. The checkout girl gave him an uneasy look when he dumped the contents of his basket – parcel tape, a screwdriver set, a torch, matches, a can of lighter fluid, a Stanley knife, gloves, a hooded sweatshirt and a Halloween mask – in front of her. He paid with cash and sprinted to his car. Twenty minutes later he was at the end of William Jones's street, scanning the vehicles parked along the kerb. His gaze fixed on a van with tinted windows opposite Jones's house. Was it an unmarked police vehicle? If, as seemed likely, it was, he was going to need some kind of diversion.

He pulled out of sight of the van, put on the sweatshirt and got out of his car. He approached a row of lock-up garages at the end of Jones's street, jammed a screwdriver into the lock of the first one he came to and twisted. The lock wouldn't budge. He tried the next garage along. This time the lock gave and he lifted the door just enough to duck under it. The garage was empty, except for some dusty old furniture. He quickly piled up several chairs, sprayed lighter fluid over them and put a lighted match to them. As flames whooshed up, he sprinted back to his car. He hunched down in his seat, burning with anticipation. It was as though he'd set a fire in his head as well as the garage. He concentrated on his breathing, focusing his mind. By the time the two men appeared from the end of the street, he'd restored an icy clarity to his thoughts. The way they moved, the way they carried themselves, told him they were plain-clothes coppers. One of them spoke into a mobile phone – no doubt phoning for a fire engine – while the other approached the garage, from which thick black smoke was billowing.

Harlan slunk out of his car, darting into the shadows of the alleyway behind Jones's house. When he saw the gate to Jones's backyard, he knew there was no way he could break through it. The gate and surrounding frame had been reinforced with steel bars. Coils of shiny new razor wire had also been strung along it and the walls. The house was as secure as a fortress, or a prison, depending on how you looked at it. There was only one way he was getting in – the front way.

He ran to the opposite end of the street from the burning garage. Slowing to walking pace, he approached Jones's front door. The plain-clothes policemen were still watching the fast growing fire. He raised his fist to knock, but hesitated. Again, flames licked at his brain, illuminating Robert Reed's blood-streaked, dead face. *Focus*, he told himself sharply, *focus. You have to forget Rob Reed. Forget you're human. You're a machine that won't stop until its job is done.* He rapped his knuckles against the door – a policeman's knock, heavy and commanding – and turned his back to it. A moment later, a familiar voice piped up nervously from behind the door. 'Who is it? What do you want?'

'Police, Mr Jones. Is everything OK?'

'Yes. Why wouldn't it be?'

'There's a fire at the end of the street. I need you to open the door, please.'

'Why?'

'So that I can visually verify you're OK. Orders from Detective Chief Inspector Garrett.'

There was the sound of several locks being undone. The door opened a crack. Harlan whirled around and slammed his foot into it with all the force of his desperate fear for Ethan, breaking a chain lock and sending Jones reeling onto his back. Pulling on the Halloween mask, he sprang inside the hallway and shut the door. Winded, gasping for breath, Jones grasped at a radiator, trying to haul himself upright with his good arm. He cried out as Harlan kicked his hand away and then grabbed his foot and twisted, flipping him onto his belly. Driving his knee into the small of Jones's back, he snatched out the Stanley knife and pressed it to his neck. 'Do exactly as I say or I'll cut your throat,' he hissed through his teeth.

'Oh Christ, oh fuck, not you again,' whimpered Jones, recognising Harlan's voice. 'I've already told you—'

'Shut the fuck up. You know how this works. You don't speak unless I ask you a direct question.'

Harlan bound Jones's mouth with packing tape. Jones let out a muffled scream as Harlan yanked his injured arm out of its sling and twisted it behind his back. He rapidly rolled the tape around and around Jones's arms and legs, before locking the front door. His ears caught the faint but unmistakable wail of fire-engine sirens as he dragged Jones into the living room. The place was in an even worse state than the last time he'd been there – cans and bottles strewn everywhere, interspersed with mouldering fragments of food that looked as though they'd been gnawed on by mice. The smell brought bitter saliva to Harlan's mouth. Swallowing it, he hurried upstairs, removing all the paintings from the walls. He dumped them in a pile on the living-room floor, before tearing the tape away from Jones's mouth. He stabbed a finger at the drawing of the figures holding hands outside the tunnel. 'Where is that?'

'I already told you, it's nowhere.'

'Wrong answer.' Harlan slashed one of the paintings with his knife.

Jones's eyes bulged as though he'd been kicked. 'Don't! Please, don't!'

Harlan reached for another painting. 'The truth.'

'It is the truth.'

The Stanley knife sliced through more layers of paint and canvas. Harlan flung aside the ruined artwork and started in on another.

'Stop,' cried Jones.

Harlan looked at him with steel-cold eyes. 'No more bullshit.

163

Either you tell me what I want to know or I'm going to shred all of them.'

Jones's tongue flicked at his lips, which quivered as though they were about to speak, but no sound came from them. Harlan re-gagged him. Then he resumed slashing at the paintings. And the more he slashed, the more his movements took on a frenzied intensity, as though some barrier inside him had broken, unleashing a barrage of pent-up rage and frustration. Once he was finished with the paintings on the floor, he started shredding those on the walls. Oblivious to the pain in his injured elbow, Jones writhed and twisted like a crazed animal, desperately trying to free his arms. Finally, Harlan attacked the painting on the easel, obliterating the scene of the children on the swings with almost gleeful savagery. Breathless and sweating behind his mask, he squatted down, peeled back Jones's gag and pointed at the only piece of artwork still intact – the little charcoal drawing.

'Where is that place?'

Jones stared at Harlan through a sheen of tears, his eyes burning with acid hate. 'You fucker, you bastard,' he hissed hoarsely.

Harlan moved the knife towards the drawing. He had no intention of damaging such a potentially important piece of evidence, but he figured the bluff was worth a shot.

'Why? Why do you want to know where it is?' Jones asked as the blade touched the canvas, a note of pleading replacing the anger in his voice.

'So, it is somewhere real and not just something from your imagination.'

'I... I didn't say that.'

Harlan took out his phone. Watching intently for Jones's reaction, he showed him the photo of the storm drain. 'Does

164

this place look familiar to you?'

Jones looked at the photo blankly – perhaps just a shade too blankly. 'No.'

'I think it does. I think you've been there.'

'Why the hell would I have been there?'

'To abuse and maybe even murder children.'

Jones's puffy alcoholic's face scrunched into a horrified red ball. 'You're off your fucking head.'

Harlan opened his mouth to ask another question but closed it again as a siren blared past the house. Soon the street would be swarming with firemen and police, making it almost impossible for him to get away unnoticed. He needed answers fast, and as he'd feared, it was clearly going to take more than questioning to get them. He gagged Jones, then looked around for something hard and heavy. His gaze fixed on the old truncheon, which was leant, handle up, against the foot of the armchair. Jones moaned through his gag as Harlan rolled him onto his side and twisted his arms so that his fingers were splayed out flat on the floorboards. Harlan snatched up the truncheon, raising it overhead, his knuckles showing bone-white where they gripped it. One second passed, two, three and still the truncheon didn't descend. Harlan's breath came rapidly through the mask's mouth-hole. *Ethan's life depends on you*, he shouted silently at himself. *Do it! Fucking do it!*

Harlan brought the truncheon down on Jones's fingers with bone-crunching force. Jones let out a scream that was loud even through the gag. Harlan hit his fingers again. He waited for Jones's screams to subside before removing his gag. 'Now will you tell me?' He managed to keep his voice cold and level, even though his insides were reeling and churning.

Jones stared up at him, eyes swollen with fear and hate, breath rasping with agony. He said nothing.

'Much more of this and you'll never be able to paint again.'
Still nothing.

Harlan replaced the gag. Jones kicked and writhed amongst the wreckage of his life's work, trying desperately but vainly to break his bonds. Holding him steady, Harlan pummelled his fingers with all the force his muscular arms could exert. Jones's screams changed into retches. Harlan tore away the packing tape and Jones vomited up what looked, and smelled, like a can's worth of cider muddied with blood. Suppressing a retch himself, Harlan said, 'It won't stop until you tell me. Understand?'

Jones's pale, mottled face contorted almost beyond recognition. He sobbed into his vomit. Suddenly, his whole body trembling from the effort as if palsied, he managed to lift his head and scream, 'Help!'

Harlan snatched up a handful of shredded canvas and stuffed it into Jones's mouth. He stuck fresh packing tape over it. Jones's eyes bulged as if he couldn't breathe. Sweat dribbled into Harlan's eyes. He blinked to clear his vision. This wasn't working. He didn't have time to gradually beat the truth out of Jones. Any second now the plain-clothes policemen might come knocking, and then the game would be up. He had to go further, faster. He had to make Jones believe it was a straight choice between spilling what he knew and death. And there was only one way he could think of to do that.

Composing his features into a mask of implacable resolve, Harlan reached up and removed the Halloween mask. He put down the truncheon and picked up his knife. He pushed his face close to Jones's. 'I'm letting you see me so you'll know I'm serious when I say this. The only way you're going to live through this is if you tell me what I want to know.' With one hand Harlan removed the gag, with the other he pressed the knife to Jones's windpipe. 'Now talk.'

Spittle stretched like an elastic band from Jones's lips as he sobbed, 'I already told you the truth. Oh God, please don't—' He broke off as Harlan pressed harder. The blade drew blood as his Adam's apple bobbed convulsively.

Somewhere in some deep, dark part of Harlan, the same frenzy that'd overtaken him earlier stirred. He pictured himself slashing at Jones until he was as unrecognisable as his paintings. The unbidden thought vibrated through his mind and down his arm. When it reached the knife, Jones flinched as if from an electric shock. 'OK, I'll talk,' he gasped, his voice deflating to a hoarse whisper as fear sucked the last dregs of resistance out of him. 'You're right. My drawing and that photo you showed me are of the same place.'

An almost euphoric sense of relief swept through Harlan, and not just because he may well have got one step closer to finding Ethan. It'd shocked him nearly as much as it had Jones to realise that he hadn't been bluffing. He really would've killed Jones if he had to. 'You've been there?'

'A long time ago. Before I went to prison.'

'What year? What month?'

'Two thousand and three. I don't remember what month. It was hot, so I guess it was summertime.'

'Did you go alone?'

There was a pause. The blade twitched against Jones's throat, prompting him to speak. 'No. Someone took me.'

'Who? What's their name?'

'I don't know.'

'Don't fucking bullshit me.'

'I'm not. He never told me his name and I never asked it. Sometimes it's best that way.'

'Well, what does he look like?'

'I dunno what he looks like now, but back then he had long

dark hair and a beard. I used to call him the Prophet, y'know, cos he looked like something out of the Bible.'

'What about height and build?'

'About the same as you, I think. I can't really remember. It was that long ago.'

'How did you meet?'

'He sold toys on the street in the city centre. This other guy I knew pointed him out to me because he'd seen him at an offenders' hostel.'

'A sex offenders' hostel?'

'Yeah.'

'What did he do time for?'

'I dunno. You don't ask questions like that, do you? Anyway, I used to buy things from him occasionally – stuffed toys, cheap plastic jewellery, things like that – and we got to talking about photography.'

'Why did he take you to the storm drain?'

'He said he had some photographs I might be interested in buying. So we drove out there to take a look at them.'

Thinking about what Jim had told him, Harlan shuddered as he felt that primal urge of frenzy nibble at the edges of his mind again. As if sensing this, Jones continued quickly, 'I only went there the once.'

'Just to buy photos?'

'Yes.'

Harlan tapped the charcoal drawing. 'That seems to suggest you went there for a lot more than photos.'

'I didn't do that drawing, the Prophet did. He started doing art when he was inside, same as me. I saw it on his wall and, well, I liked it, so I asked if I could buy it. He gave it me for nothing.'

Squinting at the drawing, Harlan saw that the lower half of the adult figure's face was indeed slightly misshapen, as if they had a beard. His brow puckered as something occurred to him. 'Are you saying that was hanging on the wall of the storm drain?'

Jones winced as if he'd let something slip unintentionally. He winced again as a slight movement of the blade brought a fresh trickle of blood from his throat. 'No. It was on the wall of his caravan. He took me there as well as the drain.'

'Where was this caravan?'

'In some woods ten or fifteen miles away from the drain.'

'On a site?'

'No. On its own. There's nothing else for miles around but trees.'

'Did it look like it had been there a long time?'

'Yeah, it was half covered in ivy.'

'And did the Prophet live there?'

'I dunno. I don't think so. I think he just used it for storing photos and other stuff.'

'What other stuff?'

'Home-made videos, stuff like that.'

'So where does he live?'

'How the hell would I know? I haven't seen him since the day he gave me that drawing.' A tremor passed through Jones's bloated frame. He swallowed a groan. 'Look, I've told you everything I know. What else do you want from me?'

Harlan's eyes flicked between Jones and the drawing as he considered the question. This guy, the Prophet, obviously had a record. He'd spent time in prison and in a sex offenders' hostel. He was, or used to be, very distinctive-looking. His fingerprints might even be on the drawing. Given time, that was probably more than enough for the police to track down his identity. But there was no time. 'I want you to show me where the caravan is.'

'I don't know if I can. It was years—' Jones fell silent at the warning in Harlan's eyes. He heaved a wheezy breath of resignation. 'OK, I'll try.'

'You'll do more than try. Where's the back door key?'

'In my left trouser pocket.'

Harlan pulled out a thick bundle of keys. 'Is the gate key on here?'

'Yes.'

As Harlan flicked through the bundle, Jones nodded to indicate the required keys. Harlan gagged him once more and hurried to the back door. As fast as his trembling hands would allow, he twisted open the half-dozen deadbolts and other locks securing the door and gate. He sprinted towards his car, pulling up sharply at the end of the alley. Peering around the corner, he saw a couple of fire engines shrouded in the smoke billowing from the garage. Firemen were aiming a jet of water at flames stretching through a hole in the roof. Others had formed a loose cordon in front of a crowd of onlookers. No one seemed to notice Harlan as he ducked into his car and drove into the alleyway. If they had, he reflected, they'd most likely assume he was removing his car from harm's way. He braked in front of the gate, popped the boot and darted back into the house. His heart gave a lurch when he saw that Jones's eyes were closed. He anxiously searched for a pulse and found one as thin as a spider's thread. He slapped Jones's face and the bound man's eyelids flickered open. He cut the tape wrapped around his legs, then thrust his hands under his sweat-drenched armpits and hauled him upright. As Harlan guided him to the car, Jones swayed and reeled like a ship in heavy seas, almost capsizing both of them several times.

Jones shook his head and tried weakly to pull away from Harlan when he saw the open boot. He squealed as if he'd been stabbed as Harlan shoved him into it, flipped his legs in after him and slammed it shut. Breathless, Harlan jumped behind the steering wheel and accelerated away hard. He braked equally hard as a couple of police cars passed the end of the alley, lights flashing, sirens wailing. Jones hammered at the boot. 'Don't waste your time. There's no one around to hear you,' said Harlan, but Jones kept at it until they were beyond the sound of the sirens. At an inconspicuous speed, Harlan drove on through the night-time sounds of the city, which seemed strangely muffled and distant, as if they came from deep inside a tunnel.

Chapter Fifteen

As Harlan passed into the sheltering dark of a street of unlit warehouses, his mask of implacable resolve slipped and his breath came in a sharp exhalation. He pulled over, tremors of revulsion running through him as he thought about how close he'd come to killing Jones. He'd been forced to go down into a place inside himself that he'd seen but never visited before, and the call of the darkness that lurked there had proved almost irresistible. He could still feel its voice at the back of his brain, like an itch demanding to be scratched. He flung open the door and sucked in lungfuls of the night. 'Focus, focus,' he murmured over and over. Gradually the tremors subsided.

He opened the boot. Jones goggled up at him, his face slick with sweat. As Harlan peeled away his gag, he gasped for breath like a drowning man pulled out of the water. 'I'm claustrophobic,' he wheezed. 'Please don't keep me in here any longer.'

'I won't, but try anything funny and it's straight back in here. Understand?'

Jones nodded. Harlan helped him out of the boot and into the front passenger seat. Jones cried out as his weight came down on his pulverised hands. Giving him a warning look, Harlan cut the tape binding his wrists. He rebound his hands in front of him.

'Which way?' asked Harlan.

'Just get onto the motorway and I'll tell you when to leave it.'

As fast as he dared, Harlan drove to the motorway. He kept one eye on the road and one on Jones. Jones watched him right back as if trying to work out what he was thinking. 'I know who you are,' he said suddenly, eyes widening with realisation. 'You're that guy who killed Susan Reed's husband. I've seen your face on the news. Your name's H... Ha...'

'Harlan Miller.'

'Yeah, that's it. You used to be a copper, didn't you?'

'Yes.'

'So you know you'll never get away with this.'

'Who said anything about getting away with this?'

'You want to go back to prison?'

'I want to find Ethan Reed.'

'I understand. I get it. You want to save the boy to make up for what you did to his old man. But you and I both know he's long beyond saving. Whoever took him did his thing and killed him weeks—'

'Shut up,' broke in Harlan, a twitch pulling at the corner of his mouth.

'Look, what I'm saying is there's no need for this. You tell your copper mates about the caravan and they'll find it in no time, if it's still there. Just let me go. Let me go now and I promise I won't give your name to—'

'One more fucking word and it's back in the boot for you.'

Jones grimaced at the threat. He fell to studying his hands. A great shudder racked him. 'Maybe it's best if you kill me,' he murmured. 'Because if I can't paint, I... I don't know what I'll do.'

I don't know what I'll do. The threat implicit in those words made Harlan go cold. He didn't doubt for a second that Jones had been, at least to some degree, telling the truth when he'd said that painting kept him straight. Without it, surely it was just a matter of time before he answered the call of his own darkness. And then more people – children, their parents, relatives and friends – would suffer. The cycle of devastated lives would continue, expanding and intersecting like ripples in a pond. And, Harlan reflected with a mounting sense of guilt, it would be his fault. Unless, unless… The itch in his mind became a burning, and spread. *No*, he said silently but vehemently to himself, *no!* He wound down his window. Tears sprang into his eyes as the air hit him like ice-water. The heat receded again. *But for how long?* he wondered darkly. *For how long?*

They stayed on the M1 and then the M62 for nearly an hour and a half, passing fields of crops and livestock, lonely industrial estates, and the sleeping outskirts of Wakefield, Leeds and Huddersfield, before crossing the black peaty spine of the Pennines. 'Come off here and head towards Saddleworth,' said Jones, gesturing at a junction, beyond which hills loomed like solid shadows in the moonlight.

Twenty minutes or so after leaving the motorway, having been directed into a snarl of narrow lanes, Harlan asked with a note of doubt and warning in his voice, 'How much further?'

'Shh,' hissed Jones, looking intently at the passing landscape. 'Let me concentrate.' He pointed at a humpback stone bridge that crossed a stream. 'I remember that. It's not far now.'

The moon was hidden from sight as they passed into a mixed wood of towering deciduous trees and pine plantations. 'There!' said Jones, pointing at a wooden gate with a sign on it that read *PRIVATE NO PUBIC RIGHT OF WAY*.

'Are you sure this is it?' asked Harlan.

'Yes. I remember laughing because some joker had scratched out the L in public.' Jones didn't smile at the joke now.

As Harlan turned off the road, the car's headlights illuminated a narrow wheel-rutted track cutting between uniform ranks of pine trees. He got out of the car and approached the gate. It was secured with a chain and padlock, but the frame was so soft with rot that he was able to loosen a nail and unhook the chain. He drove through the gate, then closed it, returned the chain to its place and pushed the nail back in with his thumb – if anyone else came to the gate that night, he didn't want to give them a hint someone had been through it.

'How far to the caravan?' he asked.

Jones shrugged. 'About a mile, I think.'

'You think?'

'Yeah, I think. What do you expect? Like I told you, I haven't been here for donkey's years.'

Harlan leaned in close to Jones, eyes glinting like steel beads. 'Well you need to do better than just think. You need to be certain. If this friend of yours, the Prophet, is—'

'He's not my friend,' Jones was quick to point out. 'He's just someone I bought some stuff off.'

'Whatever. If he's already at the caravan, I don't exactly want to announce our arrival.'

'OK, OK. Just give me a moment.' Jones closed his eyes, forehead wrinkling as he dredged through his memories. 'These pine trees go on for a couple of hundred yards, then... then the road goes down into a dip where it crosses a stream. That's where the pines stop and the oaks and beeches start. From there it's about two or three hundred yards to a clearing set off to the right of the road. That's where the caravan was.'

Harlan drove slowly along the track. Like Jones had said, after a short distance it descended into a valley with a shallow, boggy stream at its bottom. The car rocked from side to side as it wallowed through the mud and climbed the stream's far bank. The trees closed in thickly on either side, their branches brushing the car, almost blotting out the sky. Harlan had a sense that he was entering somewhere cut off from the rest of the world. He'd used to love such isolated places before becoming a copper. But the longer he'd been in the job, the more their silence and secrecy made him uneasy. Where another person saw a romantic spot to spend a night or two, he saw somewhere where someone could commit murder and hide a body without fear of being seen or heard. He switched off the headlights and crawled along for another hundred yards or so, watching for a gap in the trees where he could pull off the track. There wasn't one. He stopped the car. He didn't like leaving it in full view, but he couldn't risk continuing any further until he'd checked the caravan out. He popped the boot and turned to Jones.

'No, please, please don't make me go back in there,' begged Jones. 'I'm not gonna try to get away. I mean, come on, where would I go out here in the middle of nowhere?'

Harlan got out of the car and made his way around to Jones, who recoiled from him, shaking his head frantically. He took out his knife and brought the blade close to the man's face. Jones stopped struggling. Dragging in a quivering breath, he stood up out of the car and shuffled to the boot. He lay limp and resigned as Harlan wrapped more tape around his ankles and mouth. Harlan then retrieved the torch from the back seat, before heading along the track. He covered the lens with his fingers, letting out just enough light to illuminate his way. Again, Jones's memory proved reliable – after maybe two hundred yards, the wall of trees gave way on the right to an overgrown grassy clearing. The caravan, a tiny oval tourer furred with ivy, was set to the back of the clearing. No lights showed in its windows. There was no car outside it, but the grass was flattened in places as though one had been there recently. To its right was a roughly built shelter, a beard of vines dangling from its tarpaulin roof.

Resisting the urge to investigate further, Harlan made his way back to the car. He drove past the clearing, stopping out of sight of it around a bend. Thinking about ringing Jim, he checked his phone. It had no signal. There'd be no calling for back-up out here.

He returned for a closer look at the caravan and shelter. Rusty petrol drums and gas canisters were stacked beneath the sagging tarp. There was also an old petrol-powered generator from which wires ran to a battery beneath the caravan. A spade and pickaxe leaned against the generator. Harlan's eyebrows drew together as he stooped to inspect the spade. Its flat blade was caked with damp earth, as though it'd recently been used. Behind the shelter a faint trail was visible in the long grass. Harlan followed it to the treeline. Beyond that the trail disappeared into a mulchy mass of fallen leaves. He approached the caravan and tried its door. Locked. He turned his attention to the nearest window. The rubber seal was rotted and cracked. With a punch of his palm, he jammed the blade of his screwdriver through it. A quick jerk dislodged the latch. He opened the window, pulled aside a mildewy curtain and shone his torch into the caravan.

At first glance, the place looked abandoned – the floor was strewn with soggy newspaper, apparently put down to soak up the multiple leaks in the roof; the walls were studded with mould; several of the cupboards stood open and bare; piles of pots and pans festered in a pool of grease-filmed water in the sink. A closer look, however, revealed signs that someone had been there recently – a rolled-up sleeping bag and pillow wrapped in clear plastic to keep the damp out were stowed on a built-in sofa; a plate still glistening with baked-bean juice and a glass half full of milk stood on a fold-up table.

Harlan hauled himself through the window, wincing as he sent several plates crashing to the floor. He closed the window and drew the curtain back across it, before continuing his exploration. He tried a light switch. Nothing happened. He sniffed the milk. It was sour but not curdled. Perhaps a week old, he reckoned, maybe less. He opened the cupboards. In one there were several litres of bottled water, a jar of instant coffee and a box of matches. In another there were tins of baked beans and soup and half a pack of stale biscuits. In a third there was a coil of rope that could've been used for tying people up or hanging clothes out to dry. There was no sign of the photos and videos Jones had spoken about. A partially dismantled television sat on a shelf in an alcove, but there was no video or, for that matter, DVD player. There were two doors other than the entrance. Harlan opened one and reflexively clapped his hand over his nose. The door led to a tiny toilet cubicle. The toilet was full almost to the brim with rust-coloured, stinking water. He thought about the spade, reflecting that whoever had been staying here had probably used it to dig a toilet in the woods. The second door opened into a cupboard that contained a dustpan and brush, a couple of toilet rolls and some empty clothes-hangers.

Harlan frowned as a thought crossed his mind. Had Jones been feeding him a line of bullshit about coming here with the Prophet? Did the Prophet even exist? Maybe Jones had made him up to buy himself some time? Maybe this was just some place where he had stayed before. Harlan shook his head. The fear in Jones's face and voice hadn't lied. Still, he was relieved he hadn't had the chance to phone Jim. At least, if it came to it, he could question Jones further. A shudder passed through him as a voice piped up in his mind. *What if you lose control? What if this time you can't stop yourself from killing him?* He

178

shoved the voice away. The 'what ifs' were irrelevant. What had to be done, had to be done. It was as simple as that. His pulse jumped at a sound from outside – the whine of an engine grinding its way along in low gear.

Snapping off his torch, Harlan peered between the curtains. The approaching vehicle's headlights danced crazily as it negotiated the rutted track. He was about to climb out the window and dash into the woods, but there was no time. The vehicle was already swaying into view. As its twin beams fell on the caravan he squinted, struggling to make out what kind of vehicle it was. It wasn't a transit van, that much was obvious. But it was much bigger than a normal car. Some kind of four-wheel drive, maybe. The vehicle pulled up outside the caravan. Its engine fell silent and the driver's door opened. A figure got out and walked in front of the still blazing headlights. Before he scurried into the toilet, Harlan caught a glimpse of a masculine physique – stocky, but close enough in build to the man Kane had described to plausibly be him – beneath a head of thick, long black hair. He covered his nose with one hand as the stench hit him again, the other felt for the knife in his pocket. As a key clicked in a lock and the front door squeaked open, he raised the knife, ready, if necessary, to slash whoever was coming.

The floor trembled slightly as footsteps advanced into the kitchen area. There was a pause. A sniff, as if the footsteps' owner had caught a whiff of an unfamiliar scent, followed by a sound of clinking crockery, which Harlan guessed was the plates being picked up from the floor and returned to the sink. His muscles tensed for action. A few seconds passed. The footsteps moved towards the far end of the caravan. There was a tearing sound of Velcro being peeled apart. A low grunt as something heavy was lifted. Then the footsteps came back to the front door and went out. The door was left open. A moment later the footsteps returned. Another grunt as something else was carried outside. A minute crawled by and still the door remained open. A faint whiff of smoke – not wood smoke, but an acrid smell of burning petrol and plastic – cut through the toilet's fumes. Harlan's ears caught the crackle of flames. *The photos and videos*, he thought. *They were here and the fucker's burning them. He's burning the evidence.*

He resisted an urge to rush outside and restrain the Prophet. Assuming that was really who it was, there was a lot more at stake than the loss of physical evidence. The questions uppermost in his mind were: where did that trail in the grass lead? What did the woods conceal? He could perhaps find out by questioning the Prophet like he'd questioned Jones. But he was reluctant to do so while there was a chance that the Prophet might unwittingly lead him to the answers he sought. At the same time, whether or not the front door was open, he couldn't risk remaining in the toilet. If the Prophet suddenly jumped in his car and drove off, Harlan would lose him. Similarly, if the Prophet headed off into the woods, Harlan had to be ready to follow him the instant he made a move.

He opened the door a crack and peered out. The headlights of the vehicle, which he could see now was a mud-spattered green Land Rover, had been switched off. The glow of a fire away to its right was reflected in its windscreen. Harlan closed the toilet door behind himself and, hunkering low, moved to the opposite end of the caravan. The sofa's cushions had been removed, exposing a hollow, now empty interior. Harlan parted the curtains a finger's breadth. The Prophet, with his sleeves pushed up, was prodding at the fire with the spade, his eyes as black as the hair on his forearms in its flickering light. He was wearing loose-fitting jeans and a green bomber jacket that fitted tightly around his bull-neck. He had no beard, but there was heavy stubble on his jaw. His shoulder-length hair framed an angular face pitted with what looked like acne scars. Harlan estimated him to be mid-thirties. Forty at the most. As the Prophet watched the fire eat away at two cardboard boxes, his jaw twitched like Harlan's pulse, and his expression twisted in a grimace of rage. He flung the spade away suddenly, shouting, 'Fuck!' He lowered his head, rubbing roughly at his eyes. Then, his shoulders rising and falling with a deep breath, he retrieved the spade and continued his prodding. When the boxes and their contents, which Harlan couldn't make out from where he was, had burned down to glowing embers, the Prophet approached the caravan again.

Harlan crouched down, flattening himself against the wall between the end of the kitchen unit and the sofa. Dry mouthed but calm enough to hold himself as still as a beast of prey, he listened to the Prophet climb the little flight of metal steps outside the caravan. The door slammed shut, shaking the flimsy structure. The lock clicked back into place. Harlan lifted his head above the window sill in time to see the Prophet striding towards the woods, torch in hand, the spade resting on his shoulder. He waited until he was under the trees before opening the window and clambering out. He couldn't see the Prophet any more, but the beam of his torch was visible. As quickly and quietly as possible, he pursued it. It was dark as the bottom of a well under the dense canopy of oak and beech. Branches snagged his clothes and scratched his face, his feet stubbed against roots, but he didn't slow his pace until he was as close as he dared get to the man.

Down they went, deeper and deeper into the valley, as if they were descending into an abyss. The silence of the woods hammered against Harlan's ears. He winced at every twig that snapped or dry leaf that crunched beneath his feet. The Prophet stopped. Harlan hid behind a tree, heart loud as a drum in his chest, certain he'd been made. The Prophet swung his torch from side to side as if searching for something, then started walking again. Down, down, deeper, deeper and still deeper he unknowingly led Harlan. Harlan lost all track of time and distance in the cloying darkness. Despite his fear of being heard, he drew ever closer to the Prophet. If he lost him here, he knew chances were he'd never find him again or his way out of the woods. Suddenly, the light disappeared. Harlan felt a rush of something like vertigo as the world seemed to dissolve around him. Hands outstretched, groping blindly, he took several steps and stumbled to his knees. He crawled through the undergrowth, and after maybe a minute found himself at the edge of a grassy, bowl-like depression. The Prophet was standing at the bottom of the depression, digging up sods of turf and pilling them neatly to one side.

He's digging a grave for Ethan, was Harlan's first thought. But he quickly questioned it. The depression was open to the night sky. Why dig a grave somewhere visible from above when you could just as easily do it under cover of the trees? There was little chance of a helicopter passing overhead. Still, it was an unnecessary risk. Another possibility occurred to him as the Prophet's spade clanged against something metallic. *Maybe he's digging something up. But what? More photos? A corpse?* For the same reason, neither possibility struck him as likely.

The Prophet cleared away a square of turf about three feet by three feet, exposing a rusty sheet of metal secured with a chain and padlock. A length of plastic pipe slightly longer than the depth of the turf protruded from the centre of the sheet. *What the hell's that for?* wondered Harlan. His heart began to thump wildly against his ribs as the answer came to him: *it's an air pipe. The metal sheet's a trap door. This is where he keeps them. This is where the fucker keeps his victims.* The Prophet unlocked the padlock and, bracing his legs, lifted the inch-thick sheet. It fell back on its hinges with a dull thud. He retrieved his torch and shone it down into a round hole about as wide as his shoulders. Gripping the torch between his teeth, he lowered himself into the hole.

Harlan waited a few seconds before squirming down the bank to the edge of the hole, which radiated a faint yellowish light. The hole went straight down for about six feet, then turned at a right angle. A string of fairy lights hooked up to a battery illuminated a sandy-floored narrow tunnel whose regular angled rock walls bore the marks of pickaxes. This was obviously an entrance to some kind of disused mine or cave system that'd caused the ground to subside. The hole smelled of dank earth with an underlying faintly fetid scent that impelled Harlan to climb into it. The tunnel descended gently, curving to the left. Taking out his knife, stooping to avoid hitting his head, Harlan hurried forward. He was less concerned about being heard now than he was by what the object of his pursuit might be doing. The Prophet had already got rid of anything incriminating at the caravan. More than likely he was going to do the same down here too.

As Harlan advanced, the underlying smell grew heavier, thicker. It was a smell he knew only too well, one that always made his throat tight. The tunnel flared suddenly into a cave whose outermost fringes were shrouded in darkness. He stood motionless, ears straining. Not a sound.

The cave was natural. It had jagged walls. Gnarled roots poked through its ceiling. The fragments of rock they'd dislodged were scattered over the uneven floor. *Oh Christ, please don't let it be Ethan*, thought Harlan, as the smell drew him towards the far side of the cave, where the darkness was as impenetrable as the walls. Stomach like a clenched fist, he switched on his torch. Its beam illuminated a dirty tarp wrapped like a chrysalis around something. Kneeling, he peeled away the tarp and saw what he'd known he would – a corpse. A tiny breath of relief escaped him. It wasn't Ethan. The corpse was months, perhaps even years old. It was rotted down almost to a skeleton. Parchment-like shreds of mouldy skin encased its bones. Its stomach and eye sockets were hollow. Its mouth hung open in a grotesque parody of a smile. Wisps of boyishly short blond hair still clung to its skull. From its size, Harlan estimated the body to be that of a child of between seven and ten years old. He wondered why it hadn't been buried. He could think of only one reason: the Prophet kept it here as a kind of trophy. He'd read case studies of killers who kept parts or even the whole of their victims' bodies, using them to relive their crimes over and over again. But he'd never encountered it himself.

Harlan's face creased up so that his features seemed to turn in on themselves, leaving only his blazing eyes staring out. Even in death, the child hadn't been allowed to rest. The same feeling that'd rushed over him as he tortured Jones swelled inside him again. The same only much, much stronger. He didn't resist it. He allowed it to pick him up and carry him back to the fairy lights, which ended at a tunnel opening braced with timbers. Ducking into it, he hurried onward. As the tunnel wound deeper into the earth, its ceiling lowered until he was stooped almost double. He came to a fork. One branch angled rightwards and down. The other turned to the left, climbing gently. He paused, trying to decide which way to go. After a moment, he moved to the right, urged on by an inner voice that said, *Keep going deeper, deeper!*

The air got thicker and harder to breathe. Sweat stung Harlan's eyes. After several minutes, he heard something that caused him to pause. The sound came again. It was a faint clink, like a chain rattling. He switched off his torch and felt his way forward. His nostrils flared at a foul smell. Not a smell of death, but a smell of life festering in its own filth. The walls closed in to a gap just wide enough for him to turn sideways and squeeze through. After a short distance, they widened again and the pale electric glow of more fairy lights shimmered up ahead. Barely daring to breathe, he advanced to the edge of a roughly circular cave about fifteen feet in diameter.

The cave's floor was littered with empty soup and soft-drink cans, water bottles, crisp packets and chocolate bar wrappers. In one corner stood a metal bucket brimful with human waste. In the opposite corner was a mouldering mattress with a young boy sitting on it, knees drawn up against his chin, arms wrapped around the blades of his shins. The boy's legs and feet were bare. A chain led from a medieval-looking shackle on one of his ankles to a hoop bolted to the wall. A ragged blanket was wrapped around his narrow shoulders. His grimy, pinch-cheeked face, lank hair and the fear flowing from his trapped eyes gave him the look of some small, helpless animal. Harlan recognised him instantly, even though he no longer looked much like his picture in the newspaper. The boy was Jamie Sutton. The Prophet was sitting on a deckchair in the centre of the cave, facing Jamie, his back to Harlan. His hands were clasped at his chin as if in prayer.

Harlan padded towards the Prophet. He raised a finger to his lips as Jamie's eyes flicked at him. Ten feet. His heart hammered so loudly he was certain the Prophet must hear it. Five feet. A bead of sweat dripped from his chin and exploded on the floor. Gasping, the Prophet started to stand and turn. With the speed of a striking snake, Harlan sprang at him, wrapping an arm around his throat. With his other arm, he locked in the chokehold. The Prophet rammed his head back against Harlan's face, bringing a stream of blood from his nose. Tucking his head down, Harlan cranked his arm tighter against the Prophet's carotid artery. His breath grating like sandpaper in his lungs, the Prophet staggered around, flinging ineffective elbows at Harlan. Finally, his arms dropped to his sides and his legs began to buckle. In a last-ditch attempt to dislodge Harlan, he flung himself backward. As Harlan slammed into the sandy floor, pain crackled up his spine and all his breath was driven from him. But still he clung on grimly, wrapping his legs around the Prophet's midriff to prevent him from twisting free. The Prophet rolled onto his front and, exerting what strength remained in his powerful, thickset body, managed to rise to his hands and knees. Arms burning, Harlan squeezed and squeezed. Suddenly unconsciousness stole the Prophet's resistance away. He collapsed. But Harlan continued to squeeze, driven on by the force of what was inside. It was only the thought of Ethan flashing through his mind that stopped him from crushing the Prophet's windpipe.

Breathing heavily, he released his grip. The Prophet's face was colourless, except for a bluish tinge to his lips. Harlan felt for a pulse and found one. He quickly turned his attention to the boy. As he reached for the shackle, Jamie flinched away from him. 'It's OK, Jamie,' Harlan reassured him. 'I'm here to help you.' Jamie stiffened, trembling slightly, but remained motionless as Harlan examined the clasp. There were brownish-red, infected-looking sores where it had rubbed the skin off the boy's ankle. It was secured with a padlock. 'Where's the key?'

Jamie pointed to the Prophet. Harlan stooped over him to search his pockets and found a bundle of keys in the first one he put his hand into. He tried them on the padlock until he found one that fitted. Jamie grimaced as Harlan removed the clasp. The instant he was free, he scuttled naked to a pile of dusty clothes in a corner and began pulling them on. His body was mottled with bruises, streaked with scratches, and crusted with excrement. His ribs and backbone were prominent from starvation, like a concentration-camp victim.

Rage pushed up inside Harlan, almost choking him. He grabbed the Prophet's wrists and dragged him to the mattress. The shackle didn't fit around the Prophet's meaty ankle, but Harlan squeezed until the metal clasp bit deep enough into his flesh that he could click the padlock shut. The Prophet stirred and groaned but didn't open his eyes.

Harlan turned to Jamie, who was crouched now by the cave's entrance, tense as a rabbit near a wolf. Gently taking hold of the boy's wrist, he guided him into the tunnel out of sight of the Prophet. 'Listen, Jamie, before we can leave this place I need to ask you something. Have you seen anyone else down here other than that man in there and me?'

Jamie shook his head.

'Are you sure? This is very important. There may be another boy like you here somewhere.'

Jamie nodded. He pulled at Harlan's arm, urging him onward. Harlan shook his head, prising Jamie's hands away. He jerked his chin at the cave. 'I need you to wait here while I talk to him.'

Eyes like full moons, Jamie shook his head again more vehemently. His lips quivered, but no words came. He seemed to have been struck mute by the trauma of his experiences.

Harlan gave him a steady, reassuring look. 'Don't worry. You're safe now. I'm not going to let anything happen to you, I promise. Do you believe me?'

Jamie didn't nod – his trust in adults had been destroyed too completely for that – but he stopped shaking his head.

Harlan handed Jamie his torch, then returned to the cave. The Prophet's colour had improved but he still hadn't regained consciousness. Taking out his knife, Harlan crouched to slap him. 'Wake up!' The Prophet's eyelids flickered. Harlan hit him again, hard enough to split his lip. As the Prophet's eyes popped wide, Harlan pressed the knife against his throat. 'Where's Ethan Reed?'

'Wha... Who?' the Prophet said, groggily.

'Don't give me that. You know who the fuck I'm talking—' Harlan broke off as, out of the corner of his eye, he glimpsed the Prophet pulling something out of his jacket pocket – something that caught the light with a glimmer. He moved his arm to block the thrust, but he wasn't fast enough. He felt the knife blade grind against his hipbone as it went in. There was an intense sensation of pressure, more like he'd been hit with a hammer than stabbed. He slashed at the Prophet's hand, opening a bone-deep gash across the back of it. The Prophet jerked the blade free and made another thrust. It bit nothing more substantial than air, as Harlan flung himself sideways. Scrambling upright, the Prophet lurched after Harlan, but the chain whipped his foot from under him. Nostrils flaring like an enraged bull, he sprang back upright and stood at the full extent of the chain, knife held ready to strike.

Harlan faced him, teeth gritted, hand clutched to his side. He could feel blood seeping warmly through his clothes. A dull throbbing ache was spreading outwards from the wound. He looked at the Prophet's knife. It had a tidemark about half-way up its five- or six-inch blade. Deep enough to have pierced internal organs. *Why the fuck didn't you search all his pockets?* he thought with bitter self-contempt. *How could you make such a fucking rookie mistake?* The pain was fast intensifying, growing hotter. Soon, experience told him, it would feel like boiling fat was being pumped into the wound. He'd been stabbed once before back when he was a uniformed copper, just a flesh wound, but the pain had quickly become almost unbearable, making him shake uncontrollably. He knew he had to move fast, try and make it back to his car before that stage of shock overtook him. But his desperate desire to find out where Ethan was held him in place. He glanced around for something he could use to knock the knife out of the Prophet's hand. His gaze fixed on the deckchair. Wincing, he picked it up.

'Come on then!' snarled the Prophet, echoing Robert Reed's last words.

When Harlan heard that, he knew. If he attempted to tackle the Prophet, one of them was going to die. Either way, that wouldn't help Ethan. But if it was himself, the Prophet might have time to break free and recapture Jamie. No matter what, he couldn't allow that to happen. Better to call in the police, let them deal with him. Besides, the Prophet was already facing life in prison. So, unlike Jones, he had nothing to gain by hiding the truth.

Holding the chair up like a shield, in case the Prophet threw the knife at him, Harlan backed out of the cave. Once he was inside the tunnel he dropped the chair and limped to the boy. It felt like there was a nail lodged in the wound, pushing deeper into his hipbone with every step. A look of relief came into Jamie's eyes when he saw Harlan. But the anxiety returned to them as Harlan pulled up his sweatshirt. The wound was about two inches long, its clean edges yawning apart to a width of about half an inch. Dark red blood seeped steadily from it. Already his left trouser leg was soaked down to the knee. He pulled off his sweatshirt and cut it into two strips. One he folded into a thick pad and pressed against the wound. The other he tied tightly over the pad.

'Let's get the hell out of here,' he said to Jamie, taking back the torch.

Moving as fast as he could bear to, Harlan made his way back along the tunnel. When he came to the T-junction, he paused, shining his torch into the left-hand tunnel. 'Ethan!' he shouted. His voice echoed back at him but there was no other response. Still, he hesitated to continue, wondering if he had the strength to check out the tunnel. The tremors in his legs and the waves of dizziness crashing over him told him he didn't. Jamie tugged at his hand, urging him to take the tunnel that led to the first cave. Heaving a painful sigh, Harlan allowed himself to be pulled along. Clearly knowing the way out, Jamie moved ahead of Harlan, pausing every few paces to glance back, his eyes shining like saucers in the torchlight. Harlan's left leg dragged ever more heavily. Several times he staggered and almost fell. But when they reached the cave, and his nostrils caught the stench of the corpse, some hidden reserve of strength welled up inside him. Picking up his pace, he waved Jamie onwards. Beyond the cave, a cool draught of night air blew in from the tunnel's entrance, soothing his feverishly hot face. He gulped down lungfuls of it.

When they reached the hole, Jamie scrambled out of it as if the devil was nipping at his heels. Harlan dragged himself up after him and grasped the trapdoor. As he strained to lift it, pain exploded like a grenade in his hip. His grip on the metal sheet started to slip, but Jamie rushed forward to help. Between them, they managed to flip it shut. Harlan locked the padlock and fell breathless on the ground. He lay on his back, shivering like grass in the wind. Above him, the stars swam in and out of focus. After a moment, fighting nausea, he struggled to his feet and looked at the encircling trees. It was only then that the realisation hit him that he was lost. Without the Prophet's guidance, he had little or no chance of finding his way to the caravan. He was going to have to go back down into the tunnels, tackle the Prophet and force him to lead them there. It was either that or risk wandering in circles in the woods until he fell unconscious from the pain or loss of blood. Heart heavy as a lump of lead, he looked at the trapdoor. Jamie tugged at his arm again. 'Do you know the way to the caravan?' Harlan asked him hopefully.

Jamie nodded. Briefly closing his eyes with relief, Harlan handed him the torch and gestured for him to lead the way. They clambered up the grassy bank and entered the deeper darkness beneath the leaf canopy. Occasionally, Jamie paused, shining the torch this way and that, before continuing onwards. Even though the night was cool, sweat poured off Harlan. At shortening intervals, he was forced to lean, panting, against a tree and wring out the makeshift bandage like a wet dishcloth. The blood leaking from him was no longer blood, it was molten lava, scorching its way down his leg and squelching in his shoe. Every step now was pure agony. He stared at his feet, thinking, *One foot in front of the other. One foot in front of the other. Keep moving. Keep moving or die.*

After about twenty minutes, although it seemed more like twenty hours to Harlan, they emerged into the clearing to the left of the caravan. The car was only a couple of hundred yards up the dirt track but it might as well have been a hundred miles away. As Harlan tried to move, the world went blurry with the pain. For a moment he stood swaying on the edge of unconsciousness. Then he saw Jamie's face. The boy was staring at the caravan as if transfixed, mouth working mutely, tears streaming down his cheeks. The sight pulled Harlan back from the brink. His gaze moved beyond the boy to the Land Rover. He took the Prophet's keys out of his pocket. There was an ignition key amongst the bunch. There was a risk that in using the vehicle he would contaminate physical evidence but he didn't see any other choice. Jamie blinked as Harlan tapped his shoulder and pointed to it.

With Jamie supporting Harlan by the elbow as best he could, they moved torturously slowly towards the Land Rover. The key fitted. Harlan hauled himself behind the wheel, groaning with relief as he took his weight off his injured hip. He glanced at the back seat while Jamie ran around to the front passenger door. There was a pharmacy prescription bag sealed with a label on it. He picked it up and read the label. *Mary Webster. 1831 Wilmslow Road, Parrs Wood, Manchester.* A faint ripple of surprise passed through him. He'd assumed the Prophet would, out of practical and psychological necessity, be a loner, but that obviously wasn't the case. Who was Mary Webster? he wondered. The Prophet's wife? His partner in crime? Was he one half of a murderous duo cast in the mould of Brady and Hindley? It was possible, of course, but unlikely. More probably it was his mother. Whoever she was, she was in for a big shock when the police came to batter down her door and tear her home apart. She'd be in for an even bigger shock, one she'd likely never recover from, when she learned what they were searching for. And so the trail of devastated lives would continue on and on with no apparent end.

Exhaling a burning breath, Harlan reversed onto the track and slammed the gearstick into first. Even cushioned by the four-by-four's suspension, every bump in the dirt was like a twist of a torturer's rack, squeezing more nausea up from the pit of his stomach. Halfway to the main road he braked, threw open his door and vomited. There wasn't much to bring up. He'd eaten little other than doughnuts for days. Finally, they made it to the road. Harlan checked his phone. There was a signal. He called Jim.

'What is it?' his ex-partner asked brusquely. 'Things are kind of crazy here right—'

'I've got him,' interrupted Harlan, his voice was low and hoarse with agonised exhaustion.

'Got who? Are you all right? You sound terrible.'

'The guy who snatched Jack Holland. I found Jamie Sutton as well. He's alive.'

There was a moment of silence, as if Jim was struggling to take in what he'd heard. Then he said, 'Where are you?'

As Harlan described as best he could where they were, he examined the blood-soaked makeshift bandage. 'And send an ambulance. I've been...' His voice slurred off. Without him even realising it, his eyes slid shut and his head nodded. Suddenly he was with Tom at the park, pushing him on a swing. Tom was laughing, kicking his feet high, his thick brown hair blowing in the wind. A perfectly happy scene, but something about it made Harlan uneasy. More than that, it made him angry. So angry he wanted to scream and claw at it, tear it to shreds.

'Harlan, are you still there? Talk to me?'

Jim's voice jerked Harlan away from Tom. With difficulty, he lifted his head. 'Hurry, Jim.'

'Someone's already on the way. Don't hang up, Harlan. Stay on the line with me until they get there.'

'I'll try.' Harlan seemed to hear his own voice from a distance. He leaned his head against the window. The pain wasn't so bad any more. He knew that probably wasn't a good sign.

'We've got a helicopter up. Can you see it?'

Harlan rolled his eyes glassily at the sky. 'No.'

'Keep looking. Tell me when you do.'

Harlan gazed up at the stars. His eyes drifted as he wondered dimly about how Jamie knew the path through the woods. The answer seemed obvious. The boy had been moved from the cave to the caravan enough times that he could find his way between the two even in the dark. But for what purpose? From Jamie's reaction to the caravan, the answer to that also seemed chillingly obvious.

He looked at Jamie. The boy was sitting hunched down, hands clasped in his lap. Even after everything that'd just happened, he met Harlan's gaze warily. 'Did that man, the one from the cave, take you to see someone else at the caravan?' Harlan hated to ask the question, but he had to know.

Jamie nodded.

'Was it a man?'

Jamie shrugged.

'Were you blindfolded?'

Tears shimmered in Jamie's eyes as he shook his head.

'Did the person wear a mask?'

Another nod.

'Did… did…' Harlan stumbled over his words. The world was turning grey at the fringes. Merciful blackness beckoned. *Just one or two more questions*, he told himself, *then you can let go.* 'Did this person take photos of you?'

Jamie shook his head and gestured in the air. Harlan wrinkled his brow, not understanding. Then realisation hit him. 'They drew you.'

Jamie nodded. The tears finally spilled over.

'It's OK,' said Harlan, barely murmuring the words. 'Everything's going to be OK.'

But it wasn't going to be OK. Never. Ever. Harlan returned his gaze to the stars. One was brighter than the others. It hadn't been there before. He watched it moving nearer. He heard a distant sound. Whump, whump, whump, like a pounding heart. Then his eyelids slammed down and it felt like when Kane hit him with the bat, only this time he was falling into warm, dark water.

Chapter Sixteen

Harlan remembered being stretchered to the ambulance, flashing lights, the wail of the siren. He remembered being wheeled into the hospital, a nurse cutting away his clothes, doctors crowding around talking about blood loss and X-rays, shining lights in his eyes. He remembered a voice. 'Harlan, can you hear me?' it'd asked. 'Blink if you can.' He'd blinked. Another – or was it the same? – voice had said something about exploratory surgery. He even remembered being lifted onto the operating table. But all of it was hazy and remote as a dream. And the whole time, one train of thought kept running through his brain: *I need to talk to Eve. I need to hear her voice. I need her to be here. I need her. I need her...*

The next thing Harlan remembered was waking up to find himself lying in a hospital bed in a single room, hooked up to an oxygen mask, an IV bag and a cardiac monitor. A female doctor was standing at the end of his bed, reading his medical notes. Her face blurred in and out before his drug-clouded eyes. He felt floaty, disconnected. Noticing he was awake, the doctor asked, 'Mr Miller, how do you feel? Any pain?'

'None,' Harlan croaked through the mask. 'No bullshit, doc, how am I doing?'

'You're doing fine. There was a perforation to your small intestine that required stitching. But otherwise you've been very lucky. The knife missed your femoral artery by millimetres. If it had hit it, you'd have bled to death.'

'How long have I been out?'

'Not long. You came out of surgery about an hour ago.'

Where's Jamie? Harlan meant to ask the question out loud, but his mind was already slipping away from him, drifting back into unconsciousness. Sometime later, it might've been hours or only minutes, a familiar voice reached through the ether and pulled him into wakefulness. He cracked his eyelids open and squinted up at Jim's grizzled face. The oxygen mask and cardiac monitor were gone, but the IV remained. There was a faint throbbing in his lower abdomen. His mouth was drier than sand. He gestured to a jug of water and Jim poured him a cup. After sipping from it, he asked, 'Where's Jamie?'

'On another ward, being treated for shock, malnutrition and Christ knows what else. Poor little bugger.'

'Has he spoken yet?'

'Just a few words. Enough to let us know what you did for him.'

'So you found that son-of-a-bitch I left chained up in the caves.'

Jim nodded. 'How did you find your way down there?'

Harlan gave Jim the story from arriving at the caravan to rescuing Jamie – he figured Jones would've filled the police in on the earlier events. Then he asked, 'What about Jones?'

'We found him too. Or rather, we heard him kicking and shouting from the boot of your car. He's in hospital as well.' Jim's lips thinned into a smile, although his eyes were troubled. 'You crazy bastard. Do you have any idea of the shit storm you've brought down on me and the whole department?'

Harlan couldn't have cared less about that. There was only one thing he really cared about right then. 'Have you found Ethan?'

'Not yet. We're still searching the caves. Apparently there's mile after mile of them underneath the woods.'

'What about bodies? Have you found any more besides the one in the first cave?'

'So you saw that, did you?'

Harlan gave a slight nod.

A cleft appeared between Jim's eyebrows. 'Pretty fucking gruesome, eh. Why the hell would he keep it there?'

'I guess he got some kind of kick out of it.'

'Yeah, that's what our psychologists said, except they used the word necrophilia.' The cleft deepened. 'You know me, Harlan. I've seen plenty in my time. Nothing much gets to me, but this... I just can't seem to wrap my head around it.' Jim heaved a sigh. 'Anyway, the answer to your question is no. But if there are any more down there the dogs will sniff them out.'

'What do you know about the body?'

'Forensics is still working on that. All I can tell you right now is it's a male, aged eight or nine, and he's been dead for a good few years.'

'And what about the Prophet?'

'Who?'

'The Prophet. That's Jones's nickname for the fucker who knifed me. Is he talking?'

'Richard Nash. That's his actual name. He's a real case. A forty-year-old Geordie serial sex offender with a drug habit.'

'What kind of drugs?'

'Whatever he can get his hands on – speed, coke, heroin, prescription drugs. And no, he's not talking. In fact, he's not said a fucking word since we brought him in. We're working on the bastard day and night.'

'What does his rap sheet look like?'

'Like every parent's worst nightmare. It starts when he was just a kid himself. Only days before his sixteenth birthday, he lured an eight-year-old boy out of a garden in Newcastle with the promise of ice cream. The boy was later found semi-conscious on a nearby disused railway line. There was bruising on his throat and traces of semen on his clothing. Nash had strangled him half to death and masturbated over him. Several people had seen Nash walking with the boy, so he was soon identified and arrested. He was charged with ABH and indecent assault. But some idiot judge swallowed a psychiatrist's opinion that the assault was out of character and reduced the charges to lewd conduct.'

'Lewd conduct,' Harlan said incredulously. 'Why not just give him a slap on the wrist and send him on his way?'

'That's pretty much what happened. Nash was given a two-year suspended borstal sentence. As soon as it was over, he headed south to London and got a job as a labourer. He found lodgings with a family with three children, one of whom was a nine-year-old boy. You don't have to be a genius to work out what happened next. When the boy's parents learned that Nash was molesting him, they called the police. And when Nash's room was searched, they found a huge stash of child pornography magazines, videos, and photos he'd taken himself. Turns out Nash liked nothing better than to go to Brighton on his days off and covertly photograph kids on the beach. This time he was sent down. He did a two-year stretch.'

Harlan's lips curled in disgust. 'Two fucking years.'

'I know. It's a joke. But it was enough to teach him to be cautious. After he got out, he worked as a jobbing handyman back in Newcastle, and managed to stay off our radar for a good few years. Then, in 2001, a woman whose house he was working on caught him stealing jewellery. The police searched his digs. They turned up a small amount of cocaine and a boxful of toys.'

'Jones said Nash sold toys on the streets.'

Jim shook his head. 'These were used toys. The woman identified several of them as belonging to her kids.' His voice grew thick with import. 'Get this, Nash admitted he'd been stealing from the bedrooms of children at houses where he worked. He was always careful only to take things that would've been assumed to be lost rather than stolen – teddy bears, toy soldiers and cars, things like that. But it's pretty obvious now that he was working up the nerve to take not merely toys, but the kids they belonged to as well.'

'Let me guess, he wasn't charged.'

'He got a small fine for possession. But his business was ruined, so he was forced to head south again. This time he didn't make it as far as London. He stayed with a relative in Birmingham. That's when he met his first girlfriend.'

'Mary Webster?'

'No, but I'll get to her in a minute. Her name was Coralee Edmunds. She gave him bed and board in return for working on her house, and they started sleeping together. They'd only been together four or five months when she found child porn on his computer. She called the police, and Nash ended up with a ten-month jail sentence. He served just over half of it.'

'Another joke. Nash must've been laughing.'

'Apparently not. A psychiatric report prepared for his parole hearing says he was suicidal with remorse.'

'Remorse!' Contempt hissed through Harlan's voice. 'Remorse that he'd been caught, not for what he did.'

Nodding agreement, Jim continued, 'On his release, Nash stayed in an offenders' hostel in our own fair city for a while. After that our knowledge of his movements becomes hazy.

He seems to have travelled around a lot, doing odd jobs, often sleeping in homeless shelters. We also know now that he became acquainted with William Jones around this time. According to Jones, they met up several times over the course of a couple of years to talk about photography and exchange photos.'

'They exchanged a lot more than just photos,' said Harlan. 'Jones is in this right up to his fat neck. You know that some guy other than Nash went to the caravan and painted Jamie.'

'Yes, but Jamie never saw his face.'

'So fucking what? It was Jones. You know that as well as I do.'

'It doesn't matter what I know, or think I know. If Jamie can't ID Jones and Nash won't give him up, we need physical evidence to tie him to the crime. And as of now we've got nothing – no fingerprints, no hair, no semen, no saliva.'

'What about the painting?'

'We're searching Jones's house for that.' Jim looked meaningfully at Harlan. 'But it seems somebody's destroyed all his paintings.'

'There was no painting of Jamie there. I'm sure of it. It must be somewhere else.'

'Obviously, but where?'

Harlan was silent, eyes narrowed, thinking that five minutes alone with Jones would be enough for him to find out.

'Whatever you're thinking, don't,' said Jim, reading him. 'You're in deep enough shit already. Trust me, we're not gonna let the fucker off the hook.'

'I hope not. I really fucking hope not.' Harlan's voice cracked dryly. He took a sip of water. 'So tell me the rest of Nash's story.'

'There's not much left to tell. After Jones was banged up, Nash dropped off the radar again. We're filling in the gap between those years: 2005 and the present.'

'I'm guessing this is where Mary Webster comes into the story.'

Jim nodded. 'Mary Webster's an eighty-three-year-old spinster, all but bedridden with arthritis. From what she's told us, Nash has been her carer since late 2007.'

'Her carer? What the hell does a guy like Nash know about caring for anybody but himself?'

'According to Miss Webster, he's the kindest, gentlest person she's ever met.'

Harlan let out another hiss of breath. 'Has she been told what he's done?'

'Yes, but she won't have a word of it. You know what these old women are like, deaf to everything but what they want to hear. You can't blame her, really. She's got no family. Lives in a big wreck of a house. Without Nash, she'll more than likely have to go into a care home.'

'How did Nash get to be her carer?'

'He came knocking on her door, offering to do some repairs. They got chatting and he told her he needed a place to live. She took him in, and he's been there ever since.'

'Have you found anything at her house?'

'The transit van was in the garage. It'd been washed inside and out. Apart from that, we've found nothing. If there was anything, Nash most probably got rid of it after Jack escaped.'

That was pretty much the answer Harlan had expected. After all, Nash had been in the process of getting rid of evidence when he'd pounced on him. He closed his eyes momentarily, thought about Ethan, and sighed. 'Has Susan Reed been told what's happened?'

'She's been told what she needs to know – that we have a man in custody who we think was almost certainly involved in her son's abduction.'

'How's she holding up?'

'Not too well, by all accounts.'

Again, this was what Harlan had expected to hear. Neil had been Susan's support, her strength. Without him, she had no one to lean on. A pain that no amount of drugs could numb washed through Harlan as he pictured her waiting alone to hear news of Ethan. 'I take it you got nothing from him.'

'Who?'

'Neil Price.'

Jim shook his head. 'The only thing that guy's guilty of is being terminally naive. We released him yesterday. Guess what the stupid little prick did.'

'Tried to see Susan.'

'Got it in one. He showed up at her house, pleading for forgiveness. She called us and we slung him straight back in the cells. Apparently he was sobbing like a baby.' Jim shook his head. 'You've got to feel sorry for him.'

Harlan didn't feel sorry for Neil. But he pitied him a little. The guy had made a mistake. Now he was desperate for a chance to make amends. Harlan knew all about that. 'You were right, you are going soft in your old age.'

Smiling, Jim patted his shoulder. 'I'd better get back to it. I'll see you later.'

'Is that it?' said Harlan, as Jim stood to leave. 'Don't you want a statement from me?'

'We don't need to do that right now. The doctor tells me you're going to be in here a few more days at least.'

Harlan's eyebrows lifted. 'What's going on, Jim? I thought Garrett would be jumping all over the chance to bury me.'

'I'm sure he would be if it was up to him, but things have changed.'

'Changed how?'

'Like I said, you've brought a shit storm down on the whole department. Garrett got a phone call this morning. Rumour has it it was from some Home Office bigwig. Whoever it was, they made a big impression on Garrett. When he hung up, his face was white as an old turd. Without a word to any of us, he stormed out the office and drove off. I found out later that he went to see Jones. He was in with him alone for over an hour.'

Harlan frowned with realisation. 'Garrett's been ordered to hush up my involvement.'

'What else can it be?'

'But why?' There was no hint of relief in Harlan's voice, just curiosity.

A touch of wryness pulled down the corners of Jim's lips. 'It's always the same with you, Harlan. You see everything but yourself. Think about it. Who you are, what you've done, it scares the shit out of the politicians. They must know that if this gets out, the public will see you the same way most of us in the department do.'

'And how's that exactly?'

'A hero.'

'A *hero*?' Harlan's mouth twisted on the word. He almost laughed. 'The last thing I am is a fucking hero.'

'Maybe, but most of them don't know you like I do. They don't know what a suicidal nut job you really are.' The wryness left Jim's face. 'All they know is you risked your life to save that boy's.'

'And beat a man half to death in the process.'

'A convicted paedophile who'd been questioned and released. Just imagine the fallout if you were jailed for succeeding where we'd failed. Garrett's future job prospects wouldn't be worth shit.'

'I might've killed Jones. Nash too.'

'But you didn't.'

Harlan's eyes dropped away from Jim's. His voice dropped too. 'No, but I wanted to.'

Jim stared down at Harlan a moment, a slight frown over his jaded cop's eyes as though he wasn't sure what he thought of that comment. Then he spoke in a husky but gentle tone. 'Get some rest. Heal that wound.'

'Anyway, I didn't succeed,' murmured Harlan. 'Ethan's still missing.'

'Not for much longer. I'm going to crack that bastard Nash wide open. Believe me, by the time I'm finished with him he'll be spilling like a broken egg. And think on this, Harlan: Nash kept Jamie Sutton alive for over four months. Ethan's been missing half that time.'

'I have thought on it.' Harlan looked grimly from the plastic cup in his hand to Jim. 'Three to ten days.'

'What does that mean?'

'It means that even if Ethan's alive, he won't be much longer unless he's found. Don't you remember your survival training? Three to ten days is how long a person can survive without water.'

For a heartbeat longer, the two men held each other's gaze. Then Jim turned and hurried away. It suddenly occurred to Harlan that there was a question he hadn't asked. One he badly wanted the answer to. 'Have you told Eve what's happened?' he called. But Jim was already gone.

Weariness throbbed in Harlan's head, pulling him into sleep. Looking into the darkness behind his eyelids, he saw a parade of people. Everyone who'd ever meant anything to him was there. All of them merging, like droplets of spilled blood. Then he was facing a mirror. But instead of seeing himself, he saw Nash. He clamped his hands around Nash's throat, squeezing as hard as he could, to no effect. 'Where is he?' he desperately demanded to know. Suddenly, as if he'd dissolved into the air, Nash was gone. But Harlan was still squeezing, only now his hands were on his own throat. They seemed to be glued there. His head felt like a balloon ready to pop. 'Eve,' he choked out. 'Eve.'

When Harlan awoke Eve was there, at his bedside, like a prayer answered. She looked worried, but calm. Harlan drank in her face and felt it ease through him like whisky. Smiling, he stretched out a hand and she took it between hers. But she didn't smile back. 'How long have you been there?' he asked.

'A while. How are you feeling?'

'They've got me pumped so full of drugs I can't feel anything much at all.'

'You called out my name in your sleep.'

The dream suddenly came back to Harlan. A little shudder ran through him. 'I was having a nightmare.'

'About me?'

'No. I wanted you to save me.'

'From what?'

'Myself.'

A sad smile played over Eve's lips. 'I wish I could, Harlan, but I can't. No one can save you but yourself.' She glanced at the bulge of Harlan's bandage showing through the sheets. 'Only you can decide what's enough.'

What's enough? Harlan didn't have to think to know the answer to that question. Finding Ethan. That was the only 'enough' there was for him. He didn't say this to Eve. He didn't have to. She'd already read it in his eyes. She sighed. 'Jim's right. You do have a death wish.'

'You've spoken to him?'

'Who do you think told me you were here?'

'What else did he tell you?'

'Not much, just that you'd been stabbed. He was pretty cagey, even by his standards.'

'Did he mention Ethan Reed?' Harlan knew Jim wouldn't have, but he had to ask anyway.

'No.'

'What day is this?'

'Thursday.'

Harlan's brow contracted. He'd been in hospital two days. Which meant that at the most optimistic estimate, Ethan had seven or eight days to live. In all probability, he would already be suffering the symptoms of severe dehydration: he'd have a headache and nausea; a raised body temperature and increased pulse; his muscles would be tingling and twitching; his vision growing dim; he might even be starting to hallucinate. Of course, that was assuming he was still alive at all. Which he almost certainly wasn't.

'What's going on, Harlan?' asked Eve. 'Who did this to you?'

Harlan told Eve what'd happened. He left out any mention of Jones. Not because he didn't trust her to keep it to herself but because he was afraid how it would affect the way she looked at him. She knew, of course, that he was capable of the kind of drunken, self-destructive violence that'd led to Robert Reed's death. But cold, calculated torture? She'd always despised that kind of violence. If she found out he was capable of it, would she ever again be able to look at him with the same purity of love that she was doing now? He doubted it. And with that doubt came the realisation that he needed her love more than anything, more even than he needed to suffer for his guilt. Without it, there could be no light at the end of the tunnel for him. Just darkness.

Bright-eyed and tight-lipped with tension, Eve listened. When Harlan finished, a light of hope flickering in her voice, she said, 'So you got him. You got the guy who took Ethan.'

'Looks like it.'

'It's over then.'

Harlan shook his head. 'Ethan's still missing.'

'But surely there's nothing else you can do to help find him.'

'Assuming it was Nash who abducted him.'

'Of course it was. Who else could it be?'

Harlan thought about Jones. He thought about the prison segregation ward where he'd been housed alongside other inmates who weren't fit for general population – serial rapists, paedophiles, child killers. 'There are a lot of bad people out there.'

An edge of irritation came into Eve's tone. 'Do you think I don't know that? I lived with a policeman for over ten years, remember?'

'Sorry, Eve, I didn't mean to patronise you. You're right, Nash almost certainly is the kidnapper. But I'm just trying to point out that things aren't always as they seem.'

'And I'm just trying to find something to hold onto, something to give me the strength to endure.' Tears formed in the corners of Eve's eyes. She looked away from Harlan. He squeezed her hand. He wished he could tell her what he knew she wanted to hear – that the nightmare would soon be over. But he couldn't. When she returned her gaze to his, her tears had receded and she managed a faint smile. 'Whatever the truth is, whatever happens from now on, I want you to know how proud I am of you. You've done something...' she searched for the right word, 'wonderful. Surely it's got to make you feel better about yourself knowing you saved that boy's life and prevented that man from hurting anyone else.'

Do I feel any better about myself? wondered Harlan. *I've taken a life and saved a life. Does one cancel out the other?* He didn't know. All he knew was that the guilt was still there, festering like a pus-filled sore. Perhaps it would never be healed, not even if Ethan was found alive. 'I did what I had to do. Nothing more.'

Eve shook her head. 'There you go again, always downplaying the good things you do. In a way, I suppose it's comforting that some things about you never change.'

A nurse came to check Harlan's vitals. After she was done, Eve said, 'I've got to get back to work. Do you want me to come see you again?' There was a tentative quality to the question.

'Yes,' Harlan replied without hesitation. He suddenly found himself thinking about Susan. He wanted to see her – to try and hold her up. 'Hopefully I won't be in here much longer.'

Eve stood to leave. She looked at Harlan a moment, before stooping to kiss his forehead. A kiss he felt through the painkillers, like soft, warm hands caressing his entire body. 'I love you,' he murmured.

'I know.'

As Eve turned away, Harlan said, 'I don't have a death wish. I just want another chance.'

'I know,' Eve said again, then she left.

Harlan closed his eyes, still feeling Eve's kiss. Images came at him like bullets. He saw Ethan chained up, filthy, starving. He saw Susan trying to hold herself together for Kane, but crumbling inside. *She needs you there with her.* The thought urged him from his bed. Grimacing as his stitches pulled, he swung his legs off the mattress. His head reeled and blood pounded in his ears as he stood up. Trembling, he clutched the bedside table for support. Another nurse entered the room, pushing a medication cart. She rushed to his side, saying, 'You shouldn't be on your feet.'

Harlan didn't have the strength to resist as the nurse gently but firmly guided him back onto the mattress. 'I need to speak to the doctor and find out when I can leave.'

'I can tell you right now that you're not going anywhere for a few days at least. So you might as well just relax.'

Relax, thought Harlan. *How the hell am I supposed to do that?* As if in answer, the nurse handed him a pot of pills and poured some water to swallow them with. She wheeled the cart from the room, pausing to give him a glance that said, *Don't even think about getting out of bed again.* The pills quickly did their job, numbing his physical, but not his mental pain. As a heavy blanket of medicated sleep dropped over him, the images pierced his brain again. Ethan dying slowly. Susan falling apart fast. And there was nothing he could do for either of them. In his sleep, he wept with frustration.

Chapter Seventeen

When Harlan next awoke, a nurse was setting out his breakfast. His heart sat like a stone in his chest at the knowledge that another night had passed. Although he had no appetite, desperate to regain his strength, he ate everything there was to the last crumb of toast. Afterwards, he watched the morning news. Jamie Sutton's face was all over it. The screen showed photos of a bright-eyed, smiling, chubby-cheeked schoolboy who bore only a passing resemblance to the boy Harlan had rescued. There was an interview with a po-faced detective who, apart from stating that a suspect had been arrested, refused to answer any questions, saying only that this was an ongoing investigation. Speculation was rife in the studio as to the suspect's identity and whether there was any connection to the abductions of Jack Holland and Ethan Reed. The term 'serial child abductor' was bandied around. Jamie's rescue was a big story in itself, but the journalists smelled an even bigger one. There was a camera shot of a police car blocking the dirt road to the caravan, followed by a sweeping aerial shot of the treetops. Yellow and white forensic tents had been erected over the caravan and the entrance to the caves. A line of policemen could be glimpsed advancing slowly through the woods, combing the undergrowth.

Tagged onto the end of the report was a short piece about a lantern vigil that'd been held for Ethan. Hundreds of people had gathered at a park close to his home to launch Chinese lanterns with prayers for Ethan attached to them. The lanterns rose into the night sky like fiery jewels, borne by the wind to some unknown destination. The preacher, Lewis Gunn, said that the event had raised more than forty thousand pounds for the reward fund. There was no sign of Susan, which was hardly surprising considering what was going on elsewhere. Even so, her absence deepened Harlan's anxiety for her.

Forehead drawn into a frown, he turned off the television. It wasn't only Ethan and Susan that troubled him. It was the fact that the DI had said 'suspect' when he should've said 'suspects'. Clearly the police still didn't have sufficient evidence to bring charges against Jones.

There was a knock at the door and Jim entered the room. 'Morning. You're looking a lot better.'

Harlan read the sombre weariness etched into his ex-partner's face. 'Do I even need to ask if you've found him?'

Jim dropped heavily onto a chair. 'We're still searching the caves, but if you ask me he's not down there.'

'What makes you say that?'

'We've searched to a depth of over two hundred feet. Why would Nash take Ethan so far down, when he kept Jamie and the dead boy close to the surface?'

'Maybe he kept Ethan somewhere else. After all, he took Jack Holland to the storm drain, not the caves.'

'Or maybe Ethan's buried somewhere in those woods.'

Harlan shook his head. 'He wouldn't have buried him. He likes to keep their bodies where he can see and touch them, so he can relive the crime, extend the fantasy. Have you finished searching Mary Webster's house?'

'We've torn the fucking place apart. Pulled up every floor-board. Dug up the cellar and garden. Nothing.'

'What about Nash. Has he spoken?'

'Not a fucking word.' Sighing, Jim rubbed his craggy eyes. 'He just stares off into space like a zombie.'

'Sounds like you need some kind of fresh angle. Has he got any family or friends?'

'Both his parents are dead. No siblings. An aunt and a couple of cousins in Birmingham. No one he cares about enough to stay in touch with. Mary Webster's the closest thing he's got to a friend.'

'Then maybe she's the angle you're looking for. Why not let her talk to him? See if she can appeal to his conscience.'

Jim's nose scrunched up. 'That scumbag's got no conscience.'

'Not when it comes to his victims. They're nothing more than objects to him. Tools to satisfy his desires. But Mary Webster's something different. She's a vulnerable old woman with no family. She was totally in his power. He could easily have abused her. But he didn't. Why?'

'Because he needed her.'

'Maybe it's the other way around. Maybe she was the first person in his life who'd really needed him. And that made him feel good – good in a way nothing else had done before.' Harlan's eyes faded away from Jim's. He suddenly found himself thinking about Tom. All his life he'd felt lonely. Even after he got together with Eve. But the first time he'd cradled Tom in his arms, and gazed into his tiny, helpless eyes, the pangs of loneliness had been replaced by a warm sense of being needed that'd made him feel capable of doing anything.

Jim's voice jerked Harlan back into the room. 'When you put it like that, it's got to be worth a shot.'

'You reckon Garrett will agree to it?'

'I don't see he's got a choice. We need to come up with something fast. In fact, I'll call him right now.' Pulling out his phone, Jim left the room. He returned after several minutes, his manner more brisk and animated. 'He wasn't entirely convinced. The idea of using the old woman makes him nervous, but he's going to set it up. You know, Harlan, I've got a good feeling about this. If anyone can get through to Nash, surely it's her.' He looked at Harlan with a regretful, admiring gleam in his eyes. 'Christ, I wish you could be there when she speaks to him. I've never known anyone who could get inside the heads of bastards like him, like you can.'

'Any other developments I should know about?'

'The pathologist's report on the body came in. We got a dental ID. His name's Lee Dale. He was an eight-year-old Stockport boy who went missing on his way home from school in 2003.'

'That's the year Jones and Nash met. Don't tell me that's coincidence.'

Jim shook his head. 'You know what I think about coincidences.' The furrows on his forehead turned into ravines. 'Problem is, we still can't connect Jones to the crime scenes.'

'For fuck's sake, Jim, he took me to the caravan. What more do you need?'

'Hard forensic evidence. You know as well as I do what'd happen if we prosecuted Jones on the basis of information you tortured out of him: you'd be the one who ended up in prison, not him.'

'Don't go cutting any deals with that fucker just to keep me out of prison.'

'No one's cutting those kinds of deals. If Jones agrees not to press charges, it'll be because he knows we'll make his life a living hell otherwise. If we get any evidence on him, he's going down. It's as simple as that.'

'And if you can't get the evidence, what then?'

'We will. Even if there are no forensics and Nash refuses to crack, I'll find some way to nail the bastard. Trust me.'

Harlan did trust Jim. But he didn't trust the system. He'd seen scumbags like Jones slip through its net too many times. And until Jim's recent transgressions he'd proved himself a dutiful, if somewhat pessimistic, servant of the system. That was why he'd been partnered with Harlan – to rein in his maverick tendencies. And it'd worked, for the most part, while they were partners. But they weren't partners any more.

He thought about Jamie painting a picture in the air in his car. If bodies were Nash's trophies, paintings were Jones's. Somewhere there was a place where Jones kept his most prized trophies. Finding that place was the key to nailing him. But how to find it? Harlan heaved a sigh, hoping Jim would prove right and he'd never be forced to search for the answer to that question. 'So what else did the pathologist's report say?'

'Exactly when Lee Dale died can't be established for certain, but the advanced state of decay indicates he's been dead for around seven years. Which means Nash kept him alive for a year or so. Cause of death was inconclusive. He'd suffered more than a dozen fractures, but no single injury that was enough to kill him. Most probably he died from an accumulation of injuries combined with the effects of malnutrition.'

The dark thing that lurked in the far regions of Harlan's psyche whispered to him as he thought about Lee Dale being slowly tortured and starved to death. His fingers dug convulsively into the mattress.

'You OK?' asked Jim.

'Just a little pain in my side.'

'I'll go. Let you get some rest.'

'Any news on how Susan Reed's doing?' Harlan asked, as his ex-partner stood to leave.

Jim shook his head, but something about his eyes, some flicker of awkwardness, told Harlan that he was keeping something from him. 'Don't bullshit me, Jim. I know you too well.'

Jim dredged up another sigh. 'OK, here's the thing. Her other boy, Kane, found her collapsed unconscious yesterday.' As Harlan started to sit up in alarm, Jim added quickly, 'Don't worry, she's fine. He called for an ambulance and the paramedics pumped her stomach.'

'What'd she taken?'

'A shit load of booze and some sleeping pills.'

'She tried to kill herself.'

'She says it was an accident. Claims she just wanted to get some sleep.'

Harlan shook his head doubtfully. 'Where is she now?'

'At home. She refused to go to hospital.'

'Who's with her?'

'Just her son, as far as I know.'

Harlan's brow creased. 'Why the hell isn't there a uniform with her?'

'She wouldn't let anyone else in the house.' Jim's phone beeped as a text message came in. He flipped it open. 'The meeting's set up for half ten. Shit, I'd better get a move on. I'll call you, let you know how it goes.' He hurried from the room.

Even before Jim's footfalls had died away, Harlan was punching the call button to summon a nurse. His fingers drummed against the mattress as he waited. When a nurse finally poked her head into the room, he said, 'I need to see the doctor.'

'Dr Hill's doing her rounds right now. She'll be looking in on you in a bit.'

Irritation surged up in Harlan but before he could retort that he wanted to see Dr fucking Hill right this fucking minute, Eve's smiling face appeared at the nurse's shoulder. Her smile faded at the sight of Harlan. As the nurse moved away, Eve approached him, carrying a brown paper bag of fruit. 'What's wrong?' she asked.

'I've got to get out of this fucking place.'

'Why?'

Harlan told her about Susan. 'I need to see her, otherwise...' He couldn't bring himself to say what he feared might happen otherwise.

'But surely you're not ready to be discharged yet. Your wound could—'

'Fuck my wound,' cut in Harlan. Seeing Eve blink at the harshness of his retort, he gave her an apologetic look. 'Look, when the doctor gets here, just back up whatever I say to her, will you?'

Harlan was sitting on the edge of his bed when Dr Hill arrived. 'You should be lying down,' said the doctor.

'I want to be discharged,' said Harlan.

'I'd strongly advise against that. We need to keep you under observation for at least another forty-eight hours.'

'I feel fine.'

'You need total bed rest. If you walk, you could tear your stitches.'

'I promise I won't walk a step. Eve will make sure of that, won't you?'

Eve's lips pursed into a tight line, but she nodded.

'Before you can go anywhere, I'll need to examine you.' Dr Hill took Harlan's temperature and checked his blood pressure. Then she carefully peeled back the bandage and sterile gauze pad. The stitches looked like an ugly, puckered mouth. The skin around them was storm-cloud black, fading to purplish yellow. The colour leached from Eve's face at the sight. 'All your vitals are normal and there's no sign of infection.'

'So I can leave.'

'Are you dead set on this?'

'Yes.'

'OK then, I can't stop you from doing it, but before you go there are a few things we need to sort out.'

Dr Hill explained to Eve that the wound needed re-dressing every day for the first week and demonstrated how to apply a fresh bandage. Then she spoke about what tablets Harlan had to take and when to take them. Finally, she headed off to sort out the discharge arrangements and find a nurse to help Harlan get dressed. 'Get dressed in what?' asked Harlan. He had a hazy memory of his trousers and t-shirt being cut off him when he arrived at A&E. His wallet, phone, shoes and socks were in a plastic bag in the bedside cabinet, caked in dried blood.

'There are some shops downstairs. I'll see if I can find you something,' said Eve. She weighed him up. 'You've lost a little weight since I last bought clothes for you.'

Harlan managed a smile. 'I guess that's one good thing prison did for me, got rid of my love handles.'

Soon enough Eve returned with a pair of tracksuit bottoms and a hooded sweatshirt she'd found in a charity shop. 'Not exactly the height of fashion, but I figured tracksuit bottoms would be the most comfortable thing.'

A nurse helped Harlan into the clothes while Eve cleaned the blood off his shoes as best she could at the sink. Clapping her hand to her mouth suddenly, she rushed retching from the room. Harlan looked at her with concern when, after several minutes, she returned. 'Are you OK?'

'I'm fine. The blood turned my stomach, that's all.'

A flicker of surprise crossed Harlan's face. Gripping the bed frame, he lowered himself into a wheelchair from which hung plastic bags full of bandages and pill boxes. After he'd scribbled his signature on a few forms, Eve wheeled him to her car. He shook his head as she moved to help him into the passenger seat and gestured at the wheelchair. 'Get rid of this thing.'

'But the doctor said—'

'I don't give a shit what she said. Get rid of it.'

Sighing, Eve returned the wheelchair to the hospital building.

For some time they drove in silence, Harlan staring out the window, casting occasional thoughtful glances at Eve. 'How you feeling?' he asked.

'I told you, I'm fine.'

'It's just you're not usually the type to get queasy at the sight of blood.'

'Instead of worrying about me, Harlan, you should worry about looking after yourself. I'm assuming you don't want me hanging around once we get to Susan Reed's house.'

'I'll be OK. I'm not planning on doing anything more strenuous than talking. I just want to be there for her, make sure she doesn't try anything stupid.'

'What makes you think she wants you to be there for her?'

'Because I'm all she's got right now.'

Eve flicked Harlan a glance and he could see her thoughts. She was thinking: *what about me? Who the fuck have I got?* She didn't say it, though. However much she was hurting, she knew it was nothing compared to Susan Reed's pain. When they arrived at Susan's house, all the curtains were closed. Eve looked at Harlan like a mother would look at a child she was reluctant to let out of her sight. 'I'll wait in case she doesn't let you in.'

Harlan shook his head. 'If she sees you it'll make her angry.'

Eve frowned. 'Why? Because she can't stand to think you might have any happiness in life?'

Harlan held in a sigh. He didn't have the energy for this now. 'Thanks for the lift, Eve. I'll call you.'

'When? In the next fucking life?'

The sigh escaped. Harlan reached for the door handle.

'Wait.' Eve put her hand on his arm. Her voice came more softly. 'If you need me to change your bandage, cook you a meal, whatever, you know where I am.'

Mustering up a small smile, Harlan nodded and squeezed her hand. Their eyes mirrored each other's sadness – not the sadness of lovers parting, but a deeper, more profound sadness of shared loss. She took the key out of the ignition and offered it to him. 'Take it,' she insisted as he shook his head. 'Please, Harlan, for me. I won't be able to rest otherwise.'

He accepted the key. 'Thanks.'

Eve leaned in towards him hesitantly, as if unsure whether to kiss him. She didn't kiss him. She just murmured, 'I love you.' Then she got out of the car. Harlan watched her until she reached the end of the street, before slowly approaching and knocking on Susan's front door. No answer. He knocked again. Still no answer. Not even a twitch of the curtains.

'Susan,' Harlan called through the letter box, voice tight with the pain of bending. 'It's Harlan Miller.' To his relief, after a few seconds, his straining ears caught the sound of feet descending the stairs. His relief evaporated when the door opened and he saw Susan. He'd expected her to look bad, but her face, ashen and cadaverous with deep bruised circles under the eyes, was even ghastlier than he'd imagined. He'd seen corpses that looked more alive than she did. Gaze darting over his shoulder, she motioned for him to come inside. She closed the door quickly behind him and shot the lock.

Chapter Eighteen

The small living room was gloomy and stale smelling. *Like a tomb*. The thought popped unbidden into Harlan's head. It made him feel a little suffocated, and he resisted an urge to fling open the window. Leaflets with Ethan's picture on them were piled on every available surface – the carpet, the sofa, the hearth, the television. 'Do you mind if I sit down?' he asked, one hand pressed over his bandage. Susan shook her head. Picking his way through the leaflets, he limped to the sofa, cleared a space and carefully lowered himself onto it.

From somewhere Susan dredged up a smile that only made her face seem more deathlike. 'You look worse than I feel.' *No I don't*, thought Harlan, as she continued, 'Shouldn't you be in hospital?'

'I wanted to see you. Are you alone?'

'Kane's asleep upstairs. Poor thing, he's tired out after what—' She broke off with a sheepish glance at Harlan.

He finished her sentence for her. 'After what happened last night. I heard about that.'

'It was an accident. I didn't try to—' Susan started to say, but broke off again, her eyes dropping guiltily away from Harlan's. She shook her head. 'I can't lie to you. Not after what you've done.'

'So you did try to kill yourself.'

Susan glanced at the ceiling. Her voice dropped low. 'Maybe I did. I don't know. All I know is I wanted to sleep. Just sleep and sleep and not have to think about anything any more.' Her razor-thin shoulders shuddered as she heaved a breath.

'And what about now? Do you still feel the same way?'

'Yes and no. One minute I'm OK. Well, as OK as I can be. The next I'm having all these thoughts.'

'What kind of thoughts?'

'Ugly thoughts. But I'm not going to listen to them. I can't. Kane needs me.'

'Ethan needs you too.'

Susan's eyes filled with a bright sheen of pain. She gave a vehement shake of her head. 'Ethan's dead.'

'Don't say that.'

'But I am saying it.' Her voice had a shrill note in it, fast edging towards hysteria. 'Ethan's my son, and I'm saying to you that I feel in my bones and my heart that he's dead.'

'Not necessarily.'

'Yes, yes. He's dead, dead, fucking dead!' Tears choked her voice. Her head drooped like a flower beaten down by a storm.

'Look at me, Susan. Look at me and believe me. There's a chance Ethan's still alive. It's only a small chance. But there's hope.'

Susan lifted her eyes uncertainly. 'You wouldn't lie to me, would you?' Before Harlan could reply, she answered her question. 'No you wouldn't. You're the only one who'll always tell me the absolute truth. I see that now.'

She was right, Harlan realised. No one had more reason to hate him than her, yet she was the only person he could bare his soul to without fear. In some twisted way, he was closer to her than he was to anyone, even Eve. 'What have the police told you?'

'Only what it suits them to. Just that you were injured rescuing Jamie Sutton from that man...' Susan shook her head, a curl of hatred distorting her lips. 'No, he's not a man. Richard Nash is a sick animal.'

'Have they shown you a photo of him?'

'Yes, but I didn't recognise him. I keep asking them questions – questions like, what makes you so sure he was the one who took Ethan? And I never get a straight answer. Christ, it makes me feel like I'm a fucking suspect.'

'You are a suspect.'

Susan's eyes swelled with indignation. 'I'd stab myself in the heart before I hurt my own children.'

'I know it's hard to take, but the fact is everyone's a suspect until a case is solved. That's just the way it has to be.'

'I understand that, I suppose,' she muttered begrudgingly. She clutched two handfuls of her hair. 'But it still makes me so frustrated I feel like tearing my fucking hair out.'

'Just sit down and listen to me, Susan, and I'll tell you why there's hope Ethan might be alive.'

Susan perched on the edge of an armchair, hardly breathing as she waited for Harlan to speak. He told her everything that'd happened since he last saw her. Unlike with Eve, he gave her the whole story, leaving out no detail. When he got to the part about Jones, her eyes widened with surprise then narrowed in fury. 'I knew that animal was in on this,' she hissed. 'I fuckin' knew it.'

Harlan described torturing Jones. He spoke quickly, feeling lighter as the words poured out of him and into Susan. She took them from him gladly, her tongue flicking over her lips as if tasting something to be relished. 'I don't know how you resisted killing the bastard,' she said.

'Neither do I,' admitted Harlan.

Susan sat silent and rigid as he told her about the caravan, the woods and the caves. She trembled with the effort of holding back her tears, but an agonised sob escaped her lips when he vividly recounted finding Jamie Sutton. 'Oh Christ, it's too much! I can't bear it!' she groaned, rocking back and forth, her thin arms hugged around herself.

'I know it's horrifying to think of Ethan possibly being kept like that, but that's where our hope comes from,' Harlan said gently. 'Do you understand?'

Susan nodded. 'I don't want to, but I do.'

Harlan's wound twinged as he described the fight with Nash. Susan looked at him with what might've been concern, maybe even compassion. 'They never told me your injury was so serious.'

'It's nothing compared to what you've suffered.'

'No, it's not nothing. It's something.' There was gratitude in her voice.

Harlan suddenly found himself unable to look at her. Her hatred he knew how to handle, but not her gratitude. Lowering his eyes, he continued his story right up to leaving hospital. He didn't mention Eve – that would've somehow felt like an admission of betrayal. A hiss of breath came from Susan as she mulled over what she'd heard. 'So let me get this straight, Jones hasn't been charged with anything yet.'

Harlan shook his head. 'They need hard evidence.'

'Evidence.' The word grated through her teeth. She echoed a thought that had been in Harlan's mind for the past couple of days. 'Give me five minutes alone with him and I'd give them all the fuckin' evidence they need.'

Susan looked as if a breath of wind could blow her over, but there was such cold fury in her eyes that Harlan didn't for a second doubt her ability to carry the threat through.

'They'll find a way to get at him and Nash. The old woman, Mary Webster, might be the key to...' Harlan fell silent as a feeling of faintness welled up inside him. His head and eyes rolled slowly back.

Susan rushed to his side and caught hold of his arm, stopping him from falling sideways. 'This is crazy. You shouldn't be here.'

'I'll be fine,' Harlan mumbled, his voice blurring. 'I just need a moment.'

Susan propped him up between the sofa's arm and a couple of cushions. 'Can I get you anything?'

'Some water to take my tablets.'

Susan hurried through to the kitchen. Harlan focused on the room, fighting to keep unconsciousness at bay. The mantelpiece was cluttered with cheap ornaments, a silver carriage clock and photos. There were recent photos of Kane and Ethan in their school uniforms. Kane with his usual sullen, angry-at-the-world face. Ethan smiling timidly, his shy eyes slightly averted from the camera. In the middle of the mantelpiece stood a photo that made Harlan's heart squeeze. It showed Robert Reed and his sons on a beach with the sea shimmering in the background. Ethan was wearing a sunhat and T-shirt that came down almost to the knees of his chubby baby legs. Kane was wearing wet, sand-caked swimming trunks and a smile so broad his eyes were barely visible. Robert squatted down behind them, one arm around each of their shoulders. He was smiling too. The scene exuded happiness – a happiness soon to be fractured into bloody pieces.

Harlan wanted to look away from the photo but he was gripped in a vice of guilt. He suddenly had the feeling that he was trespassing on forbidden ground. 'She's right, you shouldn't be here,' he said to himself. But he knew he couldn't leave, either. Not with Susan as she was.

'What the fuck's that wanker doing here?'

Harlan jerked around to face the voice's owner, grimacing at the sudden movement. From the doorway, Kane glared at him, fists balled. 'Don't talk about him like that,' said Susan, pushing past her son and proffering a glass to Harlan, which he accepted with a smile of thanks.

'I'll talk about him however I want.'

Susan shot Kane a reproachful look. 'You'll do as I say while you're in my house.'

'No I won't. Not when it comes to him. Why should I?'

'Because he risked his life to try and help your brother.'

Kane stabbed a finger at Harlan, the same curl on his lips that'd twisted Susan's mouth out of shape as she spoke about Nash. 'He fuckin' killed my dad!' He turned on Susan, eyes bulging. 'How could you do this, Mum? How could you let him in here?'

She blinked, but her own mounting anger kept her from wavering under the force of her son's glare. 'He's trying to make up for what he did.'

'He can't make up for it. Nothing he can do will bring Dad back.'

'I know that, but—'

'I don't care what you say!' broke in Kane. 'And I don't care what he does. Even if he finds Ethan, I'll still hate him and want to kill him.'

'Kane!' For the first time since Harlan had been there, some colour came into Susan's face. 'I won't have you talk like that. Do you hear me? I won't have it!'

'Fuck you.' Kane whirled to head back upstairs. Susan caught hold of his arm but he elbowed her away.

'Get back down here, you little shit,' she yelled, as he hammered up the stairs.

'I won't. Not until he's gone.' The walls quivered as Kane slammed his bedroom door.

Susan started after him but thought better of it. Heaving a sigh, she dropped into the armchair. 'I shouldn't have sworn at him. I hate myself when I lose it like that.'

'Maybe I should go,' suggested Harlan.

Susan shook her head. 'I want you here.' She glanced at the ceiling, through which loud rap music had begun to vibrate. 'And boyo's just going to have to get used to the idea. When he's calmed down, I'll go speak to him.'

'It won't make any difference. He hates me, and he's got every right to.'

'So have I.' Susan frowned as if struggling to make sense of something, some sudden realisation. 'But I don't hate you any more.' She added quickly, 'That's not to say I've forgiven you. I just don't hate you.' She let out a long breath, shaking her head. 'I never thought I'd hear myself say that.'

Harlan had never thought he'd hear it either. He replayed her words in his mind several times, trying to get a handle on how they made him feel. They counted for something, he knew that. More than something, they counted for a lot, but not enough to stop him from hating himself. Nowhere near.

'If I can stop hating you, so can Kane,' continued Susan. 'He's carried too much anger for too long. It scares me. I'm scared that if he doesn't start letting go of it he's gonna hurt somebody. I mean, really hurt somebody.'

Harlan's gaze strayed to the photo and Kane's face, its smile as untarnished as the beach and the sea. An image rose into his mind of Kane wielding the baseball bat, eyes burning with hate. A monster of his making. The vice turned a twist tighter. 'By somebody, you mean me.'

'You or anybody else he takes against.' Susan's voice grew

226

hesitant. 'I've never told anyone this before. About a year ago I bought Kane a puppy, a little mongrel terrier. I thought it would, y'know, do him good to have some responsibility. And at first it seemed to, but he soon lost interest. Started kicking up a stink every time I told him to take it for a walk. One day we had this big blow up after I caught him hitting it. When things calmed down, he apologised and promised to start looking after Sandy – that was the dog's name – properly. And for a few weeks, he kept his promise. But then this... this thing happened. One morning he came running home soaking wet, carrying Sandy. Sandy was dead. He said the dog had jumped in the river. He'd tried to save it, but it drowned. That's what he said, and that's what I wanted to believe, but...' Susan's voice trailed off into uneasy silence. She sucked her upper lip a moment, before continuing, 'But something in the back of my mind kept telling me he was lying. I wanted to confront him but I couldn't bring myself to. Truth is, I didn't want to know if he'd killed Sandy.'

Harlan wondered if he'd have pushed for the truth if he suspected Tom of something so despicable. Or would he have preferred the comfort of ignorance too. He wasn't sure. 'That's understandable.'

'Yeah, but now I'm thinking I shouldn't have let it slide. I mean, if Kane really did kill Sandy, he needs help, right? Therapy or counselling, or something.'

'I dealt with a lot of counsellors when I was on the force. If you want, I can make a couple of calls, organise something.'

Forehead puckered with uncertainty, Susan sucked her lip again. 'What if he hates me for it? I don't know if I can risk pushing him away from me. He's all I've got left.'

'You let me in here. He's not exactly happy about that.'

'That's different. You give me hope.'

'There are a lot of good detectives on the case. That should give you hope too.'

Susan dismissed Harlan's words with derisive flick of her hand. 'They can't do what's necessary. They've already proved that.' She pointed at him. 'You're the only one who can bring my baby boy back to me.'

The weight of her words pushed Harlan's head down. He stared at the piles of missing-person leaflets. Some had fallen over and were scattered across the floor. *What a mess*, he thought. He pictured Kane with the dead dog in his arms. *What a fucking mess.* There was no cleaning it up. It just went on and on, turning everything it touched to shit. His head began to reel again. He shakily pulled out a blister strip, popped a pill into his palm and swallowed it.

'I'd better go speak to him,' said Susan, as the music ratcheted up a notch. With a weary noise, she headed for the stairs. After a couple of minutes, the muffled sound of raised voices came through the floor. Harlan tried not to listen to what was being said, but he kept catching words – words like 'love' and 'hate'. His phone began to vibrate. He took it out. It was Jim. He answered it.

'I phoned the hospital,' said Jim. 'They told me you'd checked out. I would tell you you're crazy, but you know that already.'

'How's it going with Nash?'

'That's why I'm calling. You were right. The old woman got through to him. She didn't even have to say anything. As soon as we wheeled her in, he started blubbing like a baby. He genuinely seems to care about her.'

'Has he said anything?'

'Not yet, but we're working on him. I don't think it'll be long now. I need you to do me a favour. We want to arrange a line-up. You remember what Kane heard the kidnapper say to Ethan?'

Harlan remembered. *Be quiet or I'll kill you and your brother.* 'Yes.'

'Well, the idea is to see if Kane can pick Nash's voice out of the line-up. I need you to talk to Susan – I'm assuming you're with her – and convince her it's worth a shot.'

'When are you arranging it for?'

'That depends on Nash. There's no point setting it up unless he cooperates.'

'Don't hammer at him with his crimes. That'll only send him back into his shell. Concentrate on Mary Webster. Make him think that if he cooperates, he'd be doing it for her.'

'That's exactly what we are doing, and I'd better get back to it. I'll be speaking to you again soon, I'm sure.'

Jim hung up. The music was still thumping upstairs but the voices had dropped below hearing range. Harlan rested his head back against the sofa and shut his eyes. *Love, hate.* Those two words turned over and over in his mind, like a coin flipping through the air. He sighed out a long breath. The painkillers were wrapping warm hands around him. The noise outside was far away now. The noise inside was fading too. *Love, hate, love, hate...*

When he awoke, the house was silent, except for the sound of pots and pans being moved around in the kitchen. He smelled the aroma of cooking. He glanced at the carriage clock. Four twenty. He'd been asleep for an hour or so. He checked his phone. No missed calls. Nash was obviously still holding out. Slowly, stiffly, he rose and made his way to the kitchen. Susan was standing at a grease-stained cooker, shoving sausages around in a frying pan. A scarred wooden table against a wall of the tiny room was laid with cutlery, salt and pepper and sauce bottles.

Noticing Harlan, Susan said, 'Hungry?'

Now that she mentioned it, Harlan realised he was. 'Yes.'

'I thought you would be after living off hospital food.' Susan nodded towards the table. 'Sit yourself down.'

Harlan did so and Susan placed a mug of tea and a plate of chips and sausages in front of him. She headed out the room with a second plate, saying, 'I'll just take this up to Kane. Don't wait for me. Start eating.'

The food tasted good – better than any meal Harlan had eaten in weeks. When Susan returned, he asked through a mouthful of sausage, 'How's he doing?'

'He's not talking to me. Won't even look at me. I left the food for him but I doubt he'll eat it. Last time I saw him like this was a couple of years ago, when I first started seeing Neil. He didn't eat properly for weeks. I ended up taking him to the doctor.'

She sat down opposite Harlan and sparked up a cigarette. 'How about you?' he asked. 'Aren't you eating?'

She shook her head. 'I can't stomach anything. Every time I think about Ethan, about where he might be, about what might've happened to him, it makes me want to puke.'

Harlan finished his meal quickly, feeling Susan's eyes on him the whole time. 'You're a good eater,' she said, reaching for his empty plate. 'Rob was a good eater too. I used to love watching him eat.'

Harlan winced internally.

'Neil eats like a bird. It drives me mad watching him peck at his food.' Susan dumped the plate in the sink and scrubbed it clean.

Noticing that she spoke about Neil in the present tense, Harlan asked, 'Is it over between you two?'

'He lied to me. I can't be with someone who lies to me.' Susan spoke with decisive quickness, but there was a quiver of uncertainty in her voice.

'Everyone lies sometimes.'

'Yeah, sure, about small things. But not about things like that at a time like this.'

'He was afraid of losing you.'

Susan turned to Harlan, frowning. 'What are you saying? That I should get back with him?' That same little quiver was in her voice.

Harlan no longer had any suspicions about Neil. And looking into Susan's sunken eyes, he could see she was desperately hoping he'd say yes. But he couldn't bring himself to. The thought came to him that she deserved better than Neil. She deserved someone who could give her a future free from debt and worries about bailiffs coming knocking, a future where she wasn't always just scraping by.

Another thought rose to his mind: *and who's going to give her that, you?*

Maybe, he replied to it.

And are you going to hold her through the night when all she can see is Ethan's face? Are you going to be a father to Kane?

Harlan didn't need to think about the answers to those questions. He could never be there for them in that way, even if by some incredible stretch of improbability they'd have him. He thought back to when Tom was born. Eve had given up work. They'd just scraped by on his salary but they were happy – happier, perhaps, than at any other time in their lives. He sighed. Maybe Neil was the right man for Susan. But then, who was he to say one way or the other? He gave a weak little shrug, dropping his eyes to his mug.

Susan flinched at a knock on the front door. 'Will you go see who it is? Don't open the door. Just have a peep through the curtains.'

Harlan crept into the living room and did as she asked. It was Lewis Gunn. He returned to the kitchen and told Susan.

The knock came again. She made no move to answer it. After a moment, she said, 'Go see if he's gone.'

Again, Harlan peeped through the curtains. The preacher was walking away. 'He's gone.'

'Thank fuck for that.' Pulling out another cigarette, Susan added a touch guiltily, 'Don't get me wrong, I'm grateful for everything Mr Gunn's done, but... the thing is, I'm sick of listening to all his God bullshit. I keep wanting to say to him, what kind of fucking god would let this happen? How am I supposed to believe in a god like that?'

'I remember thinking the same thing when Tom died.' The words were out before Harlan realised it. Straight away, he wished he hadn't said them. He'd never really spoken about Tom's death with anyone other than Eve. Not even Jim. Like Kane's anger, his grief possessed him, and he possessed it. Part of him wanted – was desperate – to let go of it, but another part of him recoiled from anything that might cause him to do so.

'Who's Tom?'

'He was my son.'

'What happened?' Seeing the pained look that passed over Harlan's face, Susan added, 'You don't have to tell me if you don't want to.'

Harlan was silent a moment, then, almost whispering, as if he didn't want to hear his own voice, he told Susan what'd happened. When he finished, he saw that she was looking at him with a new understanding in her eyes, as if what he'd said had completed a puzzle she'd been struggling to solve. 'So you know how I feel,' she said with a softness he hadn't heard before.

'I know how it feels to lose a child. I don't know how you feel, and I never want to find out.' Exhausted, more from talking about Tom than from his wound, Harlan lowered himself onto the sofa. 'Do you mind if I close my eyes for a while?'

'Go ahead.'

He slipped into an uneasy doze. He lay half sleeping, half waking, drifting in and out of dreams he didn't want to remember, thinking thoughts he didn't want to think, cracking his eyelids every few minutes to check his phone. And with every time he saw that there were still no missed calls or new messages, a heaviness grew in his chest, until it seemed as if a concrete block was resting on it. The fingers of sunlight probing the curtains had been replaced by the cindery glow of street lamps, when Susan's raised voice brought him to full wakefulness. 'How did you get this number?' she was saying. 'No, I'm not fuckin' interested... I don't give a shit... Don't fuckin' ring here again.' She stamped into the living room and slammed the phone back into its cradle. 'Fucking bastard journalists,' she said to Harlan, her voice taking on that same edge of hysteria as earlier. 'I'm going out of my fuckin' head waiting to hear if my little boy's dead or alive, and they're calling me up for a fuckin' quote.' She took out a cigarette and lighter. When the lighter wouldn't ignite, she yelled, 'Fuck,' and flung it across the room.

Harlan retrieved the lighter, shook it and got the flame going. He held it out to Susan, and she sucked her cigarette into life. 'Thanks,' she said, her voice a little calmer. As she smoked, Harlan took his next round of pills. Susan switched the telly on. The evening news was just beginning. Like a child watching a horror movie, she put her hand to her face and peered through her fingers. There was nothing new reported – the police were still searching the woods, still questioning an unnamed man. Susan switched the telly off and flung the remote aside. 'Christ!' she groaned, her voice raw with emotion. 'How much longer? How much longer?'

Not much longer, thought Harlan, *not if they're going to find Ethan alive.*

Susan pressed her hands to her head as if to keep it from bursting. 'I don't know how much more of this I can take.'

'You can take it,' Harlan said evenly. 'You can take it because Kane needs you.'

Susan took a breath and got hold of herself. She lit another cigarette, leaning back against the armchair, inhaling deeply. 'Will you stay here tonight? I don't want to be alone if... if they find anything.'

Harlan nodded.

'I'll make you up a bed on the floor.'

'The sofa will do me fine.'

'No it won't. Not the state you're in. There's a fold-down mattress—' Susan broke off at a knock on the door, her eyes twitching with nerves. 'Who the fuck's that now?' she hissed in a low voice.

The knock came again. It wasn't like Lewis Gunn's knock, it was loud and insistent. This time Neil's voice accompanied it. 'Susan it's me,' he shouted. 'I need to speak to you. Please let me in. I'm begging you. I just want a chance to explain everything.'

Susan looked from the door to Harlan, as if seeking his permission to open it. He said nothing.

'Please, Susan, please,' continued Neil. 'I love you, and I love the kids. I'd never hurt any of you. You've got to believe me.'

Susan rose to her feet, mouth working in mute uncertainty.

'I'm so sorry, Susan.' There were tears in Neil's voice now. 'I'm so sorry. Please don't leave me. Please give me another chance.'

She approached the door, put her hand on the handle, but didn't lower it.

'I won't give up on us. You're my life, Susan. I'd rather die than lose you. Do you hear me?'

Susan pressed her forehead against the door, eyes closed.

'I'd rather die, I'd rather die.' Neil's words came in a sobbing murmur. There was a moment of silence, then the sound of a car door clunking shut. Peering between the curtains, Harlan saw that Neil had got into his Volvo. The car began to pull away. Suddenly, Susan came to life, unlocking and opening the door, rushing out into the street. 'Wait,' she called, but the car didn't stop.

She came back into the house, looking tentatively at Harlan. 'What do you think I should do?'

'I think it's none of my business to say what I think,' he replied, returning to the sofa.

'Christ, I hope he doesn't do anything silly.' Susan sat down, but couldn't keep still. 'I want a drink. Do you want one?'

'I probably shouldn't, not with all the pills I'm on,' said Harlan, but it wasn't the thought of the pills that made him hesitant, it was the memory of what'd happened the last time he'd drunk around Susan.

'One won't do you any harm. Come on, don't make me drink alone.'

Harlan sighed. 'All right, just one.'

'Is white wine OK with you?' Before Harlan could reply, she added, 'It'll have to be because that's all there is.'

Harlan shuddered involuntarily as, in a flash of remembrance, Robert Reed's words came back to him, *I'll have a lager, she'll have a large white wine*. Susan fetched two glasses of wine. The smell alone nauseated him but he forced himself to swallow a mouthful. Susan drank quietly, her brow creased, seemingly grappling with some internal debate. Suddenly, as if she'd come to some decision, she gulped her glass empty, stood and returned the kitchen. There was the sound of glass clinking against glass as she poured herself a refill. Followed by the sound of tears bursting from her. Each low, racking sob jerked at Harlan's heart. He considered going to her but quickly decided against it. What would he do if he did? Hold her to him? Murmur reassurances into her ear? No. Those were things he couldn't do. After several minutes, she stopped crying with a hitching breath. She returned to the living room, her eyes dry, but red-rimmed and puffy. 'Sorry,' she said.

Harlan shook his head to indicate there was no need to be. They sat in silence, cradling their drinks. 'Jesus,' Susan sighed, after a while. 'How did my life get here?'

How did my life get here? Harlan asked himself that same question almost every day. He'd had so many plans, so many things he was going to do with Eve and Tom. And now what did he have? Sweet fuck all, that's what. For years he'd railed at the unfairness of life. And where had it got him? Here, that's where. Here in this room, stuck up to his neck in a quicksand of guilt, where the more he struggled, the deeper he sank. So what was the answer? To just accept whatever life threw his way? The idea appalled him. Maybe there was no answer. Perhaps suffering was all there was left to life. Perhaps that was all there'd ever really been, even when he thought he was happy.

Susan finished her drink and stood up. 'I'll fetch your bed.' She headed upstairs, returning a few minutes later with the mattress and an armful of bedding. She cleared a space on the floor and began to make up the bed.

'Where's your toilet?'

'Upstairs. First door on your left.'

Harlan slowly climbed the stairs, his stitches pulling with each step. As he reached the landing, a door to his right opened and Kane stepped out. He glared at Harlan, his eyes like storm clouds ready to burst. Then he jerked around and headed back into his room, slamming the door. Sighing, Harlan went into

236

the bathroom. After emptying his bladder, he swilled the taste of the wine from his mouth at the sink. He opened the bathroom cabinet – deodorant, perfume, dental floss, Savlon, Valium. His gaze lingered briefly on the sleeping pills, before he returned to the living room. The bed was ready and waiting. Susan was sitting at the kitchen table, refilling her glass. 'Did you see Kane?' she asked.

Harlan nodded.

'What did he do?'

'Nothing. Just went back to his room.'

'That's good, isn't it? I mean, at least he didn't take a swing at you or anything.'

Harlan made a dubious little noise in his throat. He still had some faint bruises on his arms from the baseball bat attack. From the look in Kane's eyes, Harlan suspected it was only a matter of time before he attempted a repeat performance. He yawned. The bed called to his tired body but he hesitated to go to it, wondering if it was safe to leave Susan alone with her thoughts, the wine and the Valium. A thin smile curled the edges of her mouth. 'Go to bed and don't worry, I'm not gonna do anything crazy,' she said, reading his mind.

'Goodnight.'

'Night. Call me if you need anything.'

Harlan undressed stiffly and got under the duvet. He thought about the violence he'd seen lurking just under the surface of Kane's eyes. It worried him. But not enough to keep him awake. Not the way he felt. His eyelids came together like heavy curtains, snuffing out his consciousness.

Something prised its way into Harlan's mind – not a sound, but a feeling, a presence in the room. For a moment he struggled against the glue of drug-aided sleep. His eyes rolled, his hands twitched across the duvet towards his face. The outline of a figure, faintly luminescent in the glow of the street lamp, swam into focus. 'Susan,' he said, slurring the word. But something – some crawling feeling of danger – told him it wasn't her. He rubbed the blur from his eyes, revealing Kane. The deep, black pools of the boy's eyes stared back at Harlan from the end of the bed. Tears glistened on his cheeks, but he made no sound of crying. His arms hung rigidly at his sides. Something he held in one hand caught the light. A blade! Harlan's heart began to throb. He pushed up onto his elbows, grimacing as his stomach flexed. Kane moved the knife threateningly. Harlan dropped back onto the pillows. The knife returned to Kane's side.

For maybe thirty seconds they faced each other silently. Harlan's heart slowed to a steady thud. His voice was calm and clear, as he said, 'Kill me. I won't stop you. Go ahead, if that's what you want. If you want to become like me.' He closed his eyes. He could hear the boy's breathing, shallow and rapid. His own breath came slow and easy. It wasn't that he didn't believe Kane had it in him to kill – he knew he did. Nor was it that he wanted to die. His desire to live, he realised suddenly, was stronger than it had been in years, maybe since Tom's death. He merely felt that he owed Kane a chance to avenge his father's death. And if he didn't take it, if his anger and hatred didn't consume him, then maybe their flame would begin to burn less fiercely.

Another thirty seconds passed. A minute. Two minutes. Harlan became aware that he couldn't hear Kane's breathing any more. He opened his eyes. The boy was gone, like a ghost in a dream. A queasy, unreal feeling struck at him, as if maybe he was dreaming. But then he heard the creak of floorboards upstairs, and the feeling receded. Releasing a long breath, he let the curtains of sleep close over his eyes again.

Chapter Nineteen

Harlan peeled back his bandage. The wound had seeped a little, probably from all the moving around he'd done the previous day. Susan's lips formed a tight O. 'Ow, that hurts just to look at.'

He dabbed the track of stitches with wet cotton wool, followed by an antiseptic wipe. Then he applied fresh gauze and a bandage. After dropping the old dressings into the kitchen bin, he looked at his phone. He knew what he'd see – in the short time he'd been awake, he'd already checked it a dozen times – but felt compelled to do so again anyway. No new calls or messages. 'Come on, Jim,' he muttered. 'Fucking call.' He felt better than the previous day. Stronger. More clear headed. Even after the incident with Kane, perhaps because of it, he'd slept the sleep of the dead. A sleep undisturbed by dreams or thoughts. As Susan turned strips of bacon in the pan, he lined up his pills on the table and began swallowing them one by one.

'Kane,' Susan called upstairs. 'Breakfast's nearly ready. Are you coming down?'

There was no reply. Susan gave Harlan a glance that said the silence was what she expected, but at that moment there came the sound of a door opening and footsteps descending the stairs. Her eyebrows lifted as Kane entered the kitchen, and without looking at her or Harlan, seated himself. She stared at him as if unsure whether to be puzzled or pleased by his presence. Eyes down, he sipped his tea and remained silent. She looked inquiringly at Harlan, as if he might know something about this development. He gave a slight shrug. Her expression unconvinced, she scooped the bacon out of the pan. 'There you go,' she said, placing a plate in front of Kane. 'Nice and crispy. Just how you like it.'

The boy gave a low grunt of thanks. After slicing some bread for Harlan's bacon, Susan leaned against the work surface, smoking and watching her son eat. When he was finished, Kane took his plate to the sink. As he headed back upstairs, he flashed Harlan the briefest of glances. His face wore its usual scowl but his eyes were shadowed with uncertainty, as though something inside him – something fundamental to his character – had been shaken.

'Well, well,' said Susan. 'What was that all about?'

Harlan gave another shrug.

'Has something happened between you two?' persisted Susan.

'No.' Harlan hated to lie to her but neither did he want to risk upsetting the delicate balance of Kane's mood. If he spilled about what'd happened, Susan would be upset and angry. Most probably, she would confront Kane. Maybe she would even change her mind about getting him psychological help. And perhaps she would be right to do so. But Harlan wanted to give the boy one more chance – a chance to deal with his hate internally, without having to go through the pain of therapy. He felt certain that last night had been some kind of turning point. Kane had faced the ultimate decision, and surely it'd made him realise what he was and what he wasn't: he was a screwed-up kid, but he wasn't a killer. Of course, Harlan realised that if he was wrong it could cost him his life.

'Well something's happened,' said Susan, her forehead crinkling as she cast around her mind for what that 'something' might be. 'Otherwise there's no way in hell he'd have sat at that table with you.' She sighed. 'I suppose I should be pleased. Perhaps he's finally coming to realise, like I have, that hate always hurts the hater more than it does the hated.'

Not always, thought Harlan. 'Can I use your bathroom?'

Susan waved her hand slightly, a preoccupied gesture that said, *You don't need to ask*. Harlan headed upstairs. As he reached the landing, Kane opened his bedroom door. They faced each other silently, Harlan keeping his expression neutral, Kane still teetering on the edge of uncertainty. Finally, his voice reluctant and thick with guilt, as if he was betraying something or someone, the boy whispered, 'So you haven't told her?'

'No.'

'How come?'

'She's got enough on her plate right now. And besides, I didn't want to get you in trouble.'

Kane's mouth twitched but no words came. He licked his lips agitatedly, then grunted – the same sound he'd made downstairs – and turned to go back into his room. This time, though, he didn't close the door. He sat cross-legged on the threadbare carpet and began playing on a games console hooked up to a small television. Harlan's gaze travelled the cramped bedroom, lingering on a mottled black damp patch above the window, before continuing to the bunk beds. The top one was a mess of crumpled sheets and magazines. The bottom one was made up with a faded duvet depicting some cartoon character or other. A few stuffed toys perched on its pillows, awaiting their owner's return. Harlan felt a stab of sadness at the sight. It reminded him of the way he'd turned Tom's bedroom into a shrine to a ghost. He wondered how long Susan would keep the bed like that if Ethan wasn't found.

The answer was as obvious as it was painful. The rest of her life. No body, no closure.

Harlan's gaze returned to Kane. 'Do you mind if I ask you some questions about the night Ethan was taken?'

'No,' said Kane, without taking his eyes from the screen. 'But I dunno what I can tell you that I haven't already told the cops.'

'Did the man who took Ethan sound like he was from around here?'

Kane shrugged. 'He just sounded like a man.'

'Did you notice anything about him other than his voice?'

'Yeah, his wrists. They were really hairy.'

'Anything else? Did he smell of anything? Did his clothes or breath smell?'

'Yeah, he had this weird smell.'

'How do you mean, weird?'

Kane gave another shrug.

'Was it like cigarettes or alcohol?'

'I dunno what it was like, but it made my throat tickle. The cops got me to smell loads of different things. Paints and other stuff, but none of them had the smell I smelled.'

Harlan was about to inquire further, but his phone rang. He snatched it out, and a flush of adrenalin went through his veins when he saw Jim's name. He pressed the phone to his ear. 'Please tell me he's talked.'

'He's talked,' said Jim.

A hiss of relief escaped Harlan's lips, drawing a curious look from Kane. 'Thank Christ.'

'Before you go getting too excited, he hasn't said anything about anything, he's just agreed to cooperate with the line-up. We're sending a car for the boy and his mother. It should be there soon.'

'I'll let them know. Good work, Jim.'

'Don't congratulate me. It was your idea to bring the old woman to see Nash. Besides, he's still not opened up about Ethan or Jones.'

'But this is a start, and that's a hell of a lot more than we had yesterday. We just need to find something to get the floodgates fully opened, then everything else will come pouring out. Maybe the line-up is that something.'

'Maybe. We'll see. In the meantime, I'm gonna work on him some more. I'll speak to you later.'

'What was that about?' Kane asked, as Harlan hung up.

Harlan told him. Kane's tongue flicked at his lips and a tightness came into his face. 'There's nothing to be scared of,' Harlan reassured him. 'Nash won't be able to see or hear you.'

'I ain't fuckin' scared of him. If he comes after me, I'll batter the shit out of him,' Kane responded defensively, but his bravado rang as hollow as the tremor in his voice.

'I'd better go and tell your mum.' Harlan hesitated to leave Kane alone with his fear. He wanted to say something more to reassure him but he knew any such words would be flung back in his face. As if to prove how unconcerned he was, Kane nonchalantly resumed his game. 'Thanks for talking to me,' said Harlan. The boy gave no sign of having heard. Harlan's eyes strayed briefly to Ethan's bed again, then he turned to make his way downstairs.

A strange, pale look came over Susan's face when she heard what was going to take place. Like Kane, there was fear in her expression, but it was tempered by an almost violent eagerness. 'What do you think it means? Do you think he's ready to come clean?'

'I don't know,' said Harlan, not wanting to give false hope.

Susan lit a cigarette and, puffing intensely on it, began pacing the kitchen. At the sound of a car pulling up outside, she darted

243

to the front window. 'It's the police.' She lifted her head. 'Kane, get down here.' A few seconds passed. No sound of movement came from upstairs. 'What the hell's he doing?' Susan ran to the bottom of the stairs. 'Kane, get a bloody move on!'

'Take it easy on him,' said Harlan. 'He acts tough, but he's just a scared kid.'

'He's scared? What about me? I'm going out of my fucking—' Susan broke off as Kane appeared and made his way downstairs with slow, reluctant steps. 'Come on, come on,' she urged, thrusting his coat and trainers at him. He put them on and sloped after her, head hanging. She stepped out the front door, but he hesitated to follow. Her eyes swelled with frustration. 'What the hell's the matter with you? You understand what's going on, don't you?'

Kane nodded, without meeting his mother's gaze.

'Then you know that every second you waste standing there may cost your brother his life. Now get in the car.'

Kane's face crumpled as if he was about to cry, but he remained otherwise motionless.

'I said get in the fucking—' Susan caught her anger with a deep breath, before continuing firmly, but gently, 'Please, Kane, do as I say.'

Kane glanced back at Harlan. 'Will you come with us?'

For a second time that morning, Susan's eyebrows lifted high. A little tremor of relief passed over Kane as Harlan said, 'Of course I will.' Avoiding Susan's enquiring gaze, Harlan struggled into his shoes and followed Kane to the police car. The boy sat between him and Susan, nervously picking at his jeans, as the car drove blurringly fast to the edge of the city and beyond. Every once in a while, a voice crackled over the two-way radio, inquiring as to their location. Other than that and the driver's response, the journey passed in silence. An hour and a half or so later, they pulled into a car park around the back of a police station on the outskirts of Manchester. Jim was waiting for them. He gave Harlan a surprised glance but didn't otherwise acknowledge him.

'This way, please.' Jim ushered Susan and Kane into the building. They made their way along a corridor to a room where DCI Garrett, DI Greenwood, DI Sheridan and several other detectives awaited them. A faint frown tugged Garrett's brows at the sight of Harlan, but as his eyes moved to Susan a well-practised smile of grave welcome chased it away. *Slimy bastard*, thought Harlan, approaching a two-way mirror, on the other side of which eight figures were lined up. All of them roughly Nash's height and build. All of them wearing black balaclavas. They looked like a gang of terrorists.

Garrett held his hand out to Susan. She was slow to take it. 'It's good to see you again, Susan. And you, Kane. Has the procedure been explained to you?'

'No,' said Susan.

'It's simple. One at a time, each of the men will approach the mirror and say, "Be quiet or I'll kill you and your brother." All you have to do, Kane, is say if you recognise any of their voices.' Garrett gestured at the line-up. 'We're confident that one of those men is the man who took your brother, but—'

'If one of them is him, it's no thanks to you he's in there,' cut in Susan, with a meaningful glance at Harlan.

Garrett's smile faltered but remained fixed in place. Ignoring the acid remark, he continued, 'But if you can pick his voice out it'll really help strengthen our case. Now take your time. And don't be afraid to ask if you want any of them to repeat the words.'

Garrett gave a signal and one of the detectives spoke into a mic. 'Number one, step forward and read the line.'

Susan laid a hand on Kane's shoulder as the first figure approached the mirror and read from a card in a flat, emotionless tone. 'Be quiet or I'll kill you and your brother.'

Harlan didn't recognise the voice. Kane indicated that he didn't either with a shake of his head. The next figure stepped forward, and the next, and the next. All of them elicited the same response: a shake of Kane's head. The fifth figure recited the line. Harlan tensed, a jolt of adrenalin shooting through him. He recognised Nash's voice instantly, even though it sounded different. It had an unusually gentle, almost soothing quality, maybe acquired through years of caring for Mary Webster, or maybe adopted to hide its owner's true nature. Po-faced, Harlan looked at Kane. The boy seemed to consider for a moment, then shook his head. 'Are you sure?' Garrett asked him.

'Yes.'

'It's just that you hesitated.'

'Only because the voice sounded kind of strange.'

'Do you want number five to say the line again?'

Kane shrugged. Garrett gestured and number five was ordered to repeat the words. This time, Kane didn't hesitate. 'It's not him.'

'Take your time, darling,' said Susan.

'I don't need to. It's not him.'

Harlan exchanged a glance with Jim. His ex-partner's carefully expressionless face reflected his own but Harlan knew him well enough to read disappointment in his eyes. Nash stepped back into line, handing off the card. None of the other voices caused Kane to hesitate. After shaking his head at the last figure in the line, he said, 'It's none of them. He's not here.' He looked up at Susan. There was the first hint of tears in his voice. 'I'm sorry, Mum.'

Susan squeezed her son's shoulder. 'There's nothing to be sorry for.'

'Your mum's right,' said Garrett. 'You've been very brave and done all you could.'

'So does this mean Nash isn't the one who took my Ethan?' Susan asked.

'Not at all. It merely means Kane didn't recognise his voice, which when you think about it is hardly surprising. In fact, I think there are some real positives to be taken from this.'

'Positives?' A frown darkened Susan's features as she glanced at the two-way mirror.

'I'll have to ask you and Kane to wait in the corridor a moment while I talk to my colleagues.'

At a glance from Garrett, DI Sheridan ushered them out of the room. 'What about me?' asked Harlan.

Garrett looked at him with his police face, not his politician face. 'You stay where you are.' There was a hard, authoritative edge to his voice. He waited for DI Sheridan to close the door before continuing, 'William Jones won't be bringing charges against you. Before you thank me, know this, if it were up to me I'd prosecute you to the full extent of the law. But it's not up to me. Apparently some people think you're a hero. I'm not one of those people.' Garrett leaned in close to Harlan, his voice dropping to a furious hiss. 'I know what you really are.'

Harlan fought a sudden strong urge to break eye contact. 'And what's that?'

'You're a menace to society. A madman.'

Madman. The word lodged itself like a splinter in Harlan's mind. Others of his own making joined it. *A killer, a potential murderer, a monster. Is he right? Is that what I am?* Not wanting to give Garret the satisfaction of seeing that he'd got to him, he forced himself to hold his gaze a moment longer. His voice

247

almost toneless, he said, 'I wasn't going to say thanks,' and turned to leave.

'One more thing, Miller.'

Harlan paused but kept his back to Garrett. He watched the fifth figure in the line-up being cuffed, ready to be returned to the cells. Garrett coughed, as if something was stuck in his craw, before saying, 'Mr and Mrs Sutton's solicitor will be in contact about the money.'

'Money?' Harlan echoed vaguely, only half listening. The line-up participants were filing out of the neighbouring room, all of them still wearing their balaclavas, but only one cuffed.

'The reward money for finding their son. The Suttons want to thank you personally too.'

Harlan shook his head. 'Tell them the best way they can thank me is by spoiling Jamie every chance they—' He was cut off by a scream so full of hysterical rage it barely sounded human. It was followed by the sound of a scuffle in the corridor. He yanked the door open in time to see DI Sheridan struggling to restrain Susan as, eyes bulging like a demented cartoon character's, she clawed at the handcuffed man, missing him by inches. 'Where's Ethan?' she shrieked. 'What have you done to my baby boy? You sick fuck! I'll fucking kill—' Her words were choked off by DI Sheridan hauling her backwards.

Harlan stepped between Susan and Nash, who was being hurried away by a couple of uniforms. She lurched forward again, hands flailing. He winced, his stitches pulling painfully as she staggered against him. Instinctively, he wrapped his arms around her. She briefly strained to break loose. Then, suddenly, her body went limp and she was sobbing, and he was doing what he'd thought he couldn't do, he was holding her head on his shoulder, shushing her. He looked at Kane, who was shrunk back against a wall, pale and staring. He tried to reassure him

248

with his eyes, before transferring his gaze to Garrett. The DCI, his face flushed with dismayed embarrassment, was already forming an apology on his lips but Harlan spoke first. 'Jesus! What is this? Fucking amateur hour?' Keeping one arm around Susan, he walked her out of the station. The sound of Garrett giving someone the hair-dryer treatment reverberated after them. When they got to the car, she drew away abruptly.

'I'm all right now,' she said. Harlan caught a flicker of guilt in her tear-swollen eyes as she turned to Kane. 'I'm sorry.' Harlan couldn't tell if she was apologising for scaring the boy or for allowing herself to be held by the man who'd killed his dad.

'It's OK, Mum.' There was still a note of shock in Kane's voice, as if he'd seen a side to her, a savagery, that he hadn't known existed. But when she held out her hand, he took it without hesitation and they got into the car.

Harlan turned to Jim, who'd followed them outside. 'What do you think? Nash was the only one Kane hesitated over. It can't be coincidence, right?'

'There's no such thing.' Jim jerked his thumb at the station. 'Sorry about what happened in there. It was unforgivable.'

'It's not me you should be apologising to. Besides, perhaps it wasn't such a bad thing. It might give Nash something to think about, seeing the face of the suffering he's caused.'

Jim made a doubtful gesture. 'He'd have to be human first.'

'He's human. In fact, he's all too human. Mary Webster proved that.'

'Yeah, well he makes me ashamed to be part of the same species.'

'How's it going with Jones?'

'Same as last time you asked: he's still in hospital, we're still searching.' Jim glanced through the car's rear window. Susan's head was rested back, eyes closed. She might've been asleep, except the muscles of her jaw were working spasmodically. He sighed. 'Look after them, Harlan, and yourself. You look like shit, by the way. Anybody told you that?'

Harlan smiled thinly. 'Yeah.'

He ducked into the car. Susan didn't open her eyes. Still gripping her hand, Kane sat hunched down in the back seat as if trying to hide from someone. As the car pulled away from the station, it started raining.

Chapter Twenty

The journey passed in silence, except for the continuous drumming of the rain on the roof. When they arrived at Susan's house, she got out without a word, pulling Kane after her. Harlan followed her into the living room. She slumped into the armchair and closed her eyes again. Kane stood staring at her, as if he wanted to say something, maybe to make her feel better, or maybe to seek reassurance himself. 'Mum,' he said, with a tentative tremor. No response. He tried again. 'Mum.' Still no response. His lips quivered, his forehead tied itself into a knot. 'It's not my fault,' he yelled, jerking around and running upstairs. A door slammed, music began to thump against the ceiling.

Harlan lowered himself onto the sofa and was reminded by a jolt of pain that it was time for his pills. As he swallowed them dry, he wondered what Kane had meant: that it wasn't his fault he hadn't recognised Nash's voice, or that it wasn't his fault Ethan had been abducted. Either was possible. After all, he might feel a coward for not trying to stop the kidnapper. Harlan was about to head upstairs and try to reassure Kane that he had nothing to feel guilty about, when Susan said, 'What if Kane's right? What if Nash isn't the one?'

'He's the one.'

Susan opened her eyes and looked at Harlan with piercing intensity. 'How can you be certain?'

'I can't,' he admitted. 'All I can do is trust what the evidence and my instincts are telling me.'

Susan heaved a breath, and a soul-destroying weariness came into her eyes as she glanced at the ceiling. 'I'd better go talk to him.'

'It's all right. I'll go. Close your eyes, get some rest.'

Susan started to frown, but she was too exhausted to enquire as to what made Harlan think Kane would speak to him. She merely made a sound as if to say, *Rest? How the hell can I rest?*

One hand pressed against his throbbing wound, Harlan climbed the stairs and knocked on Kane's door. The boy's voice rose over the music. 'Go away!'

'It's me, Harlan.'

There was a moment's hesitation. Then the music went off and the door opened. Kane had his wannabe tough guy face on – a face that made him look uncannily like his father. 'What do you want?'

'Just to talk. Make sure you're OK.'

'I'm fine. Why shouldn't I be?'

'You seemed upset.'

'Yeah I was, cos she,' Kane stabbed a finger at the floor, 'doesn't believe me about that man not being the one who took Ethan. None of you do.'

'It's not that we don't believe you. It's just that you were very scared when your brother was taken.' Seeing a frown form on Kane's face, Harlan added quickly, 'And that's nothing to be ashamed of. Anybody would've been. But what you've got to understand is, fear does strange things to people. It makes them see and hear things differently.'

An angry vein popped out on Kane's forehead. 'There's nothin' wrong with my hearing. It wasn't fuckin' him!'

There was such conviction in his voice that Harlan found

himself almost believing him. Almost, but not quite. Everything pointed to Nash. It had to be him. Who the hell else could it be? He raised a placatory hand. 'I didn't come up here to argue. I just wanted you to know that you've got nothing to feel bad about. You did really well at the line-up. I've seen grown men fall apart at those things. But you held it together. You should be proud of yourself.'

Kane's tough-guy mask slipped a little. Hesitancy replaced his anger. 'You really think so?'

'I know so.'

'You want to come in my room? We could play on my Xbox.'

Harlan looked beyond Kane. There was nowhere for him to sit comfortably except Ethan's bed, which would've been like trespassing on something sacred. His gaze moved to the damp patch over the rain-lashed window. Water was seeping down the wall, dripping in a steady stream into a cardboard box crammed full of plastic action figures and other cheap toys. 'It always does that when it rains,' said Kane, following Harlan's line of vision.

'You'd better move that box.' Harlan started to turn away.

'Where are you going?' There was an anxious edge to Kane's tone.

'To get a pan or something to catch the drips.'

Harlan went down to the kitchen and rooted through the cupboards until he found a large pan. As he made to take it upstairs, Susan opened her eyes and asked, 'How is he?'

'He's OK. A little shaken up, but OK.'

Susan glanced at the pan. 'What's that for?' When Harlan told her, she heaved a sigh. 'The roof's fucked. I had it fixed a couple of years back, but when it rains hard water gets into the boys' room.'

'Whoever fixed it didn't do a very good job then, did they?'

'It wasn't the roofer's fault. He wanted to replace some tiles

253

but I couldn't afford it. So he just had to patch it up as best he could.'

'Have you got his number?'

Susan shook her head. 'He was a mate of Neil's. I can't even remember his name.'

'Well we need to get someone out to fix it, otherwise Kane's going to end up with pneumonia.'

Susan's breath came with a tremor through her nostrils. She tugged at her hair as if trying to uproot it. 'Oh Christ, I can't handle this. Not now.'

'You don't have to. I'll sort it out. You got a Yellow Pages?'

'I think there's one somewhere around here.' Susan's gaze skimmed over the piles of missing-person posters.

'I'll take this up to Kane while you look for it.'

When Harlan got upstairs, Kane had dragged the box away from the wall, exposing a patch of black fungal mush where once there'd been plaster. Harlan placed the pan under the drip. It began to fill slowly but surely. 'We need something bigger. That'll be overflowing in no time. Can you think of anything we could—' He broke off as he turned and saw Kane's face. The mask had fallen away completely, revealing the fear that lurked behind it.

'He looked at me.' Tears hovered in Kane's voice. 'At the police station, that man Mum went for, he looked at me, and I looked at him, and, and...' He trailed off, trying to choke back the tears now forming in his eyes, lowering his head as if he was ashamed.

Harlan put his hands on Kane's shoulders. The boy tensed a little but didn't pull away. 'Look at me, Kane.' Kane reluctantly met his eyes. 'You don't need to worry about him. He won't ever be able to hurt you. They're going to put him in prison and never let him out.'

'What if he escapes?'

'He won't. They'll lock him away in the deepest, darkest hole they've got. Do you hear?'

Kane nodded. Some, but not all, of the fear left his eyes. Harlan squeezed his shoulders. 'Good. Now keep an eye on that pan.' He returned to Susan, who was in the kitchen making tea. She pointed to a Yellow Pages on the table. He flicked through it, phoning roofers until he found one willing to come as soon as it stopped raining. Susan handed him a mug. It felt heavy as a rock as he lifted it to his lips. 'I think I need to lie down.'

'What you need is something to eat. Get yourself on the sofa and I'll bring you a sandwich.'

Harlan went through to the living room and slumped onto the sofa. He was asleep within seconds. When he awoke, there was a sandwich waiting for him on the arm of the sofa. As he took a bite, his attention was drawn to the window by the clatter of a ladder outside. He rose and peered between the curtains. It'd stopped raining. A pair of workmen's boots disappeared up the ladder. 'They came while you were sleeping,' said Susan, entering the room and sitting down.

Harlan returned to the sofa and finished his sandwich. There was a knock. Raising a hand to indicate Susan should stay put, Harlan answered the door. 'All right, mate,' said a rugged-faced man. 'I've had a look at your roof and someone's done a right bodge job. They've slapped a load of bitumen over your busted slates. I ain't got nothin' with me to fix it properly today but I can put another coat of bitumen on it. That'll keep you dry for a few days, until I can get back.'

Harlan glanced enquiringly at Susan. She nodded, and he said to the roofer, 'Do it.'

Harlan sat listening to the roofer working and Susan busying herself in the kitchen, and trying not to listen to the remorseless ticking of the clock on the mantelpiece. The faint acrid smell of bitumen mingled with the scent of whatever Susan was cooking, making him feel a touch queasy. Tick, tick, tick. The clock seemed to be getting louder with every passing second. The sound of it got inside him, reverberating along his bones, echoing in his skull. How much longer? How much longer would Nash hold out? How much longer could Ethan survive? Tick, tick, tick. Even in his weakened state, he fidgeted restlessly. He wanted to do something, even if that something was only scouring the streets for Ethan or handing out leaflets. But he knew he didn't have the strength for it. All he had the strength to do was sit and wait and listen. Tick, tick, tick...

His mobile phone rang. He snatched it out. A number he didn't recognise flashed up. Heart hammering, he answered it.

'Mr Harlan Miller?' said an unfamiliar male voice.

'Yes.'

'My name's Guy Farrell of C and G Solicitors. I'm calling on behalf of Jamie Sutton's—'

'Get off the fucking line and don't tie this phone up again. You hear?' Without waiting for a reply, Harlan hung up.

'Who was that?' asked Susan, poking her worry-lined face into the room.

'No one important.'

Harlan closed his eyes, massaging his temples. The details of Ethan's abduction and everything that'd happened since reeled through his brain, like a movie on endless repeat. Occasionally he pressed pause to examine some minutiae or other, trying to figure out if it was the piece that would solve the puzzle. The piece that would deliver Ethan to him. But the solution remained maddeningly elusive. He felt as helpless and impotent as when Tom died. It made him want to shout, to scream, to weep. Tick, tick, tick. His fingers dug painfully into his temples.

His eyes snapped open at a knock on the front door. He rose to answer it.

'All done,' said the roofer. He started to bang on about prices and materials, but his words barely registered on Harlan's brain. He just kept nodding, until the man turned and got into his van.

Susan called Harlan and Kane to the kitchen. Relieved to get away from the clock, Harlan mechanically shovelled pasta down his throat without tasting it. Kane ate as if he were in a trance. He answered with only the slightest of nods when Harlan asked if he'd emptied out the pan. Once his plate was clean, he rose without asking permission to leave the table and returned upstairs. Susan didn't seem to notice, or if she did, she didn't seem to care. She wiped and rewiped the work surfaces, rubbing almost frantically at invisible stains. Harlan watched her, knowing what was coming. She stopped suddenly and her head dropped onto her arms. Her shoulders quaked in time to her muffled sobs. Harlan rose and put his hand on her back. He didn't say anything. He just stood there, willing her the strength to go on. Her head jerked up at a knock on the door.

'I'll go and see who it is,' said Harlan. Peering through the living-room curtains, he saw the dishevelled figure of Neil. 'Persistent son-of-a-bitch,' he murmured, with a wry smile of appreciation.

'Who is it?' Susan hissed from the opposite doorway.

Before Harlan could say, Neil's voice rang out as if in answer. 'Susan, it's me. I know you're in there and… and I know you still have feelings for me. If I'm wrong, tell me and I'll leave you alone.'

No you won't, thought Harlan.

'Please, Susan. I just want to talk. Just give me five minutes. Five minutes for everything we've been through together. That's all I ask.'

Susan moved slowly towards the door, as if Neil's words were reeling her in.

'I told you I won't give up on us. Not until you—' Neil broke off as Susan opened the door. His mouth worked silently, as if all the words he wanted to say to her were blocking each other's way in their desperation to get out. 'T... thank you,' he managed to stammer. The look of almost pathetic gratitude written across his face faded as he noticed Harlan. In its place, jealousy vied with nervous hostility. 'What's *he* doing here?'

'He's stopping me from going out of my fucking mind, that's what,' Susan said sharply. 'Actually, you know what, to hell with this.' She started to shut the door but Neil jammed his foot against it.

'I'm sorry, Susan. It's just that I was surprised to see him. I didn't think you'd ever let him in your house.'

'Neither did I, but things change.'

'Take your foot out of the door,' Harlan said to Neil.

'It's OK,' said Susan, reaching for her coat. 'I'm going out. I shouldn't be long. If anyone phones—'

'I'll call you straight away.' Harlan gave Neil a hard look of warning. The younger man's eyes dropped away from his. Neil held his hand out for Susan but she walked past him without taking it. Like an eager puppy, he trotted after her.

Harlan lay on the sofa. There was no sound from upstairs. The house was silent, except for the ticking of the clock. The painkillers were wearing off but he didn't reach for more. Instead, he focused on the pain, using it to deaden his psychological agony. Five minutes passed. Ten. Fifteen. The daylight began to drop, but still Susan didn't return. Whatever Neil was saying, she was obviously listening. A piercing scream clawed the throat of the silence. Heart lurching, Harlan jerked to his feet. An electric shock of pain almost sent him reeling back onto the sofa. Clutching his wound, he climbed the stairs as fast as his leaden legs could manage. Another scream rang out as he entered Kane's bedroom. The boy was laid fully clothed on his bed, eyes closed, face contorted in terror. A sheen of sweat glistened on his flushed cheeks. Harlan shook him gently. 'Kane.'

'I saw him,' Kane gasped, half sitting up, eyes popping wide. 'I saw him at the window.'

'Saw who?'

'That man from the line-up.'

'No you didn't, you were dreaming. It was only a nightmare.'

Harlan's words smoothed the fear from Kane's face. He dropped back onto his pillows. Harlan's nose wrinkled at the room's warm, mildewy air. He moved to open the window. A tang of bitumen wafted in on the cool breeze. 'Are you OK now?'

Kane nodded. 'Where's my mum?'

'She had to go out. She'll be back soon. I'll be downstairs if you need me.'

Harlan headed for the kitchen and a glass of water. He swallowed his pills, then sat perfectly still, waiting for them to kick in. Another half an hour ticked by. A new kernel of worry began to form in his mind. Where the hell was Susan? He was about to reach for his phone to find out when Kane rushed into the room and exclaimed, 'I know who it is.'

'What do you mean, you know who it is?'

Kane's words tumbled out in a breathless rush. 'He's the man I saw at my bedroom window.'

'You had another dream.'

Kane shook his head frantically. 'I don't mean now. I saw him there ages and ages ago. He came to fix our roof.'

Harlan frowned up at the boy. 'Let me get this straight, you're saying the man who fixed the roof two years ago is the man who took Ethan.'

'Yes.'

'How can you be sure?'

'Cos there was the same smell then that there is now. It's the smell I smelled on the man I saw in my bedroom. You've got to believe me. It's him. He's the one! He's the one!'

Harlan held up a hand, palm outwards. 'OK, I believe you.' As soon as he said it, he realised he meant it. Suddenly the puzzle made sense. The smell, that was the missing piece. It was so elusive that only chance could've found it, so intangible that it couldn't not be believed. That was why Nash had agreed to cooperate with the line-up, not out of some sense of guilt or some warped way of apologising to Mary Webster, but because he had no fear of further incriminating himself or Jones. He hadn't abducted Ethan. This man, the roofer, he was the one. And Neil had brought him here. All the doubts and questions about Neil came rushing back to the surface of Harlan's mind. Was he involved after all? And if he was, what the hell was this all about? Was it a sexual thing? No, if it was then he'd already got what he was after. He wouldn't be pleading with Susan to take him back. As far as Harlan could see, that left only one possibility: money. If Neil was part of this, it had to be about money. Harlan suddenly found himself hoping with everything he had that Neil was part of it, because if he was, if he and this roofer had cooked up some plan to get their hands on the reward, surely that meant Ethan was still alive. 'Do you remember the man's name?'

'I was never told it.' Kane's anxiously rounded eyes scanned Harlan's features. 'What you gonna do?'

In reply, Harlan took out his phone and dialled Jim. His ex-partner's voice came wearily through the phone. 'What is it, Harlan? I told you I'd phone if—'

'I don't think Nash took Ethan,' interrupted Harlan.

'What the hell are you talking about? Of course he did. Why are you saying this now when we're so close to cracking the case?'

Harlan told Jim why. Jim considered what he'd heard a brief moment, then he said, 'I don't buy it. You're talking about a relatively common smell. Something thousands of people come into contact with every day.'

'So you're saying this is a coincidence.'

'I...' Jim trailed off into a sigh. 'OK, point taken. I'll have someone look into this. What's the guy's name?'

'I don't know, but I can find out.'

'Well get back to me when you do. But understand this, Harlan, most of our resources are tied up investigating Nash and Jones, so it may take a few days to get round to following this up.'

'Don't give me that, Jim. You owe me.'

'I know, and I trust your instincts more than my own. But I need more than what you're telling me if I'm going to convince Garrett to pull manpower off our prime suspects and put them on this.'

'Fine.' Harlan's voice rose with irritation. 'You need more, I'll fucking get it.'

'Don't be like that—'

Harlan hung up on Jim mid-sentence. He looked at Kane. 'I want you to go to your bedroom.'

'Why?'

'Just do it. And no matter what you hear, don't come down here unless I call you. Understand?'

With sullen reluctance, Kane nodded and turned to head upstairs. Harlan dialled Susan. She answered within a ring. 'What is it? What's happened?'

'I just wondered where you are.' Harlan kept his voice carefully neutral. If Susan picked up on his anxiety, there was a good chance Neil would too. And he didn't want to do anything that might put Neil on his guard.

'I'm heading back now. I'll be there in a few minutes.' Susan's voice sounded different – lighter, stronger. Harlan guessed that she'd done more than merely listen to Neil, she'd bought what he was selling.

'Is Neil still with you?'

'Yes. Why?'

'No reason. I'll see you soon.' Harlan hung up and went through to the kitchen. He opened the cutlery drawer, chose a sharp knife with a four-inch blade and slipped it into the pocket of his tracksuit bottoms.

Chapter Twenty-One

Harlan was hunting through the cupboards for string or Sellotape or anything else he could use, if necessary, to bind Neil's wrists, when the sound of the front door opening drew his attention. Susan and Neil were holding hands now. Neil was doing his best to look grave, but there was a kind of excitability about his manner, as if he could barely contain his elation at being given a second chance. Susan looked better too. For the first time in days, there was some real colour in her cheeks. Harlan felt a pang of regret that once again he was going to shake not only her trust in Neil, but her faith in her ability as a mother. If Neil did turn out to be involved, she'd probably never be able to let a man into her life again. That'd be a tiny price to pay, though, for Ethan's safe return.

Susan led Neil into the kitchen. 'So you've decided to give it another go,' Harlan said, stating the obvious, not wanting to rush in with questions that might put Neil on his guard.

Susan nodded, giving Harlan a sheepish look, as if she wasn't sure how he'd react to the news. 'People might say I'm a fool for giving him a second chance, and maybe I am, but... well, the thing is...' She trailed off awkwardly.

'You don't have to justify yourself to me.'

'I know, but I feel I owe you an explanation. Everything that's happened this past couple of months, the way Neil's been there

263

for me, it's really made me realise just how much he means to me. I don't want to lose that, not on top of everything else I've lost.' She gave Neil a glance. 'I understand now why he lied to me. And he understands that if he ever does it again, it's over. No more chances.'

'I won't need another chance,' Neil said. 'I promise on my life.' He held out a hand to Harlan. 'Sorry about before.'

'No need.' Harlan took Neil's hand. He held it longer than was necessary, staring searchingly into Neil's eyes. They were weak-looking eyes. The eyes of someone who lacked self-esteem, someone who might be easily led. Not the eyes of a hardened criminal.

Blinking, Neil pulled his hand free.

Susan glanced at the ceiling, her mind suddenly elsewhere. 'How's he been?' Harlan told Susan about Kane's nightmare. Her face wrinkled with concern. 'Maybe I should go see him.'

'I wouldn't. I think he's sleeping.' Casually, as if as an after-thought, Harlan added, 'The wall seems to be drying out.'

'What wall?' asked Neil.

'The roof started leaking again where your mate... What was his name?' asked Susan.

Perfect, thought Harlan, *she's doing the job for me.*

Neil hesitated to reply. The faintest ripple of a frown crossed his forehead, but it was impossible to tell whether the question had sparked a flame of unease or he was merely searching his memory. 'Martin Yates.'

Susan clicked her fingers. 'Martin Yates. That was it. We had to call a roofer out today to fix his botch job.'

'Have you got his phone number?' Harlan asked Neil.

'Why?'

'I'm thinking about ringing him to ask for Susan's money back.'

264

'I haven't got his number. He was just some bloke I played darts with a couple of times. It's been over a year since I last saw him.'

'There's no need to talk to him,' said Susan, her eyes narrowing slightly, as if she was wondering whether there was more to Harlan's question than his words indicated. 'Like I said, he did the roof on the cheap. I'm lucky it's lasted as long as it has.'

'Well maybe he can do the job cheaper than we were quoted today.'

The narrowness left Susan's eyes. Harlan knew that she knew him well enough by now to know that he couldn't care less about the spending or saving of a few quid. And he saw that, even if she didn't understand his game, she was playing along, as she said, 'Um, well, I suppose it makes sense to ask. It's not as though any of us is flush with cash.' She turned to Neil. 'Where did you meet Martin?'

Again, Neil hesitated. Again, a frown gathered on his face, deeper this time. Again, Harlan couldn't tell whether he was troubled or simply struggling to remember. 'The Railway Hotel on Bramall Lane.'

Harlan knew the Railway well – as did any copper who'd ever policed a Sheffield United match. 'Come on then.' He reached for Eve's car keys. 'Let's go see if we can find him.'

Neil's eyebrows lifted. 'What? Now? Can't it wait?'

Harlan shook his head. 'It was like Niagara Falls in Kane's room this afternoon. If the roof goes again, it won't only be a few tiles that need replacing. The plaster will need stripping back, a new ceiling will have to be put in, the carpet and floorboards will have to be ripped—'

'OK, OK, I get the point,' sighed Neil. He looked concernedly at Susan. 'Will you be all right on your own?'

She nodded. Neil leaned in to kiss her, but she turned her head so that his lips brushed her cheek. A small tick of hurt pulled at his face, but he managed a smile. 'This shouldn't take long.'

They headed to the car. As Neil got into the passenger seat, Susan pulled Harlan back by the arm and hissed in his ear, 'What's going on?'

'I just want to check something out. It's probably nothing.'

'You don't think Neil's—'

'We'll talk later.'

He ducked into the car. Neil waved at Susan as they pulled away. She didn't wave back. Neil released another sighing breath. 'This is going to be a complete waste of time. Chances are, Martin won't even be there.'

'If he isn't, we'll ask around, see if anyone knows how to get hold of him.' As he spoke, Harlan watched Neil from the corner of his eye, taking in every movement, examining every detail of his face. Was his complexion a shade paler than usual? It was difficult to tell in the unnatural glow of the street lamps. His hands were clenched on his thighs, the veins showing unusually prominent on the backs of them. A sign of anxiety, perhaps. A few silent minutes passed. Neil's right hand crept into his coat pocket. *What's he got in there?* wondered Harlan. *A knife? A phone? Is he trying to send someone a text to warn them? Is it possible to send a text blind?* He resisted an urge to yank Neil's hand out of his pocket. He was glad he'd done so a second later, when Neil took out his glasses and put them on.

Sheffield United's stadium loomed up from the city skyline as Harlan turned onto Bramall Lane. Across the road from the south-west corner of the stadium stood the Railway Hotel. They pulled over and got out of the car. Neil hurried towards the pub's entrance. As with his hesitant reaction to Susan's questions, there was no way of telling whether his feet were quickened by nerves or impatience to return to her. 'Slow down,' Harlan said through gritted teeth, struggling to keep up.

'Sorry, I forgot about your injury. It's just I don't like leaving Susan alone.'

It wasn't a match day and the pub was empty except for a scattering of early evening drinkers hunched over their drinks – mostly glazed-eyed men with nowhere better to be, or hiding from their families and themselves. Harlan recognised them well from the years between Tom and Robert Reed's deaths. He watched Neil scan the bar, wondering whether he'd told the truth about meeting Yates here. A dartboard in one corner at least partially suggested he had done.

'He's not here,' said Neil, his voice flat, expressing neither disappointment nor relief.

They approached the barman and Harlan asked if he knew Yates. 'Sorry, mate, never heard of him,' came the reply. They made their way around the bar's patrons and got the same response from all of them. Harlan saw no flicker of recognition in any of their eyes to suggest they were lying.

'He's obviously not a regular here,' he said, frowning in thought. 'We could check out some of the other pubs around here.'

Neil expelled a breath of irritation. 'What's the big deal about finding this guy? He didn't even do a good job. Surely it's better to spend a few quid extra and get the job done properly.'

As he spoke, a man came out of the toilets. 'Excuse me, mate,' said Harlan. 'I'm looking for Martin Yates. Do you know him?'

'Yeah, I know Martin, but I've not seen him in months.'

'Any idea how I can get hold of him?'

'He used to drink in the Cricketers' sometimes.'

Harlan thanked him, and they headed for the car. The Cricketers' Arms was a few hundred yards further along Bramall Lane. As they drove past the stadium, Neil sat with his arms crossed, hunched forward in his seat. 'This is ridiculous,' he muttered. 'Susan—'

'Will be fine,' interjected Harlan. *He's getting panicky*, he thought. *Keep pushing his buttons, see how he responds. If he's truly involved in Ethan's abduction, maybe you can nudge him into sticking his neck out.* 'Don't worry, I'll find Yates. That's what I'm good at. Jim – that's my ex-partner – he used to say I was like a sniffer dog on a trail. Once I get the scent, I never give up.'

Neil gazed at the approaching pub, seemingly brooding over Harlan's words. As they pulled over, he turned to Harlan and said, 'This isn't only about the roof, is it?'

'What makes you say that?'

'I just don't believe you'd go to all this trouble over a few quid. I know you've got money. Susan told me you tried to give her thousands.'

Straight as a dart, Harlan looked Neil in the eyes. *Offer him just enough rope to hang himself with*, said his cop's brain. 'I have reason to believe Martin Yates abducted Ethan.'

Neil's eyes widened. 'What reason?'

'A good reason,' said Harlan, trying to judge whether or not Neil's surprise was genuine. 'That's all you need to know for now.'

'But I thought Jones and that other guy took him.'

'They did as far as the police are concerned.'

'You mean you've told them and they don't believe you.'

Harlan nodded.

Neil shook his head in indignant amazement. 'How can they doubt you after what you've done?'

'They have procedures to follow.'

'Bollocks to their procedures.' Neil's eyes flashed with uncharacteristic fierceness. 'If you say Martin Yates took Ethan, that's good enough for me.' He jerked open the car door. 'We'll find him, if we have to look in every pub in this city.'

Harlan could detect no false note in Neil's voice, no trace of insincerity in his expression. If he was acting, it was a convincing performance. He recalled what Neil had shouted to Susan the first night he'd come banging at the door. *I'd rather die than lose you!* If those words were true, surely they marked him out as innocent. Looking at Neil's nervous but determined boy–man face, part of Harlan couldn't help but want to believe they were. He wanted to believe love meant more than money, more than life itself even. But if all those years on the force had taught him anything it was to view the world with the eyes of a cynic. He motioned for Neil to enter the pub first. He didn't want to take his eyes off him. Not for a second. He realised that might prove difficult when he saw how busy the pub was. There was a band playing, and the room was wall-to-wall with bodies that reluctantly parted as the two men approached the bar. Someone swayed against Harlan, knocking him off balance. Someone else's elbow poked into his midriff – not hard, but hard enough to double him over. 'Wait,' he called to Neil, but his pain-choked voice couldn't make itself heard above the grinding music and rowdy crowd. He lowered his head, gritting his teeth, sucking up the pain, then straightened.

Neil was nowhere to be seen.

Angry glances flashed at Harlan as, eyes darting from side to side, he elbowed his way forward. People were standing three deep at the bar. Neil wasn't amongst them. His heart was pounding now. He stood on his tiptoes, craning his neck, ignoring the stretching agony in his gut. No sign of Neil. 'Fuck,' he hissed. This wasn't good. This wasn't good at all! 'Where are the toilets?' he shouted in someone's ear. They pointed to a door at the rear of the room, and he headed for it. Sweat was dribbling down his face by the time he reached the door. He yanked it open, half ran, half staggered along a short corridor and through a door with a male stick figure on it. He found himself facing a urinal trough. To its right were a couple of cubicles, one vacant, the other engaged. He kicked the locked door in, and felt something bust inside of him. Neil was standing facing him, goggle-eyed with shock, a phone pressed to his ear. Propelled by an explosion of searing pain, Harlan drove the heel of his hand against Neil's nose. There was a crunch of cartilage and plastic. Neil reeled back onto the toilet with instant tears in his eyes, his glasses broken, blood streaming from both nostrils. Harlan snatched the phone off him. A number he didn't recognise was dialling. He cut it off and pocketed the phone.

'I think you broke my nose,' Neil groaned nasally.

Harlan glared down at him. 'I'll do a lot fucking worse than that if you don't tell me who you were phoning.'

'I... I was calling my boss to say I won't be coming in to work.'

The lie was as shaky as Neil's hands that were pressed to either side of his nose. 'Bit late for that, isn't it? It's after eight. Your shift started at six.'

'Not tonight. I changed my hours so...' Neil trailed off under Harlan's gaze, which was sad and hard at the same time. Snuffling back blood, he gave a slight nod, as if to say, *OK, you got me.*

Harlan took out the knife. 'Who were you calling?'

Neil made no reply. For once there was no nervousness in his eyes, only blank resignation. The music briefly jumped in volume as someone entered the corridor to the toilet.

'Stand up,' commanded Harlan. Neil did so, and Harlan pulled him roughly out of the cubicle and jabbed the knife into his ribs. 'We're gonna walk out of here. Fuck with me and I'll stick this in you.'

Harlan put his hand holding the knife in his pocket. With his other hand closed like steel on Neil's arm, he guided him through the packed bar. His breath caught with every agonising step. Neil made no attempt to get away. When they reached the car, Harlan opened the boot. 'Get in.'

Neil compliantly folded himself into the cramped space.

'Who were you phoning?' Harlan asked again.

Still no answer.

'We can do this the hard way or the easy way.' Harlan thumbed the knife. 'I could go to work on you until you quite literally spill your guts, or you could just tell me the truth right now.'

Some of the animation came back into Neil's face. His pale, watery eyes blinked fearfully at Harlan. 'I already told you the truth.'

'Have it your own way.'

Harlan slammed the boot. He felt beneath his sweatshirt. A wetness seeped through the bandage, warm and sticky against his fingers. The wound was bleeding, but not badly enough to prevent him from doing what needed to be done – he hoped. He got behind the wheel and accelerated back the way they'd come. There was no time to follow through on his threat. Even unanswered, Neil's phone call might give warning to Yates that something was wrong – assuming that's who it was intended for. Speed was everything now. And he could see only one way to prove quickly and irrefutably whether or not Neil was lying. Yet the thought of the trauma this would cause almost made

271

him wish there was time to take Neil out to some isolated place and beat the truth from him.

He sped through the city streets, ignoring red lights, overtaking at every opportunity. Neil's phone rang. He snatched it out. The same number flashed up on its screen. The caller rang off after a few seconds. Harlan returned the phone to his pocket and pressed down harder on the accelerator. Minutes later, he screeched to a stop outside Susan's house and popped the boot. Dazed and blinking, Neil uncoiled himself from its confines. 'I don't want Susan to see me like this,' he said, resisting as Harlan pulled him towards the house. 'It'll upset her.'

There was no time to talk or reason. Harlan slapped Neil hard. As if it'd been programmed into his nervous system, Neil instantly went into a blank, passive state again. Harlan hammered on the door. Even before he stopped knocking, Susan opened it. Her eyes grew big at the sight of Neil's bloodied face. 'What happened? Who did that to you?'

'I did,' said Harlan, hauling Neil into the living room and shoving him onto the sofa.

'What? Why?'

'Cos he's crazy, that's why,' said Neil, snapping himself out of his stupor with a shake of his head. 'He's got it into his messed-up head that I had something to do with Ethan's abduction.'

Susan's face twisted into an expression caught between suspicion and fear. 'Why would he think that?'

'Because I tried to phone my shift manager.'

A look of confusion took over Susan's features. 'I don't understand.'

'That makes two of us then.'

'Kane!' shouted Harlan.

'Harlan, will you tell me just what the hell's going on here?' Susan demanded to know as the boy came thundering downstairs.

In answer, Harlan took out Neil's phone. Kane pulled up abruptly, sucking his breath in at the sight of Neil. Harlan scrolled through the phone to the missed call list and found the number. Then he pulled out the knife and held it to Neil's throat. 'Jesus,' gasped Susan. 'What are you doing?'

'I told you he's crazy,' said Neil, his tone curiously flat for someone with a blade at their jugular.

He knows he's caught, thought Harlan. Pressing the blade's edge into Neil's flesh, Harlan breathed in his ear, 'Say one more fucking word and I swear to God I'll cut your throat. In fact...' His gaze scanned the room, coming to rest on the coat hooks by the door. He pointed to a scarf. 'Pass me that, will you?'

Susan hesitated, uncertainty clouding her haggard face.

'Do it,' snapped Harlan. 'There's no time for explanations now.'

Susan passed the scarf to Harlan. He snatched up a handful of missing-person flyers and stuffed them into Neil's mouth before gagging him with the scarf. Neil struggled for breath, expelling black plugs of congealed blood from his nostrils. Harlan's features softened as he looked at Kane. 'Come closer. You need to hear this.'

Kane remained motionless, eyes shining like those of a wild animal ready to fight or flee.

'Don't worry. No one's going to hurt you or your mum.'

Kane's gaze flicked to Susan. When she gave him a nod, he warily approached the sofa. Harlan raised a finger to his lips, then pressed the dial button. He put the phone on speaker mode. With each of the phone's rings, Neil flinched slightly, causing a thin line of blood to trickle down his throat. He closed his eyes as a gravelly male voice answered the phone. 'What you calling me on your moby for? I thought we agreed to use landlines only.'

Harlan watched for Kane's reaction, mouthing silently, 'Is it him?' The boy didn't shake his head or nod, but he didn't need to. His ashen face with its expression of paralysed fear told Harlan everything he needed to know.

'Neil, you there?' said the man. 'Neil—' Harlan hung up.

Susan's eyes widened as the penny suddenly dropped. 'That was him, wasn't it?' she hissed. 'That was the bastard who took Ethan.'

Kane nodded mutely.

Harlan tore away Neil's gag. 'Where's—' he started to say but before he could finish, Susan flew at Neil, her fists and nails flailing, drawing livid red track marks across his face. He made no attempt to defend himself.

'It was you!' she screamed. 'It was you all along! How could you do this?'

Neil's reedy voice quivered in reply. 'I did it for us.'

Harlan caught Susan's wrists as she swung at Neil again. 'There's no time for this, Susan!' His mind reeled with pain as she strained against his hold, trying to twist her arms free.

'Where's my boy? Where's Ethan?'

'He's not far away,' said Neil.

'Is he alive?'

Neil screwed up his face in horror at the suggestion that Ethan might not be. 'Of course he is. I told you, I'd never hurt the kids.'

Susan stopped struggling. A shudder passed through her. Tears swelled in her eyes. Her lips twitched, unable to express the pain and joy she felt. Harlan knew there was no time for the luxury of emotion. There was no time for anything except getting to Ethan. Right this moment, Yates would be wondering what was going on. He might be starting to panic. Maybe he'd even be thinking about disposing of the evidence. Harlan gestured at Kane. The boy blinked as if emerging from a trance, before quickly moving to take hold of his mother's wrist and draw her away from Harlan.

Harlan hauled Neil to his feet. 'You're gonna take me to Ethan right now.' His voice was as deadly sharp as the blade at Neil's throat. He pushed him towards the door.

Neil twisted to look at Susan, heedless of the way his Adam's apple dragged over the knife. 'I did it for us,' he said again, with a tremor of pitifully desperate love in his voice. 'Because I wanted us to have a life together.'

Susan looked at Neil with a hate in her eyes even more toxic than his love.

Crushed by what he saw, Neil's body sagged and his head drooped. As Harlan thrust him into the street, Susan broke away from Kane and ran after them. 'I'm coming with you.'

'No way,' said Harlan. 'It's too dangerous.'

'I don't give a fuck! I'm coming!'

Kane grabbed Susan's wrist again. 'Please, Mum, I don't want you to go.'

'Let go, Kane.' She tried to shake him off but he clung on like a limpet.

Turning quickly away from them, Harlan put his hand on Neil's head and none too gently guided him to the driver's seat. 'Don't you fucking go without me,' shrieked Susan, as he rushed around to the other side of the car. He just had time to reach across Neil and press the central-locking button before Susan yanked at the passenger door. She hammered on the window. 'Open this bastard door!'

Harlan thrust the ignition key into Neil's hand. 'Go! Go!'

With trembling fingers, Neil fumbled the key into the ignition. As they accelerated away, Harlan hissed in his ear, 'Remember what I said, if you fuck with me...' He trailed off, letting the threat hang between them.

'I won't.' Neil's voice matched his ghastly grey face, as he watched Susan recede in the rear-view mirror.

Chapter Twenty-Two

'Where are we going?' asked Harlan.

'Spital Street.'

Harlan had been called out to Spital Street numerous times during his years on the force. It traversed the lowermost edge of a rundown estate of maisonettes and flats perched on a hillside just north-east of the city centre. 'What address?'

'I know where it is, but I dunno the exact address. It's a second-floor flat.'

'Who lives there?'

'No one. It's empty. That's why Martin took Ethan there.'

'Is he the only other person involved in this?'

A slight hesitation, then, 'No. His girlfriend's in on it too. Her name's Paula. I dunno her surname. She lives in the flat below the one where we're keeping Ethan.'

Harlan took out his phone and dialled Jim. 'Have you got a name for me then?' his ex-partner asked, on answering the phone.

'I've got a lot more than that. Nash didn't abduct Ethan. Neil Price did.'

Jim released an exhausted breath. 'Make up your mind, Harlan. First you tell me this nameless roofer did it, now you—'

'Shut up and listen, Jim,' Harlan interrupted. 'They both did it. The roofer – his name's Martin Yates – him and Price are in it together, along with Yates's girlfriend.'

An instant's stunned silence followed, then Jim said, 'How do you know this?'

'Price told me himself. I'm in the car with him now, on my way to where they're holding Ethan.'

'You mean the boy's alive.'

'Yes.'

'Where?' There was no relief in Jim's voice. Within seconds, icy professionalism had overcome his initial surprise. Like Harlan, he knew they hadn't won the game yet, and the clock was running down fast.

'Spital Street. It's an empty second-floor flat.'

'But we searched all the unoccupied flats around there,' said Jim. 'How did we miss him?'

The answer was obvious to Harlan: Ethan had been kept elsewhere – and that elsewhere was almost certainly Yates's girlfriend's place – until after the police were done searching. But there was no time for explanations. 'We're in Eve's Toyota. I'll make sure we park directly outside the flat. You need to get some units over there fast. Yates might be onto me.'

'I'm already on it. How far away are you?'

'Not far. Five or ten minutes.'

'You'll be there before us then. Don't go trying to be a hero, Harlan. Wait in your car and let us do our job.'

'I'll do whatever it takes to get Ethan back safe.' Harlan hung up. A woozy feeling hit him, causing the road to momentarily double before his watering eyes. Shaking the dizziness from his head, he felt his bandage again. As he drew his hand away, rivulets of blood coursed between his fingers. Grappling with Susan, it seemed, had opened his wound fully. He wondered whether he'd have the strength to 'do whatever it takes'.

'So what was the plan?' Harlan asked, more to try and

fend off the tugging fingers of unconsciousness than because he needed to know right that moment.

Neil shrugged as if he wasn't sure, but then said in a strangled sort of voice, 'Paula was gonna phone the police and say she'd heard suspicious sounds in the flat above hers. When they came and found Ethan, she'd claim the reward and we'd split it three ways.'

'And who came up with this plan?'

Again, Neil shrugged. 'Me and Martin went out drinking a few months back. I don't usually drink, but Gary Dawson,' his upper lip curled with hate around the name, 'was threatening to send his thugs to my parents' house. I was going out of my head with worry. Martin's in even deeper with Dawson than me. We were talking about ways of making some quick cash, and I jokingly said we should try to find that missing boy, Jamie Sutton, and claim the reward. And Martin said it would be easier to just snatch a kid ourselves for the reward. So we started talking about how we might do it. We weren't being serious at first – at least, I wasn't...' Neil trailed off as if he wasn't entirely convinced of the truth of his words. 'Oh God, it sounds so insane now.'

'No it doesn't.' There was a simple, ruthless logic to everything Neil had said. Harlan wasn't about to let him use madness to exonerate himself from responsibility. A couple of things didn't make sense to him, though. 'But why risk abducting Ethan from his bed? Why not just snatch him off the street?'

'That was our original plan. We wanted to make it look like the same bloke who took Jamie Sutton took Ethan.'

'So why didn't you?'

'Ethan, that's why. Outside school, he never leaves Susan's side. He's been like that since his dad died. I remember even when me and Susan first got together, he used to ask her all the time, why did Dad leave us? She tried to explain, but he just couldn't get it into his head what death means. I guess he's afraid she'll leave him too.' The familiar guilt twisted inside Harlan as Neil continued, 'We kept waiting for a chance to grab him off the street, but it didn't happen. Martin got impatient. Dawson's thugs were hounding him. We talked about taking Ethan from the house. Martin was all for it but I didn't like the idea. The problem wasn't Susan – after she takes her Valium she's out of it for the night. The problem was Kane. If we were gonna do it that way, it would have to be on a night Kane was sleeping over at a friend's or something. But then Martin, the crazy fucker, just went ahead and did it. First I heard about it was when the coppers came to see me. I swear, I nearly had a heart attack.' Neil heaved a breath, shaking his head. 'I thought Martin was all right, but he's got serious problems up here.' He tapped his temple. 'If it hadn't been for him, I don't think I'd ever have gone through with this.'

'Bollocks,' retorted Harlan, sickened to his core by the nauseatingly familiar sound of someone trying to talk their way out of their guilt.

'It's true. Martin wasn't even going to give me my full share of the reward, cos he reckons I haven't done enough to earn it.'

'Whose idea was it to take Ethan?'

Neil was silent a moment, then he admitted, 'Mine.'

'Then you've done plenty to deserve everything you've got coming to you.'

'But all I did was come up with the idea; Martin and Paula did—' Neil broke off at a glance from Harlan that warned him there would be dire consequences if he continued to insist on his relative innocence.

They were nearing Spital Street. Three- and four-storey blocks of flats loomed over them, rising up one behind another like piles of boxes. Another wave of wooziness washed over Harlan, prompting him to ask, 'That's the other thing I don't get, why Ethan? Why not abduct some random kid?'

'Martin wanted to, but I told him it had to be Ethan or I wouldn't go through with it.'

'Why?'

'I know Ethan. I knew he wouldn't try to fight or escape. Plus, that way I could, y'know, stay close to the investigation and give Martin the heads up if the coppers began sniffing in his direction.'

Harlan narrowed his eyes in scrutiny, wondering whether Neil was really as stupid as his words suggested. If they'd done as Martin wanted, maybe, just maybe, their plan would've worked. But this way they had little or no chance of getting away with it. After Paula had contacted the police, it wouldn't have taken them long to connect her to Martin, and from Martin it was only three or four short steps to Neil. 'So you did all this for seventy-odd thousand quid.'

'We expected it would be a lot more. Jamie Sutton's reward was two hundred thousand.' Neil's voice took on a sneering tone. 'But it turns out most people in this piss-hole of a city won't put their hands in their pockets to save anyone except themselves. If they had done, this thing would've been over weeks ago.'

'Seventy thousand, two hundred thousand, a million. What's the difference? No amount of money's worth this.'

'That's easy for you to say. You haven't been fucked over by people your whole life.' Neil flashed Harlan a look sodden with resentment. 'Susan told me about you. You had it all, and you threw it away.'

Neil's words pierced Harlan deeper than Nash's knife had done. Talking about himself was the last thing he wanted to do. And Neil was the last person he owed an explanation of his past to. But still, he felt compelled to respond. 'I didn't throw it away, it was taken from me.'

'Bullshit. Your son died, but you still had a career, a house, a wife who loved you. You still had a million times more than me.'

I had nothing after Tom died! Nothing! Harlan wanted to yell, but he knew that wasn't true. The truth was he'd been so torn apart by pain, fear and rage that he'd wanted to nullify his identify, make his life nothing. And he'd almost managed it. Almost.

A bitter smile spread across Neil's face. 'I know your type. I've known you all my shitty life. You were one of the popular kids, I can tell. Things have always come easy to you. Easy come, easy go. But I've had to fight for everything I've got. I found happiness for the first time when I met Susan, and I wasn't about to let it go. No fucking way! When she told me she thought maybe we should stop—' He broke off suddenly, as if he'd said more than he intended to.

Looking at Neil, his plain, mousy features quivering with emotion, his parting words to Susan came back to Harlan. *I did it for us. Because I wanted us to have a life together.* And with them came the realisation of exactly what they meant. A strange kind of relief passed over him as he said, 'This was never about money. Susan was going to leave you. You took Ethan to stop her, to make her need you as much as you need her. Didn't you?' Silence was all the answer Harlan received, and all the answer he needed. 'You never intended to follow your plan through – at least, not the plan you and Yates cooked up. That's why this thing has dragged on so long. Because you knew that if Susan ever got Ethan back, you and her would be finished. But why involve Yates and his girlfriend? It would've been a lot simpler to abduct Ethan yourself, do him in and get rid of the body.'

'I could never hurt Ethan,' Neil retorted fervently.

'No, what I think you mean is, you haven't got the balls to hurt Ethan yourself. That's why you needed Yates. You needed him to kill Ethan.' Violent twitches pulled at Neil's face, twisting one side of it like a stroke victim, as Harlan continued, 'What were you planning to do? Feed Yates some bullshit about the police being onto him and panic him into killing the boy? But you didn't even have the nerve to make that call, did you? At least, not until I backed you into a corner.'

Neil slammed his foot on the brake, throwing Harlan against the dashboard. Both he and the tyres screamed in protest. Gasping in the stink of burning rubber, he clutched his wound. Something was bulging out of it, hard and bulbous. Too winded to speak, he twisted towards Neil, expecting him to make a run for it. But Neil was crumpled against the steering wheel, tears coursing down his cheeks. 'I love her,' he sobbed through clenched teeth. 'I love her more than my own life. I told her that, and she chucked it back in my face, said she didn't feel the same way. Said she was sorry. Sorry!' He spat the word out like vomit. 'She didn't love me. She pitied me. Do you know how that feels? To be pitied by someone you've offered everything you have? Of course you fucking don't.' He ground his head against the wheel, groaning, 'What was I supposed to do? What was I supposed to do?'

You were supposed to try and convince her she was making a mistake. And if that didn't work, you were supposed to cry, shout and beg, maybe even threaten to kill yourself. But you weren't supposed to do this, you pathetic little fuck. That was what Harlan wanted to say, but there was no time, and besides he didn't have enough breath in his lungs for it. 'Take me to

Ethan.' Neil was too deep in self-pity to hear Harlan's hoarse voice. Trembling with the effort, he grabbed Neil's ear and yanked him upright. 'I said take me to Ethan.'

Neil winced but made no attempt to remove Harlan's hand. 'He's in there.' He pointed at a boarded-up window on the second floor of a scaffolding-encased block of flats that appeared to be largely uninhabited. All the neighbouring windows were also as dark as the night sky, except for the flickering bluish glow of a TV coming from the flat below. 'Looks like Paula's in.'

'What about Yates?'

'I can't see his car. It could be parked around the back.'

'Get out.'

'Aren't you going to wait for the police? Martin used to box. He's a bit slow on the uptake, but he's fast with his fists. You're in no fit state to—'

'Shut up and do as I say.'

Neil got out of the car. Grimacing, Harlan did likewise. His body felt heavy as a sack of coal. Neil was right, he was in no fit state, but he couldn't take the risk that harm might come to Ethan while he waited out here. Leaning on the car, he limped around to the boot and opened it. 'Now get in there.'

Neil shook his head.

Harlan put the knife to Neil's throat. 'Fucking do it.'

Neil's tongue flicked nervously across his lips but he held his ground. 'You need my help to get into the flat. I know where the key's hidden.'

'Tell me.'

'I'll show you. Look, we're wasting time. Martin might be up there right now, wondering what's going on and what to do with Ethan.'

For a tense moment the two men looked at each other. Knowing he didn't have the strength to force Neil to do as he demanded, Harlan gestured at the flats with his knife. 'Move.' As they approached them, he held onto Neil's arm, more for support than to prevent him from making a break for it. He caught a glimpse through a crack in some curtains of a woman he assumed to be Paula. She was slumped low in an armchair, sipping from a can of lager, eyes vacantly staring from under a fringe of peroxide-blonde hair, black at the roots. She looked thirtyish, but it was difficult to tell with all the make-up plastered on. Her heavy-set body was squeezed into pink leggings and a matching vest top. A Celtic band tattoo encircled one fleshy bicep. There was no anxiety in her face, no sign that Martin had told her about Neil's silent phone call. Drawing hope from this, Harlan hurried past the window into a gloomy, piss-stinking stairwell.

When they reached the second-floor landing, which was lit only by the glow of the street lights, Harlan leaned heavily against a wall, struggling to find his breath. Neil approached a door, felt above its frame and found a key. Harlan held out his hand and Neil handed it over. Harlan raised a finger to his lips. As quietly as possible, he unlocked and opened the door. A faint damp smell wafted out. The hallway was almost pitch black. He stood listening for a few seconds. Not a sound. He tried a light switch, and wasn't surprised when nothing happened. Neil nudged him and pointed to a torch on the floor. That decided him – Yates wasn't there. He picked up the torch and switched it on. Its pale beam illuminated a dingy blue carpet and matching wallpaper, which was peeling away in places. There were two closed doors in the right wall. A third door stood a few inches ajar at the far end of the hallway.

'Which room?' whispered Harlan.

Neil shrugged. 'This is the first time I've been here.'

Harlan gave him a narrow look. 'So how did you know where the key was hidden?'

'Martin told me in case of an emergency.'

Pushing Neil ahead of him, Harlan approached the first door. It opened onto a tiny room with bare floorboards and mould-studded white walls. Several bulging black bin liners were piled in one corner. What looked like bed sheets stained with excrement and vomit had spilled out of one of them. Just inside the door was a chest of drawers with no drawers. Brown medicine bottles and silver blister packs cluttered its surface. Harlan read their labels. Blackcurrant-flavoured codeine linctus, diazepam and Traveleeze travel sickness tablets. He glanced darkly at Neil. 'You've been drugging him.'

'Not enough to hurt him, just enough to keep him subdued. I know what dose to give from working at the hospital.'

'They don't give diazepam to kids.'

Neil blinked away from Harlan's hard, condemning eyes. With the tip of his knife, Harlan prodded him towards the second door. When he saw the drawn bolts that'd been crudely fitted to the top and bottom of the door, his heart began to pound. He quickly unlocked them and turned the handle. The first thing he saw was the drawings. The lower portion of the room's walls was covered in colourful childish pictures of houses, vehicles, trees, people, animals and cartoon characters. *Mummy*, *Kane* and *Ethan* was written above the heads of three figures holding hands. Against the opposite wall, underneath a window that'd been boarded up from the inside as well as the outside, stood a bucket containing a stinking stew of piss and shit. The sight yanked Harlan's mind back to the dungeon where Jamie Sutton had been held, and he felt a dark tide of rage and revulsion rising. It surged up his throat like choking flames when he saw the mass of crumpled blankets on a mattress. Comics, colouring pens, crisp packets, chocolate bar wrappers and Coke cans littered the bed and threadbare carpet.

For several barely drawn breaths, Harlan stared at the bed as though turned to stone. Then, from deep within the blankets, came a flicker of movement. Forgetting his pain, he dashed forward and pulled the sheets away to reveal Ethan's face, very pale, but alive. Alive! Oh God, the relief. It hit him like a punch to the gut, forcing his breath out in a rush. The boy was wearing filthy Spiderman pyjamas. He'd lost weight, making him look as if he might break at the merest touch, but there was no sign of any injuries. His eyes were closed, the eyeballs moving rapidly beneath their lids. A frown rippled across the smooth surface of his forehead. His dry, cracked lips twitched in a silent scream but he was unable to pull himself from the depths of whatever nightmare he was trapped in.

'Ethan,' said Harlan. No response. He repeated the boy's name louder, tapping his cheek. Ethan's eyelids flickered and a soft moan escaped his lips but he still didn't wake. Harlan put the torch down, its beam facing the doorway. Gently sliding one arm under Ethan's neck and the other behind his knees, he attempted to lift him. The boy was light as a pillow, but he felt heavy as lead to Harlan. His whole body shook with the strain. His head swam in a flood of dizzy agony.

'Here, let me help,' offered Neil, stepping forward.

'Don't fucking touch him!' hissed Harlan, flashing him a look of violent wrath. It was then that he saw the figure wearing a balaclava standing behind Neil. The figure was about Harlan's height and build. In one hand – the backs of which were covered with curls of dark hair – he held some kind of old-fashioned revolver with a long barrel, which was aimed at Harlan.

'Put him down.'

Harlan recognised the voice immediately. It was the same voice he'd heard over Neil's phone. He lowered Ethan back onto the mattress and stood with his body shielding him, hands spread.

The eyes staring tensely out of the balaclava flicked towards Neil. 'What the fuck's going on?' their owner demanded to know. 'Who's he?'

'He's the one I told you about,' said Neil.

'The ex-copper?'

Neil nodded. 'Put the gun down, Martin.'

'Don't use my fuckin' name.'

'He already knows your name. He knows everything.'

'What? How the fuck—'

'I told him.'

Martin's eyes popped wide. 'Why?'

A sigh heaved from Neil. 'Does it matter?'

'Course it fuckin' does. Now tell me or I'll blast a hole in your face.'

'Do that and you'll go down for murder as well as kidnapping,' said Harlan.

'They'll have to catch me first.'

'You're already caught. The police are on their way.'

Martin cocked his head, listening. 'Then why don't I hear no sirens, eh?'

'Sirens would warn you they were coming. I know how they work, and believe me, right now this building's being surrounded by armed units. If you want to get out of here in one piece, I suggest you do as Neil says and put the gun down.'

Martin barked out a harsh laugh. 'You must think I'm stupid. There's no way in hell I'm putting this—' He broke off with a sharp exclamation as Neil lunged for the gun. The muzzle flashed, there was a concussive bang. Harlan felt the bullet go by his head. He staggered sideways, the smell of gunpowder stinging his nostrils, ears ringing, momentarily dazzled. When his vision cleared after a few seconds, he saw that Neil and Martin were locked together. Martin's free hand was pummelling Neil's face with short, powerful punches. Neil had Martin pressed against a wall. Both his hands were on the gun, yanking at it, prising Martin's fingers off the grip. As suddenly as they'd come together, the two men staggered apart. Only now, Neil was holding the gun. Gasping for breath, blood streaming from his nose and mouth, he pointed it at Martin.

'Don't,' cried Martin, flinging up his hands.

'Don't,' echoed Harlan. 'You pull that trigger and your life's over.'

Neil looked at Harlan. And when Harlan saw his eyes he knew what he was going to do.

'It already is. Tell Susan I'm sorry,' said Neil. Then he put the gun in his mouth and pulled the trigger. His head snapped back. Fragments of skull, brain matter and clotted hair splattered across the wall, oozing down over Ethan's drawings, making it look as if some kind of massacre had taken place. Neil briefly rocked on his heels, smoke trickling from the shattered remains of his mouth, before dropping the gun and pitching backwards.

Harlan's eyes darted between the gun and Martin. Martin's eyes did the same. Harlan gave a slight shake of his head. For a moment, time seemed to hold its breath. Then both men went for the gun. Martin was faster. He snatched it up and brought its butt down on Harlan's head. A corona of white light flashing over his vision, Harlan collapsed onto his face. He felt Martin press the gun against the back of his head. *So this is it*, he thought, *this is how I die*. 'Don't hurt the boy,' he said in a pained, ragged whisper. Hoping to buy some time, he added, 'You can still go through with your plan.'

'How the fuck's that possible?'

'I was lying about the police.'

'You mean they're not outside.'

'They don't know about any of this. No one else does.'

Martin mulled these words over for a few precious seconds. 'So let me get this straight, all I have to do is kill you and I'm in the clear.'

'Or I could take Neil's place as your partner. Think about it, I could tell the police I followed him here and found Ethan.' Harlan knew there was no logic in what he was saying, but every word kept him and, more importantly, Ethan alive another breath. 'That way, I'd be able to claim the reward, then we could split it.'

'And what's to stop you telling the coppers the truth once I don't have my gun pointed at your head?'

'You have my word of honour.'

'Your word of honour.' Martin snorted with laughter. 'Your word of fuckin' honour! That's classic, that is. Nice try, mate, but I'm afraid I'll have to turn down your—' He was interrupted by a shrill female voice calling to him from the landing.

'Martin! Martin!'

Scowling, he bellowed back, 'What the fuck do you want?'

'I saw some people creeping about outside. I think it's the coppers.'

The scowl turned into a taut-lipped grimace. Martin pressed the gun barrel even harder into Harlan's head. 'You fuckin' lying bastard,' he hissed. 'I ought to blow your fuckin' brains out just for the hell of it.'

Harlan closed his eyes and pictured Tom – the dark eyes peering out from beneath a tousle of equally dark hair, the cute snub nose and full, smiling lips. He saw him more clearly than he had done in years. So clearly he could almost reach out and touch him. A sense of calm stole over him. If this really was it, he was ready.

'Ach! You're not fuckin' worth it,' spat Martin.

Harlan felt him take the gun away. He heard him sprint out the room, slam the door and shoot the bolts. Before he had time to feel relief or anything else, he heard a low whimper from beside him. Twisting his head, he saw that Ethan was awake – awake and staring at Neil, eyes like huge marbles as they took in the destroyed face, the widening slick of blood. He could almost hear the hiss of the image branding itself on the boy's brain. From somewhere he found the strength to rise, enfold Ethan in his arms and turn him away from the corpse. The boy whimpered again and struggled weakly, but he subsided into trembling stillness as Harlan stroked his hair, shushing him and soothing, 'It's OK, Ethan. It's OK. It's OK.' Like a mantra, he repeated the words, until he heard booted feet in the hallway. 'In here,' he shouted.

The bolts clicked. The door jerked inwards. Two officers wearing bullet-proof vests and armed with pistols entered the room. 'Show us your hands!' bellowed one of them.

Overcome by a sudden reluctance to let Ethan go, Harlan hesitated to do so. He knew it was illogical, but he had the feeling that he was the only one who could protect Ethan, the only one who could truly keep him safe.

'Do it now!'

Harlan held onto the boy.

A female detective appeared. 'It's OK, he's with us,' she told the armed officers, ushering them out of the room. She turned to Harlan and said softly, 'I need you to let go of Ethan. We have to get him… we have to get both of you to hospital.'

'Have you got Yates?' asked Harlan.

The detective nodded. 'And his girlfriend. They gave themselves up without a fight.'

Harlan turned his head and murmured in Ethan's ear, 'Close your eyes.' He waited for Ethan to do so, before adding, 'Promise me you'll keep them closed until you're a long way away from here.'

In a heartbreakingly small voice, Ethan said, 'I promise.'

'Good boy.'

Harlan nodded at the detective. At a gesture from her, a uniform came to scoop up the boy and carry him away. Harlan struggled to stand but the detective held up a hand to stay him. 'There are paramedics on their way up.'

Harlan slumped back onto the mattress. The detective looked dispassionately at Neil's nearly faceless corpse. 'Who's he?'

'He's nobody,' said Harlan. 'Nobody at all.'

Chapter Twenty-Three

Harlan waved away the nurse when she offered him a newspaper. He wasn't interested in what the media had to say about the personal histories of himself, Neil Price or anyone else. And there was nothing they could tell him about the hard facts of the case that he didn't already know. Jim had filled him in on the few details he'd been uncertain about. At first, after abducting Ethan, Yates had kept him gagged, bound, blindfolded and ear-muffled. In such a state of sensory deprivation, it was impossible for the boy to say where he'd been taken or how long he'd been held there for. All he knew was that every once in a while someone came to feed him food, liquids and tablets. At some point it seemed that, as Harlan suspected, he was moved to another place. Ethan had a vague, dreamlike memory of being lifted and carried. It was after that that he woke to find himself free of his bonds in the room where Harlan had found him. From then on, the man in the balaclava looked in on him once every day or two.

There were other details. Things Yates told the police that contradicted what Neil told Harlan – things like how the whole sorry caper was Neil's idea from start to finish. But Harlan wasn't concerned with the truth or falsity of such claims. That was for the police and courts. All he was concerned with now was tying up the loose ends of his present life – his non-life –

and moving forward. He'd given Susan the closure she needed, now it was her turn to do the same for him

Susan entered the hospital room and saw Harlan lying on his bed, and her tears started to flow. Kane lingered by the door as she approached him and took his hand between hers. 'Thank you, thank you. I...' She trailed off momentarily, her voice clogged with emotion. 'I don't know what else to say.'

Harlan smiled. It was different from any other smile that had appeared on his face in a long time. There was nothing forced or strained about it. 'You don't have to say anything else.' Thank you weren't the words he was so desperate to hear. But looking at Susan, he realised he didn't need to hear them, they were in her eyes, plain as ink on paper. 'Have they let you see Ethan?'

Susan nodded. 'Soon as he saw me, he ran to me and gave me a great big hug. Same as always.' She drew in an elated breath, her eyes shining at the memory of that moment. A slight frown nibbled at her happiness. 'I'd have brought him to see you, only the doctors want to keep him in a few more days to run some tests. Physically he's fine. Nothing a few good meals won't fix. But...' She broke off, glancing at Kane.

'You don't need to worry about me hearing what you're saying, Mum,' said Kane. 'I already know why they won't let Ethan come home. They want to make sure he's all right up there.' He pointed at his temple.

'Nothing much gets past you, does it?' said Harlan. 'Ever thought about being a copper when you grow up?'

'Fuck that.'

Susan flashed her son a sharp look. 'Watch your language or you'll get it!' As Kane lowered his gaze and muttered under his breath, she continued, 'Isn't there something you wanted to say to Harlan?'

Kane stood silent a moment, chewing his lips as if working his courage up. Then, with only a faint trace of his usual sullen indignation, he said, 'Thanks for finding my brother, and... and I'm sorry for what I did to you.'

Susan frowned. 'What do you mean? What did you do to him?'

'It doesn't matter,' said Harlan. 'Kane's apologised and it's over.'

The creases left Susan's forehead. She sucked in a big breath and let it out in a shudder. 'You're right. It's over and my beautiful baby boy will soon be back where he belongs. That's all that matters.' Some anxiety crept back into her expression. 'The only thing that worries me is taking Ethan back to that house. I mean, how's he ever supposed to feel safe enough to sleep there again?'

'So don't take him there. Put it up for sale and rent somewhere until you find a new place to buy.'

'How am I supposed to do that? I've barely got the bus fare to get home, never mind money enough to shell out on the mortgage and rent at the same time.'

'I want you to have the reward for finding Ethan.' The shadow that fell over Susan's face prompted Harlan to add quickly, 'It's not a gift. The money's yours by right. Well, to be precise, it's Kane's. Without him, Ethan would still be locked up in that flat.'

Looking at his mother with excited, pleading eyes, Kane opened his mouth to speak. But seeing her frowning uncertainty, he thought better of it and resumed biting his lips. 'I suppose you're right,' said Susan, not sounding entirely convinced.

'So you'll take the money.'

Susan thought a moment longer, then the shadow left her face. Harlan smiled again, both at the leap of joy in Kane's eyes as his mum nodded, and at the way the boy turned to him as if expecting him to somehow magic up the cash right that instant. There was relief as well as amusement in Harlan's expression. The thought of accepting the reward turned his stomach. If Susan had refused it, he would've instructed the solicitors to distribute it to whatever worthy causes they pleased. And after all, what worthier cause was there than Ethan? The money wouldn't erase the memory of what'd happened to him – only time and love might do that – but it would make things easier. After everything he'd been through, surely he deserved that much at least. Harlan was careful not to let Susan see his relief. He knew she'd reverse her decision if she got even the slightest hint that taking the money was charity.

'Does this mean we're gonna move house?' Kane asked eagerly. When Susan nodded, he continued, 'Fuckin' wicked! Can we get one of those plasma tellies for the front room?'

'Kane, what did I just say about watching your language?'

'Sorry, Mum, but can we?'

'We can't afford a new telly.'

'Yes we can. We're gonna be rich.'

'Seventy thousand pounds is a lot of money, but it doesn't make us rich.'

Kane's lips contracted into a pout. 'Harlan said it's my money. So that means I can spend it on what I want.'

'If you think I'm gonna let you piss that money away on TVs and the like, you've got another thing coming.'

'But—'

Susan raised a warning finger. 'This isn't up for discussion.'

With a huff of annoyance, Kane turned and stomped from the room. Susan rolled her eyes at Harlan. 'Honestly, kids! Who'd have 'em?'

I would, was Harlan's instant thought.

Susan blinked guiltily, as if she'd read his mind. 'Sorry. I forgot about... y'know, about your son.'

Harlan smiled, but it was the old forced smile. 'You don't ever have to apologise to me.'

'But I want to.' Susan squeezed Harlan's hand, looking into his eyes. 'I want...' For a second she seemed to be struggling to find the words she was looking for. Or maybe that wasn't it at all. Maybe she was thinking the words, but finding it difficult to say them. She cleared her throat as if clearing a slight blockage from her mind. 'I want you to be happy.'

The strain vanished from Harlan's face. *Happy.* The word vibrated through his body. Was it possible for him to be happy? He didn't know. He was certain of only one thing: it was possible now for him to try. He squeezed Susan's hand back. Their eyes remained in contact a moment longer, then she glanced worriedly towards the door. 'Go after him,' said Harlan.

'Do you mind? I can stay if you want?'

Harlan shook his head. 'He needs you a lot more than I do.'

Susan released his hand, saying in a hesitating kind of way, 'I guess we'll talk soon.'

He nodded. 'I'll call you.' Even as he said the words, he realised he wouldn't be calling Susan. As much as he wanted to keep tabs on how she, Kane and especially Ethan were doing, he also knew it wouldn't do any of them any good to remain in contact. All it would do would be to keep the embers of the past glowing. Now was the time to let that fire die and build another. From her hesitation, he guessed Susan felt the same way, even if she didn't consciously recognise it.

'Take care.'

'You too.'

As Susan headed out the room, Eve stepped into it. The two women exchanged glances. Susan smiled faintly and nodded almost imperceptibly. Eve replied in kind. There was no particular like or dislike in either of their eyes, simply acknowledgement. Eve's brow creased in a slight wince at the sight of Harlan, as if it hurt her to look at him. She made as if to take his hand, but hesitated. She stared nervously at him, unconsciously touching her belly as she waited for him to speak. 'She came to say thank you,' he told her.

'And what does that mean for us?'

'It means I want us to start again, build a new life, maybe in a new place, just the two of us – that's if you'll have me.'

The lines faded from Eve's brow, but her nervousness remained. 'Of course I'll have you,' she began in a soft, almost tentative voice. 'I don't care whether we stay here or move to the other side of the world, just so long as we can be together. But...' She broke off with a little swallow.

Harlan frowned. 'But what?'

'Wherever we are it won't be just the two of us.'

'What do you mean?'

'For an ex-copper, you sure are slow catching on sometimes.' Eve took Harlan's hand and very gently placed its palm against her stomach.

He stared up at her, feeling hope flicker in the darkness that'd grown like a tumour inside him, but hardly daring to believe it. 'You mean...'

'I'm pregnant.'

Pregnant! Was it possible? Or was it the effects of concussion and painkillers playing tricks on him. 'How?'

'How do you think? Remember, Harlan, that doctor didn't say you were infertile, he said you'd find it very difficult to conceive.' Eve smiled. 'You look as if you're wondering whether or not you're about to wake up. Well don't worry, you're not dreaming. This is real. I'm... we're going to have a baby.'

'A baby.' Suddenly tears filled Harlan's eyes, and laughter filled his mouth. 'We're going to have a baby!' He pulled Eve to him and kissed her hard and full on the lips.

'Easy, tiger,' she gasped, laughing too.

Harlan eased his embrace. He gently touched Eve's stomach and softly spoke to it. 'Sorry, little baby, Daddy got a bit carried away. I promise it won't happen again. From now on I'll handle Mummy as if she was made of glass.'

'Don't worry about me. I'm made out of something a lot tougher than glass.'

A look of guilt came into Harlan's eyes as he thought about everything he'd put Eve through. He started to drop his gaze, but she lifted his chin.

'This isn't the time for sad thoughts, Harlan. Like you said, this is the time for putting the past behind us and starting afresh. All that other stuff – the grief, the guilt – that's over with, isn't it?'

Harlan nodded, wanting to believe she was right, needing to believe it. Tom would always be with him, of course. As would Robert Reed. But maybe he could start to remember the good times with Tom. And maybe, just maybe he wouldn't feel like tearing his own guts out every time the image of Robert Reed lying on the snowy pavement came into his mind. He kissed Eve again, as gently as a breeze this time. Then he pulled back his sheets and got out of bed.

'What are you doing?' asked Eve.

'What does it look like? I'm discharging myself.'

'But you're not well enough.'

'I feel great. Better than I have done in years. And besides, I'm not letting either of you out of my sight. This time things are going to be different. No working long hours at a job that sucks me dry. No losing sight of what really matters. This time it's just going to be the three of us all the way.'

'Sounds wonderful. Unfortunately someone has to go to work and pay the bills.'

'You're forgetting. I've got a couple of hundred thousand quid coming my way. If we're careful, we should be able to live off that for a good few years.'

'And what about when it runs out?'

Harlan shrugged. 'We'll work something out.'

Eve raised an eyebrow. 'Work something out? That doesn't sound like you, Harlan.'

'Well, maybe this is the new me. And the new me isn't going to waste a second worrying about money. Hell, when it runs out we could start our own business. Nothing big, just enough to get us by. But for now...' He took Eve's hands. 'For now, let's get out of the city and go somewhere quiet, somewhere we can lie in the sun and... and pretend the last few years never happened.'

'OK,' Eve said, with an excited little laugh. 'OK, you're on. I'll ring work and hand in my notice.' She lifted his hand to her mouth and kissed it, murmuring, 'I think I'm going to enjoy spending all my time with the new you.'

Harlan gave her a wry look. 'If I were you, I'd reserve judgement on that until we've been living in each other's pockets for a few months.'

He slowly dressed. Even with all the pills there were pains in almost every nerve of his body. But he didn't care. Nothing was going to stop him from being with Eve and his unborn child. Nothing.

An hour or so later, all the forms signed and medication doled out, they headed for the car park. Harlan blinked as they stepped outside. The morning seemed so bright, so fresh. He filled his lungs as if starved for air. Eve pointed out her car. He limped towards it, heavy on his feet but light in his heart, and got into the passenger seat. As Eve negotiated the congested streets, he stared at the city, seeing the dirt and hustle, but not seeing it. He felt in a kind of daze. Suddenly, in the space of two moments, the life that'd been taken away from him had been returned. It was almost too much to take in. He kept replaying the moments. *I want you to be happy… I'm pregnant… I want you to be happy… I'm pregnant…* Susan and Eve's voices went round and round in his head until they blended and became indistinguishable, forming a perfect circle of proof – proof that life was worth it, that there was light in the darkness, that a new day really had begun. He almost didn't want to think about any of it, in case in thinking he found some flaw in the circle.

Harlan started at the sound of his phone. He took it out and a little squeeze of anxiety pressed against his chest when he saw who was calling.

'Who is it?' asked Eve.

'Jim.'

As if infected by his unease, Eve said quickly, 'Don't answer it.'

'It might be important.'

Eve shot Harlan a glance, her eyes intense, almost pleading. Her hand dropped to her belly. '*This* is important. *This* is the most important thing in the world.'

She was right, he knew. And in a way he felt instinctively, but didn't quite comprehend at that moment, that was why he had to answer the phone. Eve's blue eyes winced as he put it to his ear and asked, 'What is it, Jim?'

His ex-partner's voice came back down the line, low and apologetic. 'It's Jones.'

The squeezing became a painful weight. *Hang up*, his mind screamed. But the phone remained pressed to his ear as if glued there. 'What about him?'

'He got out today.'

'What do you mean, got out?'

'They discharged him from hospital. We've got nothing to hold him on. No forensics. Nash is still saying nothing. I'm so sorry, Harlan. I tried, I really tried, but...' Jim trailed off into a sigh of utter dejection.

As he listened, Harlan closed his eyes. With every word, the circle was crumbling, the future receding, the gap growing between his dreams of a bright new beginning and the bitter realities of his past. He suddenly felt a fool for allowing himself to hope that he could escape the darkness. There was no escape. Not now. Not ever. There was only wilful blindness. Better to face it full on, embrace it, use it. 'No need to apologise, it's not your fault.' His voice was flat, toneless, making it difficult to tell whether he meant what he said. He meant it. It wasn't Jim's fault, it was the system's. The system had failed him. It had failed Jamie Sutton. But worst of all, it had failed his unborn child. The thought of it being born into a world where William Jones walked free made his stomach churn with rage.

'I just thought you'd want to know.' Jim's voice was edged with unspoken meaning.

The bastard knows I'll go after Jones, thought Harlan. *He's using me to do what he hasn't got the balls to do himself.* For an instant, he felt like shouting *Fuck you! How could you do this to me? Why couldn't you just leave me alone?* But his anger towards Jim died as quickly as it'd flared, and when he opened his mouth all that came out was a monotone, 'I understand.'

Harlan hung up. He didn't blame Jim for calling him. How could he? After all, both of them had seen the same things, and both of them wanted the same thing – Jones off the street, one way or another. But Jim was too invested in the system to go against it. So he'd turned to the only person he knew who stood outside it, maybe realising, maybe not, how dangerous the consequences might be. Harlan opened his eyes and his vision was filled by Bankwood House tower block, its colourful exterior jarring with his grim mood. He noticed that his car had been returned.

Harlan looked at Eve, sadness, guilt and fear all mingling in his expression. But most of all fear. Fear that she and his unborn child would come to some harm – harm he might've prevented – while he was away from them. 'We're not going away, are we?' she said, reading his eyes.

Harlan shook his head. 'There's something I have to do. And I have to do it alone.'

With fatalistic resignation, Eve accepted his words. 'How long will this something take?'

'I don't know. Maybe days, maybe weeks, maybe... I don't know.'

'And when this *thing* is done, when it's over, what then?'

Harlan hesitated, only for a second, but long enough for Eve to catch it. 'We can do what we planned.'

Eve pulled over. She gazed out the window, eyes unfocused, seeming to stare off into some other place, as if she was putting mental distance between herself and Harlan. He started to reach for her but stopped when the knuckles of her hands gripping the wheel whitened. She deserved more of an explanation, he knew. She deserved more than him. But he couldn't give her either of those things. Heaving a sigh, he got out of the car. As he did so, she murmured, 'It'll never be over.' She drove away without giving him a glance.

Chapter Twenty-Four

Shoulders stooped as if he was carrying heavy bags, Harlan made his way up to his flat. As quickly as his battered body would allow, he changed into clean clothes. Then he headed for his car. Its interior had been cleaned but there were still faint brown tidemarks where Jones's blood had soaked into the front passenger seat. He drove to the garage he'd bought it from and part-exchanged it for an Audi with tinted windows. Then he bought some black electrical tape and scissors. After cutting the tape to the right width and length to alter the Audi's registration number, he headed for Jones's house. He parked a few doors along from it. Nothing had changed, except the bowed, waterlogged window boards had been replaced with metal grilles – no doubt by the police. They had a duty to protect all citizens, even scumbags like Jones. There was no way he was breaking into the house again. Not that he intended to. As far as he could see, there was only one way to connect Jones to Jamie Sutton – the painting. He had to find the painting. He doubted whether Jones would reveal its hiding place, even under torture. If he did, his life would be as good as over anyway. Besides, Harlan was convinced that sooner or later Jones would unwittingly lead him to the painting. Jones's paintings were his trophies. He needed them to keep his fantasies alive. Right now, that need, that desire, might only be an itch in his groin, but it was an itch his ruined hands were unable to scratch, an itch that in a week, or maybe a month, would develop into a craving that demanded to be satisfied.

Harlan settled down to wait for Jones to appear. He didn't have to wait long. The front door opened and, as cautiously as a rabbit emerging from its burrow, Jones poked his bleary-eyed, unshaven face out. After making sure no one was lurking around, he left the house, wheeling a little tartan shopping trolley behind him. Moving with quick, shuffling steps, gripping the trolley's handle clumsily in his plaster-of-Paris-encased hands, he made a pathetic sight. When he reached the end of the street, Harlan got out and followed him. He guessed Jones wouldn't be going far, and he was right. Jones crossed a road and went into a Co-Op. Through the storefront window, Harlan watched him load the trolley up with White Lightning. After paying, Jones hauled his liquid diet homeward. Harlan stayed well out of sight until Jones was back in his house. Then he too went into the store. He bought a six-pack of Coke, plenty of sugary snacks and some ProPlus to keep himself awake and alert through the long hours of the night.

Jones didn't emerge from his burrow again for a couple of days. When he did, it was only to visit the shop for more booze and some bread and milk. That afternoon, figuring Jones was more than likely slumped in an alcoholic stupor, Harlan allowed himself a short nap. He dreamed about Eve. She was on some swings, massively pregnant. 'Be careful,' he kept shouting at her, but she ignored him, swinging higher and higher, nearly falling. He awoke with an intense urge to call her. He resisted it, telling himself she'd call him if there was anything wrong, knowing that the sound of her voice would only cause him to question his resolve to do what was necessary, what was right.

What is right? Harlan asked himself that question a lot during the tedious hours of his vigil. He'd once thought he knew the answer: the law was always right simply because it was the law. A few years on the force had knocked that naivety out of him, but he'd still retained a basic faith in the importance of obeying the law. That, too, was all but gone now, leaving behind a chasm full of doubt and more questions. Questions like: *what if Jones leads you to the painting, and you hand him over to the police, and they somehow let him squirm through their fingers again, is that right?* He knew he couldn't allow himself to listen to such questions. If he did, he might as well just snatch Jones off the street, drive him out to some isolated spot and cut his throat. And that would make him as much of a monster as Jones. Wouldn't it? *Of course it would*, he kept telling himself. But every time he did so, his mind's voice was a little more hollow, a little less sure. Often he would raise his eyes to the sky, like a doubting priest imploring God to give him the crumbs of faith he needed. Sometimes those crumbs came in the form of news articles about criminals who'd been convicted and got their just deserts. But such crumbs never sustained him for long. Always the doubting, questioning voice returned. *What if, what if, what if…*

Harlan quickly got to know Jones's routine. At eleven p.m. Jones's bedroom light came on and stayed on all night. At nine a.m. Jones opened his upstairs curtains, but never the downstairs ones. Every two days at noon, when the street was quietest, Jones visited the shop. If he encountered anyone in the street, they would often cross to the opposite pavement, shooting him wary glances. Some stared at him with open hostility. Whichever, he would quicken his pace, gaze fixed on the ground. Harlan spent some time watching the back gate, but Jones never left the house that way, probably because he was afraid of being jumped in the alley. He never left the house after dark either. Which was just as well because gangs of hoodie-wearing teenagers often bombarded it with bricks and bottles, until the police arrived and sent them scattering in all directions. One night Harlan was awoken from another thin, troubled sleep by the sound of two drunken men trying to kick their way into Jones's house. After five minutes of vainly pounding away, they satisfied themselves with pissing on the front door, then staggered off, laughing.

After several weeks, a man wearing what looked like a medical uniform visited Jones. The next time Jones showed his face, his plaster casts had been removed. His fingers were still too swollen to fully curl around the trolley's handle. But from then on the man, whom Harlan assumed was a physio, visited every three or four days. And with each visit Jones's fingers grew a little more flexible, until finally they could curl into fists. Harlan saw them do so one afternoon when a couple of boys, maybe thirteen years old, abused Jones in the street. 'Fuckin' pervert!' yelled one of them. 'Paedo!' added the other, flinging a bottle that popped on the pavement next to Jones. He threw back an angry glance, hands balled at his sides. The boys sneered at the warning in his eyes, but didn't approach him.

After that a change came over Jones. His posture became more upright, less shuffling. He stopped lowering his gaze from the people he saw in the street. He began to venture further afield, visiting other shops. One time, he lingered outside a toy shop, pretending to read a newspaper. Harlan's blood burned as he watched Jones watching the children play in the aisles, the more so because the store had been a favourite of Tom's. The thought that Jones might've sneaked yearning peeks at his son made him palpitate with the urge to violence. That afternoon, Jones visited an art supplies shop. Harlan's heart dropped as he watched him browse its aisles. If he started painting again, his urges would be kept in check for a time, maybe for a very long time. Jones picked up a brush and practised moving it up and down a canvas. With every stroke, Harlan could feel his chance at being the father he so desperately wanted to be slipping further away. Jones's fingers fumbled the brush. He retrieved it and tried again. The same thing happened. Shaking his head in pained frustration, he stormed from the shop. Harlan released a breath of relief.

Now another change came over Jones. When he next left the house, a new haggardness had come into his face. His piggish eyes shone with a repulsive light – a light of hunger that, day by day, grew until it was feverishly bright. He often took to muttering to himself, occasionally nodding or shaking his head in response to some internal dialogue. One day the head shaking grew more agitated, until it seemed there was a full-scale row going on between Jones and his mind's voice. He looked more crazed than dangerous. Someone to be pitied rather than feared. But Harlan felt no pity. He simply hoped something was coming to a head within Jones, so that he could get far away from here and start living.

That night Jones's bedroom light came on at the usual time, but after half an hour or so it went off. Harlan frowned up at the window, wondering what was going on. Had Jones worked up the courage to sleep in the dark? He doubted it. More likely the light bulb needed changing. Several minutes passed. The window remained dark. Another thought came: what if Jones had switched the light off because he was leaving the house? He waited a couple more minutes. Still no light. No sign of Jones either. *Maybe he's sneaking out the back door.* The thought prompted Harlan to jump out of his car and sprint to the end of the street. He peered cautiously into the alley, which was patchily illuminated by house lights. Jones's house was unlit at the rear too. Harlan squinted, straining to penetrate the darkness. He thought he could see something by Jones's gate. Something moving. An arm. On the edge of his hearing, he caught the sound of a lock clicking. A figure moved away from the gate, back turned to Harlan, hurrying. It was Jones! Harlan couldn't see his face but he recognised his thin, scruffy hair and hunch-shouldered gait.

Hugging the shadows, Harlan followed Jones. After ten or fifteen minutes, they came to Lewis Gunn's church, and the thought flashed through Harlan's mind, *Is the preacher in on this?* But Jones headed past the church. He crossed the road and descended some steps at the side of a canal bridge. His pace slowed as he made his way along a towpath illuminated by the moon and the ambient glow of the city, which seeped through the hollowed-out hulks of derelict steel mills – mills where, Harlan recalled, Jones had once worked. A tall wall overgrown with vines and other creeping plants ran alongside the path. As the hum of the unsleeping city receded, Harlan became hyper-aware of every sound he made – the faint crunch of his shoes on the hard-packed pebbles, the rustle of his clothes, the murmur of his breath, the thud of his heart. He allowed the distance between himself and Jones to grow, until Jones was little more than a faint outline against the darkness. Then suddenly, as if the ground had opened up and swallowed him, Jones disappeared.

Heart lurching, Harlan rushed forward as quietly as he could. He almost missed the door. It was set into the wall at the bottom of several worn stone steps. A straggly beard of foliage overhung it. He could just about make out the words *DANGER! KEEP OUT!* daubed in white paint. Brushing aside the foliage, he looked for a handle. There was only a keyhole. Feeling around the edge of the door, he found a gap he could slide his fingers into. The paint crackled and the hinges squeaked as he pulled the door open a couple of feet. The noise reverberated almost painfully in his ears. He slid through the gap and found himself in a cavernous, dank building, its floor strewn with the debris of its partially collapsed roof. The mill had long since been stripped of its blast furnaces and other machinery, but the smell of coal and smelted iron still hung faintly in the air. His attention was attracted by the rattle of metal against metal overhead. Craning his neck, he made out the dim shape of a walkway suspended thirty or so feet above the factory floor. There was no sign of Jones, but it had to be him up there. Who the hell else would it be?

Harlan scanned the moonlight-mottled walls for a way to reach the walkway. There was no stairway. To his right a metal ladder was bolted to the wall. He picked his way through the rubble to it and grasped a rusty rung. *BEWARE! DANGER OF DEATH!* was painted in foot-tall letters on the wall. Harlan reflected that whatever was up there Jones had to be desperate to see it if he was prepared to risk hauling himself up this death trap. The ladder rattled against its bolts as he climbed. He emerged through the walkway, which was about five feet wide and attached to the roof beams by metal rods. The walkway traversed the right-hand wall of the foundry. As Harlan edged out onto the metal grating, it swayed a little, but held. At its far end was a door. Cautiously opening it, he saw it led to another walkway that bridged a narrow gap between the mill and a door to the uppermost floor of a neighbouring building. A sickly, yellowish light glimmered through the cobwebby, cracked panes of windows on either side of the door.

Hunching low, Harlan crossed the walkway and peeped through a window into an attic room maybe twenty feet wide by thirty feet long. Jones was standing with his back to him at its far end. In one hand he held what appeared to be some kind of oil lamp. With his other hand he removed bricks from the wall. He reached inside the hole and withdrew a black plastic sack. He put down the sack and took a cardboard tube from it. Very carefully, he slid a bunch of rolled up canvases out of the tube.

I've got you, thought Harlan. *I've fucking got you!* With a look of twisted glee, he burst into the room. Jones barely had time to turn before Harlan was on him. He knocked Jones to the floorboards with enough force to wind a bull. Thrusting a knee into his back, he twisted the canvases out of his grasp and unfurled them. His triumph dissolved into sick rage. There were three paintings. Two of them were of young boys he didn't recognise. The third was of Jamie Sutton. The artist had captured perfectly the benumbed horror in their eyes, the agonising vulnerability of their naked bodies, the destruction of their innocence.

What is right? The thought tolled in Harlan's mind like a death knell. He savagely dismissed it. In that instant, he didn't care what was right. He only knew that he wanted to kill Jones so badly it gave him the shakes. He snatched up a brick and raised it over Jones's head. Jones struggled weakly, whimpering, 'Please, please don't...'

Harlan's shaking intensified. Tremors contorted his face, as if he was torn between two directions, two warring identities. A wild voice – a voice he barely recognised – burst from him. 'Do it!'

In reply, Garrett's accusing voice rose into his thoughts: *You're a menace to society.*

'Kill him!'

Garrett's voice came back: *A madman.*

There was a sudden splitting, dislocating sensation in Harlan's head. 'No,' he cried, silencing both voices. He slammed the brick against the floorboards an inch from Jones's skull.

Jones screamed, then, realising he was unhurt, gasped out, 'Thank you, thank you.'

Harlan ground his knee into Jones's spine. 'Shut the fuck up or I'll change my mind.' He returned the canvases to the plastic sack. There were other things in there too – pencil sketches, bundles of Polaroids. He jerked Jones to his feet. As he did so, Jones grabbed the lantern and swung it at him. The lantern shattered, splashing burning oil over Harlan and the sack. He dropped the sack and frantically patted out the flames on his arms and chest. Scooping up the burning sack, Jones ran for the door. Harlan pursued him, catching him up as he reached the walkway. Jones flung the sack over the railings before pitching forward onto his face. Harlan watched it sail through the darkness and hit the concrete thirty feet below, bursting and scattering its contents like burning coals. He watched any chance of connecting Jones to Jamie Sutton go up in flames.

'Help me,' groaned Jones, holding up his hands, which were coated with smoking, melted plastic.

The wild voice stirred inside Harlan again. And this time no other voice rose up in opposition. He looked down at Jones, his eyes blank as the night that surrounded him. He stooped to haul him upright. 'I don't think I can make it down the ladder,' said Jones, his voice grating with pain.

'Is there another way down?'

Jones shook his head. 'You'll have to call a fire engine or something.'

'There's no need.'

'But how else am I going to—' Jones broke off as Harlan reached down, grabbed his legs and flipped him over the railing.

For an instant, his shrill scream raked across the derelict steel-mill's courtyard. There was a dull, crunching thud as he hit the floor head first. Harlan stood for a moment, listening to the silence outside and inside. Then he crossed to the opposite doorway. Holding onto the doorframe, he stamped on the walkway and felt it give a little. He drove his heel into the metal grating again and again, until all of a sudden the bolts came loose and it collapsed, swinging against the opposite wall, dangling there for a few seconds, then clanging to the ground. Even before the echoes had died away, Harlan was making his way quickly but carefully to the ladder.

Keeping his head down, sticking to side streets and unlit back alleys, Harlan returned to his car. He drove through the empty city night, keeping well under the speed limit. He kept expecting to feel something – relief, guilt, satisfaction, fear – but he didn't. It was as though the part of his brain's circuitry that controlled his emotions had burned out. He pulled over outside Eve's flat, got out of the car and pressed the intercom button. After a long moment she answered, her voice sleepy but concerned, 'Harlan, is that you?'

Still nothing. Not even a flicker of feeling. *What's wrong with me?* he asked himself detachedly. *Am I in shock? Or did my emotions die along with Jones?* A kind of numb panic closed his throat. He heard his voice come out tight, choked. 'Yes.' Eve buzzed him in, and he climbed the stairs, moving like a man unsure of what would happen next. She was waiting for him at the door to her flat. When he saw her face, when he saw the slight swelling of her belly, all he felt for her, all he'd once felt for Tom, came rushing back. He stopped a few paces short of her, tears welling in his eyes, stammering, 'I... I've done... something... I had no...' He trailed off. *I had no choice*, he'd been about to say. But he realised that wasn't true. There was always a choice.

'Shh,' soothed Eve, moving towards him, resting her head against his chest. 'I don't care what you've done. I love you.' She drew his hand to her belly. He felt a pulse of life under his palm, faint and hardly there, but strong enough to make him tremble. Tears fell from his eyes onto her neck.

'Will you still go away with me?'

Eve looked at Harlan as if to say, *Do you even need to ask?* 'Where would we go?'

'Somewhere... somewhere where it never gets dark.'

'I don't think any such place exists.'

'Neither do I,' said Harlan. 'But let's see if we can find it anyway.'

BEN CHEETHAM

ANGEL OF DEATH

REVENGE IS HER LIFE

Chapter 1

Angel examined her face in the cracked mirror, combing her fingers through raven-black hair that framed intensely blue eyes and uncommonly pale cheeks. 'You're beautiful. You're beautiful,' she murmured, as though repetition would make the words true. But she wasn't beautiful. Not any more. Her once crystal-clear eyes were yellowish and laced with spidery veins. Fine lines and dark shadows marred the surrounding skin. The cute dimples that used to appear when she smiled – not that she ever smiled these days – were gone. In their place were two sharply etched hollows, like knife cuts.

She ran her tongue over lips that appeared unusually full and sensual in her otherwise gaunt face. The best blowjob lips in the business, that's what Deano called them. On the day they'd met he'd told her, 'Those juicy babies are gonna be your ticket out of this life.' She'd believed him at the time, just like she'd believed him later when he said he loved her. She didn't believe him any more. She'd heard him say those words, or words like them, to too many other girls. She knew him now for what he was – pure poison. He'd given her nothing but had taken everything, and she'd let him. Wilfully, pathetically, she'd sold her last chance, her last grain of hope, for an earful of his sweet bullshit and a veinful of smack. The knowledge made her burn with hatred.

2

Angel's fingers curled into a fist. She hit the mirror hard enough to send a jolt of pain rocketing up her wrist. When she drew her knuckles away from the glass, she left behind a bloody smear. She closed her eyes, letting the pain wash through her, using it to block out the hate like she had so many times before. But this time it wasn't enough. The hate kept on growing, expanding like waves from a limitless ocean. Violent visions flashed across the screen of her mind. Visions of herself lashing out at a faceless figure, punching, clawing and tearing. And as she did so, tears streamed from her eyes. Not tears of sorrow but tears of pleasure. It felt good, better than any sex she'd ever had. She began to rock back and forth. A low moan escaped her lips.

The daydream dissolved like a wisp of smoke as the bedsit's door creaked open. Eyelids snapping up, Angel jerked around to see Deano poking his head into the room. 'Grace, baby, it's—' he started to say.

'I asked you not to use that name,' Angel broke in sharply.

Deano dismissed her words with a crooked smile that showed a mouthful of stained and chipped teeth. The years hadn't been kind to him either. He was a big man, although not as big as he used to be. Slowly, the smack was wearing him away, eroding a few millimetres here, a centimetre there. He was still handsome in a rough sort of way, but his complexion was pimple-blotched and his hair was fast thinning. 'What does it matter? There's no one else around.'

'Please will you just call me Angel. Will you do that for me?'

'Alright, alright. Anything to stop your whining.' Deano squinted through the dingy gloom of the room. 'Look at the state of you. You've been crying again, haven't you? What's up? Actually, don't bother telling me. Just sort your face out. It's time to get back out there. Five minutes. I want you on the

3

street in five minutes, or I'm really gonna give you something to cry about.'

Deano headed back outside, his footsteps thumping the bare floorboards as heavily as his fists would thump Angel if she didn't get her arse and all the other parts of her body that helped pay the rent into gear. Four or five years ago he would have kissed her tears away and sweet-talked her into doing what he wanted. There was no need for any of that bullshit now. He had her exactly where he wanted her, and both of them knew it. It wasn't just the smack. She knew plenty of other people she could score from. It was the things she'd told him. Thinking back on it, she wanted to slap herself for having opened up to him, for being so weak and stupid. But at the time she'd needed to talk, to confide in someone, otherwise she might have done something even more stupid. She hadn't told him everything. There were things she couldn't bear to think about, never mind talk about. But she'd told him enough.

After rinsing the blood off her knuckles at a sink in the corner, Angel put on lippy and mascara. She shrugged off her dressing-gown and slipped into a miniskirt, boob-tube and over-the-knee high-heeled boots. Picking up a can of pepper-spray and slinging a handbag over her shoulder, she hurried after Deano. As usual, he was lurking in the ginnel alongside a boarded-up terraced house a couple of streets away. A boy of maybe eighteen approached him at the same time as Angel, shoulders hunkered against the raw wind coming off the River Tees. He handed Deano a couple of crumpled tenners, and Deano's hand emerged from the shadows holding a small foil wrap. The exchange happened fast, then the boy was hurrying away.

'Looking fuckable,' said Deano, approvingly surveying Angel's freshly applied slap before dropping his gaze to her

4

outfit that left little to the imagination. Leaning forward with a sneering smile in his eyes, he added meaningfully, 'Angel.'

Hate surged up in Angel again. She had a sudden wild urge to empty the can of pepper-spray into Deano's eyes. Oh, how she would have loved to see the fucker scream and squirm. She saw herself doing it, then saw herself grinding a heel into his throat, crushing his windpipe. The far-off wail of a police siren brought her back to the moment with a slight start. 'Where do you want me?'

'Over by the bridge.' Deano scanned the street uneasily as he spoke, ear cocked towards the sound of the siren. The wailing faded away and his gaze returned to Angel. 'Do me proud, baby, and later we'll do a bit of you know what.' He rustled the foil wraps in his pocket. The sound, so repulsively yet irresistibly familiar to Angel, sent a shudder through her. It had only been a couple of hours since her last fix, but already the craving was growing. Her veins itched with it.

Angel tottered towards the Transporter Bridge, whose blue frame dominated the Middlesbrough skyline, straddling the Tees like a steel-limbed horse. She passed a scattering of other girls all dressed, like her, in high heels and revealing clothes. Most of their heavily made-up faces were familiar. Some of them smiled and nodded hello. She spotted a new girl scarcely old enough to be out of school, her eyes glazed with a tell-tale sheen. The girl shifted nervously as Angel neared her. There was a bruise on her cheek, probably put there by one of the other girls protecting her patch. The girls looked out for each other, but that didn't stop fights from frequently breaking out over who worked the most lucrative spots. Angel gave her a smile, not of sympathy – her heart was too hardened by bitterness and anger for that – but of understanding. She knew what the girl was feeling. She'd been there herself not so many years ago.

She didn't offer any words of reassurance. Some whores liked to take new girls under their wing, impart their wisdom. Not Angel. The idea repulsed her. Nothing this life had taught her was worth repeating.

A black BMW with tinted windows crawled along the kerb. One of the other girls lifted the hem of her skirt, exposing her bare crotch. But the car didn't stop. She shoved her middle finger up at it, mouthing, 'Fuck you.' The Beamer pulled over by Angel and the young girl. The driver-side window came down just enough for a massive hand adorned with chunky gold rings to beckon the girl. Flicking Angel a tense glance, the girl hurried to the passenger door and ducked into the car, which accelerated sharply away in the direction of the Transporter Bridge.

'Hope that little bitch isn't thick enough to let him take her over the river,' said the girl who'd been snubbed.

The other side of the Tees was a lonely mixture of heavy industrial land and the Seal Sands nature reserve. If you got into trouble, there was no one to hear you scream except the wildlife. Some girls came back robbed and raped. They were the lucky ones. In Angel's time, there had been two girls she knew of who never came back at all. Angel went there occasionally, but only with her most trusted regulars who were willing to pay extra to indulge their vice in the safety of isolation. She stared after the fast-receding car, trying to make out the number plate. She caught the first three letters before the car turned from view. 'B... A... D,' she read aloud, a frown gathering on her brow.

'Bad.' The other girl shook her head. 'That can't be good.'

Another kerb-crawler pulled into view. The girl yanked her skirt up again. This time the car stopped. Angel continued to her patch – a corner between two warehouses a couple of hundred metres from the river. She sparked up and took a drag, watching the bridge's gondola ferrying cars towards the north bank. She couldn't be certain, but she thought she glimpsed the Beamer amongst them. A car pulled into the kerb. She flicked away her cig and ducked down to greet her first punter of the night.

The next hour went by in its usual way – a couple of blowjobs, a handjob, straight sex that was over in less than two minutes. Even as Angel serviced her punters, her eyes kept shifting towards the bridge, watching for the Beamer or the girl. But there was no sign of them. Minute by minute, her uneasiness grew. She kept thinking of the number plate, and the more she thought of it, the more the letters seemed like some sort of omen. She returned along the street. 'Has she been back?' she asked the skirt-lifting girl, who shook her head in reply. 'What do you reckon we should do?'

'Sod all. What else can we do?'

Angel briefly considered going to Deano, but she knew what his response would be. What the fuck do I care? Her heart heavy with foreboding, she headed back to her corner. Her mind flashed back to when she'd first worked the streets. The things that had happened to her. So many bad, ugly, twisted things she'd lost count. Sometimes she wondered how she was still alive, or even if she deserved to be.

A familiar car was waiting for Angel: a red Volvo estate. Its middle-aged driver had the unmistakable look of a family man – balding and grey, a little overweight, glasses, shirt and tie. His name was Kevin – or at least that's what he said it was – and he was one of Angel's regulars, an easy customer who liked a bit of domination, but nothing too kinky. As soon as she saw him, she knew what she had to do. 'Hi there, lover. What's it to be tonight?'

'The usual.'

Angel ducked into the passenger seat. 'You're not in a rush, are you?'

'Why do you ask?'

'Fancy taking a trip to the other side of the river? I'm in the mood for a drive.'

Kevin glanced uncertainly at the bridge. 'It's already late. The wife will start to wonder where I am.'

Angel's long red fingernails crawled up Kevin's thigh. 'I'll make it worth your while,' she purred. 'No extra charge.'

Still Kevin hesitated. Angel grabbed his crotch and gave it a hard squeeze. 'OK,' he groaned, his face wrinkling into a pleasurably pained grimace. She let go and, shifting the car into gear, he accelerated towards the bridge. He paid the toll and drove onto the gondola.

'Come on, get a fucking move on,' muttered Angel, twisting to look at the bridge operator.

'You alright, Angel?' asked Kevin. 'You seem a bit tense, like.'

Angel forced a smile of pouting promise. 'I'm fine, lover. I'm always fine, you know that.'

The thick steel cables that the gondola was suspended from vibrated as well-greased wheels cranked into motion nearly fifty metres overhead. As the gondola advanced across the broad, dark waters towards the north bank, Angel got out of the car and leaned against the railings, staring at the vast sprawl of petro-chemical refineries. Flames spouted from their chimneys, illuminating colossal tangles of steel pipes. The thought came to her, What the hell are you doing? What's this girl to you? The answer was obvious – Nothing. And yet she had to do something. She didn't understand why, but she felt it in her heart. Maybe it was because something about the girl had reminded her of herself. Or maybe that wasn't it at all. Maybe it had more to do with the anger that was simmering inside her, ready to go off like a grenade at the slightest provocation.

There was a dull, heavy thunk as the gondola connected with the north bank. Angel returned to the car. 'Where are we going?' asked Kevin, accelerating away from the bridge.

'Head towards Seaton. I'll tell you when to stop.'

As they drove, Angel scanned the roadside. 'Slow down,' she said, whenever they came to a layby or anywhere else a car might pull over.

'Are you looking for someone?'

Angel didn't reply to Kevin's question. They were nearing the muddy tidal estuary of Seal Sands – pretty much the final place the Beamer could have pulled over before hitting the coastal town of Seaton Carew. They passed a small car park on their left. No Beamer. To their right a narrow lane angled away from the main road. It led, Angel knew, to a car park popular with bird- and seal watchers during the day, and lovers, doggers and stoned kids during the night. She gestured towards the lane, and Kevin turned onto it, his tongue running excitedly over his lips. He expelled a huff of breath upon reaching the car park. 'Bloody hell, someone's already using it.'

The Beamer was parked at the edge of the estuary. Its tinted rear windscreen gleamed in the Volvo's headlights. "BAD 1',' Kevin said, reading its number plate. 'What kind of dickhead has a reg like that?'

'Stop the car,' said Angel.

Kevin shoved the gearstick into reverse. 'We can use the other car park.'

'I said stop!'

Kevin took his foot off the accelerator, but kept the engine running. 'What's going on, Angel?' A little quiver in his voice suggested it had dawned on him that maybe he'd stumbled into something he wanted no part of.

'Wait here.'

9

'Listen, I don't want to get into some kind of trouble.'

Angel's nostrils flared. It was on her tongue to snap back, Don't be such a pussy! But she resisted, reflecting that she should know better than to expect anything more from Kevin – or for that matter, any man. 'Nothing's going on, baby,' she reassured him. 'I know the owner of that car. I'm just going to say hi, that's all.'

Looking unconvinced, Kevin cut the engine. 'OK. Make it quick, though.'

Nothing much scared Angel, but her heart began to pound as she approached the Beamer. Her highly developed whore's instinct for sniffing out danger screamed that something dodgy was going on. It was impossible to tell if there was anyone in the car, but a faint light seeped from the edges of the doors. She raised one hand to knock on the driver-side window. Her other slipped into her handbag and curled around the pepper-spray. Before she could knock, the window came down a few centimetres. A puff of sickly sweet ganja smoke wafted out as a deep voice barked, 'Fuck off.'

Stooping, Angel found herself looking into a pair of eyes glassy with dope and hard with threat. 'I'm looking for a girl you picked up—'

A mouthful of gold teeth flashed from the Beamer's interior as its driver broke in. 'I said fuck off, bitch.'

As the window slid back up, Angel caught a glimpse of two parallel scratches still glistening with blood on the man's cheek. Her already pounding heart surged at the sight. She took several hesitant steps away from the car. The scratches didn't necessarily mean her instincts were right. She'd been with plenty of men who got turned on by being hit during sex. Men like Kevin who desired to be dominated and humiliated. The Beamer's driver wasn't one of those men. It was plain from his voice and eyes that he was the type who liked to dish it out rather than take it. Angel had been with plenty of that kind too. She still had the scars – both visible and invisible – to remind her.

Angel came to a stop as a savage burst of anger burnt away her fear. She felt suddenly as if her head was on fire. Her barely concealed breasts rose and fell as she sucked the night into her lungs. This fucker, this bad boy, thought that because the girl was a nobody, a nothing, he could do what he wanted and there'd be no consequences. Well he was wrong. There would be consequences, painful consequences.

She scanned the ground and stooped to snatch up a chunk of concrete. Without pausing, she ran at the car and hurled the chunk at its driver-side window. The glass shattered with a loud pop. The driver reeled sideways, one hand flung up to protect his face, the other groping at something on the passenger seat. He let out a shrill yell as Angel emptied the can of pepper-spray into his eyes. She yanked open the door and dragged him out of his seat, her wiry muscles straining against his bulk. She saw what he'd been reaching for – there was a handgun on the passenger seat. Ducking into the car to grab it, she found the girl stretched out unconscious on the back seat, her skirt half torn away, blood crusting her inner thighs, her face a battered mask. She didn't appear to be breathing.

Her eyes a crucible of rage, Angel twisted towards the man writhing in agony at her feet. He blindly tried to defend himself as once, twice, three times she stamped her long, sharp heel into his face, ripping deep gouges. 'You fuck!' she shouted, spittle flying from her mouth. 'You sick fuck!'

She would have continued to stamp and stamp until the man's face was as unrecognisable as the girl's, if Kevin hadn't come sprinting over, crying out, 'Stop! For Christ's sake, stop!'

Angel jerked her eyes up to Kevin's, and he lurched to a

PREVIEW

halt as if he'd come up against a wall of flames. He spread his hands, palms out. 'Please, Angel. You'll kill him.'

'And why shouldn't I?' she snarled. 'The bastard deserves it.'

'Why? What's he done?'

'He's killed her, that's what.'

His face as pale as the moon, Kevin asked, 'Killed who?'

'The girl.' Angel gestured at the car. 'She's in there.'

Kevin edged around Angel. He reached for the back door handle, but hesitated. He pulled his sleeve down over his hand, then opened the door. 'Oh Jesus,' he gasped on seeing the girl. He felt for a pulse in her neck. His eyes widened. 'She's alive!'

'Are you sure?'

'Her pulse is weak, but it's definitely there.' Kevin pulled out his mobile phone.

'What are you doing?'

'What do you think I'm doing? I'm phoning for an ambulance.'

Angel snatched the phone away. 'No you're not.'

Kevin looked at her in stunned silence for a second. 'But she'll die if I don't.'

'No she won't, because you're going to take her to hospital.'

Kevin's forehead contracted. 'I can't do that, Angel. If I'm seen with this girl, it... well, it would—' His voice snagged in his throat at the thought of what it would do to him if word of this got back to his wife.

'I don't give a shit what it'd do to you. You're taking her.'

'No I'm not.'

Kevin recoiled back against the car, his chest heaving as Angel aimed the gun at him. Her voice as hard as the steel the nearby factories produced, she said, 'Yes you are.'

'OK, OK, I'll do it. Just stop pointing that thing at me.'

Angel lowered the gun. A groan from the prostrate man

drew her attention. He was struggling to sit up, his muscular, tattooed arms trembling from the effort. She drove her heel into his face again, sending him crashing onto his back. 'Bitch,' he choked out, blood dribbling between his lips.

'Keep your fucking mouth shut unless you want more of the same,' snapped Angel. She looked at Kevin. 'Get her into your car.'

As Kevin hooked his hands under the girl's armpits and pulled her from the car, she exhaled a whisper of a moan. Her eyelids fluttered and cracked open a fraction. Angel leaned over her like a mother over a child. 'That's it, come on, open your eyes.'

The slitted eyes closed again.

'Hold on, baby girl, we're going to get you to hospital.'

The girl's limbs dangled like broken twigs as Kevin carried her to his car and laid her on its back seat. Breathing heavily, he turned to Angel. 'You coming?'

'No.'

The creases on Kevin's forehead deepened. His eyes flicked between Angel and the man at her feet. 'What are you going to do?'

'You don't need to worry about that, all you need to worry about is getting her to hospital. Oh, and if I find out you've dumped her somewhere and rung for an ambulance, I'm not going to be best pleased.' Angel patted the gun. 'You get me?'

Kevin nodded, his tongue darting dryly across his lips. 'You're not going to do anything crazy—'

'Get the fuck out of here,' cut in Angel, her eyes flashing.

Flinching from her fury, Kevin ducked into his car. He accelerated away, wheels spitting gravel. Angel waited until he hit the main road before returning her attention to the Beamer's driver. His eyes glared at her from between swollen pouches of flesh, glistening with hate but also fear. It sent a thrill through Angel almost as heady as a hit of junk to see his fear, to know that, for once in her life, she was the one with the power. 'On your belly.' Her voice was calmer. The anger was still there, but she was controlling it now, not it her.

Groaning, the man slowly rolled onto his belly.

'Now crawl to the river. Crawl like the worm you are.'

The man dug his fingers into the cracked concrete and dragged himself forward. The light from the Beamer's interior only stretched a few metres. At the edge of its reach, estuary mud glistened palely in the moonlight. When her heels sank into the mud, Angel said, 'Stop.'

The man lay panting, agonised tremors vibrating through his body.

'Roll over,' said Angel. 'I want to see your face.'

The man heaved himself onto his back again. He stared up at Angel, his mud-smeared face invisible except for the red-laced whites of his eyes and the gleam of his gold teeth. 'You don't know who the fuck I am,' he gasped, his voice cramped with pain.

'Yeah I do. I've known you all my life.'

Angel took aim. The man flung up a hand as if he might ward off a bullet with it. 'Wait! Fucking wait! I've got money.' He fumbled out his wallet and tossed it to Angel. 'There's more than a thousand quid in there. It's yours.'

Angel took out the money and shoved it into her handbag. She didn't look to see if there was any identification – she already knew all she needed to know about the man – she just threw the wallet into the estuary. Again, she took aim. Again, the man raised a hand. 'Why are you doing this?' he asked, panic sucking at his voice.

Angel studied the man with a cold fire behind her eyes,

greedily drinking in his fear, savouring its bittersweet taste. 'The same reason you did what you did. Because I can.'

The fear in the man's eyes was joined by a hopeless rage. He spat a glob of phlegm at Angel, which left a bloody snail-trail down her thigh. 'Fuck you, bitch! Fuck all you slags. I'd kill the lot of you if I got the chance.'

'Well you're not going to get the chance.'

Angel pulled the trigger. Nothing happened. She pulled it again. Still nothing. 'Shit.' The word whistled through her teeth as she thought, The fucking thing's broken. Another thought came to her. The safety must be on. A quick examination of the gun revealed a catch marked 'Safety' above the trigger. She flicked it.

'Please, I don't want to die!' pleaded the man as Angel took aim again. An ear-splitting shot rang out. The gun's recoil jerked her hand upward. The muzzle flash set pinpoints of light dancing in front of her eyes. The man screamed and flailed in the estuary slime, clutching his right shoulder. As her vision cleared, Angel took careful aim at his chest. The man just had time to cry out some incomprehensible final words before a second bullet punched the breath from his lungs. He lay gurgling like the estuary for a moment, then fell silent.

ABOUT THE STEEL CITY SERIES

Every city has its darkness. It may be buried deeper in some cities than others, but it's there. Most people choose to look away from that darkness. A few force themselves to stare into it so that they can know their enemies. And they're only too aware that the line which divides kidnap, rape, murder and corruption from love, family, home and happiness is thinner than you could ever imagine. Sheffield is a city like any other. In the shadows of its factories, tower blocks, shopping centres and housing estates, a seemingly endless battle to hold that thin line is being fought...

To discover more – and some tempting special offers – visit
www.headofzeus.com

MEET THE AUTHOR

BEN CHEETHAM's writing spans the genres from horror and sci-fi to literary fiction, but he has a passion for gritty crime fiction. His short stories have been widely published in the UK, US and Australia. Ben lives in Sheffield, where he can usually be found racking his brain for the next paragraph, the next sentence, the next word.

You can find out more about Ben Cheetham via his website:
bencheetham.blogspot.co.uk